Where No Man Cries

Anxious to cement over their previous rift, as well as being genuinely curious, Angus asked Rosemary what sort of man Sir Alan was. As Rosemary spoke, a lifestyle completely outside Angus's experience gradually unfolded. He heard of balls. Dinner parties. Holidays abroad in France and Italy. Of huntin' shootin' and fishin'. Of fast cars and expensive ones. Of clever conversation where wit was the commodity prized above all else. In fact all the glamorous things money and position can provide. The thought of being a rich businessman fascinated Angus. And the more he thought about it the more he was attracted to himself in that image.

Where No Man Cries

EMMA BLAIR

ARROW BOOKS

Arrow Books Limited
62–65 Chandos Place, London WC2N 4NW

An imprint of the Hutchinson Publishing Group

London Melbourne Sydney Auckland
Johannesburg and agencies throughout
the world

First published 1982
Reprinted 1983 (three times), 1984 (twice), 1985, 1986,
1987 and 1988

Set in Linoterm Times by
Book Economy Services, Burgess Hill, Sussex

Printed and bound in Great Britain by
Anchor Brendon Limited, Tiptree, Essex

ISBN 0 09 927720 4

For Ina

Part I

The Dear Green Place
1921–22

1

With a final rub of the cloth Carrie McBain finished work on the grate. Sighing with contentment she sat back on her haunches and studied her handiwork. Black-leading the fireplace had always been one of her jobs until she got married and moved out of the house. Occasionally when she was back visiting, she still did it for her mother.

The windows were open and a strong shaft of warm August sunlight was beaming into the room. There were dust motes in the air which was filled with the sweet smell of grass and the perfume given off by the wild plants growing down by the river.

Carrie ran a hand over her distended stomach. It wouldn't be long now till the baby came – a fortnight, according to the doctor.

Carefully she wiped her hands on a rag before laboriously climbing to her feet. She had a pain in her back that had been with her for several months now, but it only really gripped her if she moved suddenly.

Crossing to a window she stared out at a man fishing in the River Cart. The man's long rod flicked lazily as he waded in close to the bank.

The river had once been well known for its salmon fishing, but that had been in the days before Armstrong's had been built. Now, in 1921, the ever-growing amount of effluence pouring out from the engineering firm was slowly but inexorably choking the life out of the river.

The salmon that survived were few.

Still, Carrie thought grimly, rather a poisoned river and families with food in their bellies than fat fish and starving folk.

She sighed and massaged her stomach. The wean was kicking again. There were times when it kicked so hard a limb would protrude quite plainly.

'Are you all right in there?' Winnie, a bustling, stout woman shouted from the kitchen.

'Aye, I'm fine, Ma!' Carrie called back. It wouldn't be long now till they stopped for a cup of tea. She was looking forward to that.

Carrie was always pleased to be back in the house in Tallon Street where she'd been brought up. Not that it was a house in the proper sense, being a three-bedroomed flat three flights up. The word 'house' was a euphemism. In Glasgow everyone lives in a house whether it's a mansion in Kelvinside or a rat-infested single end in the Gorbals.

There had been a time when the Chisholms were tenement dwellers, but Big Donald, Carrie's father, was an industrious man with an eye always open to bettering the family lot. Thanks to his efforts they had been one of the first to move into Tallon Street, superior accommodation with every apartment boasting an inside toilet and bath, when it had been built by the Corporation.

Big Donald enjoyed his drink and tobacco. The difference between him and many of his workmates was that he knew when to call a halt. Never once had Winnie gone without money for the rent or food for the table because Donald's wages had been blown in the pub. That was something of which very few working-class women in Glasgow could boast. Donald Chisholm was a formidable man. A strict disciplinarian who believed that children should be seen and not heard.

When the children were young, God help any of them foolish enough to cheek Winnie in his hearing. Retribution, in the form of his leather belt across their backsides, was swift and painful.

Yet it was this same Donald who nearly always slipped his children sweeties and other goodies along with their Saturday pennies, for he dearly loved his wife and family although it would never have entered his head to actually say so to them. Amongst Glasgow folk that just wasn't the done thing. Any man foolish enough to do so, unless totally drunk and maudlin with it, would be considered soft and a jessie.

For Donald, love was a practical thing. Something to be practised rather than talked about. When Harriet, his eldest daughter, had had the croup as a baby he had thought it the natural thing to stay up night after night helping Winnie nurse her, while continuing to go to work each morning. He belonged to a hardy breed who believed in action rather than words.

Carrie's man, John, was another out of the same mould. In the Armstrong foundry, where he worked under Donald, he was well liked and had a name as a grafter.

Carrie thought of her husband now as she watched the fisherman wade amongst the rhubarb-type plants which grew in profusion along the river bank and in the shallows. They'd been married two years and this child was their first. She was desperately hoping for a boy, sure that a male child was what John wanted. But her husband wasn't to be drawn on the subject. He would only say that if the child was born healthy then he'd be pleased well enough.

Warmth flooded through Carrie as she thought of that. Like her mother she'd been lucky enough to find herself a good man. It was a fact she well appreciated.

She was about to turn and make for the bathroom to wash her hands when she heard a key scrape in the outside lock. When the front door closed it was done gently as though the person who'd entered was a stranger to the house.

Carrie frowned when she heard her father's voice speaking in low undertones. A swift glance at the clock on the mantelpiece confirmed that it was far too early for him to be home for his dinner. It was only ten thirty, a full hour and a half before the works' hooter was due to sound the break.

Besides, if it had been dinner time, then John and her younger brother, Hugh, would have been with him. John always came to the house in Tallon Street for his midday meal on the days when she was visiting.

Something was wrong. It had to be. Fear clutched her insides as she waddled to the door. It opened and Donald entered. Winnie, looking completely stunned, was behind him.

Carrie came up short when she saw her father's grim expression.

'There's been an accident at the foundry, lass,' he said.

'Hugh?'

'No, John.'

The breath caught in her throat and the baby fluttered in her belly. She'd automatically assumed that any accident must involve Hugh. He was such a daft lad at times, and at seventeen just at an age to do something silly and get himself hurt.

But John was always so careful. It had never entered her mind that something might happen to him. 'Is he bad?' she demanded.

For a moment Donald baulked at what he had to say. Then the words came, slowly, evenly and without emphasis. 'John's dead,' he said.

Carrie felt as though she'd been punched squarely on the forehead. She staggered back, her hands coming up to clutch at the life moving within her. It was some sort of horrible joke. It had to be.

'There, there lass,' said Donald coming quickly forward and taking her in his arms. His large, work-worn hands patted her hair.

'Dead?' The word slipped from her mouth to hang suspended in the air.

'Aye,' Donald replied softly.

Winnie sobbed and stuck a fist in her mouth. Her large

bosom heaved in sympathy.

'Oh, my God!' Carrie cried, her face crumpling into a concertina of pain and tears. Her whole body shook as she clung desperately to her father.

'Let it come. Just let it all come out,' Donald soothed, wishing he'd had the presence of mind to bring a drink home with him. If anyone ever needed one it was Carrie at this moment.

'I've got to go to him,' Carrie said suddenly. She wrenched herself from her father's embrace and staggered towards the door.

'Not yet! Not until they've had a chance to sort him out a wee bit,' Donald called after her.

Carrie whirled, her eyes filled with horror. 'What happened?' she demanded harshly.

Donald was suddenly reticent. 'Never you mind for the moment,' he replied. 'There's time enough to go into that.'

'I want to know! I want to know!' she screamed. Then she flew back to her father and thumped him on the chest. 'Tell me! Tell me!'

For once in his life Donald was at a complete loss. He glanced beseechingly across at his wife.

Winnie hurried over to take Carrie by the arm. 'Get a hold of yourself now!' she said sternly. 'This is no way to carry on.'

Carrie was hysterical as she continued pounding on her father's chest with her free hand. It seemed to her that a great chasm was threatening to engulf her.

'Tell me! Tell me! Tell me!' she screeched over and over again.

Donald knew his younger daughter only too well. Having worked herself up into this state only the truth would now suffice. 'John was crushed,' he said.

Carrie froze. 'Crushed?' Then the enormity of what that meant, in a foundry context, hit her. Her eyes rolled upwards and she dropped to the floor in a dead faint.

Winnie bent to attend to her daughter, at the same time telling Donald to hurry through to the kitchen and get some water. He left the room at a run, surprisingly nimble on his feet for such a big man.

Carrie's face was clammy to touch and there were large drops of sweat on her forehead. Her skin was a dirty white with a greenish tinge to it.

Winnie was using the hem of her dress to wipe away the sweat when Carrie's eyes blinked open. 'The pain!' she groaned.

Carrie's back arched and her body convulsed.

Winnie knew immediately what was happening. Taking a deep breath, she told herself to keep calm. When Donald returned, she took the cup from him and held it to Carrie's mouth. While Carrie drank she said, 'Go downstairs and see if Mrs Cooper is at home. If she is, then ask her to come up right away. When you've done that, run for the doctor. Tell him Carrie's started having her wean.'

Donald didn't bother asking his wife if she was sure. A man used to issuing orders, he also knew how to obey them. He rose at once from his kneeling position and tore from the room.

'Do you think you can make your bed?' Winnie asked.

Carrie gritted her teeth as another violent pain wracked her insides. Her breath came in pants as she waited for the pain to subside. When it was on the retreat she nodded.

One flight down, Big Donald was hammering on Mrs Cooper's door. She was a widow who lived directly below the Chisholms along with her teenage son, Robert. Although she had a name for sticking her nose into other people's affairs, she was also considered to be a reliable, trustworthy and good neighbour when needed.

When Mrs Cooper finally answered Donald, he hurriedly explained to her why she was wanted upstairs. Before he'd finished speaking she was undoing her pinny.

With a backward shout over his shoulder that he was off for the doctor, he clattered on his way. His heavy, tackety workboots struck sparks from the stone stairs as he ran.

By this time Winnie had managed to get Carrie into bed and stripped of some of her clothes. When Mrs Cooper arrived the two of them worked Carrie's dress up over her head and slipped it off that way.

Carrie stared up at the whitewashed ceiling. There was a far-away, glazed look in her eyes indicating she was in a state of shock.

Winnie and Mrs Cooper both knew from the frequency of the contractions that the birth was imminent and were praying the doctor would arrive in time. Still, if he didn't then they'd just have to deliver the baby themselves. It wouldn't be the first time either of them had done that.

'Poor lamb,' Mrs Cooper crooned, stroking the side of Carrie's cheek.

'Crushed,' Carrie said hollowly. Tears welled in her eyes and streamed down the sides of her face on to the pillow.

Mrs Cooper was left with Carrie while Winnie boiled some water and then ransacked her linen drawer for old sheets and towels.

Carrie threw back her head and screamed, not aware that her fingers, hooked like talons, were digging into Mrs Cooper's arm.

Between contractions Carrie mumbled her dead husband's name.

Mrs Cooper's heart went out to Carrie. She knew only too well what it was like to lose your man. It was six long, lonely years since she'd lost hers.

Donald burst into the surgery and demanded to see the doctor right away. The receptionist took one look at his frantic face and scurried off down a passageway to the consulting room.

Donald gulped in air. His chest was on fire, and he felt as though he'd swallowed a mouthful of molten metal. The thought of metal brought him back to the accident and those last few seconds before the five-ton casting crushed the life out of John McBain.

He'd been at the other end of the foundry and hadn't witnessed what had happened. What he did know was that the casting, being moved by crane, had veered and yawed out of control to slam into John who had been walking along a gantry.

Death had been instantaneous.

The question was why John was up in that particular gantry in the first place. The gantry had been declared unsafe the previous week and out of bounds until it was made secure.

Donald's thoughts were interrupted by the receptionist telling him to go through to the consulting room where the doctor would see him.

Donald was slightly in awe of Dr Robertson for no other reason than the fact the man spoke with a pronounced southern English accent.

Donald stood deferentially with cap in hand while he explained what had happened at the foundry and the effect the news of this had had on Carrie.

Before Donald had finished his story Robertson had already begun packing his black bag.

Hurrying through to the waiting room, Robertson issued a stream of instructions to the receptionist and then, with Donald hard behind him, he rushed out into the street to his car.

'Get in, man!' Robertson barked as Donald hesitated, unsure of whether or not he was to accompany the doctor.

Robertson cranked the car and it immediately burst into life. Seconds later they were chugging in the direction of Tallon Street.

In Carrie's old bedroom Winnie was holding one hand and Mrs Cooper the other while Carrie screamed, her legs jerking upwards and in towards her swollen torso. Dilation was already well advanced.

Winnie heard the rattle of a key in the outside lock and breathed a sigh of relief when, seconds later, she heard Robertson's cultured tones.

'It's yourself then, doctor,' Winnie said gratefully as

Robertson breezed into the room.

Behind Robertson's back, Winnie and Mrs Cooper exchanged glances. Although unspoken between them, they both knew something was wrong with Carrie's labour.

Donald had hung back in the hallway where he now lit a cigarette. This would be his station until it was all over. Here he would be on hand should they need him to do anything.

Robertson washed his hands in a steaming bowl of water provided for that purpose. Above the well-trimmed military moustache the keen, darting eyes were taking everything in. He had already noted that although trying to appear to the contrary, both Winnie and Mrs Cooper were uneasy about something.

'Now then, Carrie,' he said in his best bedside manner, 'let's just see what's what.' He sat on the edge of the bed and began to probe carefully with his fingers.

Carrie lay with her eyes closed. In her mind what she was seeing was a day not long before she and John had been married when he'd taken part in the all Glasgow tug-of-war championships. She'd been there cheering him on as his team, representing Armstrong's, had fought a valiant final contest with the City of Glasgow Police.

In the end the Armstrong team, amidst much shouting and general hullabalooing, had finally managed to pull their opponents over the line to win the match and championship.

The winners had received medals, silver inlaid with red and white enamel and topped by a scroll, which had later been inscribed with each of their names on the back.

John's medal was in the top drawer of the sideboard in McLellan Street: it was taken out every so often and polished. John was fond of saying it was the only thing he'd ever won. Now he'd never win anything else.

Carrie sobbed and a lump rose in her throat. Then the pain was back and there was no time to think of medals or anything else except the terrible, searing agony doing its damndest to split her in two.

Robertson was a worried man. His probing had confirmed that there were complications with the impending birth, a fact that had not been evident when he'd last examined Carrie a few weeks previously.

The baby's head, upon entering the pelvis, had failed to rotate through the required 180 degress, resulting in it now being in what was known as a persistent posterior position. He knew that if the birth went ahead this way he'd lose the baby for sure and probably Carrie as well.

As he wiped his hands on a towel, he was only too aware of the older women's eyes on him. He smiled and nodded reassuringly. Then, bending again over Carrie, he desperately cudgelled his brains for a way to remedy or at least help the situation.

Miracles do still happen, and that day one happened for Carrie McBain. Minutes before the baby started to emerge, its head suddenly rotated into the right position.

The first Robertson knew of his was when the head had appeared sufficiently for him to see that the forehead was facing downwards. He was suddenly bathed in warm, sticky sweat as he awaited further developments.

'Oh, Christ!' Carrie moaned. A trickle of bright red blood spilled from a corner of her mouth, the result of her having bitten her tongue during a particularly violent contraction.

'You're doing fine,' Winnie said.

'Just keep pushing,' Mrs Cooper added.

The baby's face slid fully into view and, as it did so, it turned sideways so that it was facing to the left.

Robertson heaved a sigh of relief. Everything was now normal.

The baby's face was a bright blue colour which, together with the black hair lying plastered to its head, was smeared with a white cheesy substance known as vernix. The face, screwed up in an angry grimace, also bore streaks of blood.

Carrie's body suddenly relaxed and she sucked in breath after breath. 'Is it over?' she asked in a thin, strained voice.

'Not quite,' Robertson replied. But you're half way there.'

The contractions started again almost immediately. Carrie's body seemed to explode from the inside as first one and then the other of the baby's shoulders emerged.

Her fingernails raked the bedsheet. The pain was now almost unbearable, and she felt that at any moment she was going to slip into the blessed relief of unconsciousness.

Not yet. Not yet, she told herself, over and over again. She wanted the baby fully born before she allowed herself the luxury of oblivion.

It crossed her mind then she might be dying. It seemed to her there was a warm blackness beckoning, and if she only allowed herself to be embraced by this all--enveloping calm she would never again waken in the world she knew. It would be so easy to slip over. John was waiting for her after all. They would be together again, this time for eternity.

The baby, a voice seemed to whisper in her ear, don't forget about the wee one. It'll need someone to look after it. Don't leave it all alone like John once was. He'd be furious to think you even contemplated the idea.

'Push Carrie! Push!' Robertson thundered.

Carrie grunted and did her best to obey, but the message being sent so urgently by her brain didn't seem to be getting through to her body.

Winnie wiped a fresh trickle of blood from the side of Carrie's mouth, while in her mind she relived the four births she'd undergone herself.

In the hallway Donald turned to face the outside door when it opened to admit Hugh. The boy's face was haggard underneath the dirt from the foundry. His brother-in-law was the first man he'd ever seen killed.

'Well?' Donald demanded quietly.

'The undertakers came and took him away. They want

to know whether he's to stay at their place or go up in a coffin to McLellan Street.'

Donald ran a hand over his face. This decision wasn't his to make. Only Carrie should decide what was to be done. That was her right.

Hugh jerked a thumb towards the bedroom. 'What's going on in there?'

In a low voice Donald told his son about the shock of John's death bringing on the baby. Hugh paled when a fresh bout of screaming rent the air.

Gratefully Hugh accepted a Willy Woodbine from his father and lit up. As he smoked he thought of the mangled mess which only that morning had been John McBain. In a macabre way it had fascinated him to discover the human body contained so much blood. The area round the gantry where the accident had taken place had been awash with the stuff. The body itself bore no resemblance to what it had once been.

The shock of seeing John's remains had been overwhelming, and for a few terrible minutes he'd thought he was going to throw up. Not that anyone would have blamed him if he had.

It amazed him to realize he was hungry. Death and birth might be all around him, but it certainly hadn't affected his stomach any. He wondered if he should sneak into the kitchen and make himself a jam piece. One thing was certain: there wasn't going to be any dinner that day.

'Do you think I should go and get Harriet?' he asked. His elder sister worked as a machinist in a clothing factory about half a mile away. Carrie had also worked there before having to leave because of her advancing pregnancy.

Big Donald shook his head. There was no point in taking the lassie away from her work when there were already enough people on hand. Besides, Harriet was naturally squeamish about certain things and would probably have ended up being more of a hindrance than a help.

In the bedroom Carrie gave a long drawn-out sigh as her body completed the ejection. The baby, large and raw-looking, slid neatly into Robertson's waiting hands.

Winnie craned forward. 'It's a wee boy!' she breathed.

'A wee boy,' Carrie repeated.

Mrs Cooper stuck her head round the door and called the news to Donald and Hugh.

Donald beamed and smacked his meaty hands together. 'That's rare!' he said.

Winnie and Mrs Cooper both laughed when the baby opened his mouth and gave a lusty cry.

'Is he . . . all right?' Carrie asked. It was the one question every newly delivered mother feels compelled to ask, and the one they dread to have answered in the negative.

Robertson thoroughly checked the baby's fingers, toes and external organs. 'He's a smasher,' he replied eventually. 'There's absolutely nothing wrong with him.'

Carrie nodded gratefully, the ghost of a smile hovering round her bloodless lips.

Robertson tied off the baby's umbilical cord and then handed him over to his grandmother.

Winnie swathed the baby, first in a torn-off piece of clean cotton sheet and then in a shawl that had been in the family for generations. Every one of her family had worn that shawl. It was part of Chisholm tradition.

Mrs Cooper washed Carrie down and then, with Robertson's help, changed the bedding. When Carrie had been made decent, Donald and Hugh were allowed into the room.

Donald stared in wonderment at the baby cradled in his wife's arms. The miracle of birth never ceased to amaze him.

The baby's eyelids flickered and jerked open. Eyes of the palest blue stared out at the world for the first time.

The mouth twisted and seemed to be preparing to cry again, so Winnie started humming a lullaby that had long been a great favourite of hers. The mouth immediately slackened and settled back into repose.

Carrie felt more tired than she'd ever done before in her life. It was as though every particle of energy in her body had been carefully and methodically drained away.

The blackness was behind her now. She no longer felt drawn to what it had to offer. Her time for dying hadn't come yet.

Hugh was bursting with pride. He would have liked to hold the baby but didn't think that the manly thing to do. Instead he stuck his chest out and nodded knowingly as though he'd been through this sort of thing many times before.

'Please?' Carrie asked, holding out her hands.

Staring down at her newborn son, it seemed to her that his blue eyes were drinking her in, studying her every feature for future reference. But of course she knew that to be pure imagination on her part.

'He's to be called Angus,' she said. 'That was the name John and I had agreed on.'

Donald and Winnie nodded their approval. They knew that Angus had been the name of John's father who'd died before John was born.

History tragically repeating itself, Donald thought, somehow managing to retain the smile on his face.

'Angus,' Carrie said again. Laying her head back on the pillow, she closed her eyes.

A few seconds later both mother and son were fast asleep.

Mrs Cooper tiptoed from the room to put the kettle on for a cup of tea.

2

The day of the funeral dawned a scorcher. From horizon to horizon the sky was unmarred by even the vaguest wisp of cloud. The sun hung heavy and fat, looking like the centre of a perfectly fried egg.

Head bowed and supported on either side by Donald and Hugh, Carrie stepped aboard the hired black carriage which would take them to the cemetery.

All the curtains and blinds in Tallon Street had been drawn as a mark of respect. A neighbour from across the way stood with his cap in his hand. He wouldn't move until the carriage had gone past him.

It was the first time Carrie had been out since Angus's birth, and she felt a little light-headed. Anxiously she gazed up at the Coopers' window, fancying she could hear the wee fellow crying. Mrs Cooper was looking after Angus while she was at the funeral.

Winnie squeezed Carrie's arm, knowing what was running through her daughter's mind. Carrie's anxiety subsided and she shot her mother the briefest of smiles. Mrs Cooper was a dab hand with children. Angus would be all right in her more than capable hands.

The carriage moved forward at a dignified pace as they made their way up Tallon Street. Carrie had decided John was to remain at the undertakers until the time of the funeral. They were headed there now to pick up the coffin.

Harriet Chisholm stared stonily out the carriage

window as they clip-clopped up the cobbled street. She hated funerals. In fact, she loathed them so much the very thought of having to go to one was enough to make her feel sick for days beforehand. Harriet was only too well aware that one day she, too, would die and the thought terrified her.

As a wee lassie she'd had terrible nightmares about dying. Nightmares that would bring her out of her sleep whimpering with terror. With small fist stuck in her mouth and a cold sweat literally dripping from her, she'd lie staring into the darkness. Her nightmares about death were always the same: flesh-eating worms slowly devouring her body, the claustrophobia of the grave; and the awful, awful loneliness which was undoubtedly the worst thing of all.

Loneliness was a word Harriet was well acquainted with. For as long as she could remember she had been alone, with the sort of loneliness that's there even when you're surrounded by others.

Perhaps things would have been different if she'd been born pretty, or at least attractive. But she hadn't been. There had been no magical transformation for this ugly duckling. The ugly duckling had grown up into just as ugly a duck.

With bitter shame she remembered it had been a great dare at one time amongst the boys of her class to corner and kiss her. For a long time she'd wondered why she was in such demand till at a birthday party that beautiful blonde bitch, Aileen Summers, had whispered the answer in her ear during a game of postie postie.

She'd fled the room and the house, running down the road with a face awash with hot tears and Aileen's words still ringing in her ears.

The boys had been kissing her as the worst dare they could think of to test their manhood. 'Kiss Harriet Chisholm and not be sick' was how they put it. Laughing and wiping their mouths afterwards, saying it wasn't as bad as all that, as long as you kept your eyes shut so you didn't see her face.

Tall, angular and bony she'd been at school. And despite her many prayers she'd grown up exactly the same – a fact that burned resentfully in her breast, causing her to view the world through a cold and jaundiced eye.

Harriet's gaze flickered sideways to where Carrie was sitting with Winnie. Although hardly a raving beauty, Carrie was none the less far more attractive than she was. And how she'd always envied Carrie that.

If only men could see inside her, she thought. If only they would take the trouble to see the real her inside this hated shell which housed her being. But in her experience men didn't have that sort of insight when it came to women. All they were interested in were the externals.

She glanced across again at Carrie. It saddened her to see her sister so obviously suffering, but there was a side of her that was jealous of Carrie even now.

Hadn't Carrie had a man of her own? A good, loving husband who'd worshipped the very ground she'd walked on. And didn't she now have a gorgeous baby as a legacy of that marriage?

It was certainly a lot more than Harriet was ever likely to get.

Her eyes glittered as she stared out at the passing scene. She would have given anything to have landed a man like John McBain. And as for Angus, she would have sold her soul for a wean like him.

What was to become of her? she wondered bitterly. Was her fate to end up a dry old spinster? She was sure it was. Angus and any other nephews and nieces she might have would pay a duty call to Aunty Harriet on those Sunday afternoons when their parents forced them to come and see her.

'You're looking well, Aunty Harriet. And how are you today?'

Bitterness welled up inside her as she imagined how pitifully grateful she'd probably be for the visits while knowing that to them she would undoubtedly be a figure of fun, someone they laughed and sniggered about when they were on their own.

Her hands twitched towards her bag and the cigarettes it contained. But she daren't light up, even though she was desperate for a smoke. Her father would have a fit had she tried. And even though she was a grown woman she was still as scared of him as she'd always been.

She recalled the leatherings and beltings he'd given them all when they were young. Hugh and Carrie had taken their punishments in silence. As indeed had Alex. She, on the other hand, had howled the place down at the very threat of his hand or belt.

A physical coward, Donald had called her. And he was right. She couldn't stand pain and was convinced her sensitivity to it was far greater than other people's.

But Donald didn't agree. He just said she was a big feartie. Always had been and always would be.

God how she hated herself. If only she'd been born beautiful, or at least attractive. If only she hadn't been so damned clever, which seemed to put off so many men.

If only. . . . If only. . . .

Big Donald eyed Carrie closely. The loss of John had been a terrible blow to her, as indeed it had to them all. She was taking it badly but that was only to be expected. The pair of them had been so much in love.

At least she had the bairn to keep her occupied and help take her mind off matters. The wee chap would be a big solace to her in the difficult times ahead.

When they arrived at the undertakers, Donald and Hugh got out of the carriage and went inside. The hearse was already in place. The four black horses, each with a magnificent black plume flowing backwards from its head, were hooked up and waiting patiently to go.

After the coffin had been loaded aboard, the wreaths that had arrived at the undertakers were strewn decorously around it.

When all was ready, Donald and Hugh climbed back aboard the carriage, and followed the hearse to the cemetery.

Carrie felt as though she was only the shell of what she'd been before. She was learning to cope with the days, but the nights were something again. It was the early morning hours that were hardest, when she was up giving Angus his feed. Then she was all alone and, while the baby suckled, her mind filled itself with memories.

She'd lie in bed with her thoughts whirling after Angus had gone back to sleep. Once or twice it had been so bad she'd woken Harriet and kept her sister talking until the dawn came creeping over the chimney tops. She knew that was grossly unfair of her as Harriet had her work to go to, but Harriet had never complained.

The pair of them would lie there talking about anything and everything. It didn't matter what they spoke about. The important thing was they did. To her credit, Harriet understood that.

Hugh was sweating and uncomfortable because of the rigid shirt collar jabbing into his throat. He was dressed in his one and only suit with a black armband stitched round the right sleeve. He felt lost and rather lonely sitting there amongst his family. He would be glad when all this was over.

It was hard to believe that a man as full of life as John McBain had been was now dead, and that within the hour they'd be burying him in the cold, dank earth.

Gooseflesh prickled on Hugh's neck as it came home to him for the first time that he, too, was only mortal.

On the way to the cemetery men doffed their hats and caps while the few they passed in uniform saluted.

During the drive, Winnie's mind was filled with thoughts of her son, Alex, who'd been killed just outside Sherman, Texas, in 1911. Alex had been sixteen when he left home, saying in the time-honoured way that he wanted to see the world and maybe find his fortune.

He'd been gone a little over six months when word arrived back to say he'd been hurt badly in an accident. Three days later, further word came saying he was dead.

The people in the American hospital had been

extremely kind. A doctor had written them a letter which had come in the parcel containing Alex's effects. Some months later the same doctor sent them a photo of the grave.

Winnie kept that photo in her handbag so she could have it with her at all times. Never a day went by that she didn't take it out and look at it.

Occasionally on the anniversary of Alex's death Donald would go down to the pub and drink a lot more than was good for him. Those were the only times Winnie ever saw her husband the worse for wear because of alcohol.

Robert Smith and his wife, Meg, were waiting for them at the cemetery gates. The Smiths were the nearest thing John had to a family as they had taken him in when he was a bare-arsed lad after his mother died. No formal adoption had ever taken place, so John had always maintained his own family name of McBain.

After being greeted by the Smiths, Carrie had a few words with the other pallbearers. Two of these were foundrymen who had been particular friends of John and the third was a chap called Archie Marjoribanks, an old school chum with whom John had run the streets as a boy and who had kept in touch ever since.

Donald, Hugh and old man Smith comprised one line of pallbearers, the two foundrymen and Marjoribanks the other.

Once the coffin was shouldered, the six men moved slowly forward while the women followed.

A large gang from Armstrong's stood grouped round the graveside, a few of whom were in their work clothes as they would be going straight on to weekend caretaking duties after the ceremony.

The Reverend Duncan Forbes stood at the top end of the grave with a large, well-thumbed Bible open in his hand. Looking rather like an Old Testament prophet with his longish white hair and hawk-like, yet ascetic, features, he was a gentle man who genuinely cared.

Friends and neighbours from Tallon Street and

McLellan Street had turned up as well as various relatives of the Chisholm family. Chief amongst the latter was Donald's brother, Sandy, who was a merchant seaman.

The coffin was carefully laid by the graveside and the ceremony began with a prayer.

Old man Smith was heartbroken as he stared down at the coffin. John had been everything to him and his wife, the focal point of their waning lives. They had never had any children themselves, a fact to which he and Meg had never become reconciled.

It had always upset them both that John had never wanted to follow them into the newsagent and confectioner's shop they owned, which was a good, well-established business with an ever-increasing turnover.

Robert Smith sighed. If John had come into the shop, this would never have happened.

He glanced across to where Carrie was standing. He'd not altogether approved of that marriage, albeit it was obvious to anyone with half an eye in his head that John and the lassie had been daft on one another.

What had worried him at the time was the fact that the Chisholms and the Smiths – and since taking John in he'd considered John a Smith – although both working-class families, occupied different rungs on the social ladder. The Smiths were *rough*, whereas the Chisholms had bettered themselves by escaping into a *good* area. Cathcart was a far cry from Scotland Street where the Smiths lived and where John had been brought up. The Smiths were considerably well off, while the Chisholms lived from week to week on what was brought into the house.

Robert Smith greatly admired Big Donald, although the man's overpowering masculinity both awed and frightened him a little. Robert was a shy, retiring person, who, outside of business, had very little to say for himself. However, people who mistook his shyness for weakness soon learned better. In his own quiet way Robert was as ruthless as any self-made tycoon who's fought his way to the top.

What worried him now was the fact that Angus had

been left without a father, and he knew the harsh economic realities, both now and in the future. He knew Carrie would do her best by the child, and furthermore he trusted Big Donald to play his part in supporting the wee fellow, but Carrie would certainly find a capital sum handy. That was why he'd brought £200 along with him today.

The money hadn't come from a bank, but out of the safe he had bolted to the kitchen floor at home. A lot of people would have been surprised to know what was in that safe. Certainly the tax man would.

The Reverend Forbes spoke about John and the terrible tragedy that had befallen the McBain family. Then he called for them all to join him in singing 'Abide with Me'.

Carrie watched, dry-eyed, as the coffin was lowered into the grave. At a signal from the minister she stepped forward to pick up a handful of earth which she threw on to the coffin lid. One by one the chief mourners came forward and followed suit.

When the ceremony was over Carrie spoke to the men from Armstrong's who'd come along to pay their last respects. Some she knew, others she didn't.

Donald stood staring at the great mound of wreaths and flowers piled high beside the grave.

'They did him proud,' Robert Smith said, coming up to Donald from behind.

'Aye, they did that,' Donald agreed, lifting his eyes and staring out over the rolling green countryside.

Donald loved being in the country. He found it soothing after the racket and clatter of the foundry. The sky was clear now, but on weekdays when the Glasgow smokestacks and chimneys were belching soot and fug into the air, it was a different matter entirely. Then the sky was stained with a great grey cloud which hung, lowering, over the city.

It always amused Donald to think that the word Glasgow came from the Gaelic meaning 'Dear Green Place'. What a joke when you considered the filthy industrial hell that 'Green Place' had now become.

Winnie and Harriet waited patiently while the Reverend Forbes quietly spoke to Carrie. Judging from the expression on her face she seemed to be finding some comfort in what he was saying.

Winnie finally caught Donald's attention and signalled to him that they really must be away if they were to get back in time to receive those who were coming to tea.

Carrie had one last look at the grave. As she turned away the gravediggers moved into position and soon their spades were flying rhythmically.

When they had all arrived back at Tallon Street, Carrie stopped off at Mrs Cooper's for Angus.

Bella Millar, who lived in one of the ground floor apartments, and Mrs McElvey from across the street, had laid out the tea while the Chisholms were at the funeral. Both of these women were close friends of Winnie and the girls.

A few people had already arrived, the Smiths amongst them, and these had been ushered into the big room where they now stood talking and trying to be at ease.

Winnie said hello and then fled to the kitchen, leaving Harriet to play hostess, a task she performed easily.

Drinks were dispensed and then shortly afterwards everyone was asked to go through to the front room where an assortment of borrowed tables and chairs had been arranged so that the entire company could sit down in one sitting.

After the meal Big Donald asked them all to go back through to the big room where there would be more drinks for those who wished them.

Winnie, Harriet and a few of the women – Meg Smith insisted on being one of them – stayed behind to clear things away and do the washing up. They would have their own blether while they were getting on with it, and then go back to the big room.

In the big room Archie Marjoribanks found himself standing close to Carrie who was talking to the young

Robert Cooper. Marjoribanks had already consumed a large number of whiskies, some of which had come from the half bottle he was carrying in his inside jacket pocket, enough to make him half cut and querulous. Accepting another large one from Donald, he literally threw it down his throat. Turning to Carrie he said, 'I only hope Armstrong's are going to pay you a fair bit of compensation. They must be liable, surely to God, as John was killed on the premises.'

A sudden feel of unease settled on the room at these words and those who worked at Amrstrong's glanced from one to the other.

'It's not quite as black and white as that,' Donald said. He then tried to change the subject but Marjoribanks would have none of it.

Marjoribanks was a man of medium height with a stocky build and auburn hair. He would have been reasonably handsome if it hadn't been for his eyes which gave him a foxy look.

'I don't understand,' Marjoribanks persisted, his attention now centred on Donald. 'John was killed in the foundry, therefore compensation must be due. Surely that's the way it is nowadays?'

'Sir Alan might not see it that way,' Donald replied softly.'

'Sir Alan?'

'Him that owns the place. John was on a gantry that had been declared unsafe and put out of bounds when the accident occurred. You can bet Sir Alan's going to make an awful lot of that.'

'I see,' said Marjoribanks, frowning.

'The union will be meeting Sir Alan first thing Monday morning,' Donald continued. 'We should know what's what then.'

Wishing to put an end to the conversation, Donald moved to the bottles to pour out more drinks. He was furious with Marjoribanks, thinking the man crass and insensitive. Talk of compensation was completely out of order at a time like this.

Unaware of the offence he'd caused, Marjoribanks turned his attention back to Carrie. Although he'd met her several times in the past he'd never bothered to have a really good look at her. He saw now that she was a rather attractive woman and one very much to his taste.

Carrie decided to check up on Angus. She gave Marjoribanks a brief smile in passing because he was staring so intently at her.

Marjoribanks quickly returned the smile, convinced that Carrie had taken a shine to him. Later, the memory of that smile started him thinking.

Carrie was coming out of the bedroom where Angus was sleeping when she found Robert Smith waiting for her. She genuinely liked the old man, having always found him sympathetic. She didn't know about his early objection to her marriage as John had never seen fit to mention it to her.

Robert Smith pressed a buff-coloured envelope into her hand. 'A little something to help you and the wean out,' he said.

'Oh, but I couldn't!'

'Don't be daft, woman. Of course you can,' he said and folded her fingers round the envelope.

Carrie took a deep breath. This was most unexpected. 'Well, if you're sure . . . ?'

'Of course I'm sure. I wouldn't have given it to you otherwise.'

Carrie wondered whether the thing to do was to open the envelope there and then or wait till later. When she saw he was staring expectantly at her she presumed he wanted her to open it in front of him.

Using her finger she slit the envelope. She gasped when she saw the thickness of the wad of fivers that were inside.

Robert Smith wasn't a man who gave much away, but when he did he enjoyed the experience. The thunderstruck expression on Carrie's face delighted him. He would derive enormous pleasure in describing that expression to his wife, Meg, whose voice he could now hear coming from behind the closed kitchen door.

'We just ask that you bring the wee fellow to see us once in a while,' he said. Leaning across he kissed Carrie on the cheek. Then he was swiftly making his way back to the big room where he intended having a large glass of Donald's whisky.

Carrie slipped back into the bedroom where Angus was sleeping and stood with her back pressed hard against the door. Her hands were trembling as she slowly counted the wad of fivers.

'Two hundred pounds,' she breathed. Her heart was thudding and her legs felt weak at the knees. The hand holding the money was sticky and hot.

Closing her eyes, she offered up a silent prayer of gratitude. There was a halfpenny policy on John's life, but when that was realized it would hardly be enough to bury him, much less anything else.

The £200 windfall was a fortune to her and she swore there and then to put every farthing of it to good use. Now it wouldn't be necessary for her to find a job right away which was an enormous weight off her mind as jobs were so few and far between.

When she rejoined the assembled company she felt a sense of optimism for the future that she hadn't known before.

3

Early on the Monday evening Winnie was sitting at the big room window. From this vantage point she could see the bend beyond which lay the sombre-looking cluster of buildings comprising Armstrong's. The hooter had just blown and at any moment the men would come streaming round the bend, hurrying home for their tea.

Normally, Winnie would have been in the kitchen getting the evening meal ready, but that night they were having salad and the rest of the boiled ham left over from the funeral. Everything was already prepared and laid out on the front room table, waiting for Donald and Hugh to arrive.

Carrie was in the bedroom feeding the wee one while Harriet was talking to her.

Winnie gently massaged her left temple. She had a bit of a headache which had been brought on by the day's heat. It had been another scorcher. Every window in the house was wide open to any breeze that might be about to waft through.

Winnie had spoken to Carrie that afternoon about the house in McLellan Street, wanting to know what Carrie's plans were. The one thing Carrie was certain about was that she didn't want to go back there to live. The place held too many memories for her.

She had said they'd speak to Donald that night to see if he'd be agreeable to Carrie and Angus staying on permanently in Carrie's old room. As Harriet would have to share the room with the two of them, she too would have to be consulted.

The first of the men had started coming round the bend which meant that it would only be a matter of minutes before Donald and Hugh were home.

She often thought that Donald expected too much from Hugh, and consequently was far too hard on him. The trouble was that Donald couldn't seem to understand that Hugh was going through a stage he himself had never been allowed, for Donald's youth had ended abruptly when he was ten years old on the day he went to graft in the bakery.

According to Donald there had been fourteen of them, slaving away in a room little bigger than the one she was in now, and at least one-third of that space had been taken up by the two ovens.

On a number of occasions Donald had described to her what it had been like to walk into that room when the ovens were going full blast. Like being thrust into the very maw of hell itself, was one way he'd put it.

It hadn't been uncommon for grown men to suddenly keel over in a dead faint, and once a man called Barton had thrown himself to the floor where he'd cried and drummed his fists like a baby.

In those days Donald hadn't known what it was to own a pair of shoes, but he had known what hard work was. By Christ he had.

The Chisholms were a Highland family, as were her own, who'd made the long trek south to the big city because they'd been slowly starving to death on their croft outside a village called Invershuie.

Donald's father knew a lot about sheep and precious little else. But work was to be had in Glasgow, and not long after his arrival, he had landed himself a job as a labourer down at the Broomielaw, working for a well-to-do tobacco merchant called Gordon.

Alastair Chisholm was thirty-two years old the day he dropped down dead, so completely and utterly exhausted that his worn-out body had no other recourse but to up and quit on him. When he'd died, Donald had just turned ten and Sandy was thirteen. There was another brother, Willy, who was seven, and Nettie, the only girl in the family, who was three.

A week after his father died, Donald started at the bakery. Sandy had already been grafting for just over a year at a rope works.

The young Donald had worked his fingers to the bone helping to keep the family alive, and later when the chance of an apprenticeship came up in a city foundry he'd jumped at it.

By that time Willie was older and able to bring in some money, and Nettie wasn't such a tie on their mother who was able to get to do scrubbing and general housework.

By the time Donald was twelve, the hard, punishing

work he'd been forced to endure had long since knocked any vestiges of his youth clean out of him. He'd become a man in every sense of the word.

Winnie sighed and patted the greying hair piled up on her head in two side rolls. Before they went to sleep that night she'd have another quiet word with Donald, asking him to try and be more understanding with Hugh.

Winnie started, realizing she'd drifted off into a world of her own. Crowds of men were hurrying past now, while just up ahead she could make out Hugh's tall, slim figure.

Hugh looked up at the window and saw his mother's face peering down at him. He gave her a cheery wave before turning into their close and bounding up the stairs three at a time.

Winnie was waiting for him at the door.

'Papa's stayed behind to have a word with the union official. He said to tell you he won't be long .'

Winnie read Hugh's face correctly. 'The meeting didn't go well, then, I take it?'

Hugh pushed past her into the house, wanting for once to be the first at the sink. Normally that was Donald's privilege. 'No, it didn't,' he called back over his shoulder. 'But I think you'd better wait and hear the story from Papa. You know what he's like about that sort of thing.'

Harriet emerged from her bedroom to glance questioningly at Winnie who in a few terse sentences explained the situation. Harriet made a sort of harrumphing sound, a vocal mannerism of hers which could make her appear very formidable indeed, and disappeared back into the bedroom to relay the information to Carrie.

Carrie had been in a depressed state of mind ever since that morning when she'd been back to McLellan Street to pick up some more clothes for herself and the baby.

There had been the terrible moment when she'd come across some dirty clothes of John's which had been pushed into a corner. His own distinctive smell still clung to them and that had hit her like a body blow.

Then there had been his pipe; his spare collar studs lying on the mantelpiece above the fireplace, his favourite chair which he'd been threatening to repair for over a year, and the brass poker he'd made in the foundry when an apprentice.

The sight of each of these articles which she so closely associated with him had torn afresh at her still raw grief.

'Are you all right?' Harriet asked.

Carrie someow managed a smile. 'Just thinking. Remembering.' Then suddenly, 'I saw that Archie Marjoribanks giving you the eye the other day. If you ask me, I think he took a fancy to you.'

Harriet snorted and looked away. 'Don't be soft. That sort of man wouldn't be interested in the likes of me.'

'Why not, for heaven's sake?'

Harriet smiled grimly and didn't reply. Instead she started buffing her nails. She would have liked to grow them long and talonlike, but of course that was impossible when she spent five and a half days every week knocking her pan out over an industrial sewing machine.

God, how she hated the factory! With her brain she should have been able to do a lot better for herself than that. The trouble was there were so few opportunities for women and virtually none where something more than hard physical slog or a beautiful body was demanded of one.

Harriet ground her teeth in frustration, thinking that the entire world had conspired to thwart her ambitions.

Well, one day the work situation would have to ease, and when it did she wouldn't be slow in putting herself forward. Unless, of course, there were other ways to skin this particular cat?

That sudden electrifying thought was something completely new, and she wondered why it hadn't occurred to her before.

Her eyes half closed and a look of muted excitement settled on her face as she began to brood on the idea of a possible alternative.

In the bathroom Hugh finished his wash and vigorously dried himself off. It had been a terrible day in the foundry with everyone being acutely aware that young John McBain, who'd been laughing and joking with them only a few days previously, was now dead and buried.

The entire work force had paused when the casting, still with traces of blood on its side, had been hauled away by a gang of labourers to be loaded on to a wagon and dispatched to the people who'd placed the order for it. Armstrong's wasn't the sort of firm to destroy a perfectly good casting just because some poor bugger had the misfortune to be killed by it.

Going through to the living room, Hugh threw himself into one of the fireside chairs. He was ravenously hungry but knew only too well that no one would be allowed to start on their tea until Big Donald arrived home and was ready to sit down. That was one of the house rules.

It was over an hour later when the front door clicked to announce Big Donald's return.

When he entered the living room he found Winnie, Carrie and Harriet waiting expectantly for him. Hugh, head fallen to one side, was fast asleep and snoring.

Donald wasn't a man who believed in mincing words so he came straight to the point. 'There's no hope for a penny piece of compensation, lass,' he said to Carrie. 'Sir Alan just won't entertain the idea.'

Carrie hadn't believed it would be much, but she had expected something. She'd thought that Armstrong would have felt obliged at least to make a token gesture. It seemed that wasn't to be the case. She thanked God yet again for Robert Smith's £200, without which she would have been destitute.

'The mean, miserable bastard!' Harriet hissed.

'Did you speak to Sir Alan yourself?' Winnie asked.

'I did,' Donald replied. 'The trouble is that John was up on that gantry without authority. Sir Alan argues that it doesn't matter that the casting was out of control. If

John hadn't been where he was he wouldn't have been killed. Sir Alan says that as John's death was John's own fault, he daren't make even an *ex gratia* payment to Carrie in case it sets a precedent.'

'What do you think, Papa?' Carrie asked in a tight voice.

Donald's face contorted into a mask of suppressed fury. He clenched and unclenched his massive fists. A terrible injustice had been done that day and what angered him was that he'd been totally powerless to do anything about it.

'I did think of telling Armstrong what to do with my job.'

Winnie paled, and a vein in her neck began to throb.

'But, of course, there wouldn't have been any sense in that. There isn't a snowball's hope in hell of me or anyone else in the works getting another job in Glasgow at the moment, and that's why that man can treat us any way he bloody well pleases.'

'You did right, Papa,' Carrie said. 'John wouldn't have expected you to do otherwise.'

Harriet said, 'I was talking to a girl at work the other day whose husband was recently out at the Gareloch. According to him, it's chock-a-block with laid-up ships.'

'She told the truth,' Donald growled. 'That's why there are no orders on the books. There's a glut of merchant tonnage left over from the war, far more than is now needed. If things go on the way they are I can see at least half the men on Clydeside being idle before the year's out.'

'Oh, don't say that!' Winnie exclaimed, her eyes wide with fear.

Donald stalked to the sideboard where he knew there to be some whisky left over from the funeral. He poured himself a large one and gulped it down. Then he poured himself another.

He was worried sick that he might end up in the position of not being able to provide for his family. To Donald that was a horrifying prospect, and the worst sin a man like him could commit. The entire strength of his male ego was centred round two things: his virility, and his ability to be the family bread-winner.

Crossing to the open window, he gazed down on to the back green. His overriding fear was that they'd lose this house and be forced to move back to the slums from which he and Winnie had struggled so hard and so long to escape.

Winnie sighed and ran a hand wearily over her hair. The possibility of Donald being made idle was something she was going to have to face. Somehow she was going to have to find a way of cutting back so that she could put a wee bit by against that black day, should it ever arrive. Still, looking on the bright side, no matter how bad things got, there was bound to come a time when they'd get better again. That thought lightened her heart and, combined with the love she had for her family and they for her, gave her the courage to face whatever the future held in store for them.

Thinking of the slums had led to Donald remembering his mother. She'd been a beauty in her day, with long, flowing, lustrous hair and a peerless complexion. But her looks had soon withered as a result of producing four children and then struggling to cope when Alastair died. When she was thirty-five her face was heavily lined and she had grey hair which turned snow white a decade later.

Many's the time they'd all huddled together for warmth in the one bed while she regaled them with tales of Invershuie. She'd speak of her young days and the adventures she'd had in the wild glens and mountains surrounding the village.

Once she'd confided to them that she'd known their father all her life and there had never been anyone else whom she'd ever wanted to marry. Young Nettie had cried at that, saying she hated Glasgow and wanted her daddy back. Fiona Chisholm had held her only daughter tight then and in a cracked voice confessed that she too wanted their daddy back.

Donald finally emerged from his dream to remember that he still had John's last wage packet in his trouser pocket.

Crossing to Carrie, he laid the small brown envelope in her lap. 'That was what John had coming,' he said, unable to keep the bitterness out of his voice.

Winnie startled everyone by rising and declaring, 'I hope that man Armstrong rots in hell for what he did today.'

She stared defiantly round the room: it was almost unknown for her to swear.

'Amen to that,' said Donald, agreeing with his wife's sentiments. 'Now let's eat before our stomachs begin to think our throats have been cut.'

Hugh needed no further telling. He was the first one to sit at the table.

4

Summer gave way to autumn and that, in turn, to winter. Early one Saturday evening in February, Hugh answered a knock on the front door to find Archie Marjoribanks standing there with a bunch of flowers in one hand and a brown paper bag full of clinking bottles in the other.

For a moment Hugh was taken aback. Then, grinning, he ushered Marjoribanks through to the living room where the family was assembled.

When Carrie heard Marjoribanks's voice in the hallway, she shot Harriet a look which clearly said, 'See I was right. He *is* interested in you!'

Harriet frowned, an action she normally tried to avoid as it caused a deep cleft of unattractive flesh to appear above her nose.

As Marjoribanks entered the room, Donald carefully folded his evening paper and laid it by the side of his chair. Rising slowly and ponderously, he shook Marjoribanks by the hand.

The flowers were for Winnie. They were terribly expensive at this time of year, but although she protested, she was obviously delighted and touched.

The bottles were beer and lemonade.

Hugh hurried to the sideboard where the glasses were kept while Marjoribanks was urged to sit down.

Marjoribanks cleared his throat and said he hoped they didn't mind him visiting, but being an old china of John's he was naturally concerned as to how Carrie and the baby were managing.

He was hastily assured by Winnie that mother and son were doing just fine. Carrie smiled and confirmed that this was so.

Hugh poured the beers and shandies while Carrie handed them round. He hesitated over whether or not to pour himself one. Empty glass in hand, he turned to gaze inquiringly at Donald, who after only the briefest of hestitations gave him the nod to go ahead.

For a while Donald and Marjoribanks discussed the state of the country which they both agreed had deteriorated since the previous summer. Then they talked about the pay-offs which had taken place at Armstrong's just before Christmas when 180 men had been sent home at the end of the week with the words ringing in their ears that they weren't to bother reporting back the following Monday.

Amrstrong's was a marine engineering firm, manufacturing and servicing pumps for the ships built on Clydeside. It had taken time but now the general slump in the yards was feeding back to the ancillary firms depending on them of which Armstrong's was one.

Normally a person of definite opinion, Donald now

found himself in the unusual position of not being sure what he thought of Marjoribanks. The man *had* spoken out of line at the funeral tea, but perhaps that wasn't such a bad thing after all. He had been concerned for Carrie's rights. But there was something elusive about the man, some aspect of his personality which defied Donald's analysis.

He had a great deal of charm, there was no denying that. He smiled a lot. Maybe too much. And he certainly knew how to flatter, as had been demonstrated in the little speech he'd made to Winnie when handing her the flowers.

Perhaps it was the flattery which had triggered his unease, Donald thought. He distrusted people who used flattery to their own advantage.

The conversation veered on to Marjoribanks's job, and much to Hugh's delight it transpired that he worked on the railways.

Hugh was something of a railway buff, having become mad keen on them when he was only a tiny lad. He now spoke eagerly with Marjoribanks about the far-reaching changes taking place at that time amongst the many railway companies up and down the length and breadth of Britain.

Marjoribanks was a shunter with the Caledonian Railway which was soon to integrate with a new company to form what was to be known as the London, Midland and Scottish Railway, LMS for short.

A light came into Marjoribanks's eyes as he talked about the engines currently in use with Caledonian, such as the old Dugald Drummonds whose designer was renowned for experimenting with 200lb pressure – a fearsome figure at the time.

Hugh wanted to know about the new Cardean Class 4-6-0 and the Pickersgill's two cylinder 4-6-0 express due to go into general service later that year.

Donald's unease melted as Hugh and Marjoribanks delved deeper into the facts and figures of the Caledonian and its rolling stock.

It was soon apparent from Marjoribanks's enthusiastic comments that he both loved and was good at his job. This put him several notches higher in Big Donald's estimation.

After more discussion Marjoribanks extended Hugh an invitation to come along to the Central Station one weekend, promising to show him around and, if possible, give him a short ride in an engine cab.

Needless to say, Hugh was ecstatic and immediately asked if the following Saturday would be suitable. The date was fixed, and to the accompaniment of a delighted laugh from Hugh they shook hands on it.

After that Winnie rose to say she was going to make a cup of tea. She had just baked some fresh scones that afternoon and wanted to impress Marjoribanks with them. Both Carrie and Harriet offered to help, but she told them to sit down again as she could manage on her own.

Winnie had guessed correctly that there was more to Marjoribanks's visit than a mere social call. What was yet unclear to her was which of her two daughters he was interested in. Carrie with Angus to look after needed another man, of course, but in a way she rather hoped it was Harriet he had his eye on.

Harriet worried her at times. She was too introspective and given to brooding for her own good. The real trouble with Harriet was that she was extremely intelligent and refused to hide the fact. Obvious intelligence tended to put men off as she'd once tried explaining to her, but Harriet had merely glowered and thrust her chin forward.

Look at her now! Winnie thought. Sitting there staring daggers at poor Mr Marjoribanks, who so far hadn't spoken one word out of place and had, in fact, been civility itself. No wonder she couldn't land herself a man if that was the way she treated them!

Harriet was surprised by her reaction towards Archie Marjoribanks. Coldly dissecting that reaction, she came to the conclusion he both attracted and repelled her at the same time.

He was a smoothie, all right – glib and surprisingly articulate. But his accent was dreadfully common. Far more so than John's had been, who had been brought up in the same district as he.

She wondered if it was the way his eyes bent in towards one another that put her off. To her mind they made him look like a crook.

Harriet had just lit her umpteenth cigarette since Marjoribanks's arrival when she suddenly became aware that he was staring at her. Her gaze flickered towards him and their eyes locked.

The embarrassed burning sensation started in the pit of her stomach and then swiftly radiated outwards. She wanted to squirm under that gaze, knowing he was mentally stripping her with a clinical objectivity that was both exciting and disgusting. There was a wealth of sexual knowledge in those eyes so dispassionately viewing her. That and a glint of humour as though he was inwardly laughing at the pitiful object she saw herself to be.

Fury exploded within her. How dare he look at her as if she were some common tart parading on the street corner! She wanted to pick something up and throw it at him. She wanted to grind her cigarette into his leering face. She wanted Donald to thrash him within an inch of his life and then throw him down the stairs. She wanted . . .

When the full realization of what she really *did* want burst in her, she was filled with both horror and shame.

Marjoribanks's mocking eyes once more trapped hers, this time for only the briefest of seconds – just long enough for him to let her know he was aware of what was running through her mind. Then he deliberately turned his back on her and struck up a new line of conversation with Donald who at that moment had just stopped speaking.

Harriet had an overwhelming urge to leap to her feet and flee the room, but she fought it down. This is ridiculous, she told herself. She was a mature woman of twenty-eight and not some silly wee lassie to be reduced to a jelly just because a man had looked at her *that* way. Of course it wasn't the look that was really bothering her, but rather what it sparked off within her. For the first time in her life she found herself scared of a man, not merely because he was bigger and stronger than she was, but due to something that went far deeper and whose roots were lodged in the very essence of her femininity.

A few minutes later Winnie bustled in, pushing a trolley loaded down with goodies. Carrie broke off speaking to help her mother by handing out the plates while Winnie poured the tea.

Marjoribanks was highly amused at Harriet's reaction to him. It was a long long time since he'd come across a girl at that age whom he could immediately sense was a virgin. In a way she reminded him of his dead wife, Libby, who'd also had that supercilious quality which he'd found so attractive.

For a moment or two he considered changing his mind about which sister to go after, but in the end decided it had to be Carrie. At least he wouldn't mind waking up in the morning and seeing her face next to his, which was a lot more than he could say for Harriet. Jesus, she was plain! But there *was* sex there. A vast untapped reservoir desperate to burst its banks. He could have relished being the one to do the bursting.

Sipping his tea he turned his attention to Carrie. Her pins were good which was important. He appreciated good legs. The backside, belly and breasts were overweight, but that would be because she was still feeding. She had an excellent profile, and her facial skin was flawless, unlike Harriet's which was marked from childhood spots.

But what was most in Carrie's favour was that she had an extremely pleasant personality as well as being easy to get on with and always eager to please. He knew all this for fact as John had mentioned it to him more than once.

The conversation died abruptly when they heard Angus yelling in his bedroom. Carrie hurried away to attend to him. She returned minutes later to report that the wee fellow must have been having a nightmare which luckily hadn't woken him.

At first Marjoribanks had viewed Angus as a liability, but thinking the matter through he'd come to realize how the child could be used to his advantage. If he did get married to Carrie, then Angus would be an enormous lever he'd have over her.

Half an hour later he decided it was time to go. Having reconfirmed Hugh's visit to the Central Station on the following Saturday – that had been a stroke of luck as it gave him the perfect opportunity to wangle another social call – he said his good-byes.

'Well, well, well,' said Donald after Marjoribanks had gone. Thoughtfully he rubbed his chin.

'I'll do the washing up,' said Harriet and started to gather the dirty dishes together. The trolley rattled as she vigorously pushed it from the room.

Hugh excused himself and went through to the big room where he slept on a bed settee. He wanted to go over his books on railways and dream about the coming Saturday.

Carrie had another look at Angus before taking herself through to the kitchen to help Harriet. 'What do you make of that, then?' she queried.

Harriet harrumphed. 'Make of what?' she snapped in reply.

Carrie was well used to her sister's moods and rudeness. Harriet just wouldn't have been Harriet without the tartness and caustic replies. Both in looks and temperament, they were as different as the proverbial chalk and cheese.

'I'm talking about Archie Marjoribanks paying a call,' Carrie said drily.

Harriet shrugged.

'You must have made some impression!'

'If you really want to know, I think he's got an awful

big tip for himself. He's arrogant, conceited and probably in the long run a bore to boot.'

Carrie turned her back to hide the smile which crept across her face. 'I can see he impressed you,' she said, her voice crackling at the edges with laughter.

Harriet glowered into the sink. The emotions Marjoribanks had aroused frightened her. There had been a few terrible moments back there in the living room when she'd fantasized about him using her. Degrading her. Even now the thought made her shiver.

'Are you all right? You've gone all pale suddenly,' Carrie said anxiously.

Harriet shrugged dismissively. 'I'm fine. Just tired, I think. We've been busy at the factory.'

'Well, that's something to be thankful for. Being busy, I mean. There are plenty who'd give their eye teeth to be in your shoes.'

'I'm only too aware of that,' Harriet said wearily.

'He was married, you know.'

'Who?

'Archie Marjoribanks. His wife died of cancer. I remember John telling me. He knew her, of course, but I never met the woman. I hardly know him, come to that.' She paused to stare thoughtfully before adding, 'I'm pretty sure there's a daughter, but I can't remember what her name is.'

Harriet sighed. 'For the last time, I'm not interested in him nor he in me,' she lied.

'Then why did he bother visiting?'

This was another of those times when Harriet wasn't sure whether Carrie was being naïvely ingenuous or downright dense. 'Well, there *are* two eligible females in this house now you know.'

'What?'

Harriet dried her hands on a spare tea towel before taking herself through to the living room for a last cigarette before bed. She left a stunned Carrie staring after her.

Carrie's thoughts were whirling. It had just never

entered her head that she might be the one who interested Marjoribanks.

Her first impulse was to dismiss the notion of a relationship out of hand as John was only six months dead and still very much in her heart.

Taking a deep breath, she told herself to hold on a minute and give the matter some thought. If what Harriet said was true, then this wasn't an opportunity to be lightly tossed aside.

For the moment, anyway, she had no feelings for Archie Marjoribanks, but he seemed personable enough and had a good sense of humour – an important point for Carrie.

Although still only twenty-one, she was well aware of how difficult it was going to be for her to land another husband with Angus in tow. She appreciated only too well the reluctance of Glasgow men to take on someone else's family. But Marjoribanks was a widower with a wee lassie of his own which rather put him in the same boat she herself was in.

Of course no one could replace John. There was no question of that. What she had to do was consider the practicality of this possible new situation.

She could go on living here in Tallon Street – Donald had told her she and the baby were welcome as long as they wanted to stay – but with things as bad as they were and steadily getting worse it would certainly be helpful to the family if she was to get out and re-establish a home of her own.

She still had most of the £200 Robert Smith had given her, which meant she was economically independent for some time yet. But that money wouldn't last forever, and when it finally did run out, where was she going to get a job when there were virtually none to be had? She'd already been back several times to the factory trying for her old place and each time had been turned down flat.

Biting her lip, she wondered if John would have approved of her remarrying. Of course he would, she told herself. John had been a practical man who would have appreciated that life had to go on. He wouldn't have expected her to remain static. Especially not when an opportunity like this presented itself. John and Archie had been close friends when they were running the streets together. If she was going to remarry then it seemed the sensible thing to choose a man of whom John had so obviously been fond. Then there was the fact that Archie worked for the railways in a job that was known not only to be highly paid but also secure. Both these factors counted for an awful lot in these desperate times.

She decided her best policy for the moment was to go to bed and sleep on all this. If she could sleep, that is, with her mind in such a turmoil.

But Carrie did sleep and it was Harriet that the early hours of the morning found wide awake and staring at the ceiling. She was smoking a cigarette and thinking about Australia and the correspondence she'd had recently with the Australian authorities in London. It seemed her chances were high of being accepted for immigration; this was an alternative to her present life which attracted her. There was still an interview to come which meant she had to travel to London in about a month's time and, all being well with the outcome, there was no reason why she shouldn't set sail before the end of the year.

The thought of travelling to the other side of the world excited her immensely. The long sea voyage, the exotic sights, the new people she would meet. She'd already made up her mind to go to Sydney first because that seemed to be the centre of things down there.

It amazed her that she was so unafraid of leaving everyone and everything behind. Perhaps the fear and possible misgivings would come later when things were fixed and it was time for her to leave.

It was going to be so good to get away to a new life and the many things she would be experiencing for the first time. Not that her mother and father hadn't done their best by her, they had. It was just that she felt so confined and constricted by life in Glasgow. Also she felt ashamed that she was twenty-eight years old and still not married. Occasionally at work she'd catch girls looking at her in a funny way and she'd know they'd been talking about her. Pitying her.

Well, she didn't need anyone's pity. Not now or ever.

There would be a man in Australia for her. There just had to be!

She drew on the cigarette and gradually calmed down. What she was dreading most was telling Winnie and Donald she was going abroad. That was going to be sheer bloody murder.

Casting her mind back she remembered what it had been like when Alex left home. There had been an atmosphere in the house for weeks beforehand that you could've cut with a knife. Winnie's face had been continually tripping her while Donald had been like a rumbling volcano threatening to explode at any moment.

Alex had been fresh-faced and bright-eyed that morning he'd set off on his great adventure. Carrie, Hugh, Winnie and she had crowded the big room window as Alex and Donald, her father carrying Alex's suitcase, walked down the street to the tram stop.

Several of the neighbours had thrown their windows open and shouted good luck. Alex had responded with a cheery wave and in one instance with a kiss blown to an old wifey who'd been especially fond of him and he of her.

On reaching the top of the street, he'd turned and stood for a few seconds, drinking it all in: absorbing and memorizing every little detail to take with him on his journey.

Then he was gone and that was the last they ever saw of him.

Now she was going to have to tell her parents that she, too, was going to leave them by going overseas. It would break their hearts.

Sighing, she reached for yet another cigarette. The night had been a long one.

5

Nobody was surprised when Archie Marjoribanks turned up with Hugh after the lad's visit to the Central Station. The idea of being invited to tea had of course been craftily planted by Marjoribanks himself who'd accepted immediately Hugh made the proposal.

Arriving at the Chisholm house, Marjoribanks announced he'd just had a marvellous idea. He'd noticed a fish and chip shop round the corner and why didn't he take them all there for their tea, his treat? He beamed Carrie a winning smile which left no doubt that it was definitely Carrie he'd set his sights on.

Harriet said she was sorry but she had to wash her hair while Winnie came up with the excuse she was a wee bit chesty and going out in the cold might aggravate it. Donald said he would bide at home with his wife.

That left Hugh and Carrie with Hugh mad keen on the idea. Carrie swithered for a moment or two, saying that it wasn't all that long till Angus's feed. She finally agreed after Marjoribanks promised to get her there and back again within the hour.

As this was to be Carrie's first time out with Marjoribanks, Winnie didn't think it a bad thing at all for Hugh to be going along with them. That way things didn't look too obvious for either party and it would also take the pressure off a little bit.

The fish and chip shop was almost deserted, which meant they had no trouble getting seats at one of the marble-topped tables. Having helped Carrie sit down, Marjoribanks slipped Hugh a ten bob note and asked him to go up to the counter and do the ordering.

Carrie was suddenly shy and self-conscious as it had been a long time since she'd been out with a man other than John. She was grateful when Marjoribanks offered her a cigarette as it gave her hands something to do.

While Hugh waited patiently to be served Marjoribanks reminisced about the days when he and John had been youngsters together. Because he had a marvellous way with a story he soon had Carrie laughing so much she had to fumble in her handbag for a hanky with which to dab her streaming eyes.

Marjoribanks had enormous charm and he knew how to use it to best advantage. He now set to work on Carrie, breaking her down, reaching out to her with his personality, enveloping her with warmth and good feelings. By the time Hugh brought over their fish teas he'd sold himself to her lock, stock and winning smile.

While they ate Carrie inquired about his daughter. She nodded sympathetically when in hushed tones he told her how dreadfully the wee lass – who was six and called Sheena – was missing her mum. No matter how hard he tried to compensate for this loss, it just wasn't good enough by a long chalk.

Carrie commiserated about how difficult things must be for the pair of them and he, pulling a wry face, agreed.

Suddenly it dawned on Hugh that there was a lot more going on around this table than at first met the eye. Carefully he listened and watched till, with a shock, he realized Carrie and Marjoribanks were actually making up to one another.

Self-righteous anger blazed in him. John was hardly dead and buried and here was Carrie all set to get off with the man's supposed china!

But Hugh wasn't a fool and he had reached the stage

where he was learning to think twice about things before opening his mouth and making comment.

He recalled the funny look his mother had given his father just before they'd left the house and which he'd momentarily puzzled about at the time. Now the meaning of that look became clear to him. It had been one of connivance, which could only mean that not only were his parents aware of what was going on but that they actually approved!

Now he knew why Marjoribanks had wanted him to do the ordering. It was so these two could have time to chat on their own.

He was inordinately pleased with himself at having figured all this out and decided the best thing he could do would be to remove himself for a little while longer.

Hastily he finished what was left on his plate. Then with a cough he announced he was just going to pop out for an evening paper.

When Carrie said she needed some cigarettes it was Marjoribanks who insisted on handing him the money for them.

He rose and excused himself saying he wouldn't be long but already he'd made up his mind to spend a good fifteen or twenty minutes in the snooker room round the corner. When he strutted out into the drizzle that had started to fall he felt very grown up and wise in the ways of the world.

After Hugh had gone, Carrie told Marjoribanks about her trying to no avail to get her job back at Ballogie Clothing where she'd worked alongside Harriet before having to leave on account of her pregnancy.

This time it was Marjoribanks's turn to make sympathetic noises. When he asked her how she was managing, she told him about the money Robert Smith had given her.

'A good man, old Robert. One of the best,' Marjoribanks stated. His face suddenly creased into a dark scowl as he added, 'but you should have had some compensation from Armstrong's. It was criminal right enough that you didn't.'

There was black bitterness inside Carrie whenever she thought about Armstrong's and Sir Alan in particular. It wasn't an act of charity she was after. The very suggestion would have horrified her. But when a man had worked as hard and diligently as her John had done for Armstrong's then surely his life was worth something!

The flowers and wreaths at the funeral from Armstrong's had all been from John's mates. There hadn't been one solitary bloom from the management. And you would have thought that inquiries would have been made. A word to Donald or someone sent down to chap the door. But no. Nothing at all. Only silence. As far as Sir Alan Armstrong was concerned she and Angus might just as well never have existed.

Dragging herself back from her thoughts she discovered Marjoribanks was talking about where he lived.

His house was in Laidlaw Street which ran off Scotland Street where the Smiths had their shop. What he had was a room and kitchen one flight up. A good house, he assured her, with a range and cavity bed in the kitchen. This latter Sheena slept in while he was through in the front room.

'Tell me about your wife?' Carrie asked. 'I'd like to know.'

A sad, pained expression clouded Marjoribanks's face. She'd been a local girl whom he'd first met when he was Hugh's age. They'd taken an immediate liking to one another and started winching right away. A year after they'd met they got married and a few years later Sheena came along.

It had been a happy marriage. Although mind you they'd had their ups and downs, but then what couple didn't?

With a laugh Carrie agreed. She and John had been known to have had a few right old barneys in their time.

The laughter between them suddenly died as Marjoribanks's face became hard and his cheeks seemed to sink in upon themselves.

In a flat voice he said Sheena had been three when
Libby's pain started. Excruciating pain that had caused
her to shriek and scream in agony.

Various doctors had been consulted, all of whom
agreed on the diagnosis and also on the fact there was
nothing they could do for her other than try to alleviate
the pain.

At twenty-two years of age Libby had advanced
stomach cancer. Her torture had lasted just under a year
until a few days before Sheena's fourth birthday when
she'd passed away one night in her sleep. As far as he
was concerned that final release was a blessing.

Carrie's heart went out to Marjoribanks and the wee
lassie whom she hadn't yet met as she listened to all this.
Finally after a long silence she said, 'I'd like to meet
Sheena sometime.'

Marjoribanks immediately brightened and asked if
she'd like to bring Angus over to Laidlaw Street the
following Saturday when they could all have tea together?

Carrie replied she'd enjoy that. The arrangement was
that she'd take the tram to Scotland Street where
Marjoribanks would be waiting to meet her. He did offer
to come to Tallon Street and collect her but she laughed
that off saying she was perfectly capable of making the
journey on her own.

Shortly after that her breasts began to ache and she
felt the tell-tale wet which told it was time to feed the
bairn. Luckily, Hugh arrived back with his paper and her
cigarettes, having been gone almost a full half-hour.

Once outside, Marjoribanks took hold of her by the
arm and together the three of them dashed down Tallon
Street while above them the heavens opened and heavy
rain fell in thundering sheets.

Later, when Carrie emerged from feeding Angus she
found Marjoribanks had gone, having taken advantage
of a break in the rain.

When she told Winnie and Donald about the
arrangement that had been made in the fish and chip
shop, Donald's reply was a non-committal grunt while

Winnie's only comment was that it wouldn't do her any harm to get out and about a wee bit more.

Sitting by the fire reading a book, Harriet looked up but didn't speak. She was convinced Carrie was making the biggest mistake of her life but refrained from saying so in case it was misinterpreted as jealousy on her part.

When the following Saturday arrived and it was time to embark on her visit, Carrie wrapped Angus up warmly and bound him to her by means of a tartan shawl. Donald himself saw her to the tramstop.

The journey was a familiar one for Carrie; she'd done it a number of times in the past with John but also on several occasions since the funeral when, true to her word, she'd taken Angus with her over to see the Smiths.

Marjoribanks was waiting for her as arranged and side by side they set off down Scotland Street.

With a new eye, Carrie viewed the area, for if things worked out between her and Marjoribanks this would be where she'd be coming to live.

She had to admit she didn't view the prospect with any great enthusiasm. The streets were manky and in parts choked with litter and refuse. The air smelled strongly of sewage and toilets. Many of the people they passed looked as though they hadn't seen a wash flannel in weeks, while others were so filthy they stank to high heaven.

Faces were pale and thin, features pinched, and although it was February nearly all the children were barefoot.

A couple of tough looking young boys clattered by propelling an iron hoop from a beer barrel by whacking it with a length of wooden stick.

A little girl sat with her feet dangling in the gutter and nursed a dolly made from rags. The doll was tattered and falling apart. She was singing a haunting lullaby about poverty and deprivation she'd learned at her mother's knee, and she sang it with feeling.

Carrie couldn't help comparing Scotland Street with

Tallon Street, something she hadn't actually consciously done before. And on this same conscious level she began to appreciate just how far her father's strivings had brought the Chisholm family.

She told herself that if Donald and John had been able to escape with squalor then so could she and Archie Marjoribanks. All it needed was incentive and determination and she had plenty of both.

Her heart plummeted when they turned into Laidlaw Street. Several of the houses were lying empty with their windows smashed in. They looked like eyeless and toothless monsters who'd succumbed to a combination of internal rot and old age.

Women sat by open windows chatting to their neighbours on either side and occasionally calling to one another across the street, even though it was raw and bitter out.

Carrie gulped as she turned into Marjoribanks's close. There was water running down the walls while from the back of the close came the distinctive stomach-churning smell of an overflowing outside lavatory.

'We're nearly there,' Marjoribanks said quickly ushering her up the stairs. 'I can't tell you how much Sheena is looking forward to meeting you.'

Pulling a large brass key from his pocket he opened the door to his first landing room and kitchen.

Expecting the worst by now Carrie was surprised to find the hallway immaculate, the linoleum on the floor dazzling in its brightness.

Sheena was waiting for them in the kitchen. She was standing in front of a blazing range on which a blackened kettle busily boiled its head off.

The first thing Carrie noted about the lassie was how scared she looked. No doubt it was at the prospect of meeting her. The second thing she saw were the scrapes and bruises on the girl's face.

Archie introduced them and very shyly Sheena extended her hand for it to be shaken. Although the room was warm the hand in Carrie's was as cold as ice. It was also limp as though Sheena wasn't used to shaking hands or else was frightened to put any expression into the gesture.

Carrie beamed Sheena a smile which seemed to put the girl at ease a little. Then Archie mentioned that the kettle was boiling and immediately Sheena scuttled to make some tea.

The kitchen gleamed just like the hallway and on mentioning this Carrie was informed by Archie that Sheena did all the cleaning round the house. Carrie was most impressed by this and said so. This earned her a grateful look from Sheena who was busy spooning tea from the caddy into the pot.

At the back of the range a soot-blackened crock hung on a hook and from this a tantalizing smell wafted forth. Carrie asked what was cooking. Sheen responded that it was an Irish stew.

Carrie was amazed at Sheena's capabilities. Not only was this chit of a girl running the entire household but she was making a damn good job ot if to boot!

Having been instructed to sit in what was obviously the best chair Carrie was then handed a cup of tea by Sheena. Before the girl could draw away Carrie clasped her chin and turned her head to one side. The scrapes and bruises were worse than Carrie had first thought; one bruise in particular was very angry and inflamed.

Prompted by Carrie the girl explained she'd missed her footing on the landing one night and tumbled down an entire flight of stairs.

Having said that, Sheena broke away from Carrie and hurried over to the range where she made herself busy.

Since their arrival the light had faded rapidly leaving the kitchen dark and filled with dancing shadows from the glow from the range.

Marjoribanks lit a spill which he used to light the two gas points jutting out above the brass rail running along the mantelpiece. The kitchen was instantly saturated with warm yellow light.

Carrie asked Sheena if she'd like to hold Angus and

wasn't at all surprised at the enthusiastic reply she received. After all, what little girl doesn't like to fuss with a baby.

Sheena very sensibly said she'd better sit down first before she held Angus. This she did in an old mothering chair which it seemed she'd long since claimed as her own.

Sheena had long, dark hair which fell rather limply in loose waves. Her eyes were two enormous blackcurrants far older and wiser than normal for girls of that age. Her nose had a slight droop at the end giving her something of a witchy appearance. Strangely sensual and provocative mulberry coloured lips added to the effect.

As though she'd been handling babies all her short life Sheena snuggled Angus deep into the crook of her arm and began to hum a popular tune of the day.

For a few seconds Angus showed concern at being deprived of his mother. Then his face burst into a smile and he frothed bubbles. He'd found a new friend.

Carrie rose and crossed to the sideboard on which stood a picture in a frame. As she'd guessed, it was of Archie and Libby's wedding.

Libby was small, dark and looked just like a grown up version of Sheena.

Carrie was suddenly aware of Marjoribanks standing beside her and that he to was gazing down at the picture. His lips were pursed and the sadness she'd seen in the fish and chip shop was back in his eyes.

'She looks nice,' Carrie said.

'I thought so and so did John. He always maintained I got the better bargain by far.'

Carrie couldn't think of a reply to that so she returned to her chair. Staring into the fire's flickering flames, she was aware of being closely studied by Sheena.

She liked the girl and was certain she was liked in return. All that was needed was a little time for the pair of them to get used to one another. If all went well it shouldn't be too long before they were great friends.

Carrie turned and indicated Angus. 'He's certainly

taken to you,' she said.

Sheena smiled, suddenly wide open and vulnerable. 'I like him too. I could sit here cuddling him all night.'

Angus cooed and stuck a chubby fist in the air. From the look on his face it was an idea he heartily approved of.

'Libby and I had hoped to have more children,' Marjoribanks said softly, then shrugged philosophically, 'But of course that wasn't to be.'

'Who knows how these things finally turn out?' Carried said enigmatically. A brief glance in his direction told her he'd got the point.

A little later she took Angus back to let Sheena get on with the business of setting out the meal. She thought the best thing to do was sit back and not interfere. Sheena might be young but for the time being, anyway, this kitchen was her preserve.

When everything was ready Carrie laid the now fast asleep Angus on his rug in front of the fire, close enough to benefit from the warmth but far enough away to escape any flying sparks.

She knew he wouldn't sleep too long as it was his feed time soon and he was notoriously prompt in his demands when it came to that.

The stew was excellent, certainly as good as anything she could have turned out and she didn't hesitate in saying so.

Besides the stew there were jacket potatoes and thick slices of bread and butter – navvies' doorstops, Winnie would have called the latter – all of which went down a treat.

It transpired that Libby had been teaching Sheena to cook ever since the lassie was old enough to take things in, which was just as well, Archie joked. His cooking was so abominable as to be completely inedible.

As soon as the meal was finished Sheena cleared the table and started the washing up.

Having asked Archie to remove himself to the front room Carrie lifted the now grizzling Angus and started feeding him.

While Angus sucked lustily Carrie sat watching Sheena working at the sink. With her sleeves drawn back, the girl was standing on a chair humming to herself as she attacked the pile of dirty dishes in front of her.

Carrie shook her head in wonderment. The girl was so grown up. It was hard to remember that Sheena was six and not sixty, for that was how she continually came across. A wee old wifey who'd seen and done it all and consequently would stand no nonsense from anyone.

Carrie winced as Angus nipped her nipple, his way of telling her that that breast was empty and would she please change him over. 'Beast!' she grinned.

For a while she tried to engage Sheena in conversation about school but the girl was vague and unforthcoming on the subject.

When Angus had been fed she called Marjoribanks back through and told him it was time she was going.

She changed the baby's nappy and then wrapped him up warmly. After shrugging herself into her coat Archie helped bind the baby to her by means of the tartan shawl.

When she was ready she solemnly thanked Sheena for the meal and said she hoped she would be seeing her again soon. Sheena seemed pleased by that prospect.

As they walked down the stairs Marjoribanks said the people on the ground floor had been on to the factor about the overflowing cludge and the factor had promised to have it seen to within the next few days. He didn't refer to the water running down the close walls.

Carrie had hoped to call in on the Smiths but there was no time for that now.

On the previous occasion she'd been up to see them, Robert had let drop several times that she'd be surprised if she knew what was in the black metal safe he kept bolted to the kitchen floor. There had been sly references to pearls and other extremely expensive items. When she'd obviously looked doubting he'd hurried from the room to return with a gorgeous piece of scrimshaw which she'd duly admired.

Thinking about it afterwards she'd come to the conclusion the fly old devil must be acting as a receiver for illegal merchandise brought in from abroad. The docks weren't all that far away and as a consequence the area was well frequented by merchant seamen.

She hoped old man Smith wasn't going to land himself in trouble, for his wife Meg's sake as much as his own.

When they reached the tramstop Archie asked to see her again and suggested the following Friday. He said he would like to take her dancing or if she wasn't up to that yet how about the pictures?

Carrie replied the pictures would be the best idea and a time was agreed when he would pick her up at Tallon Street.

Carrie immediately made a mental note that she was going to have to wean Angus onto a bottle so she wouldn't be as tied as she was now. She decided to buy the necessary paraphernalia first thing on Monday morning and try him on it.

During her journey home she thought about her meeting with Sheena. She'd been worried in case the girl turned out to be a problem but her fears had proved groundless. She and Sheena were going to be the very best of pals. She was sure of it.

As soon as Carrie let herself into the house she knew something had happened. Through the open doorway to the living room she saw her mother sitting at the table with a face like fizz.

She settled Angus in his bed before taking her coat off and going on through.

Donald sat hunched in his chair, pipe clamped between his teeth, glowering into the fire. Underneath the glower he looked angry and hurt.

Harriet was sitting on the pouffe by the window. Her face was pale, her expression one of defiance.

'Have you heard the latest?' Winnie demanded.

Carrie shook her head.

'Harriet is emigrating to Australia.'

It was a bombshell which left Carrie literally stunned. It was so unexpected, so completely out of the blue. 'When?' she finally managed to get out.

'I'll have to go to London in three weeks for an interview. If I'm successful I'll know sometime after that,' Harriet replied.

Winnie rose and, looking to be on the verge of tears, left the room.

After the door had closed behind her mother Harriet said, 'It's my life. Surely I'm allowed to decide what I want to do with it?'

Donald didn't reply but savagely poked the fire instead.

'Well?' The word cracked between Harriet and her father like a rifle shot. But there was no disrespect in her tone. Rather a plea to be understood.

'You're within your rights, lass,' Donald said reluctantly. Then as an afterthought, 'It's Alex, you see. She can't forget what happened to him.'

'I don't want to hurt anybody, Papa. I just want to do what I think is right for me.'

Carrie wasn't sure whether or not it was her imagination but it seemed to her that Donald had aged since she'd seen him last earlier in the day.

Donald took a deep breath and knocked out his pipe. He saw a lot of himself in Harriet. Good points as well as bad. Losing her this way would be like losing an arm. Of his children she was the one he'd always most closely identified with.

'I'd better see to your mother,' he said, adding, 'we won't stand in your way, lass. As you say, it's your life. Best do with it as you see fit. Tonight was . . . well, let's just say tonight was a wee bit of a shock, that's all. No doubt we'll have grown to accept it by the morning.'

'Thanks Papa.'

He followed Winnie through to their bedroom where, as he'd known he would, he found her lying crying in the dark.

'I knew it wasn't going to be easy and it wasn't,'

Harriet said.

'Want to talk about it?'

'No. Tomorrow maybe but not now.'

Carrie understood. She stayed long enough to smoke a last cigarette and then she left Harriet alone and gazing into the fire.

In times like these great comfort and solace could be found in a fire.

This would be first time Harriet had ever been out of Scotland and naturally enough she was excited at the prospect.

It was bitterly cold in the train compartment due to the heating not working so she was grateful for the woolly rug Winnie had insisted she bring with her, and for the flask of hot tea Carrie had made and packed.

It hadn't been easy getting time off from Ballogie Clothing but luckily she was chums with Jakey Sanderson, the supervisor. He'd managed to wangle it for her after she'd explained the position to him, having first of all sworn him to secrecy.

What Harriet didn't know was that Jakey had a cousin who'd been pestering him for months to get her a job which he'd promised to do the moment one of his girls left. That was why he'd been so obliging in helping Harriet get a few days off so she could travel to London.

As the train thundered through the night Harriet reflected that the days following her telling Winnie and Donald about her plans to emigrate hadn't been nearly so bad as she'd expected. There had been a weary, resigned quality about Winnie but there were no further words of either argument or recrimination. Regardless of hurt, acceptance had been total.

She'd gone into the big room one night to find Winnie sitting quietly by the window staring at the photo of Alex she always carried in her handbag. With guilt lying in her stomach like a lump of lead she'd turned and left the room.

Hugh's reactions to her news had been different to

anyone else's in the family. He'd been so excited you'd have thought it was him who was going rather than her.

The rhythmic clickety clack of the wheels finally lulled Harriet into a fitful sleep. When she woke the train was pulling into Euston Station.

Punctual to the minute, she presented herself at the address in the Strand where she'd been instructed to go.

For half an hour she sat on a hard wooden bench and then an official came out to see her. Gravely he told her the person she'd been due to see was off sick and could she possibly stay overnight at their expense and come back the following morning.

She was delighted as she'd been dreading the long return journey. Quickly she agreed and a taxi took her to a small hotel in Euston Square.

The room she was shown into was far grander than she could have afforded, so this little touch of luxury was an added bonus. She had a cup of tea and a token rest. Then she took herself out onto the streets of London.

Midday found her in Soho standing outside a little restaurant. Thinking herself terribly daring, she went inside and ordered something to eat.

Filled with all sorts of exquisite things and, as a consequence, feeling extraordinarily happy and alive, she strolled to Regent Street where she spent a long time window shopping.

Eventually, exhausted and foot sore she made her way back to the hotel in Euston Square where she slept for several hours like the proverbial log.

In the hotel the evening meal was called dinner and served a lot later than the tea she was used to.

At the appropriate time she made her way down to the dining room where she found a number of guests already gathered. Spying a small table set to one side she decided that was for her and sat down. She was unfolding her napkin when a deep voice said, 'Excuse me ma'am but I think you've made a mistake. This table is reserved for me.'

Harriet looked up, flushing as she did so. The man had

no sooner spoken than she'd seen the 'reserved' sign set out quite plainly in front of her. 'I'm terribly sorry,' she said and started to rise.

The man was short, paunchy and balding with a round, jovial face and laughing eyes. 'No please!' he said laying a restraining hand on her arm. 'Now that rights have been established it would be my pleasure if you would join me.'

Harriet was at a loss to know what to do. Her mind was made up for her when the man said, 'That's settled then,' and sat down facing her.

He was a lot older than she was. Nearly fifty she guessed. With a voice that came out as a lazy drawl and had a rather hypnotic quality about it.

'My name's Lou Dansie,' he said sticking out his hand.

'I'm Harriet Chisholm,' she replied as they shook.

'Scots?'

She nodded.

'Aaah! I thought so. Unmistakable, that brogue. I knew a lot of Jocks during the war.' He leaned across and whispered confidentially. 'I was sure as heck pleased those guys were on my side. Yes siree!'

She had to laugh. 'You must be an American.'

'From Los Angeles. And you?'

'Glasgow.'

'I've heard about there,' Dansie said. 'I think it would be too heavily industrial for my taste. Too dirty.'

Thinking that Dansie was being disparaging about her city, Harriet's temper flared. Then she realized from the look on his face that he'd merely been passing comment. Instantly she relaxed again, contrite at her hotheadedness.

'Aye well a place is *who* you know. If you're ever in Glasgow come and see my family and me. We'll try and see to it that you go away with a favourable impression.'

'I might just take you up on that,' Dansie replied, thinking that Harriet's spontaneous offer of hospitality was just like the Jocks he'd known in France. Those guys would share their last grain of food with you rather than let you go without.

Because he was easy to talk to Dansie soon had Harriet chattering on about her family and their life in Cathcart.

'Now, how about some claret?' he finally interrupted.

Harriet was taken aback. The fact of the matter was she'd never tasted wine in her life, it being viewed with the utmost suspicion north of the border.

Dansie saw her hesitation. 'Perhaps you'd prefer a burgundy or a beaujolais?' he asked.

Harriet decided frankness was always the best policy. She admitted that wine was totally unknown to her but as he seemed so keen on the idea she wasn't averse to trying some.

Dansie was aghast, declaring this to be a situation that would have to be remedied. He immediately summoned the wine waiter.

Harriet could hardly believe her ears when he ordered champagne. 'But that must be so expensive!' she gasped.

Dansie chuckled, enjoying the gesture he was making. The women he normally mixed with wouldn't have shown as much enthusiasm or delight had he been showering them with fistfuls of diamonds. 'Nothing less will do to mark the occasion!' he stated firmly and dispatched the wine waiter with a flourish.

Harriet had already decided she liked this little, stout man from America. Despite the differences in their ages and backgrounds there was an empathy between them.

Dansie was an expert at getting people to unburden themselves and this talent he now exercised on Harriet, who began to speak at length about her plans for emigration.

When the champagne came Dansie proposed a toast to Harriet wishing her success and happiness in her new life. Harriet declared she would drink to that and did so with a laugh.

She liked the champagne. It was light and tickly like cider only a lot more so. But it didn't seem to have a kick to it.

Dansie smiled enigmatically when she said that.

There was a bloom in Harriet's cheeks and a sparkle in her eyes that had nothing whatever to do with the wine. The dry spinster was being transformed into a desirable woman, desirable because she knew the man sitting opposite saw her as such.

After a while it dawned on Harriet she'd been doing all the talking. So telling Dansie it was his turn she shut up.

'Do you ever go to the motion pictures?' he asked.

The unexpectedness of the question and its seeming irrelevance caught her off guard. She nodded. She and Carrie often went, enjoying the sheer escapism the cinema had to offer.

With a smile Dansie informed her he was a contract writer with United Artists, the company formed two years previously by Mary Pickford, Douglas Fairbanks, Charlie Chaplin and D.W. Griffith.

Harriet was rocked. She was with someone who actually knew the fabled stars of the silver screen! Men and women who were like gods to her.

She listened eagerly to Dansie's account of life in Hollywood. The parties. The swimming pools. What a cut-throat business the movie industry was. The ambitions of the young hopefuls who flocked there. The bitter disappointment that lay in store for so many of them.

The razzle-dazzle of an opening night; what it was like to discover you'd been involved in a success, a failure.

Personalities who worked for Metro, Universal, Cosmopolitan, Vitagraph, First National, Paramount, Selznick. The names rolled off Dansie's tongue as naturally as Glasgow districts would have rolled off hers.

Films of the previous year he'd personally seen being made: 'The Four Horsemen of the Apocalypse', 'The Queen of Sheba', 'The Square Shooter', 'The Lotus Eater', 'Camille', 'A Virgin Paradise'.

Harriet was completely entranced by the spell of words that Dansie wove. She'd been transported to a world a million miles away from Tallon Street and

Ballogie Clothing. Here was glamour, excitement, all the things she so desperately craved in life. Dansie went on to describe how he'd been irresistibly drawn towards movies having seen Florence Lawrence in 'The Biograph Girl' and a one-reel version of Tolstoy's 'Redemption' in 1909.

To start with he'd worked as an actor, it seeming the obvious way to get into the industry. But as time went by he'd grown more and more frustrated by the actor's role until one morning it had come to him like a bolt from the blue that writing was his true vocation. He had realized his destiny in life was to be a motion picture script writer.

He laid his right hand on the table and pointed to a heavy gold ring he wore. 'Mary herself gave me that,' he stated proudly.

'Pickford?'

He nodded.

Harriet gingerly reached out and touched the ring. She might have been touching the Holy Grail so reverential was her gesture.

The courses came and went while Dansie explained he'd been sent to Britain to gather background material for a new picture he was to write for Fairbanks and Pickford.

The previous year Fairbanks had starred in 'The Three Musketeers' and the production had been so successful that he was to star in another costume drama. The subject chosen had been Bonnie Prince Charlie. Fairbanks would play the Prince, of course, while Pickford would be Flora McDonald.

So far Dansie had been in London for a fortnight and during that time he'd been researching Charles Edward Stuart at the British Museum. This would take him at least another week and then he was travelling north by motor car to Scotland where he would tour round all the places known to be associated with the Young Pretender's uprising.

Harriet put up no resistance when Dansie ordered brandies. She'd have drunk turpentine by now had he suggested it. Anything so long as this conversation continued.

Over coffee Dansie suggested they go on to a night club where they could talk further and perhaps dance. Harriet accepted instantly.

Sheena Marjoribanks lay in her cavity bed in the darkness listening to the sound of her father snoring through the wall. She shivered at the memory of the thrashing he'd given her a few nights previously with the thick leather belt he wore round his work trousers.

He'd been drinking. Not too much but still enough to spark off one of his terrible rages.

She could remember the many times he'd used that same belt on her mother and her mother screaming and pleading in the front room while she lay huddled here in her bed listening to it all.

'Oh, mummy!' she whispered stuffing her hand into her mouth. Tears burst from the corners of her eyes. Her mother's face danced before her. Those sad, forlorn features crammed full of misery and despair.

Some day she was going to escape from all this, she promised herself. As soon as she was old enough she was going to walk out through that front door and never come back.

In the meantime it would be good to have an ally about the place. She saw Carrie could be an ally and she would bring a baby to hug when the nights were long and cold and it was lonely to be on your own.

Thinking of Angus made her smile, and with him still in her thoughts, she drifted off to sleep.

Beside Harriet, Lou Dansie lay sleeping with his arm thrown over the top part of his face. His mouth puckered every time he exhaled, which he did often and noisily.

Harriet was glowing inside. The aftermath of lovemaking had left her for the first time in her life feeling fulfilled. She'd waited long enough for this moment but the wait had been worthwhile.

She ran her hands over her breasts and down her long, lean flanks, the flesh tingling to her touch. It might have been slumbering through the years until this small, paunchy American had come along and with a wave of his magic wand (she smiled at that) brought it ecstatically alive.

Dansie groaned and turned on to his side so that his back was towards her. She stared in fascination at the thick matting of black hair which started at the nape of his neck and grew downwards. Reaching out she stroked the hair on his shoulders, causing him to quiver.

'What are you thinking about?' he asked without turning round.

'You.'

'What about me?'

'You've told me nearly everything about yourself except the most important thing. Are you married?'

Dansie thought of his wife, Bess, and their daughter, Bonnie Sue who were 6000 miles away in Hollywood. It had been years since things were good between him and Bess but they'd stuck it out together because of the kid.

Hollywood was filled with children whose parents were divorced. Both he and Bess knew only too well what the majority of these kids turned out like. Lost souls. Neurotic messes. Bums. And in some extreme cases all three combined.

Neither he nor Bess could bear the thought of their daughter ending up like that, so they'd clung on to the few tattered remnants of their relationship.

'Well?' Harriet prompted.

'I'm married.'

He'd had to be, of course. It would have been too easy otherwise.

'Harriet?'

She drew him to her while placing a hand over his mouth. 'There are only a few hours left before you have to go back to your own room. Use them to love me,' she whispered.

6

Sitting by the window watching the men from Armstrong's trudge home from their work, Winnie's heart sank within her. The spring had gone out of their step, and without exception they walked with eyes downcast. Instead of the usual hum punctuated by the occasional laugh or piece of horse play, there was an air about them that was dark and sombre.

Winnie knew the signs. There had been a big lay-off. The only question remaining was how many had been made idle?

Closing her eyes and clasping her hands in her lap, she offered up a brief prayer. Luckily Donald was a gaffer and as such would be among the last to go. Hugh was still an apprentice which was an advantage at a time like this. Apprentices were always kept on to the end because they were cheap labour.

It was a strange night out, the sky peculiarly overcast and everything very still. The only sound to disturb the brooding silence was the tramp of the men's tackety boots on pavement and road.

There was Mrs McElvey's man, Bill, looking as though he'd lost a pound and found a tanner. Dazed and bewildered, he turned into his close and vanished from view.

Wee Tommy Taylor who always whistled to and from his work turned into Tallon Street. He wasn't whistling now.

Behind Tommy Taylor came Davey Beattie who

every Hogmanay came out onto the street directly after the bells to play his pipes. The expression on his face was the one he'd worn for weeks after receiving word that his two boys had fallen at Ypres.

Winnie rose and went through to the kitchen to make sure the tea was ready to go onto the table. That's where she was when the front door opened.

Wiping her hands on her pinny she hurried into the hall where she found Donald staring at the yellow distempered wall as though some profound truth was being unfolded to him there.

'Donald?'

When she got no reply or even a flicker of recognition she tried again. 'Donald?'

Coming out of the deep trance, he shook himself.

'How many?' Winnie asked, trepidation large within her. She'd never seen Donald in this sort of state before.

It took him a full minute, but finally he got that one terrible word out. 'Everyone,' he rasped.

She slumped and had to hold on to the wall for support. It was the nightmare come true. '*Everyone?*'

He nodded. 'Every last man jack of us laid off until further notice.'

Somehow she found the strength to stagger back to the kitchen where she sat on the edge of the opened coal bin.

Big Donald ran his wife a glass of water and then called through to Hugh that he wanted him.

Hugh was handed money by his father and told to run down the road and get a bottle of whisky.

'God knows but we all need a dram,' Donald said, adding, 'And if we don't get one the night who knows when we'll get the chance again?'

'This means we'll have to get by on Harriet's money and whatever Carrie can put into the kitty from what's left of old man Smith's two hundred,' Winnie said.

Donald and Winnie looked at one another, each with the same thought in mind. When Harriet went to Australia there wouldn't even be her money coming in.

Winnie buried her head in her hands, her mind numb at the prospect of what lay ahead of them.

Donald sat on the coal bunker beside his wife and, in a gesture that was both rough and gentle, put his arm round her shoulders. 'We'll get by somehow, lass. You just wait and see. After all, we've never died a winter yet!'

His voice was jocular and full of hope. Exactly the opposite to what he was feeling.

Sitting there, he noted that the linoleum under the sink was beginning to go. Well, it would be a long time now before that was replaced.

He clasped and unclasped his fist in frustration. There had to be work somewhere! And even as he was trying to reassure himself he knew in his heart of hearts the position was hopeless. There were tens of thousands out of work on Clydeside and now he and the rest of the men from Armstrong's had joined their ever swelling ranks.

Sneeringly he thought of Lloyd George and the coalition government. What a fiasco! What a shambles! It was long overdue for the working man to take power into his own hands in order to shape both his and his country's future. Only with the Labour Party in control would the ordinary man in the street get a fair crack of the whip. That was something Donald believed fervently and with total commitment.

Donald and Winnie were still sitting on the edge of the bunker when Hugh arrived back with the whisky. Carrie was with Hugh, having met up with him at the bottom of the stairs. She'd already heard the news on the street and had come straight home from her shopping.

Standing now just inside the kitchen door, Carrie watched Donald pour out four very large glasses of whisky.

Holding his glass, Hugh opened his mouth to make a flippant toast, but clamped it shut again when he saw the brooding volcanic expression on his father's face.

Sipping her whisky Carrie thought about Archie Marjoribanks. He'd already hinted at marriage, but she'd contrived to let him know that out of respect for John she wanted to wait a little while yet. Now it seemed she was going to have to think again due to this sudden alteration in circumstances.

She'd arranged to meet Archie in two nights' time when they planned to go to the jigging. She would sort it out with him then.

Hugh felt strangely lightheaded, a state which had nothing whatsoever to do with the drink but rather because it was gradually sinking into him that he'd been laid off and was now without a job.

Long, boring days stretched endlessly before him. The prospect was depressing. He'd seen what enforced idleness had done to other men, turning them into cabbages with no hope. No future. No nothing! It terrified him that he, too, in time would become like them.

He remembered then what Aly Paterson had said to him when he'd given up running with the milk to start in at Armstrong's. 'You're the best lad we've ever had and it breaks my heart to see you go,' Aly had said. Well, Aly still had the dairy up at Muirend and still did morning deliveries. It was certainly worth a try.

Harriet arrived home several hours later, having taken the midday train from Euston. Harriet thought it's an ill-wind which blows no one any good when she was told the calamitous news about Armstrong's. This was precisely the excuse she needed on which to hang her change of plans. She announced she had no intention of going to Australia now as it was essential she stayed at home and kept on her job at Ballogie Clothing.

Both Donald and Winnie were most humble at what they thought to be their daugher's enormous self-sacrifice.

What neither of them knew was that Harriet had already decided not to emigrate and hadn't even bothered to attend the interview for which she'd gone down to London especially.

Lou Dansie had paid the hotel bill. The arrangement between her and Dansie was that he would come to

Glasgow and see her before motoring through to Edinburgh where he intended making his base of operations while in Scotland.

She would be travelling through to stay with him at weekends.

Shortly after Harriet's return, Hugh slipped down to the wash-house where he kept his bike. He'd decided there was no time like the present to find out what the current situation was at Aly Paterson's dairy.

It was several miles from Tallon Street to Muirend and all of it uphill.

As Hugh strained at the pedals he recalled that a lot of the enjoyment of running with the milk had been the horses whom he'd liked enormously and who'd liked him in return.

There had been one which had been his favourite, an old black beast named Squinty whose eyes were so crossed as to almost disappear into one another.

He thought now of Squinty with affection and wondered whether the old horse was still going strong or if it had finally got past it and been put down.

He turned the bike off the hill and into Aly Paterson's driveway. The house situated at the end of the long run up was an imposing edifice of grey stone which Aly had built many years previously to replace the very old and tiny one already on the site.

In front and to one side of the house stood the dairy building; facing that across the yard were the stables.

Besides this small complex Aly also owned a farm on the road to East Kilbride from where he supplied the dairy with milk.

Aly himself answered Hugh's ring and after shaking hands and being pounded on the back Hugh was ushered straight into the parlour where several logs were crackling away cheerily in the large stone fireplace.

Aly's wife, Greta, greeted Hugh as a long lost son. Kissing him on the cheek, she announced she would away through and put the kettle on and see if she could find a nice wee bit of shortie.

Aly pooh-poohed this idea saying that as Hugh was a man now and doing a man's job – Hugh winced at that – he should be given a man's drink. The whisky decanter was then duly taken from the sideboard and a large one poured.

Acting on doctor's orders Aly didn't drink any more, what with a weak heart and high blood pressure. Thinking it unfair to indulge when her husband couldn't, Greta had also forsworn alcohol.

'To Stewart!' Hugh toasted bringing grins of delight to the Paterson's faces. Stewart was their only child and the apple of their eye.

Hugh had first met Stewart when he'd come to work at the dairy and the pair of them had taken an instant liking to one another. After a few weeks the two of them had become almost inseparable.

Now Stewart was at agricultural college in Dumfriesshire where he was learning the very latest in farming methods. On leaving college he would take over the farming side of the business.

Greta confided in Hugh that Stewart had met a lassie and it seemed an engagement was in the offing. But before Hugh could offer his congratulations, Greta went on to say in a sepulchral tone that, nice as the lassie was, she had one terrible drawback. She was, horror of horrors, *English!*'

Hugh was astounded by this disclosure. He wondered what had come over his old pal. Stewart married to an Englishwoman! It was unthinkable.

'Dear me,' he said, shaking his head.

Greta sniffed.

'It's enough to drive a man to drink,' said Aly, looking longingly at the decanter. But a sharp glance from Greta was enough to dispel the notion. When it came down to it he enjoyed living more than he did the booze.

Quickly changing the conversation Greta asked Hugh to what they owed the honour of his visit? In a few terse sentences he told them about the closure of Armstrong's which meant he was now out of a job.

Both the Patersons were shocked by this news and Greta immediately rose and refilled his glass.

'There have already been marches out in Rutherglen,' Aly said, grim faced. 'Thousands of men protesting that there's no work for them and demanding something be done about it. There's nearly two million unemployed in the country now, you know.'

'Two million?' Hugh repeated. He found the figure staggering.

'Thing are as bad as they've ever been,' said Aly. His own particular business hadn't yet felt the squeeze but if the present downward spiral continued then it was only a matter of time.

The white collar workers who comprised the majority of his customers had so far escaped the ravishes of being thrown out of work. But they were far from immune.

Hugh then bluntly asked if he could have his old job back and was told he could start first thing Monday morning. The going rate was three shillings a day which added up to twenty-one shillings a week. Only a shilling less than he'd been earning at Armstrong's!

Hugh was jubilant and profuse in his thanks, but Aly would have none of it, saying what were friends for if they couldn't do you a good turn when it was needed.

Hugh said his good-byes. Outside the house he whistled as he mounted his bike. He couldn't wait to get home and tell Donald and Winnie.

After Hugh had gone Greta said gently, 'You didn't really need another boy, did you?'

Aly shrugged and stuck his hands in his trouser pockets. 'What else could I do?'

Smiling, Greta crossed to her husband and hooked her arm round his. 'You're a big softie and I love you for it,' she said.

Clutching one another like teenagers they made their way upstairs.

Hugh arrived home just as Winnie was making a last cup

of tea before going to bed. Unable to contain himself he burst into the kitchen and blurted out his news to her.

Winnie's eyes were decidedly dewy as she folded him in her arms and hugged him tight. She then called out to Donald to come away through and hear what his big son had to tell him.

Donald listened in silence while Hugh reported the outcome of his visit to the Patersons. When Hugh had finished Donald cleared his throat and said gruffly they had a big son right enough.

Winnie knew how hard Donald was taking all this. It was going to tear him apart inside for the family to be dependent on what Hugh and Harriet brought in. But better that than them all slowly starving to death on the pittance the broo* would allot them, she thought grimly.

That night Harriet tossed and turned. Her newly awakened body was afire while her mind churned with thoughts about the man who'd started the blaze.

What had really changed her mind about emigration was finding out that as well as researching the Bonnie Prince Charlie film in Scotland, Lou intended remaining on there while he wrote the first drafts of the script – at least six months' work. That and the fact that his marriage was on the rocks.

A lot could happen in six months. And she would see that it did.

Early next morning Donald's eyes flickered open at their usual time. With the customary grunt at Winnie he climbed out of bed and stretched himself by the window. He was about to pull on his work trousers when Winnie quietly said, 'You've forgotten, Donald.'

It all came flooding back to him in a wash of resentment and sour bile. He was laid off. Useless.

His shoulders sagged and something of his masculinity seeped out of him. He was no longer the provider. Instead he would have to go down and join the dole

* Unemployment exchange.

queue, making himself in his own eyes no better than a common beggar. It was a galling thought and made him feel bitterly ashamed.

He sat on the edge of the bed and started to speak. Out came many ideas and theories that had been percolating in his mind since the end of the war.

'They've got it all wrong,' he said slowly. Choosing his words with care. 'There are all these capitalists like Sir Alan Armstrong who've got the wind up and instead of spending their money they're hoarding it away in banks where it isn't doing anyone any good. If they keep on like that then the damn money will eventually become worthless. Not even worth the paper it's printed on. What they should be doing is spending and expanding trade. It's as obvious as the nose on your face but none of them has the sense to see it.

'Trade! If we don't do that then we stagnate, which is exactly what's happening to the country today. The capitalists are running scared and all they can think to do is hide away in their big houses assuring one another it'll all blow over. Well I've got news for them. This time things could get so bad that none of us will come out of it.'

With eyes blazing he continued, 'They must find the courage to take their money out of the banks and spend great chunks of it. It's the only way. Our only possible salvation!

'They have to recognize that for the truth before it's too late because if they don't it'll be the end of Britain as a country, far less a world power. God help us!'

Folding his pants, he laid them over the arm of the chair and then crawled back into bed where he lay with his arms by his side, staring at the ceiling.

Eventually he fell into a fitful sleep to dream of the first Labour government putting the country to rights and sorting out all social injustices.

Like everyone else who worked at Ballogie Clothing Jakey Sanderson had long since got used to the continual roar of more than 200 heavy industrial sewing machines clattering away flat out.

He strode down the back row of machines till he came to Harriet's where he stopped and waited till she realized he was there. When she looked up, he nodded in the direction of the cubicle that served him as an office. She gesticulated back she'd be right with him as soon as she'd finished off her present seam.

Jakey and Harriet were old pals, having known one another for many years, ever since Jakey had moved to Cathcart from Govan, in fact.

For a while they'd seen each other regularly at dances, and he had always come across and asked her up. The pair of them were excellent dancers and were rated highly amongst the Glasgow crowd. This was praise indeed as dancing was and always has been a sort of second religion in the city, the first of course being football.

As he let himself into his office, Jakey thought long-ingly of the cup of tea due to be served him soon. He had a terrible hangover from the night before, having run into his cousin Isa's man, Matt. It was to Isa that he'd promised the next available job.

The first thing Matt had asked about was the job, and it had been to Jakey's great delight that he'd been able to say one was coming up soon.

Matt had insisted they celebrate the news on him. Repairing to the nearest pub, pint after pint had been called for till they were both nearly awash. Then again at Matt's insistence they'd changed to big whiskies which had flowed in a seemingly never-ending stream.

Not once had Jakey been called on to put his hand in his pocket.

There was a knock on the cubicle door and Harriet entered to find Jakey sitting behind his desk beaming up at her.

'Well?' he demanded.

She couldn't think what he was talking about. 'Well, what?'

'How did the interview go?'

Of course he would want to know. He had gone to the trouble of arranging time off for her, after all. Normally she would have thought, but since meeting Lou Dansie her mind had become preoccupied with the American to the exclusion of all else.

'I'm afraid I got turned down,' she lied smoothly. Then with a wry smile, added, 'So it looks like you'll have to keep putting up with me.'

Jakey had to turn away so she didn't see the brief flash of combined anger and panic which contorted his face. This was terrible. More than that it was disastrous! He'd assured Matt the job was in the bag and as a consequence eagerly accepted all those drinks bought him by Isa's grateful husband. He'd committed himself, damn it to hell!

Things wouldn't have been quite so bad if it hadn't been Matt he'd promised, for Matt was a notorious hardman who carried a razor and had the reputation of breaking people's limbs just for fun. In local parlance Matt was a right heidcase.

He mopped sweat from his brow and then leaned back in his chair to stare up at Harriet. He liked the woman. Always had done. And she was a great partner at the jigging, unlike his wife who danced as though wearing clogs and two left ones at that. But now she'd landed him in a proper pickle and no mistake!

One way or another Isa was going to have to be found a job, and soon, because if she wasn't Matt would be round wanting his pound of flesh. And like Shylock, Matt had a nasty habit of putting a literal interpretation on things.

'Are you all right? You're looking awful funny,' Harriet asked.

Jakey forced a laugh and replied he was suffering from a wee touch of indigestion which he was sure would soon pass.

He then muttered a few words of sympathy to Harriet about not being accepted for emigration and she played along by pretending to be disappointed.

After she'd gone he hunched forward and stared morosely at his desk. There wasn't a hope that any of the other girls would hand in her notice in the near or even distant future. They would all be hanging on to their jobs like grim death. Even more so now that Armstrong's had closed down, throwing many of their relatives and boy-friends out of work.

But a solution to his dilemma would have to be found, and even now he knew what that solution was going to be.

Sighing, he reached for a cigarette and lit up. Much as he liked Harriet he feared Matt Walker even more.

At five am on the Monday morning Hugh presented himself at Paterson's dairy. As he was the first to arrive he went into the stables to have a look round for Squinty, and it was with a whoop of delight that he found his old friend munching away on some feed. A welcoming neigh told him he hadn't been forgotten.

He made a big thing of the horse, rubbing and scratch-ing its head while in response it nuzzled him under the armpit.

'Who the hell are you?' the voice demanded roughly.

Hugh turned to find himself staring at a squat, middle-aged man of less than normal height. Normally an easy-going, affable chap who rarely took exception to any-one, Hugh did so now. The moment he set eyes on Ronnie Sproat he knew he'd met an enemy.

He explained who he was and why he was there and then waited while Sproat considered this news.

What Hugh saw filled him with apprehension. Sproat was a walking powerhouse, his chest thick and burly, his thighs and biceps chunky with muscle. His face was concave, the nose no more than a button. His neck was short and sat atop his shoulders rather like a main branch sprouting from an oak. His eyes were dark and in this particular light like two empty holes punched on either side of his nose.

Hugh, on the other hand, was tall and willowy slim. It

would be a number of years yet before he came into his full strength.

Hugh knew that Sproat could beat the living daylights out of him without even half trying.

'I've heard of you,' Sproat sneered, showing badly decayed teeth, several of which were green with infection.

'Oh aye?' said Hugh, a little scared and not quite sure what was going to happen next. What he couldn't understand was why a discerning man like Aly Paterson had taken on a brute like this.

'You were a pal of Stewart's, were you no'?' Sproat demanded, picking his nose.

Hugh nodded, wary, waiting for anything to happen.

Sproat cogitated again and from the heavy frown on his face it was obvious his thinking processes were somewhat on the slow side.

Hugh found himself twitching and desperately wishing Sproat would say something. These long silences were unnerving.

'Did you know Stewart, then?' he asked finally, more to break the silence than because he was curious.

'I knew him all right,' Sproat replied, his eyes glittering ominously. 'I took over from him as head boy when he went away to college.'

Squinty snorted and tried to poke his nose back into Hugh's armpit.

Sproat's eyes narrowed as he watched this interchange between Squinty and Hugh, nodding to himself as though he found this of great significance. Then turning abruptly on his heel he strode from the stable.

Hugh breathed a sigh of relief and sank back against a wooden wall support. He didn't know what all that had been about, but one thing was sure – Stewart and Sproat were enemies and somehow the emnity between these two had reached out to include him. He just prayed Sproat wouldn't assign him to the lead cart which would, of course, be driven by Sproat personally.

He could hear Aly's voice now out in the yard so he

walked to the stable door. He saw that Aly was deep in conversation with Sproat.

Sproat was completely transformed from the brute who'd confronted him. The man's face was wreathed in smiles as he bowed and scraped obsequiously to Aly Paterson. Ronnie Sproat looked as though butter wouldn't melt in his mouth.

Glancing up, Aly caught sight of Hugh and beckoned him over. Hugh was introduced to Sproat who, with a grin, said they'd already met.

The other lads were arriving. Several of them had started to drag the gaudily painted carts from the back of the stables where they were kept. A shout went up from one of them to announce the arrival of the milk from the farm.

Hugh had just finished helping to load the last of the churns when he witnessed an incident which confirmed for him the sort of man Ronnie Sproat was.

A youngster of about twelve had arrived late, and Sproat, having manoeuvred him into a quiet corner, was now chiselling him about it.

Abruptly and savagely Sproat's hand swung to connect with the side of the boy's head, which knocked him off his feet and against a wall.

Just about to put the boot in, Sproat hesitated when he saw Hugh staring at him. Turning, he strolled slowly away, leaving the boy coughing and gasping on the ground.

Hugh ran forward and helped the boy to his feet. There was an angry weal on his face but no real damage had been done.

The lad thanked Hugh profusely, saying in a small scared voice that Sproat was a holy terror and God help anyone who crossed him.

It was obvious to Hugh that Aly Paterson couldn't know what was going on and the lad verified this by telling him Sproat had Aly eating out of his hand.

The lad then scampered off to his cart and climbed aboard. He and another young boy bent their heads together to discuss what had just taken place. They glanced fearfully across to the centre of the yard where Sproat stood with chest thrown out and thumbs hooked into his wide leather belt.

Judging from the expression on Sproat's face he thought himself the cock of the walk.

With a flash of insight Hugh realized that Sproat was mentally unbalanced. The man was a nutter and as such to be feared all the more.

Minutes later Sproat shouted Hugh across. Pointing to the stables he told Hugh to go in and get Squinty plus another horse to make up a pair.

When Hugh had led the two beasts out Sproat told him to couple them up to the lead cart. Having done that Sproat gestured him to find a seat amongst the churns.

Hugh's heart sank as he swung himself up over the tailboard. He was wondering just what he'd let himself in for.

7

Once the decision was taken, Carrie and Archie didn't waste any time. He took out a special licence and arranged for the ceremony to take place that Saturday at the old registry office in the Candleriggs. A quiet affair was planned with only the immediate family plus a few select friends.

Big Donald offered to have everyone back to Tallon Street after the marriage had taken place but Archie discreetly suggested it might be better if the gathering was held at what would be his bride's new home. Big Donald was only too happy to comply as it meant he wouldn't have to pick up the tab.

Things were extremely tight in the Chisholm household, the budget being literally managed on halfpennies and farthings.

Early on the big day, Harriet casually announced to the rest of the family that a friend of hers from London would be dropping by and furthermore he was coming to Laidlaw Street with her. She had, of course, first spoken to Carrie about this to obtain Carrie's permission.

This shock announcement was further compounded when at a few minutes past ten o'clock a magnificent 1920 Sunbeam 16 Tourer drew up outside the close.

Children playing in the street abandoned their games to come and gawp while all around curtains twitched as the neighbours peeked out, trying to see what all the commotion was about.

Never a shy woman at the best of times, Mrs McElvey threw her window right up and leaned out across the sill so she could get the best possible view.

The Sunbeam was a dull silver colour with a hood that folded back. It was Lou Dansie's pride and joy and the only one of its kind in California.

He'd ordered the car originally as a bit of one-up-manship but had soon come to love it for itself. He had brought it to Britain – the land where it had been built – for the simple reason he hadn't been able to bear leaving it behind.

Dansie was still shaken from his drive through Glasgow. He'd seen slums in America but nothing to compare with what he'd just witnessed.

It was a relief to find the street Harriet lived in a paragon of working-class respectability. He wouldn't have to worry about getting his throat cut here.

Carrying various packages containing presents he mounted the stairs to the top landing where the Chisholms lived. Harriet met him at the door and kissed him on the cheek. Then she ushered him inside to where the family were waiting in the living room.

Hands were shaken all round and the packages handed over to Winnie, who was momentarily flummoxed: this was the last thing she'd been expecting.

Carrie excused herself saying she had a lot yet still to do and Dansie replied he fully understood.

When Winnie discovered one of the packages contained a bottle of best malt whisky she handed it to Donald who went to the sideboard for glasses.

It was customary for drink brought into a house to be at least started on, if not finished, in the presence of the giver.

Big Donald was stumped for a second when Dansie said two ounces of liquor would do for him but in the end resolved his quandary by pouring out a large one which seemed to meet with Dansie's approval.

In the kitchen Winnie was unpacking large bars of chocolate and all sorts of strange and exotic foods.

Besides the food there were three beautiful silk headsquares, one for each of the women.

Donald was naturally curious about how Dansie and Harriet had met in London. Bluntly he asked how the meeting had come about?

Dansie's reply was near enough the truth. He said he and Harriet had been staying at the same hotel and had been forced through circumstances to share a table at dinner. Learning he was coming north to Scotland, she had extended an invitation for him to come and meet her family, an invitation he had been delighted to accept.

For over an hour the two men talked about the terrible unemployment ravaging the western world until Winnie interrupted them by announcing it was time she, Harriet and the baby left for Laidlaw Street where a meal was waiting to be prepared and laid out.

Dansie said it would be his pleasure to run them over there providing someone navigated for him.

Winnie was thrilled at the prospect of riding in the Sunbeam. It would be her first time in a motor vehicle.

Dansie was delighted and promised her she would sit

up front with him.

With Angus wrapped up tight against the cold they trooped downstairs where Dansie made a bit of a fuss ensuring Harriet and her mother were seated comfortably.

The neighbours were back at their windows as the Sunbeam moved sedately off down the street with children running screaming behind it.

During the drive Winnie asked Dansie if he'd ever been to the town of Sherman in Texas? When he said he had, she sighed and sank further back into the car's ample upholstery. In a small voice she requested he tell her what sort of place it was and what its inhabitants were like?

The request puzzled Dansie who knew nothing about Alex. But it was obviously important to Winnie so he did his best to comply.

All the time he spoke of Sherman, Winnie listened intently, drinking in every word.

When he had finally exhausted his knowledge of the subject she thanked him courteously and for the remainder of the journey sat tight-lipped and introspective.

By the time they reached Laidlaw Street they'd passed through some of the worst slum areas and it was an extremely humble Lou Dansie who parked the Sunbeam outside Marjoribanks's close.

His own problems which had seemed so enormous were really of little consequence when compared to all this. For the first time he began to view his life and the job he did in perspective. It was a sobering thought.

After seeing the women and baby upstairs he returned to the Sunbeam, worried that the rough looking crowd surrounding it might damage it in some way. For a few minutes he dithered, not sure how to tackle the situation. Then he had a brainwave. Approaching two of the toughest looking men there he politely asked if they'd be willing to do a job for him.

Both men were gaunt from hunger. They glanced at each other and then one growled they might be interested providing Dansie made it worth their while.

In actual fact they were desperate for work and would have done nearly anything to earn a few bob but their pride demanded they didn't appear too eager, especially as it was a foreigner they were dealing with.

Dansie handed them five shillings each and told them to sit in his car and see no damage came to it. When it was time for him to leave he would give them a further ten shillings each providing the car was just as he'd left it.

The two men couldn't believe their luck. This was a Godsend. And money for old rope, to boot! They climbed into the Sunbeam from where the larger of the two announced in a very loud, gravelly voice that if any so and so as much as breathed on the gentleman's motor then he and his good friend Sammy here would personally mollicate the unfortunate.

Dansie went back up the stairs with a lighter heart, convinced his car was in good hands, as indeed it was.

In the house he was introduced to Archie and Sheena who were both in a fluster trying to get dressed. He was grateful for the huge fire stoked up in the kitchen range. The Chisholm place had been terribly cold, he'd thought. And he'd no sooner seated himself close to the roaring flames than Winnie plonked Angus on his lap telling him to mind the wean.

He liked children so it was no hardship for him to entertain Angus while Winnie and Harriet got on with the business of preparing the meal.

As Archie and Sheena finally left for the registry office Archie called out that they shouldn't be too long and that there was drink in the sideboard. Everyone was to help themselves.

After Archie and Sheena had noisily clattered their way downstairs Harriet opened a screwtop of beer and handed it to Dansie. When their hands accidentally touched she smiled as did he.

In a surprisingly short time those who'd attended the ceremony were streaming in through the front door. Carrie and Archie were covered in confetti and laughing like excited children.

Dansie was introduced round while Archie got out the drink.

Big Donald and old man Smith found themselves together and for a few minutes chatted about Carrie and Archie. Then Robert brought up the subject of Donald having been laid off.

There was a hollowness where his belly should have been as Donald described what it was like signing on the dole. The queues that stretched seemingly for miles. The ranks of men shuffling forward inches at a time for the indignity of being given a few miserable shillings' charity.

The air of degradation and hopelessness that hung over these men like a pall. The lined faces twisted with worry and fear.

The collective sigh that seemed to go up from time to time as though the men had just realized anew that they were of no further use to society and had been discarded on the Corporation midden.

Donald threw whisky down his throat and followed that with the remains of his beer. He shuddered and exhaled slowly.

There was no self pity in him. He knew what he was and that he was as good at his job as the next man. Better probably. He had a reputation as a grafter and a perfectionist who took pride in his work which was why he'd been the youngest foreman Armstrong's had ever appointed.

Robert Smith wanted to express his sympathy with the situation but wasn't quite sure how to do so. Words seemed so inadequate. In the end he offered to get Donald another drink.

Standing by himself in a corner Hugh was already a little tiddly as he brooded about Ronnie Sproat. Life had been hell for him since he'd started back at the dairy, Sproat making him do the work of two, if not three. Every time there was a full churn to be moved or lifted Sproat saw to it that he did it on his own. On top of that he'd been forbidden to ride on the cart which meant he had to run alongside all the time.

He'd made a few discreet inquiries amongst the other lads but none of them knew what the trouble had been between Sproat and Stewart. Or if they did they were keeping stum.

He'd considered going to see Aly Paterson to tell him what was going on but that was before he'd realized how much Aly relied on the odious Sproat, who toadied up to Aly at every occasion.

Aly wasn't a well man. The trouble with his heart had slowed him down a lot and as a result he'd sloughed off more and more of the dairy's running onto Sproat's shoulders. Sproat was only too pleased to accept the additional responsibility as, apart from increasing his pay packet, it also gave him more power. And power was something Sproat liked very much.

Hugh knew now that, albeit he and the Patersons were close, should it come to a showdown, he was far more likely to be shown the door than Sproat. Aly had come to rely on his head boy.

There had been the incident at the stables just the other day when things had nearly flared into an all out confrontation. He'd been gathering some feed to place in Squinty's stall when suddenly a pitchfork had come plunging down from the hayloft to miss him by inches.

Sproat had been full of apologies, a combined sneer and half laugh in his voice as he spoke them. He'd said that his hands must be greasy for the pitchfork to have slipped out of them like that.

Completely drained by shock, Hugh had stood there for a few moments while anger alternated hot and cold within him. Pulling himself together, he bent down and picked up the pitchfork. Its prongs were bent at their tips from the impact with the stone floor.

Monkey-like Sproat leapt onto a dangling rope and descended. When he faced Hugh his eyes were mocking and full of malicious glee.

Hugh desperately wanted to lash out, to have a go at

this horrible man whom he detested so much. But somehow he managed to keep his fury under control, reminding himself that a blow up on his part was precisely what Sproat was after as it would merit Sproat giving him the sack.

Knowing Hugh was dying to hit him Sproat smiled and thought perhaps one more turn of the screw might do it.

Sproat was convinced Hugh was after his job as head boy. After all, wasn't Hugh a great china of the high and mighty Stewart? The same Stewart who'd once threatened him with dismissal should he ever be caught bullying any of the boys again.

Fear grabbed at Sproat's stomach as he thought of Hugh being made up to head boy: if that was ever to happen his little secret would be out with dire consequences for him.

Still smiling Sproat took the pitchfork from Hugh and on turning away pretended to slip. With a yell he fell over while bringing the pitchfork sharply down so that it cruelly raked Squinty's left flank.

Squinty squealed as blood spurted. Hunching his head, he frantically drummed his rear hooves and then lashed out with them.

Hugh was well aware that this had been a deliberate act on Sproat's part. The bastard had definitely had it in for Squinty ever since his first day back at the dairy when he'd said he and Squinty were old pals.

'Whoooa there boy!' Hugh shouted, running round to the side of the stall and clambering up its side so that Squinty could see him.

As soon as the horse's hooves had started flashing Sproat had rolled to safety. He frowned now as he lay on the floor. His plan wasn't going to work. Instead of coming at him Hugh had gone to the horse.

'It's all right! It's all right!' Hugh soothed, stroking the side of Squinty's head. The beast's eyes were rolling with fright and pain. Every few seconds a fresh wave o' tremors rippled through its body.

Hugh looked at Sproat now standing well back fron

the stall. 'It seems to be your day for accidents,' he said, not even bothering to hide the sarcasm and contempt in his voice.

Sproat didn't like that and for a moment it seemed he might made an issue of it. Instead, he shrugged and threw the pitchfork clattering onto the floor which caused Squinty to whinny and lash out again.

'That animal should have gone to the knacker's yard long before now,' Sproat said. 'It hardly does enough work to earn its keep.'

Hugh bit back the angry words crowding his mouth. Squinty might be old, but he grafted damned hard and what's more Sproat knew it. The thing was Aly would believe what Sproat told him and it could well be that out of sheer spite and maliciousness Sproat would arrange for the horse to be done away with.

As casually as he could Hugh said, 'I know a farmer who's on the lookout for an old cuddy. He'll pay reasonably for one too. Certainly more than the knacker's yard would. I'll mention it to Aly as it would mean a few more quid in his pocket should he decide to replace Squinty here.'

It was a complete fabrication which he'd made up on the spur of the moment and judging from the sour look on Sproat's face it would seem his bluff was going to work. Squinty was safe for a while yet.

After Sproat had left he washed Squinty's flank down and painted the wounds with antiseptic. Luckily for the horse they weren't nearly as bad as they looked. The scores were long but shallow, and, providing infection didn't set in, should heal quickly.

While Hugh continued to brood about Ronnie Sproat his uncle Sandy had at last managed to get Winnie on her own, something he'd been trying to do since they'd arrived back from the registry office.

Nodding in the direction of the hallway he whispered for her to follow him as he wanted a quiet word.

Out in the hallway he drew the living room door to

before turning to a puzzled Winnie. Slipping some crumpled white paper into her hand he said that was a wee something to help her and the family get by.

The crumpled white paper was two fivers which expanded from the ball they'd been crushed into when she unclenched her hand. 'Och Sandy,' she said gratefully. He and his wife Mary had their own family to keep which couldn't have left them with all that much to spare at the end of the week.

'I had some good overtime on my last voyage,' Sandy said, 'And I'm away again within the next fortnight so we'll be sitting pretty for a while at least.' Slightly embarrassed now he added. 'There's no need to say anything about this to that soft brother of mine. He'd probably make you hand it back.'

Winnie knew that Sandy was right. This was best kept quiet between her and her brother-in-law.

'It's just a loan, mind!' she insisted, coming to terms with accepting the money that way.

'Aye of course. If that's how you want it.'

'I do,' she replied, knowing in her heart of hearts there was a certain futility about her promise to pay it back as Donald could well be idle for years.

Standing on her tiptoes she pecked Sandy on the cheek. 'I won't forget you and Mary for this,' she said, a catch in her voice.

Poor Mary who was so fat that a trip down to her local shops and back again was the best she could manage. Hence the reason why Sandy had attended all the official family functions on his own for the past few years. 'Once round aunt Mary, twice round the block' had at one time been a saying that would always raise a laugh. But that had been in the days when a joke could still be made out of Mary's fatness.

Opening the front door Winnie rushed down the stairs to the toilet on the half landing. Having bolted herself in she stuffed the fivers down her bra. Then she sat down and had a right good bubble to herself.

*   *   *

Early the next afternoon Jakey Sanderson used his keys to let himself into Ballogie Clothing. There was nothing unusual in this as he often worked an hour or two on a Sunday in an effort to try and keep pace with the ever increasing amount of paperwork expected of him.

The machine room floor was a different place without the constant roar that filled it during the week. His footsteps echoed hollowly as he made his way to the back row where Harriet's machine stood.

Sitting, he thumbed the switch which caused the gun metal grey machine to surge with power.

There were three bundles of finished trousers lying beside the machine. Each tied with string and bearing Harriet's personal marker. Every machinist had her own personal marker so that it was always known who had done what and that way any item could be referred back to the person responsible for it.

Jakey untied the first bundle and lifting the top pair of trousers onto the machine set to work.

In a little under an hour he had altered various seams on half a dozen pairs of trousers in such a way as to make it look like faulty workmanship on Harriet's part.

When he was finished he switched off the machine and retied the bundles. Having checked that everything was just as he'd found it he left the factory and headed for home.

On the Monday afternoon Winnie was down on her hands and knees waxing the hallway linoleum when the front door opened and Harriet appeared.

'What brings you home at this time?' Winnie demanded, thinking Harriet must have been taken ill.

Harriet stood staring numbly down at her mother and looking as though the question hadn't got through to her. Her face was strained and there was a puzzled expression in her eyes.

Donald entered the hallway from the living room where he'd been idly carving Angus a wooden boat for when the lad was older.

'What's going on then?' he asked.

'I've been given the sack,' Harriet stated bluntly.

Winnie sucked in her breath and her hand came up to her mouth.

'What happened, lass?' Donald asked quietly, not betraying by the merest flicker just how shaken he was by this latest calamity.

They all went through to the living room. Harriet told them how Jakey Sanderson had come storming up to her with several bundles of trousers saying her work on these was a bloody disgrace.

The entire factory had come to a halt as hot words were bandied between herself and Jakey who'd proceeded to humiliate her by waving the offending articles in the air and shouting in a voice loud enough for everyone to hear that an apprentice could do better work than she could.

At that, her temper had boiled over – as Jakey had known it would – and she'd traded insult for insult till in the end he'd trumped her acid retorts by declaring she was fired.

Stunned, she'd collected her few things together and gone through to the accounts office where she'd had to wait half an hour while they made up her time.

Some of the girls had made a few voluble remarks about the sacking but they weren't in a position to do anything about it. Not one of them would stick her neck out in case she, too, lost her job.

After hearing all this Winnie groaned and sat back in her chair. Closing her eyes she gently massaged her forehead with workworn hands. With Harriet's money now gone it meant they were reduced to having to live off Donald's broo money and what Hugh brought in from the milk.

Harriet shook her head. She was at a complete loss to understand how she had turned out seams like the ones Jakey had confronted her with. And yet they were undeniably hers. The bundles they'd come from had all borne her personal marker.

Donald asked if there was any chance Jakey would change his mind. Harriet's reply was that he wouldn't.

If the sacking had been done in the privacy of his office then she would have gone back to him and pleaded for another chance. But as it had occurred with the entire factory listening on – and bearing in mind some of the things she'd called him which everyone had heard – there was no likelihood whatsoever of him reversing his decision. Too much face was involved.

'I'm sorry, Papa,' Harriet ended up saying.

Donald rose and crossed to her. He tried to smile but didn't quite manage to pull it off as he patted her on the shoulder.

He desperately wanted to be out of the house. He felt hemmed in. Claustrophobic. He would walk down to the river and watch the water swirl by. There was a certain therapeutic effect to be gained from watching running water, he'd always thought.

'It seems you've sacrificed the Australian idea for nothing,' Winnie said. Dejectedly she headed for the kitchen to put the kettle on.

Donald left Harriet sitting staring into space. As he made his way down to the front close he patted the one remaining Willy Woodbine in his pocket. All that remained of the five packet Carrie had slipped him earlier on in the week. He would smoke that as he watched the water. He had nothing better to do.

Harriet and Lou Dansie sat in the Bluebird Cafe. He listening while she recounted what had happened at Ballogie Clothing.

Dansie was secretly pleased at this turn of events. He'd managed to secure a rented house for himself in Edinburgh and all that week had been puzzling about how to get Harriet to come and share it with him. Now he knew.

When he put his suggestion to her she sat back and stared at him as though he'd just pulled a rabbit out of a hat, which, in a way, he had.

Naturally she didn't want Donald and Winnie to know they were living together. Dansie's reply to that was she would take digs, which he would pay for. And as far as anyone in Glasgow was concerned that would be where she was staying. In reality, however, she would be living with him in St Stephen's Place.

Harriet was a realist who was never slow to grasp an opportunity when it presented itself. Dansie's plan solved both her major problems in that it meant she would not only be working again but would also be with him.

After they'd finished their ice creams they walked to the nearby Queen's Park where they hammered out the details. Harriet was elated after the week's depression. Everything was going to be all right after all, thanks to Lou.

On an impulse she stopped and throwing her arms round him kissed him deeply. Several passers by stopped to stare but that didn't bother her. She was truly happy which was all that mattered.

When they arrived back at Tallon Street she announced straight off that Lou had engaged her as a researcher for his film about Bonnie Prince Charlie at the marvellous wage of three pounds ten shillings per week.

Winnie gasped when she heard. It was as much as Donald in a good week with lots of overtime had ever earned at Armstrong's.

Harriet hurried on to say she would also be taking typing lessons and when she was proficient would be helping Lou type out his script.

Of course all this meant she would have to stay in Edinburgh where the job was and she had decided that digs were the most suitable thing.

When Harriet mentioned she'd be sending home two pounds per week Winnie was so relieved she collapsed into a chair and for a moment it seemed she might even burst into tears.

Dansie then suggested Harriet return with him to

Edinburgh where he would put her up in a good hotel until she found suitable digs. He stressed the fact he was desperate for her to start as soon as possible.

Harriet hid the elation bursting within her. The idea of the hotel was merely a sop for her parents. That night she'd be ensconced in St Stephen's Place. In bed with Lou Dansie where she belonged.

With everything now neatly arranged Harriet hurried through to the bedroom to pack. While she was doing this Dansie reflected on the great changes wrought in his life since meeting her. The long stale years with Bess had been blown away, leaving him gloriously alive again. He and Harriet were no two ships passing in the night. He'd known that instinctively as had she. Theirs was a relationship with a long term stamp on it.

And hadn't Harriet pointed out to him that Bonnie Sue was now at an age where she wouldn't be nearly as affected by a divorce as she would've in the past?

That thought had certainly given him a lot to chew on, just as Harriet had intended.

8

It was early in the summer when things finally came to a head between Hugh and Ronnie Sproat. So far Hugh had been able to ride everything Sproat had thrown at him; in fact the more he'd done so, the more desperate Sproat had become.

Enormous changes had taken place in Hugh since he'd come back on the milk. His experiences with Sproat had toughened him both mentally and physically, transforming him from a boy/man into a fully fledged male.

He'd also broadened out a lot and the constant exercise of running miles per day plus hauling and humping heavy churns had increased his strength to the point where he thought he could at least give Sproat a good go of it should they ever square up to one another, a situation Sproat seemed determined to bring about.

Having just returned from the morning round Hugh led Squinty to his stall where he left him standing just in front of the opening into it. First he would rub Squinty down and then when that was done to his satisfaction he'd feed the old horse. Humming to himself, Hugh reached for the hand brush hanging from a beam.

Hidden in dense shadow Sproat stood at the back of the stables watching every move Hugh made. He had a brown feed sack clutched in one hand which every so often twitched as something stirred inside.

A few days before Sproat had noticed that Hugh was terrified of rats. He wasn't too keen on them himself, come to that, but they certainly didn't frighten him the way they did Hugh.

There are always rats around stables although there weren't many in this one thanks to the big ginger tom Aly kept who was a notorious and fearless ratter.

The previous evening Sproat had returned to the stables where it had taken him several hours of patient waiting in order to trap the long sleek beast now held prisoner in the sack.

Grinning in anticipation, he thought of the terror and blind panic Hugh would experience when the rat landed on him. He was going to enjoy this. He was going to enjoy it a lot.

He flexed the thick, corded muscles running the length of his shoulders and down his arms. If only Hugh would lose control and take a swing at him then his day would really be made. Given the slightest provocation he would beat Hugh to a pulp and relish every second of it.

But Hugh had to make the first move. That was a prerequisite. When the story came to be told to Aly Paterson he must be able to protest that he'd only been defending himself.

Stealthily he crept forward, watching out that he didn't tread on anything that would make a noise.

He froze when the rat squeaked and scratched its claws on the inside of the sack. But Hugh, completely engrossed in what he was doing, heard nothing.

Sproat continued his advance only to freeze a second time when he heard the voices of several of the lads outside. For a moment it seemed the lads would come into the stables, but having paused by the doorway they continued on past.

Sproat breathed relief. He would have been furious had the lads intruded to spoil his fun, the more so as he'd specifically detailed all of them to be working across at the dairy for the next half hour. It was no accident he and Hugh were the only ones in the stables.

Masking himself behind a partition belonging to one of the horse stalls, he felt for the thick leather glove tucked into his belt. Once the glove was on he laid the sack down on the floor in such a way that its opening was spread out in a taut line. Hurriedly he placed his feet so that most of the opening was blocked off, leaving only a narrow passage for the rat to get through.

Minutes later he was cursing inwardly. Although the rat was running around inside the sack it seemed too stupid to be able to work out what it had to do to escape.

'Come on, damn you!' he breathed. He was crouched over the sack, his gloved hand poised to swoop once the beast began to emerge.

Suddenly the rat found the passage and wriggled through so quickly he almost lost it. Three times he grabbed before he managed to get his fingers round its neck.

With vicious looking claws tearing the air the rat was hoisted up off the ground. Its black beady eyes glared malevolently as it looked for someone, something, on which to vent its fury.

Sweat was coursing down Sproat's face and back as he held the rat at arm's length. Raising himself up on his tiptoes he peered over the partition to see what position Hugh was in.

Hugh pulled the brush in long even strokes along Squinty's pelt. The horse was still steaming a little from its morning's exertions and the warm animal smell it gave off was one Hugh found extremely pleasant.

When Squinty snickered he didn't pay any attention thinking the old horse was telling him to hurry up so he could get his nose into the feed which was next on the agenda.

This time Squinty whinnied with a note which caused Hugh to pause in mid-stroke and look round.

The scream was torn from him when he saw the rat, claws extended and eyes ablaze, hurtling through the air straight towards him. His right hand with the brush still banded to it struck out and with good luck more than good judgement he connected with the rat, knocking it squealing to one side.

Sproat stood with hands on hips silently roaring with laughter. The look on Hugh's face as the rat had come hurtling towards him had been absolutely priceless.

The rat twisted in mid-air and as it dropped towards the floor its flailing claws managed to catch onto and sink into soft, warm flesh. Its teeth guillotined down to bury themselves in Squinty's leg.

Squinty reared up and shrieked, an almost human sound that raised the hair on the back of Hugh's neck.

Again and again the rat's claws cruelly raked Squinty's leg. Freeing its teeth it took its time about selecting a fresh target. This time when it bit a jet of darkly coloured blood shot out from a severed artery.

Numb with fright Hugh stood watching Squinty rear and plunge. He desperately wanted to help but the only thing he could think of was to grab hold of the rat and tear it free. But with the best will in the world there was just no way he could bring himself to do that.

Sproat's silent laughter stilled when he heard the distinct sound of Aly Paterson's voice at the stable door. It wouldn't do for him to be found standing by watching while one of their horses was in obvious trouble. With a shout he rushed forward to try and knock the rat off Squinty's leg with a piece of harness.

Eyes rolling and frothing at the mouth, Squinty thought this was some new enemy come to attack him. Wheeling suddenly round he lashed out with his rear hooves, catching Sproat full in the chest.

Surprise was written all over Sproat's face as he flew backwards to land with a sickening thud on the stone floor.

'What in the name of the wee man is going on here?' Aly demanded, Greta by his side.

The rat tore itself free and jumped to the floor where it went scampering away to disappear behind a bale of straw.

Hugh ran forward to try and grab hold of Squinty but the horse would have none of it. Iron hooves stamped savagely down, causing sparks to fly from the stone floor as it backed away.

Sproat saw his danger and tried to roll to safety but the excruciating pain tearing his chest apart forced him to stop and gasp for breath. As Squinty's flicking tail and backside reared over him he just had time to cover his face with his arm before the animal's hooves came pile-driving down.

Sproat yelled in agony as his legs broke under the impact. He fainted clean away when a sliver of white bone came jabbing through his trouser leg.

Squinty staggered and then sank to his knees in a pool of arterial blood. His eyes were already glazing in death when Hugh took hold of his head and began stroking it.

'There, there old boy,' Hugh whispered, letting Aly and Greta attend to the stricken Sproat.

'I'll send for the doctor!' Greta yelled to no one in particular as she ran from the stables.

'And a vet!' Hugh called after her, knowing full well

that long before a vet could arrive it would be all over for his old pal.

Sproat was still out cold, blood trickling from a corner of his mouth.

Squinty's exhaling breath rasped out causing his nose to flutter. His flanks heaved while all around him the pool of blood grew wider.

At the end of a mighty convulsion it was all over. What light was left in his dulled eyes winked out as death claimed him for her own.

'What happened?' Aly Paterson asked. He could see how moved Hugh was by the old horse's death.

Hugh shook his head, still shocked by the speed with which events had taken place.

Of one thing he was certain, however: Sproat was behind all this. The only trouble was he had no way of proving it.

In a voice husky with emotion he told Aly the literal truth of what had happened. Concluding his story, he was aware that Sproat had come to and was watching him from behind half closed lids.

Any lingering doubts about Sproat's involvement were blown away. The bastard was guilty as hell!

Greta returned to say one of the boys had been dispatched for the doctor.

Sproat was in terrible pain which, to give him his due, he bore remarkably well. Both his legs were broken and several of his ribs.

In a croaking voice he said he wasn't to be moved till after the doctor had examined him. He was scared that if he was, one of his broken ribs might puncture a lung.

A number of the lads came crowding round the stable door to see what had happened, a few of them not bothering to hide the triumphant glint in their eyes when they saw Sproat lying there in obvious agony.

Hugh pulled himself together and took command. He ordered two of the horses brought from their stalls and hitched to a delivery cart. When it was time for Sproat to be removed to hospital this would be as good a way as any to do it.

The boys accepted Hugh's commands willingly and set about their appointed tasks with a lightness in their step that hadn't been there before.

Sproat asked for a cigarette and got one. He coughed a little as he smoked and there was a strange, resigned look in his eyes. Occasionally he smiled in a lopsided, cynical way as though amused at some private joke.

The doctor arrived a quarter of an hour later and got on with his examination.

Greta was sent into the house for an old sheet which was torn into strips and used for bandages. After Sproat's chest had been strapped up rough splints were fashioned and bound tightly to his legs.

That done, all the available lads were called in to help as Sproat was manhandled onto a plank which was lifted and slid onto the waiting delivery cart. Two of the boys were designated to drive the cart to the hospital while the doctor followed on behind in his car.

There was nothing left for Hugh to do now but organize Squinty's burial. This he did in a piece of ground at the back of the dairy building which was nicely secluded with lupins and other wild flowers growing in profusion.

Insisting on digging the grave alone, he sweated over it for what seemed an eternity. When it was finally ready he got those boys still remaining to help him load the carcass onto a bogey which they trundled to the graveside.

When Squinty was deposited at the bottom of the grave he sent the lads away again while he filled it in.

When the burial was completed Aly Paterson brought him over a screwtop of beer and together they stood looking down at the mound of freshly turned earth.

It was then Aly asked him to take over as head boy. He immediately accepted. Both of them were aware it would be a long time before Sproat was fit to work again. Those legs alone would take months to heal. The job paid two pounds a week.

He was invited over to the house where he once more

went over his version of what had happened in the stables. As he spoke Greta tut-tutted and shook her head. She wasn't particularly partial to rats either.

On the first Friday after the incident Hugh did a money collection of all the rounds. It didn't take him long to work out that what he'd taken was in excess of Sproat's figures. Furthermore, no matter how hard he tried, he couldn't make this discrepancy resolve itself.

Armed with both money and books he went straight to Aly Paterson and the pair of them sat down to work out just what was what.

It became clear that Sproat had been on the fiddle to the tune of five pounds a week, a sum he'd gradually built up to and thereafter maintained.

Aly was shocked and heartbroken by this revelation, so much so he broke his rule and had a drink. Over their dram he sought Hugh's advice. Should he prosecute or merely cut his losses and let things go at that?

Hugh took his time in replying. He wasn't a vindictive person but not only was Sproat a bully and a thief, the villain was also responsible for Squinty's death and that was something he could neither forgive nor forget.

'Prosecute,' he advised.

When Ronnie Sproat finally did appear in court he was found guilty of embezzlement and sentenced to three years in Barlinne Prison. Hugh was there to hear sentence passed and it was with a grim smile that he watched Sproat being led away.

Squinty was revenged.

Harriet had never been happier in her life. She and Lou Dansie had long since settled into St Stephen's Place where they spent long hours working, he on his script which was coming along famously and she either researching or typing up his pages for him.

She'd discovered she had a natural aptitude for typing and had consequently picked it up easily and quickly. She was studying shorthand which she found more difficult to assimilate but was none the less becoming proficient at.

She adored the researching side of her job, taking great delight in visiting museums and other such places to pore over ancient and usually musty tomes, ferreting out snippets of information which she then fed to Dansie as though they were rare treats.

Nor was her research confined solely to the academic. Several times Dansie sent her off to various parts of the country where her brief was to quizz the locals and write down stories that had been handed down by word of mouth from generation to generation about the Prince and the Jacobite rebellion.

Harriet thrived on all this. Her new life seemed as far removed from Cathcart and Ballogie Clothing as St Stephen's Place was from the far side of the moon.

A bloom had appeared in her cheeks. The sort that love, happiness and a full sex life brings.

They often ate out, frequenting the best restaurants the capital had to offer. Other times they stayed cosily at home while Harriet cooked. She was a good cook who'd got a lot better since being encouraged to experiment, something Donald would have viewed with horror.

They drank a lot of wine. Dansie bought it by the case and had it delivered to the door.

They attended many concerts and plays – a whole new world for Harriet.

It was after just such an excursion to the theatre that they returned home one night to find a telegram lying on their front door mat.

Neither were particularly perturbed by this as telegrams were commonplace to their household, United Artists often cabling Dansie and he replying by the same method.

This one was different, however, as it came from Bess.

Dansie sat and read the telegram several times before looking up. When he did so it was obvious the wire contained bad news.

Crossing to the brandy decanter, he poured himself a stiff one.

With narrowed eyes Harriet sat patiently by waiting for the worst. She knew instinctively something momentous had occurred.

'It's Bonnie Sue,' Dansie said, his eyes filling with sudden tears. 'She's been taken into hospital. The doctors don't know what's wrong yet but whatever it is, it's serious.'

Harriet had never seen a grown man cry before and for a moment was quite mesmerized by it. Where she came from a man would rather die than be seen in such a state. Only women and weans cried. A man was above such a blatant show of emotion.

Finally she roused herself to ask if this mightn't be a ruse on Bess's part to lure him back to Los Angeles?

Dansie's brow creased as he considered this possibility. There was no reason why Bess should know about him and Harriet. Certainly he had never mentioned it in any of his letters home. But these things do have a way of leaking out and it wasn't impossible that news of their liaison had somehow travelled 6000 miles.

When he spoke it was to say Bess was capable of many things but not of using Bonnie Sue in that particular way. As far as he was concerned the telegram was genuine and he would treat it as such. Anyway he couldn't afford not to.

It was too late for him to do anything that night other than draft a reply. In the morning he would go straight to Waverley Station and catch a train for London from where he'd embark on the first available New York bound ship.

Harriet was shaking inwardly as she went upstairs to pack Lou's things, while he drank more brandy and pencilled out his reply.

There was to be no sleep for either of them that night. Instead they lay in bed and talked in whispers about what was to happen while he was away.

It was agreed between them that she would stay on at St Stephen's Place doing what research she thought might be beneficial and getting on with her shorthand studies.

He would give her a cheque before he left in the morning and once back in Los Angeles he would make the necessary arrangements for her and the house's up-keep through his bank.

The Sunbeam he would leave behind for his return.

They made love after that until it was time to rise and get ready to go to the station.

Harriet was desolate as she climbed into the cab Dansie had hailed in the street. Everything had happened so quickly she still couldn't believe that within the hour he would be on his way back to America.

There was an air of unreality encompassing her as she gazed through the cab's window at the cobbled streets and passing grey stone tenement buildings. She imagined this must be something like how Carrie had felt when told about John McBain's death.

Her left hand was opened and something cold slipped onto her wedding finger. When she looked down she saw she was now wearing Dansie's heavy gold ring, the one given him by Mary Pickford.

'Keep that for me till I get back,' he said, closing her hand into a fist again.

There was so much she wanted to say but the only words that would come seemed trite and meaningless. Looking into his eyes she could see it was the same with him so she snuggled close and they stayed that way till they arrived at the station.

It was cool inside the station with sudden gusts of wind that caused men to hold onto their hats and women to clutch at their skirts.

She went to purchase newspapers and a few magazines while he stood in line to buy his ticket. As they walked the length of the platform Harriet felt as though someone was hacking at her insides with a blunt knife. She wanted to shout, scream, throw her arms round Lou.

Instead they kissed one last time and then he said he thought she should go, that way would be better for both of them.

For a few seconds more they remained clutched to one

another, and then tearing herself free she turned and walked back the way they'd come.

Time passed.

There was a letter from New York, another from Los Angeles, and after that silence.

The long weeks became a month and the month became two, then stretched to three. During this time Harriet busied herself as best she could and tried to delude herself that everything was all right.

Then one day while she was busy round the house and for once had neglected to go down to see what the mailman had delivered, the long awaited explanation came.

With trembling fingers she ripped open the envelope and sat down to read what Lou had to say.

Bonnie Sue had been stricken with a brain tumour which had come within an ace of killing her. A surgeon called Krantze had developed a brand new technique for dealing with this most horrible ailment and as a last resort had been instructed to operate.

The result had been only partially successful. Bonnie Sue's life had been saved but a terrible price had been paid. From now on the girl would be little better than a vegetable, her mind permanently that of a six-year-old.

An ice cold wind blew through Harriet when she read that. She knew then that Lou Dansie would never be coming back to her nor would she be going to him.

In that instant her whole life crumbled and fell apart. Her lips thinned to become a bloodless slash and her face sank in upon itself to become pinched and shrewish. She'd become the epitomy of an ageing spinster.

She continued reading: Bess knew nothing at all about their affair nor was he going to tell her now. There would be no divorce. As Bonnie Sue desperately needed both her parents from now on there was no way he could bring himself to break up his marriage, inflicting further pain and anguish on his mentally crippled daughter.

He was truly sorry. He still loved Harriet as much as

he had on the day they'd parted. But their affair was ended.

Harriet stopped reading to light a cigarette. She stared at her hands, wondering why she'd never noticed before how close her veins were to the surface? What a peculiar observation for a time like this, she thought.

Gazing round the room it seemed to her everything was just that little bit more so than it normally was. Colours more vivid. The ticking of the clock more resonant. Her senses of smell and touch more acute than usual.

It crossed her mind that she might be in a state of shock or on the verge of a nervous breakdown.

She returned again to the letter.

United Artists had cancelled the film about Bonnie Prince Charlie and a new project on the life and times of Robin Hood with Fairbanks again scheduled for the title role, was being set up.

This was a further blow to Lou who had invested a great deal of time and effort in his Bonnie Prince Charlie script.

He didn't elaborate on why the film had been cancelled but as he was working on a new assignment for United Artists she assumed it wasn't because of any fault on his part.

The latter pages of the letter consisted of instructions for winding up the let on the house and the disposal of the Sunbeam. She was to keep the money realized from the sale of the car. The various bits and pieces he'd bought she was to do with as she wished.

He ended the letter by repeating his love for her, adding that he wanted her to keep his Mary Pickford ring as a memento in the hope she would never forget him. He was never going to forget her till his dying day.

She laid the letter down and lit another cigarette from the butt of the first. Crossing to the whisky decanter she poured herself an extra large one.

Memories of the happy times they'd spent together came flooding back to her. Large, fat tears welled from the corners of her eyes to meander slowly down her cheeks. The dream was gone, the illusion burst. Hollywood and her love had somehow blown away, leaving only the reality of impending spinsterhood behind.

Finishing her drink she poured herself another. She wished Carrie had been there for her to talk to. Of all the people she knew her sister was the one most likely to understand just how she felt.

Picking up the letter and decanter she started for the bedroom. Tomorrow would be soon enough to begin what had to be done.

For the rest of the day she would lie womblike in the bed they'd shared together. She'd drink a lot and cry even more. Tears might be futile but they did bring some sort of relief.

The thick gold ring weighed down her wedding finger. Sometime soon she'd buy a gold chain on which to hang it round her neck. Bringing the ring to her lips she kissed it. 'Oh my darling!' she whispered.

Part II

Rosemary for Remembrance
1931–1938

9

Angus was ten years old when the Marjoribanks moved to Holmlea Road just round the corner from Tallon Street. The new house had three bedrooms, a kitchen, a living room, and an inside toilet cum bathroom. Carrie had never got used to either the stairhead closet or the zinc tub in front of the fire, so she appreciated the bathroom most of all.

Angus had a bedroom all to himself which he thought a grand thing, although at night he missed Sheena's heavy breathing, which had always been a great comfort to him, and the long whispering sessions they'd often secretly indulged in.

Now Sheena had left school and was employed as a conductress on the trams.

The work situation had eased over the past few years. Armstrong's had re-opened and one of the first people to be re-employed had been Donald, taken back in his old capacity as foreman moulder.

Although asked, Hugh hadn't returned to Armstrong's. He preferred staying on at Paterson's Dairy.

Aly was dead. His heart had finally given out and he'd passed away peacefully in his sleep three years previously. Stewart had married his English sweetheart and was now boss at Muirend and the farm just off the East Kilbride Road.

Hugh was still called head boy although he was really more of a manager as Stewart spent nearly all his time out at the farm where he and his wife lived.

Hugh had no regrets whatsoever about his decision. He enjoyed his work and loved being with the horses. The offer of a few pounds more per week wouldn't have enticed him back to the bedlam of the foundry.

On Angus's first day at Holmlea Primary he was taken along to a Mr Barr's class where he was told to sit beside a boy called Robin Kirkpatrick. The lesson at the time was spelling and during it the two boys stole surreptitious glances at one another, each trying to size the other up.

When the bell rang for playtime Angus followed the rest of the class downstairs and out into the playground where he found a quiet corner by some palings to eat the jelly pieces Carrie had packed for him.

He was in the middle of his second piece and watching some lassies playing peerie when Robin Kirkpatrick and several other boys came strolling across. Inside Angus was tense but, trying to appear nonchalant, he wiped jelly from his chin. He knew whatever happened next would decide whether or not he was accepted.

Robin Kirkpatrick was roughly the same height as Angus but a lot broader in the chest and shoulders. He had a rather ruddy face inclined towards pudginess. His hair was a deep auburn and hung limply in long and somewhat greasy strands.

Thinking it might be interpreted as a sign of weakness Angus decided not to speak first so he continued trying to look nonchalant as he switched his gaze from the peerie-playing lassies to a game of footer taking place further up the playground.

Robin Kirkpatrick noted Angus's interest in the footer and that gave him inspiration for his first question. 'Which team do you support?'

Angus turned to stare at Kirkpatrick, acting surprised at being addressed.

'What?'

The aggressiveness in Angus's voice threw Kirkpatrick a little. He was used to other boys being wary of his size.

'I said, who do you support?' This time he matched Angus's aggressive tone.

'The 'Gers are the boys,' Angus stated, as though it were Holy Catechism.

'Aye. That's right enough!' Kirkpatrick replied with grudging approval. Angus's answer had been the correct one.

By this time Angus had come to the conclusion that with the possible exception of Kirkpatrick none of the boys surrounding him were nearly as tough as some he'd known in his old school. There had been a number of real hardmen in his class there, all right.

'Where do you stay then?' Kirkpatrick continued doggedly.

When Angus replied he was living in Holmlea Road he was asked which number. It transpired he and Kirkpatrick were neighbours, living next close to one another.

The next question was what did his father do?

Angus replied that his father was dead – that caused several blank stares and shuffling of feet – but that his step-father was an engine driver. He added the last bit not out of deference to Archie but because flyly he knew the effect it would have.

Several of the boys gaped and even Kirkpatrick was taken aback. An engine driver! Probably the ambition of half the lads in that crowded playground.

'For LMS,' Angus threw in for good measure, smiling inwardly at the effect his words had produced.

'Gosh!' exclaimed one of the boys, his face full of awe.

Kirkpatrick broke the spell by stepping forward and slapping Angus on the back. He and the others were about to play a game of Cowies and Indians and would Angus care to join them?

Angus groped in his jacket pocket for the rubber dagger he had there and announced he would be only too happy to take part.

When it came to choosing up it seemed everyone

wanted to be on his side. Having an engine driver in the family did have its advantages.

After that Angus and Kitty – Robin hated the name but it was what everyone insisted on calling him – became the best of pals and through his new found friend Angus soon learned his way round Cathcart and all the best play places.

As summer gave way to autumn the pair were often down at the Cart, a place called Sandybank being their favourite spot, where they fished with string and jam jars for baggy minnows and the red bellied tiddlers known, for some obscure reason, as 'doctors' or 'docs'.

Snow came early that year and with it Hugh to Holmlea Road humping a present for Angus.

When Angus arrived home from school that day he found Hugh sitting in front of the fire chatting to Carrie. The present, wrapped in canvas bagging, took pride of place in the centre of the kitchen floor.

Hugh was extremely fond of his nephew and now that Carrie and Archie were living in the neighbourhood he was hoping to see a lot more of the lad than he'd done in the past. The present was by way of an overture to Angus who he hoped would soon find time to visit him at the dairy.

Angus ripped the canvas bagging away and whooped with delight at the newly made sledge, smartly painted in dark green with a red and black lightning flash running its entire length.

For Hugh, the beam on Angus's face was ample reward for the couple of hours it had taken him to make the sledge. He'd got the idea of knocking it together when he'd come across the runners stuck in a corner at the back of the hay loft. They'd been pretty rusty but with a bit of elbow grease he'd soon had them gleaming like new. The wood had come from an ancient cart in the process of being cannibalized.

Thanking Hugh profusely, Angus bolted down his tea, dying to get out in the snow and try out his new sledge. It was a brammer and far better than any the boys round about possessed.

He would call on Kitty and together they'd away up to the Queen's Park Reccy Ground, the most popular sledging site in the district.

After Angus had gone Hugh asked Carrie if everything was all right? She was dreadfully pale with dark heavy rings under her eyes. He'd also noticed some bruises on her arms and suspected Marjoribanks was knocking her about. This wasn't the first time he'd spotted black and blue marks on her.

Carrie knew precisely what her brother was driving at but shrugged it off, saying she wasn't sleeping too well with Archie working so many lates and nights.

When Hugh stared pointedly at the bruising she added casually she'd slipped the other day and banged her arm against the coal bunker. Having told the lie, she promptly changed the subject by putting a fresh kettle on for Sheena's tea and announcing the lassie would be arriving in from her work at any minute.

Carrie's attitude to Archie was complex. Over the years he'd worn her down to the point where she now dully accepted her lot.

It wasn't as though Archie was all bad, she'd often told herself. He did have his good points. He'd never been a day out of or off work since they'd got married and every Friday he came straight home and paid her the housekeeping money without fail.

He was also a generous man. All she had to do was ask and if it was possible he'd get it for her. Occasionally he would even surprise her by bringing home a gift which he'd hand over, saying gruffly it was a wee minding he thought she might like.

She'd long since come to the conclusion there was something wrong inside Archie's head. He could be pleasant and charming one minute, a raging animal the next, capable of almost anything.

Sexually there was a perverted side to him which he often indulged in. At such times all she could do was grit her teeth and pray the ordeal would soon be over.

Why she didn't leave Archie? In the beginning she had often considered it. But her options were strictly limited: getting a job – which still wasn't all that easy to come by – and finding a place where she and Angus could live together or, failing that, returning to Tallon Street.

There was no question of her finding another man. She wouldn't have wanted to even had it been possible.

What it boiled down to was she had reconciled herself to making the best of a bad job. Archie might be a sadistic bastard but he wasn't entirely unlivable with.

What she had made crystal clear to him was that if he ever beat up Angus the way he beat her up that would be the end of it. She would pack what few things she and the lad had and go.

Running a hand through greying hair she took a deep breath and wished she could find more energy. She was always so tired nowadays, drained to the point where she found it a terrible struggle just to get through the daily grind.

She had developed a permanent stoop and her skin had a washed out look about it.

At thirty-one she looked in her mid forties.

On arriving at Queen's Park Reccy Ground Angus and Kitty immediately joined in the fun, taking alternating shots to zoom over the hard packed snow, lying face down on the sledge or else sharing the same ride together by sitting one in front of the other.

It was Angus who first noticed the two lassies in trouble. The girls were about the same age as himself and Kitty, maybe just a little younger, and both dressed in extremely smart uniforms. They were surrounded by a gang of toughs intent on mischief.

'Yeh toffee-nosed Parkies!' one tough jeered, spitting at the taller of the two girls who recoiled in disgust as the gob landed on her coat.

Angus had never heard the expression 'Parkies' before. Kitty informed him Park School was up the town somewhere and catered for the daughters of the very rich.

Angus had no sympathy with rich girls. Or rich anyone come to that. But he did think it a bit thick that ten boys had ganged up on two puny lassies.

The tough who'd spat darted in and, catching the taller girl's scarf, yanked it from round her neck. The girl showed a lot of spunk in lashing out at him but missed and would have gone toppling over if it hadn't been for her companion catching and steadying her.

The second girl was close to tears which she was desperately trying to hold back. The taller girl stood proud and defiant with a look of utter contempt for their tormentors written across her face.

The tough with the scarf tied it round his waist and, wiggling his hips provocatively, taunted the taller girl by proposing she come and take the scarf back off him.

Hoots of strident laughter and obscene suggestions made both girls blush with embarrassment.

Angus knew the sensible thing would be to ignore what was happening but there was something about the taller girl which struck a sympathetic chord in him, making him want to go to her defence. When she caught his eye and silently pleaded with him he knew he was going to have to get involved.

At that moment one of the toughs ran at the taller girl and catching her by the shoulders sent her spinning to the ground. The tough immediately sat on her back and proceeded to rub her face with a handful of slush.

The girl spluttered and choked as the slush was driven into her mouth and up her nostrils. Her hat had been picked up by a tough who was now sporting it on his head.

'That's enough. Let her go now,' Angus said quietly, his fists balled by his side ready for action.

The tough sitting astride the taller girl stared incredulously up at Angus. 'What did you say, Jimmy?' he demanded.

'Let the lassie go,' Angus repeated.

Slowly the tough rose from his sitting position till he was fully upright on his rather bandy legs. With a nod to his mates he started moving in on Angus and Kitty who were now standing back to back. With a sudden roar all ten toughs simultaneously launched their attack.

For a few minutes Angus and Kitty held their own with hard blows given and taken by either side.

The beginning of the end came when Angus's feet were kicked from under him and with a strangled yell he went crashing to the ground. With no one to guard his back, Kitty was soon overpowered and when he fell, he landed heavily on Angus.

Kitty grunted with pain as a boot came thudding into his side. What he couldn't understand was why Angus had got them into this fight in the first place, over two lassies who undoubtedly had more money than sense. It was beyond him.

Angus and Kitty would have been onto a right doing but for the sudden intervention of Robert Cooper, Winnie's downstairs neighbour's son, who was now a houseman in the nearby Victoria Infirmary.

Robert and a few of his friends had been out for a breath of fresh air when they'd caught the sound of the fight. Seconds before he fell Angus had been recognized by Robert who immediately strode into action.

Tough after tough was hauled of the still struggling Kitty and Angus and thrown unceremoniously to one side. When the toughs realized they were facing new adversaries, and grown up ones at that, they lost heart and took to their heels.

The only injuries Angus and Kitty had were a few scratches plus a cut lip on Angus's part. They were both extremely lucky and knew it. The toughs could just as well have been carrying weapons which they wouldn't have hesitated in using.

A shaken Angus blurted out to Robert Cooper what had happened but when he came to look round for the Park School girls they'd both vanished. He was hurt, feeling the least the lassies could have done was to say thank you.

It was Kitty who pointed they'd probably run off when

they'd seen he and Angus were getting the worst of the punch up.

Robert and his pals insisted Angus and Kitty accompany them back to the hospital so that their cuts could be attended to. Despite protestations that they were both all right, the pair of them were taken back to the infirmary's casualty department to have iodine painted on their faces.

Several nurses came in to see the heroes – the nurses' words, not theirs – who'd been so gallant in going to the assistance of the put upon wee lassies. Angus and Kitty squirmed with embarrassment and couldn't wait to flee the building. But first they were taken along to a side room where tea and fancy cakes had been put out, a treat from these self same nurses whom Angus and Kitty now concluded weren't so bad after all.

Finally they did escape out into a night filled with swirling snow. Deciding it was getting late, they agreed to go home. As the pair of them trailed along the road Angus's mind was filled with images of the taller girl who'd had her face rubbed with slush. It was the queerest thing but in that moment when their eyes met and she had silently pleaded with him it was as though he'd known her all his life.

Arriving home he found Sheena sitting by the fire engrossed in a romantic novel. She looked up to tell him word had come for Carrie to go to Tallon Street as Winnie had taken ill.

Angus was immediately concerned as he was very fond of his granny. From what little Sheena knew he gathered Winnie had come down with a bad cold which had suddenly turned into something else.

Carrie's instructions were for him to go to bed when he got in and if she wasn't back by morning Sheena was to get the breakfast.

He then had to explain the iodine marks on his face. Not wanting to mention the Park School girls in case Sheena thought him soft he told a version of the story that excluded the two lassies.

Then he hurried through to his bedroom where he dried down the sledge before changing into his pyjamas.

Having changed and pulled the bedclothes back he decided on a last trip to the bathroom.

His feet pattered on the linoleum as he made his way along the hallway. The bathroom door swung open to his touch to reveal his step sister in all her naked glory.

Angus gawped. This was the first time he'd seen Sheena with no clothes on since she'd reached puberty. His eyes travelling from the generous swell of her breasts down to the furry clout protruding from between her legs. His mouth was suddenly dry and his heart palpitating fit to burst.

Sheena stared at Angus, as surprised as he was at his barging in on her. She was sure she'd locked the door! When she saw the transfixed expression on his face, her mouth slowly curved into a smile.

Angus wanted to turn and run but his feet were rooted to the spot. There was a terrible compulsion in him to reach out and touch his step-sister's naked flesh.

Sheena realized what was going through his mind and that excited her. 'Come here,' she said crooking a finger at him.

Like an automaton Angus moved towards her.

He stopped when he was only inches away, his eyes riveted on one of her nipples.

The hand that took his sweaty one was cool. 'Oh Sheena,' he mumbled as his fingers enclosed a breast.

At the back of his mind he was terrified the outside door would open to admit either Carrie or Archie. He daren't even think of what would happen should he and Sheena be found like this.

Sheena knew what she was doing was unforgivable but she couldn't help herself. There was a lot more of Archie in her than either he or she knew.

Angus started to tremble as his hand was guided down the length of his step-sister's body to come to rest on the woolly clout between her legs. The hair was a lot more wiry than he'd expected and it was damp which surprised him as he'd walked in on her before she'd had her uppey and downey.

The bathroom was warm. Heated by a small stove standing by the wc, the paraffin aroma mingled with the sweet and distinctive smell given off by Sheena's naked body.

'Are you scared?' she asked softly.

He lyingly shook his head.

Sheena's face was glistening with sweat and her lips parted in a way that made her look catlike. There was a burning sensation in her throat and between her legs where Angus's hand was. At that moment she would have given anything for him to have been a few years older.

Letting his hand go she said, 'You'd better run along to bed now and leave me to get washed.'

Angus nodded, not trusting himself to speak. His thoughts were whirling and confused, part of him wanting to run away from there as fast as his legs could carry him while another part wanted to stay.

It came to him consciously then that the Sheena he'd known these past ten years had changed beyond all recognition and in doing so had left him behind. She was no longer the same She-she who'd mothered him and held him tight in bed while strange things were happening between Archie and Carrie through the wall.

'Go Angus!' she commanded, turning her back on him and fumbling with the taps.

This time he wanted to reach out and touch her for quite different reasons than before. He couldn't bear the thought that the She-she he'd known was now lost to him. It was like losing an arm or leg.

'Go!' she repeated.

And he did.

When he was in his bed he hid under the covers and cried softly to himself, not because of what had happened but because he knew it marked the end of an era in his life.

That night he dreamt of the taller of the two Park School girls standing stark naked in the centre of the Reccy Ground.

Only it wasn't her own but rather Sheena's body she was flaunting beneath the falling snow.

Winnie was hot, sweaty and bordering on delirium. Although Carrie had changed the bedclothes not half an hour since, again they were saturated.

With hands clasped and shoulders hunched Donald sat by Winnie's bedside where he'd been since she'd taken a turn for the worse not long after he'd arrived in from his work.

He looked lost and very scared, for once not bothering to mask his emotions with manly indifference.

Dr Robertson had already been and gone and would return later. Solemn on arrival, he'd been downright grave on leaving.

Winnie blinked as globules of sweat rolled down her forehead and into her eyes. Instantly Carrie was there with a wrung out cloth to dab away the sweat and cool down her flushed cheeks.

Winnie turned her head to one side so she could look at Donald. She hadn't noticed before, probably because it had been a gradual thing. But she could see now just how much he'd aged during his six years of being idle.

There was skin hanging where his jowls had been and the neck below had gone thin and scrawny. Those magnificent broad shoulders which had been his pride and joy were now bent and bony, their muscles having withered with the onset of old age.

Closing her eyes she allowed herself to drift, seeing Donald as he'd been when they'd first met. He'd been tall and straight then and she the envy of every woman who saw them walking out together. She could remember thinking him a braw but serious young man whose one line of conversation consisted of what he was going to make of himself in life.

Whenever she could arrange to have a Sunday off he'd come and collect her and together they'd go walking down by the River Kelvin or in the Botanical Gardens, both of which were just across the way from the house in Bellhaven Terrace where she'd worked.

It wasn't long before they'd discovered they had a lot in common, coming from the same Highland stock: in her case from the clachan of Fanagmore on the banks of Loch Laxford in the wilds of Sutherlandshire.

For eighteen months Donald courted her. Then one summer's evening down by the Kelvin he'd asked her to marry him. She'd been so excited that for a full minute she hadn't been able to speak while he, poor man, died the death thinking she was going to turn him down.

But of course she hadn't, and the wedding, conducted by the young Reverend Duncan Forbes, had been one to remember.

Sandy Chisholm had been there with his wife Mary, as well as his other brother, Willy, his sister, Nettie and her man.

And Donald's mother, Fiona – looking grim and for-bidding and every inch the Chisholm matriarch – had come, softening a little as the night wore on and more than just a few drams vanished down her throat.

From her own side two of her sisters had made the journey from Fanagmore. Her father and mother wouldn't dream of leaving the croft while the third sister didn't come because they only had enough money to send two.

Both Kathy and May had arrived looking prim and proper at the Orange Hall, intent on showing that any-one from Fanagmore was just as good, if indeed not better, than anyone from the heathenish Glasgow where it was well known all sorts of unspeakable things hap-pened to a body if she wasn't careful. But time and whisky had loosened their reserve as well till in the end they'd been wheeching it up with the best of them.

Then it had been home for Donald and Winnie to their

own wee hoose in the Calton where after three years of marriage their firstborn came into the world. Alex had a wild look in his eye even as a baby. He grew up to be smaller than his father but just as broad-shouldered. Alex with the silvery laugh, which always made Winnie's insides jump just to hear it. And so clever with his hands he even won grudging praise from Donald. Grudging only inasmuch as Donald didn't want the lad to get swollen headed. Privately Donald was delighted, although he'd never dream of saying so to anyone other than her.

Winnie's eyes blinked open and she realized she must have fallen asleep and been dreaming. Everything had been so real – as though she'd somehow managed to step back in time.

'Oh Donald!' she husked, her throat parched from fever.

'I'm here lass. I'm here,' he said, taking her hands in his. Putting a strained smile on his face he told her to rest easy and she would soon be better.

He didn't believe that and neither did she. But they were both wrong.

For three days Winnie was at death's door and then, as suddenly as its onset, the fever broke and she started to mend.

During this time she'd been nursed by Carrie and Harriet taking it in shifts while Donald had remained steadfastly by her bedside only leaving the room when nature demanded it.

Learning that his mother wasn't going to die after all, Hugh was so relieved he decided to lash out and buy her something really special to cheer her up.

He took a tram into town where, because the capital outlay was beyond him for the moment, he bought her a wireless set on the newly introduced idea of hire purchase.

Winnie was delighted with the gift, though scandalized by its extravagance.

He left her listening avidly to a discussion about house

plants on the Home Service.

It was during tea that night that Harriet quizzed him about the wireless and he let slip he'd bought it on the never never.

The moment the words were out of his mouth he realized he'd made a terrible mistake. He should have known Donald would view with horror buying anything on hire purchase.

'What did you say?' Donald demanded, his voice tight with suppressed fury.

Hugh carefully laid his knife and fork on the plate before him. Taking a deep breath he sat back in his chair.

Before replying, he re-examined his motives for using the hire purchase agreement and came to the conclusion they were good ones.

He'd wanted to buy his mother a present and what he'd known she'd appreciate most had been for the moment outwith his pocket. The hire purchase scheme was merely a device allowing him to get round this temporary shortage of funds and enabling Winnie to have the set when she could most use it.

Speaking slowly and carefully he repeated his earlier statement.

The thick hairs protruding from Donald's nose quivered, the nostrils dilating and the nose itself flattening. He was appalled. What Hugh had done was unforgivable!

Fierce Highland pride welled up inside him. The creed was simple. If you couldn't afford to buy something then you went without until you could. The last thing you did was to enter into some sort of Shylock arrangement. Hands once renowned for their strength knotted into fists. He wanted to reach over and slap Hugh, to knock some sense into his son's head. Where was Hugh's pride? His self respect?

It didn't matter that Hugh's motives were laudable. If he hadn't been able to pay cash for the present then no present should have been made. Winnie could well do without. She'd survived fifty-seven years without a wireless so a wee while longer wasn't going to make all that much difference.

It was a matter of principle. He had his standards which were his father's and his father's father before him. He expected his family to live the same way. Donald's chair scraped back as he rose to his feet. Silently he strode from the room and a few seconds later the wireless playing by Winnie's bedside was switched off.

Hugh sighed and looked from Carrie to Harriet. What upset him most was that Winnie was going to lose her wee bit of comfort because he hadn't the sense to keep his mouth shut.

The living room door banged against the wall as Donald entered carrying the wireless. Crockery and cutlery jumped as the set was dumped on the table.

'Take the wireless back and we'll forget all about it. And you've your mother to thank for that. I was all for throwing you out of the house for doing such a damned stupid thing.'

Normally Donald wouldn't have over-reacted the way he was doing now but he was bone tired and not thinking straight. Nearly losing Winnie had exacted a terrible toll from him: it was affecting his judgement and sense of perspective.

'You would've thrown me out for that?' Hugh said, completely stunned.

'Oh Papa!' Carrie breathed.

All eyes turned as Angus entered the room. The happy expression on his face died as he realized something was going on. When Carrie beckoned him to her side he ran there to stand wide eyed and silent.

Driven by an inner demon Donald rattled on. Alex would never have passed up the chance of going back to Armstrong's. Alex would never have dreamt of playing milkie when there were men's jobs to be had. And most pertinent of all Alex would never have shamed his mother by buying her a present on hire purchase!

Harriet sucked in her breath.

Carrie bit her lip,

Awed and frightened by what was going on Angus clung tightly to Carrie's skirt. He didn't want his grandpa and Uncle Hugh to be like this. He wanted them to be friends.

Hugh had never realized how bitterly Donald had resented the fact he'd never resumed his job at the foundry. Nor had he realized his father had found him so much wanting compared to his dead brother.

'So there,' said Donald glowering. And coming forward he reached out with the intention of poking Hugh in the chest.

In the space of a few seconds Hugh's whole life had altered dramatically and would never be the same again. With a snarl he pushed his father's hand away and taking a step backwards said, 'Lay a finger on me and so help me God I'll flatten you.'

Donald laughed cruelly. 'Do you think you're man enough then?'

'Aye. I think I am,' Hugh retorted.

'This is ridiculous,' said Harriet. But before she could continue she was interrupted by a voice from the doorway.

'What's going on here?' Winnie said, the words little more than a whisper. She was in her nightdress with a shawl slung over her shoulders. She clung to the door frame for support.

'Winnie! You shouldn't be out of your bed, lass!' Donald exclaimed and hurried over to her.

'I could hear the shouting,' she said.

He ignored that and, turning her round, led her back towards their bedroom.

'You stay here,' Carrie instructed Angus before dashing after her parents and Harriet who'd gone ahead to straighten out the bed.

Suddenly Hugh was trembling and like a jelly inside. Not wanting Angus to see the emotions playing over his face he walked swiftly to the window and stared out over the backgreen and the River Cart beyond.

Donald had been right about one thing. The time had come for a break to be made. After what had been said it was impossible for him to remain in his father's house.

'Have you ever considered running with the milk in the mornings?' he asked.

Angus was taken aback at this coming straight out of the blue and for a moment or two was at a loss for words. It had been an ambition of his for some time now to go out with his Uncle Hugh on the milk rounds. Finding his voice again, he blurted this out, adding he had a pal who was just as keen as he was.

Pleased by the lad's reply, Hugh said that when Carrie pronounced Angus old enough he was to come out to the dairy where he and his china would be fixed up with jobs.

Going through to the big room Hugh packed his few possessions. He couldn't bring himself to walk out without saying goodbye to his mopther so tapping on her door he went in to tell her he was going.

'Oh son!' was all Winnie could say.

'Where will you stay?' Harriet asked.

Hugh shook his head. He hadn't got that far yet. With a lump in his throat he kissed his mother and turned to go.

'Don't forget to take the wireless with you,' Donald said uncompromisingly.

When Carrie let her brother out the front door he had his suitcase in one hand and the offending wireless on his shoulder. He walked up the street to the tramstop without once looking back.

Donald was a lot more shaken by what had happened than he let on. He hadn't meant to say some of those things to Hugh but somehow in the heat of the moment they'd come thundering out.

'I think I could sleep for a wee while,' Winnie lied. She wanted to be alone.

Harriet left the room to join Carrie and Angus through in the kitchen where the two women set about washing and drying the dishes while Angus sat watching.

Donald entered the kitchen carrying a bottle of whisky a little over half full plus two screwtops. 'Out,' he said, signing towards the door.

When Angus made to leave Donald restrained him. 'The men stay,' Donald growled, closing the door behind the bewildered females.

Donald poured two drams, one large, one small. The latter he topped up with water.

'Slainte!' man and boy chorused in unison.

The rawness of the alcohol caused Angus to scrunch up his face and cough. Donald chuckled. There were times when Angus reminded him of Alex as a boy. The eyes were the same, as was the way they both had in certain moods of thrusting out their lower lip.

But if Angus had Chisholm characteristics there was also a lot of John McBain in him. The same stubbornness. The same ability to withdraw into himself and view the world as though from a great distance. The same basic common sense which had made John McBain admired and respected by so many of his workmates and pals.

Donald poured himself another dram and added a beer as a chaser. He could see Angus was struggling with his drink but obviously determined to get it down.

'What do you want to be when you grow up?' he asked abruptly.

There was no hesitation about Angus's reply. He'd known the answer to that question for a long time. 'To start with I'd like to work at Armstrong's like my Da,' he said.

Donald grunted his approval, moved by the light shining in the boy's eyes, a light that was always there when Angus spoke of John McBain.

'You could do a lot worse than Armstrong's,' Donald said. 'A lot of good men have learned their trade there.'

For a while both of them were silent, Angus imagining

138

what Armstrong's was like, Donald thinking of the reality.

'After I'm time served I'd like to go to sea. Do you think my Da would have approved?' Angus asked.

Donald considered that. 'I don't see why not,' he replied. 'It's a good life at sea if you enjoy that sort of thing and if you find it doesn't suit you or get tired of it there's nothing to stop you coming ashore again. There's lots hereabouts have done that.'

Angus stared into the pale amber of his drink and, as though it were a crystal ball, imagined some of the exciting and exotic places he would visit with the Merchant Navy. The prospect sent shivers up and down his spine and goose bumps on his arms.

'To Armstrong's and the sea, then!' Donald toasted.

'To Armstrong's and the sea!' Angus responded.

'What are you two up to in there?' Carrie demanded anxiously from behind the closed door.

'Men's talk!' Angus replied, at which he and Donald burst out laughing.

10

Angus had to wait until the following autumn before he was given permission by Carrie to run with the milk. In just under a year he'd grown nearly a foot which had changed him from a compact, chunky lad into a tall, gangling one.

Carrie knew it was just the age he was but nonetheless it worried her to see how drawn and haggard he'd become. It was only after a long talk with Hugh that she agreed for Angus to go to work for the dairy, the theory being fresh air and exercise couldn't help but do him good.

It was still dark that first morning when Angus dragged himself out of bed at four thirty to stand hopping on the cold linoleum floor while he struggled into his warmest clothing. He was bleary-eyed, with a sour, bilious feeling in the pit of his stomach as he made his way through to the kitchen where Carrie was waiting for him with a cup of tea and a hot bacon roll.

Spirits revived, he rushed downstairs and out to the backgreen where his bike was kept chained to a railing, the same bike that had once belonged to Hugh and which he'd fallen heir to when big enough to reach the pedals.

Kitty, sitting astride his machine, was waiting for him outside the front close and together they headed for Muirend.

Kitty had also grown during the past year but with him there had been none of the runaway stretching that had so elongated Angus's body. Whilst steadily inching upwards Kitty had managed to retain his powerful physique, which was, if anything, even more burly than before.

The friendship between the pair of them had gone from strength to strength till now it was hard to imagine them apart. They practically lived in one another's pockets.

When they arrived at the dairy Hugh was already busy about the yard. The day he'd left his father's house he'd taken himself to the dairy where he'd explained his plight to Greta Paterson. Greta's response had been immediate. He was to stay with her in the big house where she was fed up and sometimes a little scared of living on her own. He would be her lodger paying a nominal rent.

It hadn't taken him long to settle in and soon he'd come to regard the house as a home away from home.

The dairy with Hugh in charge boomed and before long he began to think of expanding.

After considering Hugh's plans – for if the outlet side of the business expanded then the production side would have to as well – Stewart Paterson came to the conclusion that what Hugh had in mind was viable and immediately set to work organizing his end of things.

The first thing Hugh did was to order four new delivery carts and a few weeks before taking delivery, he travelled down to a farm he knew of in Selkirkshire where he bought eight young horses to add to the dairy's complement.

New rounds meant more staff, which had made him think of the promise he'd made Angus the previous year. He and Carrie had talked the matter through and it was finally agreed Angus could make a start. They would see how the lad got on.

Apart from his health, Carrie's main worry was, at eleven, Angus was still a little young to run with the milk. After all, for five days a week he would still have a full day's schooling to get through after he'd done his round. But Hugh had been able to put her mind at rest with a few well chosen arguments, plus the promise that if Angus's schoolwork suffered in any way then the lad would be made to give the job up.

The first thing Hugh showed Angus and Kitty how to do was harness the horses and after that the correct procedure in loading churns and stacking the crates of bottles.

Hugh had timed the boys' start to coincide with the first day of the new rounds and, much to their delight, they discovered he would be in charge of the cart they were to be on.

When it was time to set off Hugh shouted to them to climb aboard and the moment they'd done so he flicked the reins and the cart jolted forward.

As they went, Hugh explained he'd already solicited the area they were to service and as a result they had a considerable number of orders to start off with.

Over a bridge across the River Cart they went, the air filled with the thunderous noise from a nearby weir, and then on towards the Old Castle Road.

This was new territory for both Angus and Kitty who gazed about with unbridled curiosity.

Although still dark, they could make out many large houses of the type favoured by the rich and well to do. There was a rural, village-like atmosphere about the place which they took to right away, it being such a contrast to Holmlea Road.

Soon they were sweating profusely as they raced from door to door filling the orders while Hugh moved the cart slowly along and kept an eye on them to see no mistakes were made.

Hugh was inordinately proud of Angus and secretly wished that Angus was his son.

During the past few years it had become a fetish with Hugh to have a son of his own but, try as he might, he just couldn't seem to find a woman whom he wanted to marry.

There were girl friends in plenty, and even a few affairs. But although he enjoyed the company of all these girls there wasn't one of them he was interested enough in to marry.

There were times when he was convinced he was destined never to meet a girl with whom he could fall in love and his fate was to remain a bachelor to the end of his days. When that mood was on him he would become depressed and take to the bottle, often sitting in his room drinking alone and sinking deeper and deeper into melancholia.

Dawn was breaking when they stopped at Young's Bakery, where Hugh treated Angus and Kitty to a bag of freshly baked rolls and a pint of milk each to wash them down. He had brought a flask of tea for himself which he now drank while smoking a cigarette.

It was Kitty who spotted the apple orchard behind a high stone wall completely encircling a house far bigger and grander than any of its neighbours. Nudging Angus he gestured towards the orchard, muttering in a low voice that the apples looked ripe and ready for plucking.

Casually the pair of them sauntered round to a better vantage point and after a whispered discussion came to the conclusion the wall wasn't as formidable as it had first appeared and that a couple of bright sparks like themselves shouldn't have too much difficulty in getting over it. They decided Saturday night would be the best time for a raid and that they would come back and try their luck then.

When the round was over they returned to the dairy, where Hugh showed them how to brush down and feed the horses. Having completed both these tasks to Hugh's satisfaction, they climbed onto their bikes and headed for home, where they would have a proper breakfast before going to school.

Carrie was waiting anxiously for Angus but her fears were allayed somewhat when she saw the sparkle in his eye and the colour the fresh morning air had brought to his cheeks. Nonetheless she would watch him closely for the next couple of weeks to make sure he wasn't over-taxing himself.

As the week passed Angus and Kitty came to know their milk round inside out. Every morning they'd stop at Young's the bakers for rolls and every morning they'd eye the apple orchard and discuss their plans for the forthcoming raid.

Finally Saturday arrived and after tea that evening they cycled over to the Old Castle Road and the tall imposing grey stone house with the orchard in its grounds.

It was that curious Scottish phenomenon, the gloaming, when they made their move.

Angus stood with his hands pressed against the wall while Kitty climbed onto his shoulders and from there leapt up to catch hold of the top of the wall. Once atop the wall Kitty lay along it and dangled an arm which Angus was able to grab hold of. Kitty then hauled Angus up beside him.

For the space of a few seconds they straddled the wall and then having made sure the coast was clear dropped down the other side to land in thick, luscious grass.

Angus's heart was thudding as he snaked towards the nearest tree, nearly jumping out of his skin when a large hoodie crow cawed shrilly overhead and went flapping past to disappear round the side of the house.

Reaching the tree, Angus grasped hold of the lowest branch and hauled himself up.

The trees, like most cultivated ones, were ridiculously easy to climb and soon the pair of them were pulling apples from the branches and stuffing them into their many and voluminous pockets, the garments they wore being chosen for this particular asset.

'You there! Boy! Come down this instant!'

The voice was female and rang with authority, its owner standing with hands on hips beneath Angus's tree, glowering furiously up into the foliage.

'If you don't come down right away I'll set the dogs loose in here while I ring for the police.'

Angus peered down but all he could see was a pair of legs beneath a crumpled skirt. Feeling sick, he decided the only thing to do was as he was bid. The thought of the police being called in terrified him for if they reported to Archie what he'd been up to then Archie would undoubtedly leather the backside off him.

'I'm coming missus!' he called out and started to descend, thinking he mustn't give Kitty away as, so far anyway, it seemed he was the only one to be spotted.

When he jumped from the lowest branch, he landed badly, causing him to topple over and go crashing to the ground. Ruefully he picked himself up and turned to face the female who'd caught him.

With a shock, he realized it wasn't a woman confronting him, but a girl, and furthermore one whose face was vaguely familiar.

'You!' the girl exclaimed and frowned.

Suddenly Angus placed her. The girl was the taller of the two from Park School whom he and Kitty had rescued from the toughs.

'I didn't know it was your house,' he mumbled and immediately felt a right fool as that seemed such a daft thing to say in the circumstances. Then accusingly, 'Why did you run off that night?'

Thrown onto the defensive, the girl sniffed, 'Well, if you must know, my friend and I could see you weren't going to win against those awful boys so we decided to run and fetch a policeman, only by the time we returned with one everyone had gone.'

'Oh!' said Angus, quite deflated.

'Were you badly hurt?'

Angus stuck out his thin, bony chest, an action which made him look ridiculous. He had one sock up and one down. His knees were covered in dirt and there was a jagged tear in his short grey pants from scrambling down the tree.

'We did win,' he tried to say casually, but instead it came out somewhat pompously.

The girl smiled and fractionally raised an eyebrow.

'We did!' Then in a smaller voice because he could see written all over her face she thought him a liar, 'A man I know and some of his friends happened by and they helped us out.'

Suddenly they were grinning at one another, he remembering how at their previous meeting he'd got the impression he'd known this girl all his life.

'My name's Rosemary,' she said, tilting her head to one side and studying him.

'Mine's Angus.'

'Angus,' she repeated, tasting the word as though it were something strange which had found its way into her mouth.

'And I'm Kitty and is it safe for me to come down now?' Kitty called from the tree in which he was hiding.

Rosemary thought that very funny and asked with a giggle if there were any more of them?

Kitty replied there weren't and dropped out of his tree, landing amidst an explosion of apples which seemed to burst from every part of his person.

Rosemary beckoned them into the shadow cast by the wall, explaining as they moved quickly through the grass that her father would be furious if he caught them and would certainly prosecute.

They left the orchard by the front gate, Rosemary having first checked they weren't being overlooked from the house. And once outside the three of them made their way to the bikes parked round the corner.

As they walked Rosemary questioned Angus about where he lived and how he and Kitty had come to know of her father's orchard.

Angus explained about his Uncle Hugh and the dairy and that he and Kitty came past her house every morning on their milk run. The fact that a milk run had been started up in the area interested her and she told Angus to call at the house next morning. She would see an order was waiting for him.

She said her mother had mentioned only a few weeks previously that the house could do with having its milk delivered so this was her opportunity to see her mother's wishes were carried out. At least so she told Angus.

Bidding Rosemary goodbye, Angus and Kitty slowly cycled in the direction of Holmlea Road, munching as they went.

They hadn't gone very far when Kitty started to tease Angus, saying Angus had a fancy for the Parkie girl and was she now to be regarded as Angus's girlfriend?

Angus's reply was a well aimed apple which caught the jeering Kitty on the side of the head causing him to momentarily lose control of his bike and very nearly come off.

The next morning Angus informed Hugh that the occupants of Arnprior House – the name of the mansion where Rosemary and her parents lived – wanted to place an order for a daily delivery.

Hugh was curious as to how Angus knew this but Angus just shrugged and said it was so.

With Angus in tow Hugh personally went up to

Arnprior House where at the rear entrance a servant girl answered their ring and placed a sizeable order.

Angus had been hoping for a glimpse of Rosemary but when he failed to see her he told himself it was ridiculous even to think she might be up and about at that time of morning.

When he got home after the round Carrie informed him she was going over to Scotland Street later in the day to see Robert and Meg Smith, and she wanted him to come with her. She'd never stopped being grateful to Robert for his generosity to her after John died.

Carrie knew the Smiths had fallen on hard times of late. Several business deals of Robert's had gone awry and he'd had to sell the shop to cover his losses.

That afternoon Carrie and Angus took a tram, getting of at the stop closest to the tenement where the Smiths lived. They hurried up the close to chap at the Smiths' door. It was opened by Meg looking a lot older than either of them remembered.

Meg was delighted to see them and ushered them straight through to the kitchen where Robert was sitting hunched in front of a mean fire.

If Carrie had been shocked by the change in Meg then she was positively stunned by Robert's transformation. Countless stitches laced one side of his face with the surrounding flesh yellowy purple and angry looking. The really big change in him, however, was in the eyes, which had a vacuous, glassy stare about them. When he tried to greet her and Angus all he could manage was to mutter incoherently in heavily impedimented speech.

Meg explained what had happened as she went about putting on the kettle for a cup of tea.

Robert had been over the Clyde on business when he'd run foul of a gang called the Conks currently terrorizing the Bridgeton area.

'The Norman Street Conquerors', to give them their full title, were a product of the times, a bunch of violent although not always stupid men who derived pleasure from terrorizing other people. Usually they'd gang up on their victim at night, invariably razoring him before getting him down on the ground where they would then either stab or kick him to death.

Robert had been lucky. Two patrolling policemen had whistled up reinforcements, forcing the Conks to give him the boot and flee.

He'd been taken to Duke Street Hospital where his slashes had been attended to. He'd then been examined by a consultant who'd confirmed the Casualty doctor's suspicion that brain damage had been sustained.

Meg tried to keep a brave face as she recounted this tale of woe but there was a catch in her voice and several times she had to turn away in order to restrain the tears threatening to engulf her.

No matter how hard she tried for it not to be, Carrie's gaze kept being drawn back to Robert, whose mouth hung slack and whose chin was covered in running streaks of spittle.

She noted the black safe had gone from its place on the floor, the safe Robert had been so fond of boasting about and around whose contents he'd always woven such a shroud of mystery.

Meg went on to tell Carrie that what little money she and Robert had left would soon be gone and then heaven alone knew what would become of them.

Carrie felt guilty thinking about the two hundred pounds Robert had given her but there was just no way she could return so large a gesture. Archie might well be in regular work but at the end of most weeks what he'd earned had gone.

Totting it up in her head she estimated she had just under fourteen pounds rainy day money hidden away at the bottom of an old tea caddy in her kitchen press, hardly a fortune but at least something to give Meg Smith.

Robert grunted and squirmed in his seat and a few seconds later a terrible smell began to permeate the room.

Meg sighed, a defeated almost at the end of her tether

look settling on her face. Smiling wryly at Carrie, she crossed to Robert and helped him to his feet.

Carrie offered to help but Meg said it wouldn't be necessary. The tea was now masked and if Carrie would pour herself and Angus out a cup she would take Robert through to the other room and do what had to be done.

Angus knew by hearsay a great deal about the Conks and over tea proceeded to tell his mother about the big battle they'd had recently with a rival gang called the 'Savoy Indians'.

Angus was still chuntering on about gang warfare when Meg arrived back to tell them Robert had started to doze off so she'd bundled him into bed where he'd stay for a good couple of hours at least.

Carrie, profoundly moved by the succession of tragedies that had befallen the old couple, commiserated with Meg.

In her anguish Meg let slip that the dealings Robert had been involved in for some years outside the shop and which had finally ruined him hadn't been entirely above board. This was, of course, what Carrie and her family had suspected for a long time. Well, Robert had more than repaid the penalty for his avarice and no man would ever reproach him now.

When it was time to go, Meg kissed Carrie on the cheek and then insisted on doing the same to Angus.

During the journey home both Carrie and Angus were silent. Once Angus shivered but his mother didn't notice. She was too wrapped up in her own thoughts about the old couple they'd left behind in Scotland Street.

Sir Alan Armstrong was a small, blunt-faced man with broad powerful shoulders and piercing blue eyes. He looked more like a man used to hard physical labour than the executive he was.

He sat now in his wood-panelled office overlooking the River Cart with a frown on his face and a cup of coffee in his hand.

His desk was neat and tidy, everything squared away

in its place. And that was the trouble! He would have preferred the desk to be littered with papers and plans: that would have meant there were orders coming in.

There were still a few orders waiting to be filled but once those were gone there none to take their place.

Sir Alan grunted with annoyance and swallowed the remains of his coffee. Laying down the cup and saucer he rose and strode to the window where he stood with feet slightly apart and hands clasped behind his back.

He was an angry man, but angry with himself more than anything else. Years ago he'd been advised to diversify his interests, to partially retool and turn out new products as a back up to the traditional Armstrong marine pumps.

There had been that desalination idea which he'd finally rejected because it meant investing a considerable amount of venture capital of which he'd had more than enough at the time, profits for the preceding few years having been exceptionally high.

Well, one thing was certain, he swore to himself. If he did somehow manage to survive this crisis then there would be no need to urge him to diversify in future. He'd learned his lesson and he'd learned it the hard way.

On a sudden impulse he strode through to his secretary's office and instructed her to book him on that night's London sleeper. Then he gave her the names of various London bankers and told her to make appointments with them for the following day.

He'd already been to London several times trying to secure a sizeable loan or second mortgage – his house already had a second mortgage on it – the buildings, plant and machinery that made up his firm. The trouble was that London banks had no confidence in Glasgow any more; to them the Clyde was dying a slow lingering death and any investments made by them would only prolong the agony.

Naturally this was a belief he contested and tomorrow he would once again try to argue them round to his way of thinking.

What was needed was for something cataclysmic to happen, not only to Glasgow but the country as a whole. It was a dreadful thought but he couldn't help thinking another war would be the answer.

He stood by the window watching the gulls fly overhead. The last war had been a terrible affair but how private enterprise had prospered while it lasted! The Clyde had never been so busy, every yard bustling like a beehive as ship after ship was built and launched.

He smiled grimly remembering what Armstrong's had been like in those days: everyone working as many hours as he was able and the order books filled to overflowing.

Sir Alan sighed. Great days! Great days! But would their like ever come again?

He and Cordelia had been married during the war and, my God, but they'd been in love! His heart swelled now just thinking about it. He'd taken her on honeymoon to Dunoon where they'd had the most glorious week before returning to the house he'd bought and had done throughout in the Old Castle Road.

Anxiety fluttered within him at the thought he might lose that house along with the firm. Virtually every ha'penny he owned plus a lot more he'd borrowed was sunk into making Armstrong's once more a viable proposition.

For the umpteenth time he told himself there had to be a way out of his present financial predicament. There just had to!

Taking out a clean white hanky he dabbed hands suddenly clammy with sweat. If the worst came to the worst he knew he wouldn't be able to face Cordelia and the girls. He would kill himself first.

That was why there was a small automatic pistol locked away in one of his desk drawers which he wouldn't hesitate to use if there was no other recourse left open.

He glanced sideways at the painting of his father hanging above the fireplace. That craggy, battle-scarred face had never know either defeat or failure. Or if it had, they'd been only little ones and nothing like the unholy mess he was now neck deep in.

His father would have known the right thing to do in the circumstances because his father had always known the right thing to do: that had been his father's particular genius.

He hadn't exactly liked his father but he had admired him. Sir William Armstrong had been a man you might hate. And plenty had. But at the end of the day you just had to admire him for the clever conniving double dealing devious bastard he'd been.

Still thinking about his father, Sir Alan strode from his office and down stairs that would take him to the yard below. It was a long-standing policy of his to try and make a surprise visit once a day to a part of the works and that day he decided on the foundry.

Big Donald wiped sweat from his brow as he watched white hot molten metal being poured in a sizzling, eye blinding stream into a mould that was the last of a batch of three. Beside him stood Gemmill, the chief pattern maker, who was waiting to discuss a mould that had been ordered and which Gemmill had run into difficulty with because of the peculiar dimensions involved.

Big Donald made a waving sign which was the signal for a foundryman to tap off the streaming metal. Sitting securely atop a brace of joined bogeys, the mould was then wheeled away by another two foundrymen who steered it by means of long iron poles with hooks on the end fitted into rings projecting from the mould's side.

'Now then,' shouted Gemmill – it being necesary to shout because of the constant roar that was part and parcel of foundry life – and immediately launched into a technical explanation of his problem.

As Donald listened his eyes were continually roving over every part of the foundry visible from where he stood; he kept a continual watch over his domain. Consequently he was the first one to see Sir Alan enter the foundry through a side door from a back part of the yard.

His eyes flicked again, rechecking that every man was

hard at work and everything was as it should be. Then he interrupted Gemmill to shout instructions to a crane operator working overhead.

'Morning Chisholm. Morning Gemmill,' Sir Alan said.

Gemmill jumped as though stung. He'd been totally unaware of Sir Alan's approach.

'How is everything going then, Chisholm?' Sir Alan demanded.

Donald said everything was fine and went on to explain the current stages of the various jobs in hand. While he was doing this, Gemmill shifted uneasily from foot to foot and every few seconds shot an ingratiating smile at Sir Alan.

Donald knew Gemmill to be a crawler and detested him for it, not that Gemmill was alone in his arse-licking attitude towards the management. There were many who were just as bad, if not worse, than him. With a few of them it was because that was the way they naturally were but with the vast majority it was because they were continually terrified of putting a foot wrong and losing their previous jobs.

Donald sympathized with these men but at the same time found it difficult to stomach what they did. The whining subservient tone they invariably adopted when talking to the management made him want to puke with disgust.

Gemmill was speaking now, taking up a point Donald had made and needlessly elaborating on it.

'You there!' Sir Alan shouted and strode away, leaving Gemmill in mid-sentence.

Donald quickly glanced round at the man Sir Alan had called out to and noted with relief that it wasn't a foundryman but one of the electricians who serviced the works. The electrician who'd been with Armstrong's for many years doffed his hooker doon as Sir Alan crossed to speak to him.

What Sir Alan wanted to know was why the electrician had put a sixty watt bulb in as a replacement for one that had blown in his private cloakroom when he had specifically asked for a hundred watt to be used?

The electrician bobbed his head in acknowledgement of Sir Alan's question. In a subservient voice he explained a hundred watts were too much for the tiny cloakroom and that sixty were more than sufficient.

To Sir Alan the electrician's reply was no less than sheer insolence. He had personally issued the instructions and no matter that the man may well be right he expected all his instructions to be carried out without question.

A frown furrowed Donald's brow as he listened to the exchange between Sir Alan and the leckie, who was cringing with a terrified expression stamped across his face.

'I beg your pardon, sir?' the electrician queried. Sure he'd heard incorrectly.

'You're fired,' Sir Alan repeated, adding with a snarl, 'Collect your time from the office and then get out.'

Donald opened his mouth to intervene. Then caution warned him if he wasn't careful he'd be the next to get his marching orders. He slowly shut it again, promising himself never to have the temerity to despise Gemmill and the like again for, by keeping quiet now, wasn't he just as bad as they?

Feeling sick, he turned away, unable to stand the sight of the grovelling electrician clutching at Sir Alan's trouser bottoms. He noted that Gemmill was watching with bulging eyes.

Sir Alan snorted and tore himself free from the leckie's frantic grasp, his eyes narrowing when he saw the way Gemmill was staring at him.

With a gulp Gemmill turned to Donald and started talking absolute nonsense about the job they'd been discussing before Sir Alan's arrival.

Donald knew the electrician vaguely. The man was married with a large family to support. Donald didn't envy the poor bugger having to tell his wife he'd been sacked and that from now on they were going to have to exist on the dole.

One thing was certain: having been sacked from one
job it would be many a long day before the leckie found
another, if indeed he ever would.

Crossing back to Donald and the chief pattern maker,
Sir Alan said, 'Now then Gemmill. You were saying?'

Gemmill's voice quavered as he spoke but somehow
he managed to pull himself together enough to make
sense out of his reply.

No one looked at the electrician who, with head
bowed, dragged himself from the foundry floor.

Angus was jolted from his sound sleep by a howl of
anguish reverberating round the house. For several
moments his mind remained fuzzy and then he snapped
wide awake with the realization that it was his mother's
voice he'd heard.

Carrie lay sprawled across the bed with Archie tower-
ing over her. She was sobbing and desperately trying to
protect herself from the blows raining down.

She cried out in agony as a fist thudded deeply into her
stomach. Half out of his mind with drink Archie grabbed
hold of her nightdress and savagely jerked it down to
expose her breasts. Laughing, he fell across her and
began to suck.

Archie lifted his head as the door flew open and Angus
burst into the room. 'Get out!' he slurred.

Angus was horrified at what he saw. Apart from the
fact Carrie was near naked her face was horribly puffed
and swollen, the flesh round one fast-closing eye rapidly
assuming a greeny-purple colour.

'Angus!' Carrie croaked and thrusting Marjoribanks
from her hastily yanked her nightdress back into place.

Angus started towards the bed but he'd only gone a
few paces when arms restrained him and Sheena's voice
whispered in his ear, 'Don't!'

Marjoribanks glowered at his daughter and stepson.
'Go back to bed!' he rumbled. Beside him, Carrie
grimaced as his hand tightened on her thigh.

'You leave my Ma alone!' Angus screamed and

desperately tried to break away from Sheena who, luckily for him, was able to retain her hold.

Carrie swung her legs over the side of the bed and started to stand up only to be knocked back again by a sudden swipe from Archie who grunted she was to lie as she was.

Sheena stared in contempt at Archie. Her mind filled with memories of similar scenes from her early childhood when it had been *her* Ma he'd been abusing.

The breath caught in her throat and she drew back, dragging Angus with her, when she saw the look on Archie's face as he stared hard at her body. She, like Carrie, was clad only in a nightdress. It was the sort of look a girl should never experience from her father.

'You're obscene!' Sheena spat, drawing Angus even closer to her so he effectively covered her front.

For a man who'd consumed so much alcohol Marjoribanks moved astonishingly fast. One moment he was squatting atop his bed. The next he'd streaked across the room to backhand Sheena across the face.

Sheena screamed as she tumbled to the floor. Angus's anger gave way to fright as he was spun to one side where he stood gawking at Marjoribanks and wondering where all his courage had suddenly disappeared to.

Archie stood over his daughter staring down at her. 'You're a whore just like your mother was,' he breathed. 'I've seen it in you for years.'

'My Ma was no such thing. You're a fucking liar!' the girl retorted.

His hand flashed again to crack against her mouth, the force of the blow causing her head to bounce off the floor and her lower lip to split.

'Mind your tongue!' he roared.

Carrie slid from the bed. She had to get Angus and Sheena out of here. Better she take what he had to dish out than either of them. When he was in this sort of mood there was only one thing would calm him down. The sooner she got it over with the sooner he'd be snoring like a pig.

'Come away back to bed, Archie,' she pleaded, at the same time signalling to Angus to get out of the room.

'My Ma was not a whore,' Sheena insisted, her voice quiet and filled with dignity.

Marjoribanks stared hungrily at his daughter's voluptuous body lying spreadeagled before him and strove to remind himself that she was his own flesh and blood and as such untouchable. But by God she was beautiful!

His pulse quickened and there was a stirring in his groin which Sheena couldn't help but notice as he was stripped down to his long johns.

She averted her gaze and momentarily closed her eyes. There was a great pain inside her which had nothing to do with physical hurt. She felt lost. That and alone and terribly afraid.

Ignoring Carrie's signalling Angus ran to his mother and threw his arms round her waist, wishing fervently he was a grown man able to tackle Marjoribanks.

As he clung there an idea was born to him. He had to start making money, lots of it, so that one day he would be in a position to rescue Carrie from this brute she was married to.

Resolve hardened within him. He would buy her a nice wee house where the pair of them could live happily together. Sheena, too, if she wanted to join them.

Sheena slid herself away from Archie and cautiously stood up. Blood from her split lip dripped onto her nightdress.

'Run away through now. There's a good boy,' Carrie whispered to Angus.

'Everything is going to be all right, Ma. I'll see to it,' he whispered in reply.

Carrie frowned, realizing from his tone there was far more to his words than their apparent surface value.

Letting Carrie go, Angus crossed to his step-sister and took her by the hand. 'Goodnight Ma,' he said. Pulling Sheena so that she followed him, the pair of them left the room.

Less than a minute later Carrie was sprawled across

the bed with Archie heaving on top of her.

Big Donald was no fool and had known for a long time that Archie was beating Carrie. But according to the unwritten laws of the society they lived in it wasn't his place to interfere unless approached directly by her.

He was so angry the night Carrie appeared with a black eye and badly bruised face he had to go for a walk down by the river in order to bring under control the fury boiling within him.

During that walk Donald decided that although it wasn't his place to interfere, there was nothing to stop him conniving to find out just how bad the situation was. He would do this by arranging for one of the women to sound Carrie out on the subject.

After much cogitation he came to the conclusion Harriet was best suited for the task as Carrie was far more likely to open up to her sister than she would be to Winnie.

It was well known in the family that Marjoribanks invariably worked late on a Wednesday so Harriet chose that night to present herself at the house in Holmlea Road.

Physically, the past ten years hadn't been at all kind to Harriet. Her face had sharpened while her body had become sticklike. She smoked incessantly and drank cup after cup of black coffee. These two items to a large extent formed her staple diet.

Businesswise Harriet had prospered greatly since her affair with Lou Dansie. She'd sold the Sunbeam and used the money to buy her own small house in Wilton Street in Glasgow's fashionable West End area.

Having completed her typing and shorthand courses, she'd returned from Edinburgh with a wardrobe of smart business clothes to set about finding herself a job suited to her new skills.

The Scottish Amalgamated Insurance Company was situated in Hope Street where in a large gothic building it had both its Head Office and Glasgow Branch.

Harriet's position had been in the communal typing pool serving the Head Office's Accident Department and the Glasgow Branch but after a few years she'd landed the plum post of personal secretary to the manager of Glasgow Branch. This position was the second highest post open to a female within the company, the highest being personal secretary to the general manager himself.

During this time Harriet received several wistful letters from Lou Dansie asking after her and also informing her he and his wife Bess were succeeding in making something of a go of it for Bonnie Sue's sake.

Ruthlessly she'd never replied to any of these letters. A finish had been made that was neat and clean which was how she wanted it to stay.

After a while the letters had stopped coming and now her only reminders of Lou Dansie were Mary Pickford's ring which she wore on a gold chain round her neck and his name when it flashed up on the cinema screen credits as it did from time to time.

There had been no more men after Lou, partly because for a long time after he'd gone she hadn't wanted another relationship, but also because she hadn't been given another opportunity.

So Harriet had thrown herself into her work, so much so that within the company she'd soon gained enormous respect for her ability and dedication.

Carrie was less than delighted to see Harriet as she'd been trying to avoid as many people as possible until her face was more or less back to normal. However she made her sister welcome, ushering her through to the kitchen where she put the kettle on for tea.

The first thing Harriet did was to light the inevitable cigarette. She had a dreadful smoker's cough and as a result of this was forever clearing her throat. The second thing was to inquire after Angus whom she was told was out playing with one of his pals. That pleased Harriet as with Sheena also out of the house it meant she'd managed to catch Carrie on her own. At first Carrie was reluctant to be drawn, but, with a little bit of coaxing, the words were soon tumbling forth.

Even before Carrie had started telling her about how Marjoribanks carried on Harriet worried about her sister. She found Carrie terribly pale and drawn with skin the colour of fresh putty and ribs that jutted where once they had been encased in firm flesh.

Harriet roughly estimated Carrie had lost a stone in weight since the pair of them had last been together a little over six months previously.

Carrie was philosophical about Archie, considering his tempers and violence something that had to be endured. According to her, the beatings weren't as frequent as they'd once been nor were they as severe. The incident of the black eye was a particularly harsh one.

As Carrie spoke, a tale of sleepless nights, headaches, abdominal pains and a more or less general loss of interest made Harriet even more convinced her sister was seriously ill. Whether or not this illness had anything to do with the beatings she could only speculate on.

Completely caught up now, Carrie began to describe some of the sexually perverted practices Archie was so fond of indulging in and which she found totally repugnant.

Harriet swallowed hard, her insides fluttering as her imagination ran riot. Despite herself she couldn't help but picture Archie doing to her some of the things he did to Carrie.

Ten years was an eternity to go without a man, especially for someone like her who was a passionate woman. Besides there was a dark side to her nature she'd long been aware of which secretly hungered after the sort of treatment Archie was so fond of dishing out.

In the end it was established Carrie would stay on with Archie – unless he attacked Angus in which case she would leave – intent on making the best of it.

Harriet's advice to her sister was to go and see Dr Robertson for a thorough check up as it seemed obvious to her there was something physically wrong with Carrie which needed attention.

Shortly after that Sheena arrived home and Harriet took her leave to pay Tallon Street a quick visit in order to give Donald an edited version of what she'd learned.

That night Harriet had great difficulty in getting to sleep.

11

Weeks passed and Angus didn't see Rosemary again until the Christmas holidays which meant a fortnight's glorious release from school.

On the third day of the holiday he went personally as usual to deliver the milk to Arnprior House where he found a note addressed to him stuck in one of the empties. It was from Rosemary asking him to meet her at one-thirty inside the castle.

Foolishly he mentioned the note to Kitty and for the rest of the morning had to endure taunts and innuendoes which, no matter how much he threatened Kitty, laughingly persisted.

The castle was situated just up the hill from Arnprior House and was now a mere shell of its former glory. It went back at least to Mary, Queen of Scots but beyond that Angus knew nothing of its history.

After his dinner, Angus cycled to the castle. Then, leaving his bike, he climbed the stone wall surrounding the ruin on three sides.

Rosemary was waiting for him, sitting in a downstairs

window opening staring across at the heavily wooded area on the other side of the Cart.

'Hello. I'm glad you could come,' she said and smiled.

Angus was so overcome that what was supposed to be an accomplished lighting of a cigarette turned into a ham-fisted fumble. He succeeded in getting the cigarette alight only after two matches had blown out and he'd very nearly burned himself.

Rosemary had changed considerably since their first meeting the previous year. Her face was well on its way to losing its childish lines while her figure now boasted small firm breasts.

'I thought I might have seen you before this,' Angus said, immediately wishing he hadn't as it tipped her off he'd been thinking about her.

Before replying Rosemary asked for a cigarette, and using a lighter produced from her pocket, proceeded to light up in precisely the sort of expert manner he'd intended impressing her with.

There was a teasing note in Rosemary's voice when she informed him he might not have seen her but she'd seen him when he was delivering the milk.

Part of him was gratified to know she'd also been looking out for him but another part was mortified because of the many times he'd stood unashamedly goggling up at Arnprior House wondering which window was hers.

My God, but he must have looked glaikit standing there with his mouth hanging wide open! Quickly he turned away so she couldn't see the sudden flush which flooded his face.

Rosemary puffed on her cigarette and wondered what it was about this tall, gangly boy which intrigued and attracted her so much? Certainly there was an affinity there which she hadn't encountered in any other man and that puzzled her, as she couldn't think why it should be.

'Come and sit here and tell me about yourself. I'd like to know,' she said, sounding strangely grown up.

Angus sat on the spot indicated and instantly became aware of the warm, soapy smell emanating from her. It had the effect of making him feel all sort of jumpy and peculiar inside.

He couldn't bring himself to stare directly into her eyes so he pretended great interest in his cigarette.

'Well?' she prompted.

Slowly and hesitatingly he began telling her about life in Holmlea Road. How he hated his step-father. And how someday when he'd saved enough money he would buy a small house where he and his mother and step-sister could live in peace away from Archie Marjoribanks.

The more he spoke the more confidence he gained and soon he was telling her all about his real father who'd been killed the day he was born in an accident at Armstrong's. As he talked about John McBain his voice filled with pride and his eyes shone with a combination of admiration and love for his dead parent.

His tone became bitter as he recounted to Rosemary how Sir Alan Armstrong had refused his mother compensation for his father's death and because of this Carrie had been more or less forced into remarrying a brute who bashed her about.

Having finally found enough courage to look directly into Rosemary's eyes, he glanced up to find her shrunk back against the side of the window staring at him as though he'd turned into some sort of horrible monster.

'What's wrong?' he asked.?

'Don't let me hear you speak about Sir Alan that way ever again,' she replied coldly.

In that instant it clicked with Angus the name on the milk book for Arnprior House was Armstrong but he'd never made the connection as there had to be hundreds with that name in Glasgow.

'An uncle?' he queried.

'My *father*,' she stated.

How could Angus speak about her father like that! Why, everyone knew daddy was the most warm hearted, generous man you could ever hope to meet.

'How was Mr McBain killed?' she asked eventually, her voice dripping ice.

'He was crushed to a pulp by a casting that got out of control,' adding as though an afterthought, 'strawberry jam.'

The colour fled Rosemary's cheeks.

Angus went on. 'The union tried to get Sir Alan to give my Ma compensation but your father wouldn't entertain the idea. He maintained my Da was responsible for getting himself killed which meant he wasn't liable.'

'And was it your father's fault?' Rosemary asked quietly.

Angus thought of the snapshots he'd seen of his dad. A man of medium height. Broad-shouldered. With an open smiling face. Hair cut short. Greased and swept back from the forehead.

Apart from the snapshots the only mementoes Carrie retained were the medal John McBain had won in the tug-of-war championships when he'd been a member of the Armstrong team, and an old black leather wallet, ripped on one side, with the initials J.McB. in faded gold lettering on its front.

Angus had always found it difficult to broach the subject of his father's death with Carrie, partly because he found it acutely embarrassing to do so and partly because of the pain and anguish it caused her to be reminded of that day. Consequently it was his uncle Hugh he'd turned to for the details of what had happened in Armstrong's foundry on the morning of 12 August, 1921 when John McBain was killed.

'Well?' Rosemary prompted.

'My father was on a gantry that had been declared out of bounds because it was unsafe. We don't know why he was there, only that he was. The casting was being moved when the craneman lost control, allowing it to smash into the gantry. That was the end of my dad.'

Angus paused before continuing. 'My father was in

the wrong but then so was the craneman. Also what Sir Alan might have taken into consideration were the number of years my dad had worked for him. And my grandfather. But he didn't. Despite union pressure he disclaimed all liability and that was that.'

While Angus spoke Rosemary was fiddling with her charm bracelet, hooking a finger under it and tugging outwards. Her anger had dissipated, the last vestiges of it blown away by the sad and hurt expression on Angus's face as he told her about his father.

She desperately wanted to reach out and touch Angus. To draw him to her. To mother him. At that moment she felt as old as Eve.

'I'm going to marry you when we're grown up,' she stated abruptly and in a matter of fact tone of voice.

Angus blinked, not quite sure he'd heard correctly. 'Eh?' he queried.

'I'm going to marry you when we're grown up,' Rosemary repeated. 'I knew it that day at the reccy ground when you saved me from those roughs.'

Laughing when she saw the stunned expression on his face, she went on, 'Don't ask me how I knew. I just did.'

Angus tried to digest that. There was an inevitability about the pair of them he had felt that first day same as she had. But marriage! He hadn't quite got round to projecting their relationship that far ahead.

'Aren't you going to kiss me?' she asked, dropping her head fractionally to one side and looking at him quizzically.

'If you like.'

'Well, if you'd rather not!' she said mercurially and made to move. Her huffiness was replaced by a smile the moment he reached out to restrain her.

Angus knew he was being awkward and clumsy but somehow it didn't matter. All thoughts of denied compensation and Sir Alan Armstrong fled his mind as he took her in his arms.

He started when her tongue licked out to probe the

inside of his mouth. He'd heard about french kissing but this was his first experience of it.

Her hands worked up and down his back and as they did so her bracelet caught in his coat. Snapping open, it flew from her wrist.

'Oh no!' she cried as she saw the bracelet bounce and slide down the rockface to land in a crevice about twenty feet below the window.

The pair of them leaned out of the window to stare at the bracelet so plainly and tantalizingly in view below them.

Rosemary was distraught. Not only was the bracelet an expensive one it was also her favourite piece of jewellery.

Angus knew he was going to have to make an effort to retrieve the bracelet. He studied the sheer rockface falling away beneath them to the Cart below.

Section by section, hold by hold, he worked out a route that would take him down to the crevice where the bracelet was lodged. It wasn't too difficult a descent, he told himself. The trick would be to go slowly and whatever happened not to panic.

Taking off his coat he folded it and placed it on the castle floor. He was nervous. His stomach turned over and his heart thudded in his chest.

He wiped sweaty hands on his trousers before taking off his jacket and placing it neatly on top of his coat.

'Don't be daft!' Rosemary said, placing a hand on his arm.

'Did you really mean what you said?' he asked.

'About what?'

'Us getting married when we're old enough?'

Her mouth creased into a grin. 'Of course.'

Angus took a deep breath. 'It'll be all right,' he said moving to the window and swinging himself up on the sill. 'You'll see.'

He dropped his legs over the side and carefully groped with his right foot for the toe hold he'd picked out. There was a stiff breeze blowing which caused his hair to flap and the back of his shirt to fill out like a sail.

Adrenalin pumped through him as he crabbed his body down. Sliding his left hand across the rockface in search of the grip he knew to be there. From the safety of the window twenty feet hadn't looked very far but once out on the rockface that twenty feet was more like twenty miles.

Rosemary was leaning out of the window staring down. She thought Angus a crazy, impetuous fool and she loved him for it. Without taking her eyes from him she offered up a silent prayer on his behalf.

Angus paused to catch his breath. Already his arms and legs were aching with strain. What really worried him, however, was the possibility of a paralysing cramp setting in, the outcome of which didn't bear thinking about.

A sudden picture flashed through his mind of himself and Rosemary dressed in wedding clothes coming out of a church together. Hand in hand they climbed into a car and then he was throwing handful after handful of coppers out the window, while on the pavement a horde of children dived and swooped, grabbing what they could from the scramble.

With a shake of his head he chided himself to concentrate or it wouldn't be an imaginary wedding he'd be playing a chief role in but rather a very realistic funeral. Glancing up he saw Rosemary staring anxiously down at him.

'Are you all right?' she called.

He nodded and then brought his attention back to the rockface. He was more than halfway to the bracelet and coming up to a traverse which would be the most difficult part of the descent.

Inch by inch he edged his way down and then across. Crying out once in pain when his hand slipped, tearing a patch of skin from his palm.

The wind was worrying him a lot now. It had changed direction in the last few minutes and seemed to be both trying to pry him off and suck him from the rockface at the same time. Gritting his teeth he pressed his body hard against the rock and continued on into the traverse.

He was well aware he was being foolhardy if not downright stupid in trying to retrieve the bracelet. But after what Rosemary had said to him it was important to him to do this thing in order to prove what he felt for her – tangible proof of what he truly felt and believed.

Coming out of the traverse he descended a few more feet which brought him to the crevice where the bracelet was. Carefully bending down, he picked it up and dropped it into his pocket.

He took a few moments to catch his breath and then he started retracing his steps.

Rosemary wanted to shout words of encouragement but wisely decided not to in case she distracted him.

Angus was tiring fast now. His shoulders ached abominably and his legs threatened to buckle under him at any moment.

He wondered what the sensation would be like if he was to fall? Would he be conscious all the way down or would he know very little about it, having been knocked senseless on the first bounce? Was there life after death, or nothing at all?

Rosemary knew something was wrong. Three times he'd reached up to grasp the next hold and three times his hand had fallen away again.

Angus laid his cheek against the cool rock and sucked lungful after lungful of air down the raw barbed tunnel of his throat. He could go no further. He was buggered.

Far below he could hear the fast flowing Cart while in the distance there were voices calling to one another. Off to the left a number of herring gulls were crying as they wheeled towards some unknown destination.

A muffled sob escaped him. He didn't want to die. He didn't want to die at all!

'Angus?'

The word was a whisper in his ear. A vocal caress that might have been an angel beckoning him.

'Are you ok?'

Of course he wasn't bloody ok! Any second now he

was going to fall backwards off this bloody rockface to be smashed to smithereens.

Suddenly he started to chuckle and that eased the tension which had seized his body. He was desperate for a pee! Of all the times and places for that to happen! His chuckle became a giggle with a hysterical ring to it.

He nearly jumped out of his skin when a hand touched his. 'Jesus!' he exclaimed and twisted his head round to find Rosemary right there beside him.

'I'll help you the rest of the way,' she said.

Her hand on his was the contact through which strength poured from her to him. He could feel his body recharging, coming alive again.

And he knew then he was going to make it. With Rosemary beside him there was nothing he couldn't do.

'Careful now!' he warned as she broke the grip and started to make her way back up to the window.

When she reached the window she swung herself onto the sill. Dropping her legs into the room and then screwing round to grasp hold of Angus's extended arm.

She pulled him up till his head and shoulders were framed in the window and then, grabbing his braces, hauled on them so he came tumbling headlong into the room where they both landed in a heap on the floor.

For what must have been been a full five minutes Angus didn't attempt to speak, happy just to lie there revelling in the fact he was still alive.

Finally he produced the charm bracelet from his pocket and laid it in her hand.

Rosemary's eyes were shining as she snapped the bracelet round her wrist. 'Thank you,' she said.

'It was nothing,' he replied and they both burst out laughing at how silly and masculinely vain that sounded.

'I'll never forget today as long as I live,' Rosemary said.

This time he put his tongue into her mouth causing her to squirm and rub up against him.

When they eventually broke apart he had to excuse

himself as the desperate need to relieve himself had returned.

Going to another part of the castle he did it against a lichen spattered wall.

He was fastening his buttons when he became aware of being watched from the doorway.

'I've never seen a man doing it before,' Rosemary said, no hint of awkwardness in her voice.

Angus was acutely embarrassed and quickly did up the remainder of his buttons. 'You gave me a fright sneaking up like that,' he said, forcing out a laugh.

Rosemary stared at the long ribbon flowing along the floor and said men must have far bigger bladders than women to be able to pass as much water as Angus had just done.

The streaming pee reminded Angus of an old Scots custom which he now told her about. He felt he had to say something this was the first thing that came to mind.

According to tradition if a couple were to join hands, jump over a stream and on landing proclaim themselves man and wife then this was as binding in the eyes of God and the community as if they'd been legally married in church.

Hearing this, Rosemary came straight to his side and took one of his hands in hers. Nodding towards the still flowing pee she said if that didn't constitute a stream then she didn't know what did and would he marry her here and now, please?

They had to run to catch up with the pee. Jumping over it they declared they took one another for spouse.

Rosemary was suddenly shy then, giggling a little till Angus sealed their oath with another kiss.

Once over the outside wall and back on the road they crossed over and squeezed through a hedge which brought them out onto a cleared part of the hill. Climbing to the memorial to the ill-fated Mary, Queen of Scots, they stood looking out over Glasgow lying before them.

Anxious to cement over their previous rift as well as being genuinely curious, Angus asked Rosemary what sort of man Sir Alan was?

As Rosemary spoke a lifestyle completely outwith Angus's experience gradually unfolded. He heard of Balls. Dinner parties. Holidays abroad in France and Italy. Of huntin' shootin' and fishin'. Of fast cars and expensive ones. Of clever conversation where wit was the commodity prized above all else. In fact all the glamorous things money and position can provide.

The thought of being a rich businessman fascinated Angus. Not for him the total renunciation of the capitalist class as propagated by Big Donald. And the more he thought about it the more he was attracted to himself in that image.

Intense excitement gripped Angus with the realization that he'd arrived at a major juncture in his life. Suddenly the way ahead was crystal clear and he knew precisely the direction he wanted the rest of his life to take.

There would be no apprenticeship and going to sea after it was completed. Instead he would stay on at school to take his Highers, after which he'd enter the business world. That was where his destiny lay. He was convinced of it.

In a halting voice he told Rosemary of his revelation and as he spoke she too was caught up in the mesmeric dream now holding him fast in its spell.

Of course, all this was a long way ahead, an eternity it seemed at the moment. But all would come to fruition with the passage of time.

Just how he was going to make his fortune wasn't clear to him yet but he had no doubt the details would come with more thought on the subject. The important thing for the moment was the overall concept which lay dazzling and glittering with promise in his brain.

Not for him the anonymity of the proletariat. He was going to be a *somebody*.

In mock anger he shook his fist at the dirty industrial metropolis that was his birthplace and where his roots ran deep. 'I'm going to beat you! I'll have you dancing to my tune before I'm finished! Just you wait and see!' he roared defiantly.

Radiantly happy Rosemary put her arms round his waist. The world was truly a marvellous place. Angus had found his dream and they'd both found one another.

Her cup was running over as hand in hand they ran back down the hill towards the hedge.

When Rosemary eventually returned to Arnprior House she found her father back from the latest of his many recent London trips. There were also several guests being entertained, Sir Hamilton McLaren, a wealthy landowner and friend of her father, and his two sons, Iain and Peter.

Although she'd met Sir Hamilton before she'd never met his boys so when introductions were made they all trooped through for tea.

Iain was the elder son, being several years older than she was. While Peter was a year younger than she.

Iain, several years older than Rosemary, was dark and brooding with thick, heavy eyebrows and a face that had a saturnine quality about it. His skin was sallow and shone as though polished. His eyes black introspective and inclined to flash from time to time. He was an extraordinarily handsome young man in the blazer and tie of the Glasgow Academy.

Peter, a year younger than she, was the complete antithesis of his brother. Chunky in build, with yellow hair, he had a marvellously outgoing personality.

Cordelia Armstrong was the perfect hostess as she presided over tea, happy because for the first time in a long while her husband was too.

Before Hamilton's surprise arrival he'd had time to tell her the good news. The money he'd been so desperately in need of to keep the works afloat had been found. Armstrong's had been saved, or its fate postponed for some time anyway – literally at the eleventh hour, for if the money hadn't been forthcoming within the next few days then final notice would have had to have been served on all employees.

Sir Alan was jubilant as he sipped his tea. Later when the girls were in bed he would crack a bottle of their favourite champagne and together he and Cordelia would toast this last minute reprieve.

My God, but it had been hard graft convincing the board of the merchant bank he'd been conferring with to part with the capital he needed. But by dint of perseverance and hard fought argument he'd eventually won them round.

Mind you, he was paying a terrifically high rate of interest on the loan but what else could he expect? If he could only survive the next couple of years he was sure the works could establish itself in the black once more. His reason for thinking this was based on the disturbing rumours that were beginning to reach Britain from the continent. Mutterings of discontent with the threat of more than words to come.

Over in Spain the new republic wasn't proving at all popular while the Fascists under a certain General Franco were growing in strength daily. Those in the know were convinced an armed conflict between the two parties was inevitable.

Then, of course, there was this fellow Herr Hitler and his National Socialists over in Germany. Now if that man attained power then Germany would be bound to initiate an expansionist programme to try and win back some of the territories she'd lost as a result of the Great War.

It didn't matter if Britain was directly involved or not. Any hostilities in Europe were bound to stimulate the British shipbuilding industry. In fact this stimulation had already begun if he was reading the signs correctly. Weren't many of the ships that had been lying in mothballs for years being dusted off and sold to a suddenly demanding market in secondhand tonnage.? Something was afoot all right. Every instinct he possessed told him so.

Perhaps he hadn't been so persuasive in his arguments to the merchant bank after all. It might just be they knew even more than he did about the current European situation.

He was musing on that when his eye lit on Rosemary. How grown up she'd become recently. When she left Park it would be a finishing school for her. In Edinburgh perhaps or else one down in England. The continent was, of course, now ruled out.

His ruminations were interrupted by Sir Hamilton McLaren suggesting the entire Armstrong family come over to the McLaren house in Carmunnock for dinner sometime in the near future.

Hearing Cordelia accept, a date was set there and then.

This invitation secretly pleased him as he'd been cultivating McLaren for a number of years now and this family get together heralded a breakthrough in their relationship.

It was some hours after the McLarens had departed before Rosemary was able to get her father alone, finally cornering him in his study where he was attending to a pile of personal correspondence.

What Angus had told her about John McBain had been preying on her mind so she'd decided to ask her father for his side of the story.

Sir Alan was astonished when she put the question to him and asked how she'd come to hear of the case after so many years. She shrugged her shoulders and made some vague reply.

Sir Alan took time to collect his thoughts by pouring himself a stiff brandy and soda. He remembered the details of the John McBain affair quite clearly. At the time it had been a stroke of luck that he'd managed to wriggle out of paying the then Mrs McBain compensation, as money had been tight.

What no one knew apart from him was that McBain had been up on that gantry on his express orders to deal with a small matter that had needed attending to.

After the accident he'd naturally kept stum. To have

done otherwise would have been to admit liability. He'd felt sorry for Mrs McBain. But it was a hard world they lived in. Then and now.

Putting a smile on his face he recounted what had happened to Rosemary. The only detail he omitted was the one that mattered most.

When the interview with her father was finally concluded Rosemary was in no doubt that he'd been in the right.

When Angus arrived home after being with Rosemary he was bursting with good humour. The good humour and the whistling died when he discovered Archie to be the only one in.

With a glass of neat whisky in his hand and a half bottle at his feet Archie sat gazing into the kitchen fire. The ruddy glow from the flickering flames giving him a demonic look that accentuated the closeness of his eyes.

Archie had been at times viciously cruel to Carrie but in his own twisted way he'd come to love her. So it was with a sense of shock he'd taken a telephone call in the station manager's office that afternoon to be informed by Dr Robertson that Carrie had collapsed while out shopping and had been taken to the Emergency Department of the Victoria Hospital where she'd been found to be suffering from advanced TB. Tuberculosis. The very mention of the word was enough to still conversation and cause the heart to grow chill with fear. How many poor souls had died from that dread killer in Glasgow alone? The answer was incalculable.

Archie gulped back his drink and then poured himself another. He knew Angus hated him but it wasn't an emotion he returned. If anything, he rather respected the boy for the obvious guts the lad had. He would have liked to get close to Angus but somehow had never been able to.

Archie sighed. He was still in his dungarees with hands and face black and ingrained with oil. He knew he should get up and wash himself but he couldn't find the energy.

Sheena would be back from work soon and he'd get washed then while she made the tea. If there was anything in the house to make that was. Carrie had been out shopping when she'd collapsed.

He'd wanted to go round to the Victoria right away but had been dissuaded from doing so. He was told that Carrie would have already been dispatched by ambulance for Bellfield Sanatorium near Lanark where a bed was waiting for her.

It had been agreed he'd go to the sanatorium first thing in the morning, taking along a number of articles Dr Robertson had suggested Carrie would need.

He could hear Angus through in the boy's bedroom and knew the lad would stay there until teatime, it being Angus's habit to stay well clear of him whenever possible.

He hawked into the fire and watched while the thick phlegm sputtered and hissed on a burning coal, offering up a silent prayer of gratitude that it wasn't he who'd come down with TB. He certainly wasn't a coward but there were things he was deathly afraid of and illness was one of them.

He would go to the sanatorium but hate every second he was there. The smell common to all hospitals always succeeded in putting the fear of God into him.

The outside door opened and banged closed again which meant Sheena was home. He'd been waiting her arrival before breaking the news to Angus.

'Angus! Sheena!' he called out. 'Come away ben. I want to talk to the pair of you!'

Sheena came first, taking the long pearl-tipped pin out of her hat and allowing her hair to fall free to her shoulders. Somehow she contrived to remain voluptuous and seductive looking in spite of the severe green uniform encasing her from neck to mid-calf.

Angus entered the room, annoyance at being disturbed written all over his face. He'd been cutting up a length of red inner tubing which was going to form part of his new catapult.

Archie stared Angus straight in the eye. 'I've got some bad news for you lad,' he said. 'Your Ma collapsed in the street this afternoon and has been taken into hospital. The doctors say she's got TB.'

Angus's mouth fell open and he stared blankly at his step-father. It was some sort of cruel joke. It had to be! Archie was having him on. Taking the mickey.

'Jesus Christ!' Sheena said and sat down.

'You're kidding me?' Angus husked, wilting when Archie shook his head.

'She's been taken to a place out by Lanark. I'm going to see her in the morning. You can come with me if you like,' Archie said.

Angus looked down, seeing nothing. He wanted to run away. To hide. In fact to be anywhere except where he was. Turning abruptly, he fled the room.

Sheena was about to go after him when she was brought up short by Archie telling her to look in the press and see if there was anything there they could have for tea. When she replied there was only a loaf in he said he would go over to Tallon Street and break the news to the Chisholms. He'd pick up some fish suppers on his way back.

He had another dram before going through to the bathroom for a wash. Ten minutes later when he quietly let himself out the front door Sheena's voice could be heard coming from Angus's bedroom where she was doing her best to comfort her distraught step-brother.

The next morning Angus didn't run with the milk nor did Archie go to work.

Angus went down to the front close at his usual time to find Kitty waiting for him. He explained to his pal why he couldn't manage that day and Kitty promised to relay what had happened to Hugh.

Sheena made them a cup of tea and a slice of toast each for breakfast and then he and Archie, both dressed in their Sunday best, left the house to catch a tram.

During the entire journey Angus sat rigidly beside Archie staring out at the passing scenery. His eyes were red and puffy from being awake most of the night.

Arriving in Lanark, they inquired the way to Bellfield Sanatorium from a passer-by who informed them they had a mile and a half hike in front of them. It was either that or wait nearly two hours for the next local bus. They elected to walk.

The sanatorium was a large, imposing early Victorian building surrounded by well-tended lawns and a sprinkling of trees. It sparkled in the weak sunlight, giving the impression it was regularly scrubbed outside as well as in.

Loathing all institutions, Archie hated the place on sight. He shuddered as he and Angus walked through the heavy wooden doors opening into the marbled reception hall.

For half an hour they waited and then a young nurse arrived to escort them to the ward where Carrie was. The nurse's eyes opened fractionally when she saw Angus but she didn't pass any comment.

With the nurse leading the way they tramped along a seemingly endless maze of wood and marble corridors.

The thing that struck Angus most about the sanatorium was how cold it was. Despite the time of year every window was open wide so that the temperature inside the building was the same as it was out.

At the entrance to Carrie's ward they were again instructed to wait and this time they had to stand as there were no chairs or benches available where they might sit.

Within minutes a hatchet-faced woman approached them and announced herself to be Sister McMillan in charge of the ward.

The sister's next words caused Angus great consternation when she declared it was against the hospital's rules for children under the age of fifteen to be allowed into the wards.

Angus shot Archie a beseeching look which he transferred to the sister who stared back at him pityingly but resolutely.

Archie Marjoribanks may have done some terrible

things in his life but he did something then which went a long way to absolving many of them. Putting a winning smile on his face, he asked Sister if he might speak with her in private and together they moved off to a nearby alcove where Archie began exercising his not inconsiderable charm.

Angus never did find out what Archie said to Sister McMillan but, whatever it was, it secured for him the rare privilege of breaking the hospital rule.

Visitors were only allowed in one at a time and it was Archie's suggestion that Angus go first. Before going behind the screens masking the entrance to the ward Angus was handed a bagful of grapes and a box of chocolates by Archie and told to give them to Carrie, saying they came from him.

'Ach away and don't be daft!' said Archie when Angus tried to thank him.

Angus found Carrie near the end of a long row of beds. She was lying flat out with her eyes closed and the blankets pulled up to her chin.

She looked terrible. Her face was the colour of curds and her cheeks so sunken it gave her a skeletal appearance.

For a few moments he stared at his mother while she dozed. His chest heaved and he had to swallow repeatedly to hold back the tears.

'Ma?' he whispered, a catch in his voice.

Carrie's eyelids flickered and then slowly opened. Pain and suffering stared out. 'Hello, son,' she smiled.

He couldn't help what happened next. With a sob he threw himself beside her and, as his warm cheek touched her cold one, a dam seemed to burst inside him. The tears he'd been desperately holding back since Archie broke the news to him came flooding out.

Carrie stroked his hair while he cried and cried, his face buried in her pillow to try and stifle the racking sobs bursting from him.

'Just let yourself go, son,' she said quietly, thinking how much like his father he was becoming now his face had started to mature. Her guess was he'd end up a far taller, slimmer version of his father. She was still worried by the fact he was painfully thin but she'd reconciled herself to the idea that only time would alter that. It would be another year or two before he started to fill out and lose the gazelle quality he now had.

When his crying had finally run its course he used the corner of her top sheet to dry his eyes. He glanced round to see if any of the other patients were staring at him but they were all busy pretending they'd neither seen nor heard anything. The two ladies on either side of Carrie kept their noses buried deep in newspapers.

He wanted to know how long Carrie would be in the sanatorium but all she could tell him was she'd be there until better which could be anything from nine months to a year. Then she'd be back on her feet and singing like a lintie, she said, which brought a smile to Angus's face and even wrung the faint beginnings of a laugh from him.

A tremendous will to live was born in Carrie at that moment. She had to hang on. Her son needed her.

Angus had reached that terribly difficult stage of puberty and adolescence and if, during this time, the additional burden of being orphaned was thrust on him the consequences could well be disastrous. As the doctors would come to tell her again and again. They could do only so much to affect her cure. The real key to her getting better lay in her wanting to do so. For her, Angus became the key. The prime motivation.

They talked a little while longer and then it was time for Angus to go if Archie was to see Carrie as well.

At the screens he turned back and waved, knowing this would be the last look he'd have of her till she came back home again.

'Oh Ma!' he muttered. His heart felt it must surely snap in two. Swinging round he vanished from the ward.

As things turned out, Carrie's prediction of nine months to a year was somewhat optimistic. It was to be over two years before Angus saw his mother again.

When Archie arrived to sit by her bedside he was told

she'd come to a decision: Angus was to go and stay at Tallon Street until she was better.

Thinking it was him and his temper Carrie was worried about Archie wisely agreed. What he didn't realize was he was only part of the problem.

Carrie had often said she wasn't as green as she was cabbage looking. She knew there was a bond between Sheena and Angus that transcended normal step-sister/brother relationships. She would have trusted the young woman that Sheena had become with her life but she did not want her to be constantly alone with her son.

Archie promised faithfully that Angus would be packed over to Tallon Street that very day. Then and only then did Carrie begin to truly relax.

After a few minutes stilted conversation, Archie cleared his throat and in a whisper said he was going to try and control himself a lot more in future. Picking at his fingers he said he was going to miss her terribly and hadn't realized until this happened just how lucky he was to have a wife like her.

Carrie was astounded by this. These were the first intimate words she'd heard from Archie since their courting days. Furthermore, she could tell by his tone of voice and the expression on his face he meant what he said.

'Is it too late for us to start again?' he asked.

There was something boyish and appealing about Archie when he was like this that made you almost forget the cruel, roaring bully he could be.

Carrie lay back and watched a nurse making a bed on the other side of the ward. The nurse was young and fairly pretty with a face full of hope and expectation. Just like she'd once been so long long ago.

She wondered what she'd ever done to lose John McBain. Get saddled with Archie Marjoribanks. And now contract tuberculosis.

Archie was incorrigible. She knew no matter how hard he tried to reform he'd always revert back to type. The man was sick, not in the body like she was but in the mind where it lay darkly hidden. A malignancy that could be truly awesome when it manifested itself.

She was so tired she felt she could close her eyes and sleep for a hundred years. It was as though her very substance had nearly all melted away, leaving her a pale imitation of the woman she'd once been.

Looking a picture of melancholy, Archie sat staring at Carrie. He might have been a cur who'd been temporarily whipped into submission.

'We'll try again,' Carrie replied, knowing it was a futile gesture but feeling this reaffirmation of commitment was the best thing in the circumstances.

Archie nodded his gratitude, genuinely intending to keep his side of the bargain.

A few minutes later when he started to speak again he discovered she'd drifted off into what looked like a very heavy sleep.

With a rough tenderness he tucked her arms under the bedclothes and kissed her on the forehead. Then with a flashing smile to a hovering nurse he walked swiftly from the ward.

Hugh hadn't been back to Tallon Street since the day he'd left with the wireless on his shoulder. He came now knowing as it was the afternoon Donald would be at work. He didn't want to see his father. It was Winnie he wanted to speak to.

His mother answered the door wearing her pinny, her hands and arms covered in flour.

Exclaiming in delight, Winnie threw her arms round Hugh and hugged him tight. He didn't care that flour was deposited in streaks all over the good tweed jacket he'd bought only a few weeks ago.

When they finally disentangled themselves he was taken through to the kitchen where Winnie put the kettle on.

Hugh hardly recognized the kitchen. To begin with, electricity had been installed in the house which meant the old gas lighting outlets were gone. On one side a brand new cooker stood proudly. The small copper had been replaced by a washing machine. The kitchen had also been repainted as indeed had the hall and living room.

Winnie washed her hands at the sink and then, having masked the tea, buttered some piping hot scones fresh from the oven.

As they were going through to the living room Hugh broached the subject of his quarrel with Donald and was sad to hear his father was still angry with him. If there was to be a reconciliation it obviously wasn't going to be for some time yet.

They talked about Carrie and the shock it had been to hear of her being taken to Bellfield Sanatorium. It was unspoken between them but each blamed Archie for Carrie's present state. By now the entire family had come to know Archie Marjoribanks for what he was and if Carrie found understanding and perhaps pity for her husband she was the only one to do so.

Winnie went on to say Angus was sleeping in the room his mother had once shared with Harriet and seemed to be settling down well although at fifty-eight she was finding him quite a handful to have around the house.

This was just as Hugh had suspected and was the principle reason for his visit. He had come to ask Winnie if Angus might not be better off at the Paterson house with him? His idea was that when he eventually married – as he presumed he would someday – he would adopt Angus as his son.

Winnie could see that although Hugh's intentions were admirable he hadn't quite thought this proposal through. Tactfully she explained it was doubtful if Carrie would be willing to part with Angus or Angus with her.

If Angus had been a babe in arms and Hugh married to someone Carrie knew and approved of then that might have been a different kettle of fish. But it was her opinion, as she was certain it would be Carrie's, it was best for things to remain as they were.

Winnie added she was sure Carrie would be pleased to

know Angus had another place to go where he would be welcome. After all, she and Donald weren't getting any younger and who knew what the next day would bring?

Winnie was pleased Hugh had brought up the subject of marriage. At twenty-eight she thought it high time he settled down and raised a family of his own.

Hugh was in full agreement with this and in fact would have liked nothing better but as he hesitatingly explained he just couldn't seem to meet the right woman.

Somewhat embarrassed he said he'd chaffed enough personable lassies at the dancing but none of them had ever struck the right chord in him. He didn't want to get married just for getting married's sake. He wanted to marry someone he genuinely felt something for, someone he could see himself spending the rest of his life with.

There was very little Winnie could say to that except she was sure it would come out all right in the end.

The last thing she wanted was for Hugh to turn into some sort of eternal bachelor, knowing that would be totally wrong for him.

'I'll know her when I meet her,' Hugh said, eyes clouding with introspection.

Winnie sighed. 'I hope you do, son,' she replied in a voice full of sympathy.

While Winnie washed the tea things and saw to a pineapple upside down cake she had in the oven Hugh went through to the big room where he stood by the window looking up the road to the bend round which Armstrong's lay.

It was a bitter cold day and there was ice on the Cart. The air was heavy with grey chimney smoke while from beyond the bend came the thick black fug which proclaimed the Armstrong furnaces to be going full blast.

He lit a Willy Woodbine and wondered if there was something wrong with him that he couldn't meet a lassie he liked well enough to settle down with? He found it difficult to put into words just what he was looking for. Decent looks certainly. He couldn't see himself being drawn to somebody who was ugly. But the looks were only part of it. There was a lot more to what he was after than that.

He stood at the window pondering till the light faded into late afternoon darkness. Finally he shrugged and dismissed all thoughts of women from his mind.

One thing was certain though whomever he married he'd expect her to deliver him a son in time. Lassies round the house were fine and dandy but a boy was the thing. That was what he wanted.

He said goodbye to Winnie through in the kitchen, slipping a pound note into her pinny pocket and telling her to buy a wee extravagance for herself.

All the way up the road to the tramstop he dreamed of being a father with a son by his side.

Aye, boys were the ticket right enough. They made a man immortal.

12

During the next few years Angus and Rosemary saw as much of each other as was possible and all the while their relationship strengthened and developed.

Angus had moved back to Holmlea Road the same day Carrie returned from Bellfield Sanatorium. The reunion had been a joyous one but it had nearly broken his heart to see how gaunt and pitifully thin his mother had become. She was so changed it had taken him a moment or two to recognize her when she and Archie walked through the front door.

True to his word Archie tried to mend his ways, never

drinking and not once losing his temper, forever fussing round Carrie and even bringing her treats such as flowers and sweets.

At first it was thought amongst the family that Carrie would soon recover her former strength but as the months passed it became evident she would never be the same again.

As Donald remarked, all the sap had been drained out of her leaving only a shell of the woman who'd married John McBain and given birth to Angus.

Sheena had gone from the house and no one knew where. Not long after Carrie had been taken into Bellfield Archie had come home from work one night to discover a note which baldly stated she was leaving for good. Inquiring at the tram depot at the top of Holmlea Road he'd been told she'd handed in her notice with the intention of going south. Several clippies said she'd mentioned London while one was adamant it was Birmingham she was headed for.

From that day on not another word was heard from Sheena. Angus sorely missed her.

Angus was now at Queen's Park Secondary School where he was doing extremely well. An incident occurred in his first year which became legendary and marked him out as something of a wit and character. When asked in music class what a violin concerto was he'd blithely replied it was a small violin.

Perhaps it was the way he said it or the extremely serious expression he wore that convinced the rest of the class he was taking the mickey for, with a sort of combined hoot, they all dissolved into helpless laughter.

That reply earned him four of the belt and for a long time the nickname of Concerto McBain.

Physically Angus had grown even taller so that now he topped six feet, still skinny but wiry with it. He walked with a permanent stoop which made him look rather like a coat hanger on legs.

He'd been staying at Tallon Street only a short while when he'd secretly taken on an evening paper round which had been something Carrie had been completely against in case he overtaxed himself.

When Donald eventually found out he'd summoned Angus through to the front room where the pair of them thrashed the matter out. The upshot was that Angus would be allowed to continue running with the milk in the mornings and papers in the evenings just as long as it didn't interfere with either his health or school work, which it never did.

Week after week Angus put money by and soon his savings began to mount up. He bought a metal box with a padlock on the front and it was in this he kept the pound and ten shilling notes which began to accumulate.

His business ambitions remained as strong as ever and often he and Rosemary would discuss what it would be like when they grew up and were able to marry.

In this particular vision of the future Rosemary had replaced Sheena and the house the new triumvirate lived in was considerably more grand than the simple room and kitchen that had been his first conception.

The one fly in the ointment so far was he hadn't been able to decide what line of business he should go into. But he had no doubts whatsoever this would be revealed to him in time.

So far he'd been most secretive about his ambitions, not even disclosing them to Carrie when she came out of the sanatorium. Only Rosemary knew of his plans and the motivation behind them.

As the spring of 1936 gave way to summer Rosemary became much preoccupied with trying to think up something unusual to give Angus for his birthday. Birthdays were a big thing between them due to the fact they'd both been born on the same day, he the twelfth of August, 1921, she exactly one year later.

One of their favourite haunts was Paterson's Dairy, where Hugh always made them welcome no matter what the time of day or how busy he was. Although Hugh knew Rosemary lived in the big house in Old Castle Road he still wasn't aware she was Sir Alan

Armstrong's daughter.

It was there one Saturday afternoon when she and Angus were helping to muck out the stables that the idea came to her.

Hugh had recently bought a stallion called Royal Standard with the intention of breeding, which would add another string to the dairy's bow.

Angus had been called out of the stables for a few minutes, leaving Rosemary at work on her own. What happened next caused her to catch her breath: Royal Standard having got out of his own stall, reared onto his hind legs and mounted a mare called Gypsy.

The enormous penis sunk to its hilt to be drawn out and sunk again and again. With a most unhorsy low grunt Royal Standard pulled himself free and, as he did so, a gush of sperm exploded from Gypsy's rear.

The most marvellous sensations invaded Rosemary's stomach, making her flesh go all prickly. All she could think about was having that done to her.

She and Angus had petted of course but she'd limited this to her breasts and not beyond. Now she felt she wanted to go further and in that instant it dawned on her what the perfect birthday present for Angus would be.

When Angus returned to the stables he found her flushed and with a peculiar glint in her eye as she wielded her pitchfork with gusto. Asking her what was up he was told to mind his own business and all would be revealed, she giggled, in good time.

Mystified, Angus set to work beside Rosemary and falling into the rhythm of the job the incident passed from his mind.

Sir Alan Armstrong was a happy man as he sat in his office sipping his morning sherry.

Like some great beast, the works rumbled below and around him proclaiming Armstrong's to be in full production once again.

The books lying open in front of him were healthier than they'd been in years with more orders flooding in every day.

As he sat staring out of his window, Sir Alan mused on the fear and trepidation that was abroad in the land and had been ever since 7th March when the German Chancellor Herr Hitler's armed columns had streamed into the Rhineland where they'd reoccupied the main German towns.

All Europe was in a furore over this, especially the French government under M. Sarraut.

France was now looking to Great Britain as the British had guaranteed the French frontier against German aggression. Earlier, they'd put a great deal of pressure on France for the evacuation of the Rhineland.

At one fell swoop Hitler had not only violated the Peace Treaty but also the Treaty of Locarno, throwing into great consternation those powers ranged against him.

Lloyd George's response to this flagrant breach of faith had been placatory: 'In my judgement Herr Hitler's greatest crime was not the breach of a treaty because there was provocation.'

Lloyd George's statement was interpreted to mean Hitler's provocation was the failure of the Allies to disarm themselves more than they had done.

Now massive fortifications were being built in the Rhineland which, according to Winston Churchill, meant a great barrier of concrete was being raised which would effectively alter the whole aspect of Middle Europe.

Sir Alan smiled as he sat back in his chair to light up one of his favourite Cuban cigars. War was now inevitable. There could be no doubt about it. Those appeasers in Whitehall would eventually have to stop playing the ostrich and face reality. Herr Hitler was intent on expanding Germany's diminished colonial power and like Napoleon before him his ultimate aim was the conquest of Europe.

A frown flitted across Sir Alan's face. War meant work, which in turn meant Armstrong's was bound to make money hand over fist. If properly handled, the works would never again be in danger of closure. The other side of the coin was that many good men were bound to die, which genuinely saddened him.

Guilt niggled his insides as he thought of how much he'd hoped and prayed for this coming conflict. He'd been thinking of himself, his family and the works, not the poor sods who were going to get chopped or maimed and the loved ones they'd leave behind.

'Damnit to hell!' he exclaimed and poured himself another sherry. It was a rare occasion when he indulged in more than one at this time of the morning.

He pondered for a little while, desperately trying to salve his conscience and dispel the terrible guilt feelings growing in him with every passing second.

His face lit up in a smile as the idea came to him. When war finally did erupt those working in Armstrong's would find themselves in reserve occupations. Well, the least he could do was take on as much staff as possible thereby assuring a few more local men the chance of escaping the front line.

His conscience now assuaged, he picked up the small brass bell standing on one side of his desk and gave it two sharp rings.

He would dictate a memo immediately and see it was posted on the works noticeboard without delay. Slitting his eyes, he worked out just how many additional time served men he could take on and for good measure tacked on a number of apprentices.

Sir Alan's memo duly appeared on the noticeboard that afternoon: Donald read it en route to the pattern makers' offices. He forgot about it until the evening when the hooter had blown and he was on his way home. He recalled then how Angus had once confided in him he wanted to work for Armstrong's just like his Da before him.

Donald made a mental note to go over to Holmlea Road and speak to Carrie and the lad after tea.

Carrie was sitting knitting while Archie sprawled in the

chair facing her reading the evening paper.

Angus was through in his room counting his money. It was a Friday and he'd been paid for both his jobs.

When Carrie called him to come away ben the kitchen he carefully padlocked his metal box which he then placed in its hiding place behind some odds and ends on a shelf in the cupboard.

Satisfied everything was in order, he went through to see his grandfather whom he'd heard arrive while he was in the middle of his weekly count.

Donald disliked intensely being in Archie Marjoribanks's company nowadays. He always had the overpowering urge to backhand the man for the way he'd treated Carrie and still did as far as he knew, although according to Winnie things were a lot better between them of late.

Fancying he could still take Archie in a fight, Donald didn't appreciate just how much he'd deteriorated during the past few years. He'd shrunk several inches while his chest was now a parody of its former burly and muscular self. The fact was Donald had become an old man without realizing it. In a stand up fight he wouldn't have stood an earthly against Archie.

Carrie told Angus to sit and when he'd done so went on to tell him of the marvellous opportunity that had come his way.

With Donald being a senior gaffer it was certain anyone he put up for a job – and certainly John McBain's son – would be accepted.

Angus was thunderstruck. It had just never crossed his mind this sort of thing might happen. In a great rush of words he told them he didn't want to go to work for Armstrong's any more but wanted to go into business instead.

His confession was greeted by surprise – none of them had even the faintest inkling of Angus's change of heart. When Archie asked Angus what sort of business he would like to go into all Angus could do was blush and reply he didn't know yet. Archie snorted and muttered something about delusions of grandeur.

Donald was filled with consternation as he lit up his pipe. What had happened to the common sense he'd always credited the lad with having? Business wasn't something people of their class got mixed up in. That was strictly for those who went to fancy schools and spoke with a plum in their mouths.

Besides being in business meant you became one of *them*. A capitalist! It was the very nature of the beast.

Carefully Donald unscrewed the bowl of his pipe and knocked dottle into his hanky. As he cleaned the mucky inside of the bowl he thought that it was common for lads of Angus's age to have flights of fancy. Well there was nothing wrong with that as long as they were eventually made to realize the difference between those and the reality of their situation.

He sucked his pipe back into life and then began to speak in the calm, reassuring voice he employed when faced with a difficult situation on the foundry floor. He said Angus wanting to go into business was all very well and good but did Angus appreciate just what he'd be up against?

Angus replied rather stiffly he wasn't quite sure what his grandfather was getting at, wincing as Donald then went on to make pertinent point after point.

Angus hung his head under the gentle but penetrating and most disconcerting onslaught. He didn't have the answers to any of this. All he did have was a dream and enormous faith in his own ability to accomplish what he set out to do.

The more questions thrown at him the more frantic Angus became. He desperately wanted to try and explain his dream but found no matter how hard he groped for the words they just wouldn't come. It all seemed so clear when he was discussing it with Rosemary but here talking to adults it was a different matter altogether.

What he did manage to get out was he considered it imperative to get his Highers for without those behind him he would be at a definite disadvantage for getting on.

As the words jerked from his quivering mouth it suddenly dawned on him with resounding clarity that to men like Donald and Archie formal education beyond being able to read, write and count meant very little. To them a trade was the thing, the be-all and end-all.

Archie was in an irritable mood. The rheumatism which had suddenly started bothering him lately was giving him gyp. He thought if only he could have a wee half gill it might ease the terrible nagging pain.

Archie considered what Angus was saying to be a right load of nonsense. The lad didn't realize just how lucky he was, being handed an opportunity like this on a plate. Times might have eased but there still weren't that many jobs going you could afford to pick and choose. Silly bugger with his high-faluting notions. Secretive, too, the way he hoarded the money Carrie allowed him to keep in that metal box through in his room.

The boy was becoming miserly and that was something he detested. Money was for spending, not for hiding away in the back of a cupboard. It was high time Angus was taught a lesson regarding money (in the hope it would bring him to his senses).

Archie grimaced and rubbed his arm. Bloody rheumatism! He would get Carrie to make him a hot bread poultice after Donald was gone.

Carrie appreciated Angus was highly thought of scholastically at school and that his teachers were keen for him to stay on and take his Highers. The trouble was she'd never thought all that much about it, her assumption being he'd still want to leave Queen's Park when old enough to go up by.

At the end of a further half hour's argument Donald was still maintaining Angus should forget this daft business notion and sign apprenticeship papers with Armstrong's where he would learn a useful trade.

Folding her arms across her chest Carrie declared her mind was made up. Angus would not be going back to school at the end of the summer holidays but would be starting with Armstrong's.

'It's for the best son. I know you'll agree with us in a few years time when you come to see things in perspective,' Donald said slightly pompously.

Angus jumped to his feet. He couldn't bear to stay in this room a second longer. He had to get out. It didn't matter where as long as it was a quiet spot where he could sit and nurse his anguish.

'Angus!' Carrie yelled. But it was no use. He was gone. The front door banged behind him.

'Delusions of grandeur,' repeated Archie, shaking his head and kneading his arm.

Carrie stared at the doorway through which Angus had vanished. She knew she was right in insisting he get settled into a good job, especially now her health was giving her cause for concern again.

Angus leaned into the wind and forced his legs to pump harder and harder. His chest was heaving while his short hair spiked out behind him as he sped along the road on his bike.

It wasn't fair. It just wasn't fair! he raged. His knuckles turned white as he strained at the handlebars as though they were a length of steel he was trying to bend in half.

He would never marry Rosemary now. How could he! She was the boss's daughter while he would never be anything more than an employee. A journeyman. A nothing!

His long legs whirled faster and faster till he and his bike were a blur flashing through the night.

Suddenly as though a stopcock had been opened, his anger was gone leaving him feeling washed out and taut as a thinly stretched wire. His hands were trembling as he stopped pedalling to stare round and see where he was.

Instinctively he'd taken the road he travelled every morning to Paterson's Dairy and even now was coasting into Muirend. That pleased him for if there was anyone he could speak to at a time like this it was his uncle Hugh.

Hugh was humming merrily to himself as he put a Windsor knot in his tie. He was off to the jigging and looking forward to it. Outside the house stood a brand new Wolseley Hornet he'd bought for £175 and which had been delivered from the saleroom that very afternoon.

Moving to the window he twitched back the curtain and gazed down at the bright red car. It was a beauty all right and in his estimation well worth every penny.

For months now he'd been coveting the saleroom models and wondering where he could get £175 from. Then he remembered the wireless set he'd bought for Winnie and which now stood on top of his dressing table.

The Wolseley people had been only too happy to enter into a hire purchase agreement and as a result the shining wee beauty now standing outside was his.

He was still at the window, reluctant to take his eyes off the Hornet, when Angus appeared cycling towards the house.

He frowned when he saw the look on Angus's face. Moments later he was hurrying down to the front door where the bell was already clanging.

'You'd better come away up and tell me all about it,' he said. He gestured towards the stairs leading to his bedroom.

There was a packet of Pasha lying beside the wireless and without asking permission Angus helped himself to one.

Hugh closed the bedroom door and stood with his back to it. 'Your mother?' he queried, for his first thought had been something had happened to Carrie.

'No,' Angus said huskily, smoke rising from him as though he was a newly stoked chimney. He declined when Hugh suggested he sit. Instead, striding up and down the room, the words poured from him.

While Angus ranted Hugh crossed to the press from which he produced a screwtop whose contents he poured equally into a brace of tumblers. Angus accepted his on the move and greedily drank it down.

All the words that had steadfastly refused to come earlier now poured from him as he told Hugh about Rosemary and the plans they'd had for their future.

One of the main reasons for the words not coming in Holmlea Road was because he hadn't wanted to bring Rosemary into it, knowing only too well the derisory reaction he would have had from Donald had he announced that he planned to marry Sir Alan Armstrong's elder daughter. But here with Hugh he had no such inhibitions.

Hugh sipped his beer and listened in silence, thinking about something his mother had once said about still waters running deep. He'd thought he knew Angus and yet here was a completely new side to the boy he hadn't even suspected existed.

It amused him greatly to learn Rosemary was Sir Alan's daughter. Jesus, but Angus aimed high!

When Angus spoke about his ambitions in the business field his eyes glowed, only becoming dull again when he remembered these ambitions would probably never be fulfilled.

Finally he stopped talking and turned to Hugh with an expectant look on his face, waiting for his uncle's comments and advice.

Hugh was well aware of the responsibility now resting on his shoulders. What he said next could well affect Angus for the rest of the lad's life.

The damnable thing was he could see Donald's point of view only too clearly. Angus came from a working-class background and people from there just didn't aspire to the heady levels inhabited by Armstrong and his family.

It was obvious there was a great deal of love between Angus and Rosemary but how was she going to feel in the future when able to look beyond the bounds of passion? And if she and Angus did get married how would he be affected in the years to come?

A man like Sir Alan would denigrate the lad and treat

him as both an inferior and a lackey, to say nothing about how Angus could expect to be treated by the Armstrongs' friends.

Angus would be a misfit, the proverbial round peg in a square hole. And no matter how strong his relationship with Rosemary this could only lead to friction and eventual unhappiness between the pair of them.

Hugh knew that when Donald spoke of *us* and *them* his father had the rights of it. Maybe someday things would be different. He wasn't a prophet and couldn't say. But certainly in the year 1936 that was how it was.

'Well?' Angus prompted.

Hugh took a deep breath and then proceeded to speak for a good ten minutes. When he finally finished Angus looked the most miserable young man there had ever been.

Hugh's words were a death knell to Angus, each one another brick in the wall that had suddenly sprung up between himself and Rosemary. He'd come to Hugh looking for hope and all he was getting were reasons why he should give up all idea of marrying Rosemary Armstrong.

Hugh could see Angus thought he'd let him down so he apologized saying that was how he saw the position and surely Angus wouldn't want him to lie or pretend otherwise?

For Angus two things were crystal clear. The first was that he loved Rosemary and no matter what happened to him in life she would remain his rightful partner.

The other thing was that he wasn't cut out any longer to work at Armstrong's. There had been a time when he would have slotted neatly into that niche but that was before he'd met Rosemary and the candle of ambition had been lit within him.

They sat and talked for a while longer and then Hugh took Angus down to the front of the house to admire the Wolseley.

Hugh had the idea then of forgetting all about going to the jigging and taking Angus out for a run in the car. But

Angus declined, saying he just wasn't in the mood and perhaps they could go another time.

Angus clambered onto his bike. Hugh reached out and shook him by the hand. Angus appreciated the gesture as it signified that Hugh now accepted him as a man.

After Angus had gone Hugh went through and sat with Greta Paterson for a while. She listened sympathetically as he told her about Angus's problems. When he asked her opinion she said he'd done all he could and to have advised the lad otherwise would have been the sheerest folly.

The Plaza Dance Hall had the name of being a right toffee-nosed place where anyone bearing even the faintest resemblance to scruff was definitely not welcome. Dressed in his good suit with a brand new shirt and tie on Hugh didn't anticipate any difficulty in being admitted.

Having parked his car he made his way to the Star Bar directly facing the dance hall.

The interior of the pub was blue with smoke and there were the usual raucous Friday night voices everywhere. He ordered a pint of heavy and a half of whisky. Knocking the whisky back, in a single gulp, he washed it down with a gulp of beer.

He was deep in thought about Angus when he heard himself being hailed from the other side of the bar. Looking up, he saw a chap called Kenny White whom he'd been friendly with at school edging through the crowd towards him.

The two men shook hands, genuinely pleased to see one another. Kenny offered to buy Hugh a refill which Hugh readily accepted. They toasted each other and drank. Kenny informed Hugh he was waiting for a china who was going to make up a foursome with his girlfriend's pal.

They were deep in speculation about the forthcoming football season and how the 'Gers would do when Hugh saw the two girls enter the pub to stand rather self-consciously while they stared round.

One girl's face lit up when she spied Kenny and after a hurried whisper to her companion the pair of them began making their way over.

'Your bird and her pal I think,' Hugh said out the side of his mouth, thinking Kenny had acquired a bit of taste in his old age as both women were classy looking.

Introductions were made, Kenny's girl being Mary Maude and her pal Janey McIver. Hugh shook hands with both of them and then asked what they were having to drink as it was his round.

Once the drinks were in Hugh found himself standing beside Janey and as Kenny and Mary were deep in conversation on their own he felt duty bound to chat with the lassie, not that talking to her was all that much of a hardship. Besides being pretty like many Glasgow women, she had an incisive wit which could make you laugh one minute and cut you to the bone the next.

Janey informed Hugh they were also off to the Plaza that night. Usually she and Mary went to Barrowland but had decided on a change because she had recently broken off with a boyfriend of long standing and didn't want to run into him in case he caused trouble.

While Janey talked Hugh wondered how Kenny had come to get mixed up with a couple of left-footers like these. For it was obvious to him that was what they were, each having the map of Ireland written clearly across her face.

Half an hour later Kenny glanced at his watch and looked anxiously at the door. Fifteen minutes after that he was downright embarrassed as it was now obvious his china wasn't going to show which meant Janey had been given a dissy.

He went up to the bar and got yet another round. Then, surreptitiously, he gestured to Hugh to follow him to the cludgie.

Kenny was frantic and straightaway pleaded with Hugh to fill in for his missing friend.

With the thought that Janey was a fenian uppermost in his mind, Hugh tried to decline but Kenny wouldn't take no for an answer. Kenny confessed he was loopy about Mary and had been trying to get her to go out with him for weeks. Mary wasn't his girlfriend at all, although he desperately wanted her to be. This was their first date together.

Having made his impassioned plea, he produced a small silver flask from his pocket which he thrust into Hugh's hands, urging him to have a dram.

Under the circumstances Hugh felt he had no option other than to agree to be Janey's partner, leaving Kenny free all evening to dance with Mary rather than having to share himself between the two women.

Kenny was delighted and much relieved by Hugh's capitulation and they each had a large swallow from the flask before heading back to the bar where they found both girls looking miserable as sin.

They chatted for a few minutes and then Hugh suggested that as he was also going to the Plaza why didn't he join them to round off the numbers?

Janey flashed him a grateful smile. Finishing their drinks, they left the pub and crossed over the road.

The decor of the dancehall was very genteel with acres of plush and a great many potted plants. The ages of the clientele varied from teenagers to couples in their late forties and early fifties. A number of the older men were wearing tails.

Janey fitted snugly against Hugh when they took to the floor and soon they were enjoying themselves, having a 'rer ter', as the expression goes.

Much later they were cooling themselves with soft drinks when Kenny materialized to announce with a sideways wink to Hugh that he and Mary were off. Without actually saying so, he made it quite clear he and Mary wanted to leave alone.

Having gone this far Hugh decided he might as well go the whole hog and lumber Janey. During the last waltz he put it to her and she rather shyly agreed.

Reaching the Wolseley, he proudly showed it to her, having first made a quick tour of inspection to ensure it hadn't been vandalized in his absence. Janey was most impressed by the fact he had a car and said it was the first time she'd ever been driven home in one. Hugh replied she was the first Catholic he'd ever taken home. He'd meant it as a joke but somehow it didn't quite come out as one. Janey's eyes flashed as she bit back the retort that had sprung so readily to her mouth.

There it was, out in the open at last, the unspoken barrier that had existed between them all night. Religion.

'Aye, well,' said Hugh sadly, helping Janey into the car.

Janey knew exactly what he meant. There was an enormous gulf of bitterness and hatred between their two sides, a gulf that was rarely successfully crossed. Conditions, environment and prejudice bred at the breast saw to that.

As they drove into the festering area that was the Gorbals, Janey mumbled she wanted to thank him for coming to her rescue earlier on and he mumbled back it had been his pleasure.

Thistle Street was a grey canyon whose floor was strewn with garbage and with walls looking as though they were suffering from an advanced case of leprosy. It was a miracle of human will that such an immaculately turned out lassie as Janey could have come from a slum like this.

Hugh killed the engine and for a moment or two they sat in silence. Hugh finally cleared his throat to say he'd better get on back home as he had to be up at the crack of dawn.

In a flash Janey was out of the car, a wry smile on her face as she reached back in again to shake him by the hand. 'Perhaps we'll bump into one another some other night,' she said.

Then turning on her heel she was gone, clattering up her close.

'Aw to hell with it!' Hugh said savagely, angry and

upset and not wanting to admit to himself the reason why.

The Wolseley roared into life, peeling so fast down the street it left a long strip of rubber behind as a souvenir.

As he glared through the windscreen he told himself Kenny White was a mug. There was no future in getting involved with a left footer. That road could only lead to the worst sort of trouble.

The car had already turned out of sight when a wan face appeared high up in one of the tenement windows to stare out onto a street now empty apart from a drunk clinging for dear life onto a lamp standard while he spewed his guts into the gutter.

Sadly, Janey left the window and started to undress. When she crawled into bed it was to lie beside three of her sisters, two of whom slept up the way while she and the fourth slept down.

There were ten McIver children and all of them slept in that one tenement room.

It was a long time before she fell asleep but when she did it was to dream she was back amongst the plush and potted plants of the Plaza dancing with Hugh Chisholm.

'Property,' Sir Hamilton McLaren boomed, 'That's the thing. You can't go far wrong with property. Mark my words.'

There were four of them round the wrought iron lawn table, Sir Hamilton and his wife Elizabeth – Lize as she was known to her friends – plus Sir Alan and Cordelia.

This was the third time the Armstrongs had visited the McLarens and, as Sir Alan had wanted, a strong bond of friendship was growing up between the two families.

Sir Alan mused on Sir Hamilton's word as he sipped a cold glass of Sauterne and watched his daughters, Rosemary and Diane, riding with Iain and Peter McLaren in the far distance. He thought speculatively and not for the first time how well his girls got on with the McLaren boys, a fact he might well be able to exploit at a later date.

'Take industry like you're in,' Sir Hamilton went on, warming to his favourite subject. 'That comes and goes according to the state of the country's and the world's economy, but with property you don't have to worry because it's a permanent fixture. Well, almost permanent anyway. And as long as there are people needing a roof over their heads you're in business. Recession or boom, it's all one to the property owner.'

Sir Alan wondered if this was the diversification he'd long been looking for. Another two or three years the way things were going and he'd be in a position where he could afford to hive off a substantial amount of venture capital. Property might well be the sort of secondary investment which would suit him down to the ground and ensure he'd never again have to think of using that small automatic pistol lying in the dark recesses of his desk.

A little later Cordelia caught her husband intently eyeing Iain McLaren, sizing the lad up. Then she saw his gaze move from Iain to Rosemary and back again. The hint of a smile blossomed at the corners of her mouth as she correctly guessed what was running through his mind.

Well, why not? she thought. The boy was handsome, intelligent, and one day would be worth a fortune. She doubted there was a better prospect in all Scotland.

With a gracious nod to the attendant butler she accepted more wine. It was turning out to be a most interesting and enjoyable afternoon. Giving a brittle laugh, she turned her attention back to Hamilton who'd just delivered the tag line to some absurd joke he'd been telling.

While her parents and the McLarens laughed Rosemary attacked the plate of salmon set before her. She munched hungrily and as she ate she wondered for the umpteenth time why it was so long since she'd heard from Angus.

Twice she'd been up early enough to look out on the milk cart doing its rounds and neither time had he been with it. Could it be he was ill or had been involved in an accident?

She came to the decision she would rise early again next morning and if he still wasn't on the cart she'd go down and have a word with Kitty to find out just what was what.

With her mind now partially at rest she glanced across to where Diane was deep in conversation with Peter. Those two certainly got on like a house on fire, but then everyone got on with Peter. He was such a laugh and always tremendous fun to be with. Not at all like Iain who was quiet and intense with the loner's habit of often retreating within himself.

She watched Iain carefully wipe his mouth, every gesture neat and precious.

Her thoughts were interrupted by Diane shrieking with laughter as she tumbled down a grassy bank while Peter, who was obviously the culprit, stood grinning from ear to ear.

'Come on!' Diane yelled to Rosemary, as she got to her feet, her face red from heat and exertion. 'Let's give him some of his own medicine!'

Rosemary smiled and jumped up. As she did so, she stretched out her hands and waggled her fingers, knowing Peter was hypersensitively ticklish. Even the threat of it was enough to send him into paroxysms of laughter.

Peter yelped as both girls advanced on him. He'd gone too far and would now have to pay the penalty. 'That's not fair!' he protested and turned to run.

Iain smiled thinly at the goings on, rather enjoying them although horseplay wasn't something he personally liked getting involved in. He invariably found it undignified and degrading but only in himself and not in others.

As Peter ran off with Diane and Rosemary in pursuit a white vapour trail suddenly appeared in the sky above them.

Iain shielded his eyes as he followed the aeroplane from whose fuselage the vapour was streaming. The plane roared closer and then banked to come winging directly overhead.

He held his breath. For a split second every detail of the plane's underbelly was visible to him. Then it was gone, disappearing fast towards the horizon while behind it the vapour trail very slowly began to break up and disintegrate.

His mind filled with the excitement the plane had generated in him. He began to think what it must be like to be high in the air flying like a bird. What a glorious sense of freedom that must be!

Staring up at the sky he pictured the plane zooming overhead with himself at the controls. He found the image almost unbearably exciting.

It was mid-afternoon when Carrie and Winnie alighted from the tram into Scotland Street. It was quite some time since Carrie's last visit to the Smiths so another was well overdue.

Mounting the close stairs they rapped on the Smiths' door. They were about to turn away thinking no one was home when the door opened a few inches and an eye peered out.

'Robert?' Carrie queried. The sudden and bizarre appearance of the eye had given her a fright.

There was a pause during which the eye studied her curiously and then the door swung open to reveal old man Smith.

Both Carrie and Winnie were shocked at the sight of him. His face was ingrained with what looked like coal dirt while his hair was long, matted and tangled.

His shirt was open and collarless and, judging from its state, hadn't been changed in weeks. His trousers were tied round the middle with a piece of manky string below which his flies were completely undone. When he moved his flies opened wide revealing the fact he wasn't wearing any underpants.

His face broke into a sudden grin and extending a gnarled bony hand he invited them inside.

The poor man's completely off his chump, Winnie thought, wondering what Meg was thinking of to allow him to get into such a state. She gestured Carrie to go in first and then followed closely at her daughter's heels.

Both women gagged as the overpowering stench filling the house hit them. Winnie gulped and held a hanky to her nose as she followed Carrie and Robert through to the kitchen.

Despite the fact it was high summer and exremely warm out, there was a fire blazing in the grate but the fire wasn't a coal one. Broken pieces of furniture which had evidently been chopped by the hatchet lying just inside the fender, burnt away.

'Where's Meg?' Carrie asked, trying to act as though everything was normal and just as it should be.

Robert's eyes took on a faraway look and his mouth twisted into a secret smile.

Snapping out of his dwam, Robert started humming to himself, a strange discordant tune of his own composition. And crossing to where the hatchet was lying he picked it up and hefted it in his skeletal hand. Without warning the hatchet hissed through the air causing Winnie to give an involuntary little scream and hastily step backwards.

The hatchet crashed into the remains of a wooden chair, breaking the seat part jaggedly in two. Again and again Robert swung the hatchet till the chair was reduced to an untidy pile of kindling.

With dribble running over and through the growth on his chin he piled every last sliver of this kindling onto an already stacked and roaring fire.

Sweat dripped from Carrie as she squatted beside Robert Smith and forced herself to look into those demented eyes. 'Where's Meg?' she asked again, her voice soothing and coaxing.

The scars from the stitches lining Robert's face appeared angry in the reflected firelight. His mouth opened and he tried to speak but all that came out was more spit and animal grunts.

Then for a brief second his eyes cleared and once more he tried to speak. But it was no use. What emerged had no meaning, at least none Carrie could decipher.

Reaching out, he laid a begrimed hand on Carrie's arm and as he did so several large tears burst from the corners of his eyes. The sanity vanished as swiftly as it had appeared. He snatched his hand away and, hunkering on his feet like a dog, began to snigger.

'I think we'd better look around,' Winnie said.

Carrie nodded agreement and came to her feet while Robert ceased sniggering to gaze in fascination into the roaring blaze.

Side by side Carrie and Winnie ventured out of the kitchen and back into the hallway where the terrible stench seemed stronger. When they entered the bedroom they found it pitch dark and the stench stronger still.

'Oh my God!' exclaimed Carrie when she'd swept the curtains back.

Encased in a thick flannelette nightgown, Meg's decomposing body lay stretched out under the bedclothes. Her white hair was fluffed out halo-like round her head while what remained of her eyes stared sightlessly at the ceiling.

For a minute, Winnie thought Robert might have done for his wife with the hatchet or some other such weapon but a cursory glance was enough to verify Meg had died in her sleep or from natural causes while in bed.

Catching hold of the window, Carrie jerked it open to allow some of the stink out and fresh air in. She then asked her mother what they should do and Winnie replied the best thing would be to inform the police.

The problem was solved for them when from the kitchen came a great whoofing sound, unmistakable to those who have ever had a chimney catch fire.

Carrie dashed back through to make sure Robert was all right to discover him capering in front of the flames, cackling like a banshee.

When the firemen arrived they came charging up the

close to be met at the door by Winnie who explained to them what the situation was.

Carrie and Winnie waited on till the fire had been extinguished and the police had taken Meg away for an autopsy and Robert to Gartnavel Hospital for the mentally disturbed.

Badly shaken by their ordeal, they returned home bearing the sad news of what had happened to the Smiths.

Robert died in Gartnavel before the year was out and was buried alongside his beloved Meg. Officially, the cause of death was heart failure but those who'd heard him keening and calling for his dead wife were convinced it was really a broken heart he'd died of.

But then one is merely a romantic version of the other.

Head bowed and hands sunk deep into his overall pockets Angus trudged homeward having just finished his daily stint at Armstrong's.

He'd been working there for several weeks and, as he'd known he would, he hated every minute of it.

Once he'd seen the big white chief himself stalking across the yard and had been filled with a combination of anger, resentment and shame to think he'd been literally forced to work for the man whose daughter he'd planned to marry.

He now thought of Rosemary in the past tense, convinced their relationship was at an end.

He'd also seen Donald a number of times and had avoided his grandfather, blaming Donald for the fact he'd been apprenticed when where he really wanted to be was back at school studying for his Highers and planning his entry into the business world.

He started out of his melancholic reverie on hearing himself hailed and, turning round, saw it was Kitty who'd shouted and was hurrying to catch him up.

Kitty had also applied for an apprenticeship at Armstrong's but had been turned down. There had been a host of applications but only the lucky and the well connected had received a letter of acceptance, enclosing indenture papers to be signed.

After talking it over with his parents, Kitty had decided he, too, would leave school: with the way things had generally picked up, surely it wouldn't be long before he could land himself a decent job?

In the meantime, he was still running with the milk and had taken over Angus's paper round. He'd just made his final delivery for the evening.

'I want a word with you,' Kitty said, falling in beside Angus.

'Oh, aye?'

'Rosemary came out to see me this morning, asking why she hadn't heard from you. And I may tell you the poor lassie was worried stiff. She thought you must have been ill or had an accident or something.'

The blush swept up Angus's neck to invade his face. Stopping he fumbled for his cigarettes. Somehow managing to keep his face averted, he offered one to Kitty and then struck a match which they both used.

The plain fact of the matter was that he'd been putting off and putting off contacting Rosemary to tell her what had happened. He just couldn't seem to summon up the courage to tell her all his plans for the future lay in ruins and there was now no way he could ever see the pair of them getting married.

His wretchedness showed clearly as he strode along the street, his long legs going at such a pace that Kitty several times had to break into a trot to keep up.

Kitty had been all set to jibe Angus but now wisely decided not to. As they hurried along, Kitty told Angus that Rosemary had sent the message she would meet him in 'their place' at three on the Saturday afternoon after their birthday which was the following week.

What Rosemary was referring to as 'their place' was a spot upstream on the Cart which she and Angus had stumbled onto by accident some years ago on an exploring trip.

It was a small cave halfway up a steep bank, screened by trees and a mass of foliage. They called it the bear cave – the pretence being that it had once been a bear's lair – whose existence they kept secret.

Kitty went on to say he'd told Rosemary the story of the apprenticeships coming vacant at her father's works and how Angus, at his mother's insistence, had been made to apply and that the application had been duly accepted. He'd added ruefully that his had been turned down.

'How was she looking?' Angus asked, his voice shaking a little.

Kitty grinned and replied she hadn't sprouted a moustache if that was what Angus was worried about. Angus laughed and snapped out of his mood.

'Three o'clock on the Saturday afternoon?' he queried.

Kitty nodded and then playfully punched his pal on the arm. 'Go on, you great big long streak of misery,' he said. 'Do yourself a favour. Go and see the lassie.'

Arriving home, Angus quickly washed and then went through to his room where he would wait until called for his tea. As he changed out of his working clothes all he could think of was his forthcoming rendezvous with Rosemary.

Now a move had been made, he couldn't wait to see her again.

The day had dawned a beautiful one – just what Rosemary had been praying for. She was carrying a picnic basket in one hand and an old mac slung over her shoulder as she made her way through the undergrowth towards the bear cave.

There was something primeval about this section of the riverbank, she'd always thought. It wouldn't have surprised her in the least had she suddenly come face to face with an ancient Celtic tribesman daubed with woad, or if a sabre-toothed tiger had suddenly appeared on a branch of one of the many trees surrounding her.

She was feeling nervous and rather tired, having had trouble sleeping the night before. Her mind had been racing with thoughts of today and what she planned to make happen.

In a pocket of her mac was a packet of contraceptives which she'd finally obtained from a school chum called Margie McIntyre who had a reputation for being wild and a great one for the boys.

In the picnic basket were all sorts of goodies she'd scrounged from cook plus a bottle of wine she'd managed to lift when everyone's back was turned.

She stopped when she heard voices and, from a vantage point behind a tree, watched four wee boys dressed as Red Indians making their way in the direction she'd just come from. Judging by the way they were creeping along they were in the middle of a game, so no doubt there would be another band of them somewhere around.

A little further on she had to climb the steep bank, working her way behind masses of foliage, to the spot where the bear cave lay hidden.

The first thing she did was to lay the mac on the ground and then she began setting out the picnic things.

She heard him coming before he actually appeared. Suddenly he was there, standing in the mouth of the cave grinning down at her.

It might have been years since they'd last spoken, both were that awkward and shy.

'Happy birthday!' Angus said and thrust a brown paper parcel into her hands. He sat on the mac beside her and watched while she undid the string.

Rosemary exclaimed with delight when she opened the box. Inside were a pair of matching tortoise shell combs which she knew would look marvellous in her hair.

Although Angus had developed a fetish about making and saving money he wasn't scared to spend it when the occasion arose and could be extremely generous at times. To him money was always the means to an end and never the be-all and end-all in itself.

'They're gorgeous,' Rosemary breathed, her face beaming. Leaning across she kissed him on the lips.

'I'll give you yours later,' she added, a mischievous twinkle in her eye.

Like a lot of people who consider themselves to be at fault, Angus couldn't wait to explain himself. In a great rush of words it all came tumbling out.

According to Angus, his life lay in ruins and their relationship in tatters but Rosemary knew this just wasn't so. His having to go to work for her father might appear a setback but who knew how time might transform this into a positive advantage?

A little perspective was needed, she told him sternly. After all, school certificates were never a guarantee for success. What really mattered was determination and a willingness to work longer and harder than anyone else. An astute mind – if you didn't have that no amount of school certificates were going to give it to you – a shrewd business sense and, above all, motivation.

There was a fierceness in Rosemary as she spoke these words – the mother hen cajoling her favourite chick.

She wanted to take Angus by the shoulders and shake all this ridiculous defeatist talk out of him. So what if he had to spend the next few years learning to be a fitter? With the right motivation spurring him on being a fitter need only be the first rung on the ladder.

Angus stared at Rosemary in amazement, a new shame growing in him at how ready he'd been to throw in his hand. As she was now making abundantly clear there were more ways than one to skin the proverbial cat.

In a moment of insight it came to him that their love was only on the threshold of its potential. There were depths he could plumb with Rosemary that would take them a lifetime to fulfil.

'Well?' she demanded.

He smiled wryly. 'With you beside me I doubt if there's anything I couldn't do. You're all the motivation I'll ever need.'

Her nostrils flared and her breathing became laboured. She'd suddenly started thinking about Royal Standard again and what she'd seen him do to the mare, Gypsy.

She poured wine into cups and having passed one to Angus offered up a toast. 'To us!' she murmured. Her eyelids drooped to give her a catlike appearance.

Lying back on the mac, she beckoned him to her. Mouth met mouth and as they did so she guided his hands to the swell of her breasts.

His hands slid under her blouse to stroke and knead her flesh. He fumbled with her bra, cursing himself for having a handful of thumbs, till she came to his assistance by deftly flicking open the hooks and eyes.

She could feel how ready he was, strong and hard pressing down through her skirt.

She ran her hands over his back and then down to clasp his bottom. When she looked into his eyes he was staring quizzically back.

Groping in the mac pocket she pulled out the packet of contraceptives. 'Happy birthday!' she smiled.

He was dumbfounded. 'You mean . . . ?'

She nodded and then shrugged herself free of her blouse and bra, throwing them to one side where they lay in an untidy heap.

Angus gulped and his face drained of colour. This was a moment he'd often thought and dreamt about and now, incredibly, it had arrived.

'Come on!' she urged, undoing her skirt.

Angus was trembling as he took off his jacket and shirt. He unbuttoned his flies, feeling embarrassed and strangely vulnerable.

'Don't forget your socks,' Rosemary said with a giggle.

The giggle relaxed him with the reminder that it was his Rosemary he was doing this with and not some strange girl who meant nothing to him. There was no need for fear or embarrassment. Not with Rosie.

'Angus?'

She was laying stark naked with her hands by her sides and a soft smile on her face.

His stomach muscles rippled and although it was warm in the cave goose bumps broke out on his back and along the length of his arms.

'Scared?'

'Of course not!' he replied indignantly and just that little bit too emphatically.

'I am.'

'There's nothing to worry about. I won't hurt you. I promise,' he said.

They kissed again and as they did so his hands slid down her body.

'Don't forget the johnnies,' she whispered throatily in his ear.

Somehow he managed to rip the packet open but his hands were shaking so much he would never have got it on if she hadn't helped him.

Theoretically he knew what to do next but faced with the reality it was a different matter altogether. It just wasn't as straightforward as he'd been led to believe. If only he could see what he should have been getting at but he couldn't bring himself to visually examine her there as that would have seemed so clinical.

He poked but didn't seem to be getting anywhere until she reached between them to grasp him. Then there was yielding flesh and he was sinking deep inside her.

Her face screwed up in pain and with a hiss she told him to stop, which he did with alacrity, thinking he'd done something wrong. But after a few seconds the pain passed away and she told him to continue.

'Oh Rosie!' he whispered, feeling he should be saying something and not quite knowing what.

The laughter suddenly filling the cave was like an ice cold douche to the pair of them. Each froze in mid-action, not willing to believe their ears.

Rosemary nearly died of shame when she turned her head to see a group of wee boys gawping at her and Angus from the cave entrance. There were five of them all dressed as cowboys. The other half of the group she'd seen stalking through the undergrowth earlier.

Angus knew he had to do something and fast. Pulling himself free he made a roaring noise and simultaneously contorted his face in simulated anger.

Screeching and laughing the boys turned and fled back down the bank as fast as they could go.

'And don't dare come back again!' Angus yelled, shaking his fist after them, not realizing how utterly ridiculous he looked standing there with a condom hanging from his dangling penis.

In a flurry of cowboy hats and brightly coloured chaps the wee boys were gone.

'It seems our secret place isn't so secret after all,' Rosemary said, and started to laugh hysterically.

Seeing the funny side of the situation Angus joined in and when he sat beside her tears were streaming down both their faces. When the laughter finally subsided he poured them both more wine.

'Are you *sure* they've gone?' Rosemary asked after she'd drained her cup.

He crossed to the cave entrance and peered but of the wee boys there was no sign.

Rosemary had that craving feeling back in her stomach. She stared hungrily at Angus who stared hungrily back.

This time there was no fumbling or uncertainty.

'Oh!' she gasped.

A little later he cried out and as he did so she wrapped her legs tightly round him and exhaled a long, satisfied sigh.

Angus lay limp in her arms. 'That was definitely the best birthday present I've ever had,' he said.

In the years to come, if he'd been asked to pick out the happiest moment in his life, he would have had no hesitation in picking that one.

13

By the winter of the following year Angus had grudgingly become reconciled to working at Armstrong's. He'd also set himself up a rather lucrative sideline by keeping book on the Scottish horse and dog races and was to be found every race day taking bets during the breaks in the toilet.

The idea of making book had come to him when he noticed many men in the works were keen on having a flutter. The nearest bookie operated nearly a mile away, so here was a heaven sent opportunity to cash in on a situation crying out to be exploited by some bright spark like himself.

First of all he'd had to learn the intricacies of betting and this he'd done by paying a fitter and dedicated punter called George Edgar to teach him.

For finance he'd used his savings which at the inception of the book stood at an astonshing £235, most of which he'd saved from his milk and paper rounds.

It appealed to Angus's sense of irony that, as time passed, he was making far more from his book than the pittance he was being paid in his position as apprentice.

He rarely took home less than a fiver a week from his book and on several occasions it had been as much as a tenner – more than double what the highest paid worker at Armstrong's was getting.

He was seeing Rosemary as often as he could and sleeping with her whenever possible.

By now Diane and Kitty had become friendly as it was always easier for Rosemary to get out at night with her sister. Kitty had been introduced to make up the foursome and luckily he and Diane had hit it off right away.

Rosemary and Diane always told their parents they were going somewhere locally – to the pictures or dancing – but invariably went further afield to lessen the risk of being seen with Angus and Kitty.

Their luck held out for a long time until one Saturday evening at a dance in the Croftfoot Boy Scout Hall Angus and Rosemary were spotted by a lad called Tod Gemmill. Tod was the son of Ronnie Gemmill, Armstrong's chief pattern maker and as big an arse-licker as his father.

Tod was an apprentice same as Angus although older and in the third year of his apprenticeship. And he recognized Rosemary, having seen her several times at the works with her father.

It was obvious to Tod that Angus and Rosemary were close and he judged from the easy way they had with one another they'd been winching for some time. That gave him food for thought. He made a mental note to mention it to his father.

Hugh was also at the dancing that night, only in his case he'd gone to the St Andrew's Halls in the centre of the city. It was the back of ten when he decided he'd had enough and would drive home to Muirend.

He was passing another dancehall called the Locarno when he noticed a girl struggling with a burly chap. The girl's face swung round into full profile and it was with a shock he recognized Janey McIver whom he hadn't seen since the night he'd dropped her off outside her house in Thistle Street.

He pulled the car into the kerb, rolled down the window and caled out, 'Everything all right, Janey?'

With a sob Janey succeeded in wrenching herself away from the man and, running across to the car, quickly climbed inside. 'Get the hell out of here quick,' she gasped, looking thoroughly frightened as the man she'd been struggling with started fumbling with the door handle.

Hugh let the clutch out and the Hornet leapt away. The man uttered a curse as he was sent spinning into a passer-by, causing the two of them to go crashing to the pavement.

It took a few minutes and a cigarette to calm Janey down. Once she was capable of speaking coherently she explained the chap had been her old boyfriend who was refusing to get the message and take no for an answer.

She'd been at the Locarno that night when suddenly Francey had appeared at her side, demanding she dance with him.

She'd agreed to have one dance to humour him but at the end of it when she'd tried to excuse herself he'd physically forced her to stay on the floor, at the same time declaring in a loud voice to all and sundry she was his girl and the sooner she learned to accept the fact the better.

She'd been scared stiff by then as she'd known from the smell of his breath and the glassy look in his eye he'd been drinking heavily and in that mood was capable of almost anything.

She'd danced the next half hour with him and then pleaded to be allowed to go to the toilet as she was bursting. It was a request Francey couldn't very well refuse so he'd reluctantly consented saying he'd be waiting for her when she came out again.

Knowing he'd be watching, she'd made a show of entering the Ladies. Chancing her luck, she sneaked out less than a minute later, hoping he'd be looking elsewhere and not expecting her to reappear so soon.

Her luck had held as far as the cloakroom. But as she was hurrying from there with her coat over her arm, Francey had spotted her. The ensuing argument had continued out into the street at which point Hugh had come driving by.

As Hugh listened to all this he couldn't help but think

what an attractive woman Janey was. Furthermore she had a certain something which made him feel relaxed and easy in her company.

When they reached St Enoch Square she thanked him again for coming to her rescue and suggested he drop her off on the corner where she could catch a tram.

Hugh wouldn't hear of it, insisting that as Thistle Street was en route to Muirend anyway, the least he could do was take her home.

Both of them were delighted at seeing one another although neither would have dreamt of saying so. Occasionally Janey glanced at him out the corner of her eye while he used the windscreen mirror to catch a glimpse of her.

When they arrived at Thistle Street there was an awkward pause between them which Janey finally broke by asking if he'd like to come up for a cup of tea and a biscuit?

Hugh agreed. Enjoying Janey's company so much he was reluctant to be parted from her.

They climbed the close stairs to arrive at a badly chipped green door.

The kitchen he was ushered into was warm and friendly. It was also crammed with children of all sizes, shapes and ages.

What caught and held his attention were the holy pictures on the walls. There was one of the Virgin Mary with the infant Jesus, another of Jesus wearing a crown of thorns. One of a kind-faced man surrounded by animals whom he guessed was St Francis. Plus a very large one in a gilt frame of Pope Pius XI. There were also two statues on either side of the mantelpiece – Mary and Joseph.

He gulped at this overpowering display of Popery. Here were all the things he and every other Protestant boy in the city like him had been brought up to hate and despise. Involuntarily he shrank within himself, rueing his folly in allowing himself to come into such close contact with the Roman Church.

Mrs McIver was a stout woman of his mother's age who came forward to shake him by the hand after Janey had recounted what had happened both inside and outside the Locarno and how his timely intervention had saved her from something which might well have ended up nastily.

McIver was furious, saying Francey was a bad lot and should he run into Francey he would give him what for. In the meantime would Hugh care for a wee drop of the cratur rather than the tea his good wife was offering? Before Hugh could reply glasses were out and a bottle was being opened.

Hugh's apprehension about his surroundings melted a little as the whisky warmed and soothed him. And soon he began to relax. It transpired that McIver was even more of a radical left winger than Big Donald and soon he and Hugh were arguing the toss about the pros and cons of the new Coalition Government led by Neville Chamberlain, and the attitude of that government in relation to Spain which was being torn apart by the most dreadful civil war.

After a while a small child of about three came and clambered onto Hugh's lap. Hugh stroked the wee lad's hair and then tickled him under the chin, causing him to snort with laughter.

'You like weans, then?' Mrs McIver asked.

Hugh smiled and admitted freely he did, adding that one day when he was married he was hoping to have lots of his own, especially boys whom he was particularly fond of.

Janey sat silent through all this watching Hugh as he talked with her mother and father, admiring his well-spoken manner and the way he held his own against her Da who was a notorious bully when it came to exchanging views, particularly political ones.

When Hugh finally rose to go he was told by Mrs McIver he'd be welcome any time he cared to call. They shook hands all round, then Janey showed him to the front door. The kitchen door was diplomatically shut behind them after they'd made their exit.

Hugh was in a terrible quandary. He liked Janey tremendously – there was no doubt in his mind about that, just as there was none about her liking him in return. But what use was it trying to start a relationship that was bound to founder on the rocks of religion? Words from the old song came leaping to mind.

T'was in County Tyrone in the town of Dungannon,
Where's many a rumption myself had a han' in.
Bob Williamson lived there a weaver to trade,
And all of us thought him a stout Orange blade.

On the twelfth of July as it yearly did come.
Bob played on his flute to the sound of the drum.
Well you can talk of your piano, your violin or lute,
But there's nothing to beat the old Orange flute.

But Bob the old bastard he took us all in,
He married a fenian named Brigid McGinn.
Turned Papish himself and forsook the old cause,
That gave us our freedom, religion and laws. . . .

'I enjoyed meeting your family,' Hugh said, hating what was coming next.

Janey smiled and nodded, waiting.

Outside a cat began to yowl while from a house somewhere close by came the unmistakable sound of a couple having a barney.

'It wouldn't work Janey. You know that as well as I do,' he mumbled.

Her smile stretched and stretched till it seemed her face must surely be sliced in two. Her eyes had a dead, marbled look about them. She'd known he was going to say this but would have given anything to have had herself proved wrong. He was right of course. Trying to mix the green and orange was just asking for trouble, especially if children were to become involved.

'Goodbye,' she whispered, hesitating for a brief second before going to him and kissing him full on the mouth. Then she was gone. The badly chipped green door closed behind her with a click that had the ring of finality about it.

Hugh stuck his hands in his pockets and trudged downstairs. He felt as though he'd just lost both arms.

He was fumbling for his car keys as he came out of the close but when his gaze lit on the Hornet he stopped dead in his tracks. 'Oh no!' he exclaimed, fury bursting within him.

The Hornet's beautiful red paintwork had been viciously scratched and scraped from nose to boot while the upholstery had been ripped and slashed to shreds.

He felt sick, cursing himself for being so stupid as to leave the car parked in a Gorbals street.

The laugh was low and evil and came from directly behind him. Swinging round he found himself facing a grinning Francey.

'Like your fancy car now, Jim? Maybe that'll teach you to take off with my bird and make me look stupid,' Francey spat.

'You fucker!' Hugh hissed and stepped forward intent on smashing Francey in the face.

Laughing again, Francey brought his right hand from behind his back to reveal a rusty iron bar. The bar whistled through the air in an overhand arc that brought it smashing against the side of Hugh's head.

Hugh's legs were suddenly jelly, buckling under him to send him crashing to the filthy pavement.

Again and again Francey's foot thudded into his ribs and back.

He tried to wriggle out of the way but instead got it full on the chin. There was a splintering sound and blood everywhere as he flipped over onto his back.

He must have passed out, for the next thing he knew Francey was gone and he was staring up at a night sky filled with clouds and smoke from tenement chimneys.

He grunted with pain as he rolled onto his side and shuffled himself to the tenement wall which he used as a steadying post to bring himself to his feet.

He spat out gobs of congealed blood and gritty

fragments of teeth. Many of the teeth left were broken, jagged and excruciatingly sore, as indeed were his chest and back.

Coughing up more blood he staggered into the close and, like a drunken man, made his way upstairs to the McIvers' door which he hammered on with his fist.

Suddenly Mr and Mrs McIver were there and arms were being thrown round him.

'Francey,' he croaked.

There was so much pain wracking his mouth and body it was with relief he greeted the darkness.

Donald fidgeted as he and Winnie sat outside Ward 5 of the Victoria Infirmary. The staff nurse had been in to inform Hugh they were waiting and he'd sent back word his present visitor wouldn't be long.

A few minutes later the swing doors opened and an extremely pretty girl emerged from the ward, smiling to the staff nurse as she passed. The nurse then turned to the Chisholms and said they could go away in now.

Winnie and Donald turned to stare at one another, both of them having noted the Saint Christopher dangling from Janey's neck and wondering what business a Catholic girl could have with their Hugh?

Now the moment had arrived for Donald to go in and see Hugh he was reluctant to do so without first knowing he'd be welcome. Voicing his fears to Winnie she agreed to sound out the ground.

Hugh was a sight, his face puffed up like a balloon, from the combination of the kicking and having the remainder of his teeth extracted.

When Winnie confirmed the staff nurse's message that his father was also here, he fell silent for a few seconds before mumbling she'd best call him in.

'It was his own idea, I assure you. You two might have had your differences but that doesn't alter the fact he still loves and worries about you, son,' Winnie said before walking back to the swing doors and beckoning Donald to come away through.

The two men solemnly shook hands. Then Donald asked what the damage was and how it had come about?

According to Hugh, he'd been lucky. Apart from the loss of his teeth he was merely bruised, which looked a lot worse than it actually was.

He went on to tell them about rescuing Janey McIver and how her ex-boyfriend had been waiting for him after he'd said goodnight to her and her family.

Winnie sat quietly on the one chair provided, listening to the men talk about the violence that was an inter-woven part of the city's fabric. She would wait till Hugh was better and out of hospital before chiselling him about this McIver lassie.

She prayed to God there was nothing serious between him and the girl, because there would be the most almighty ructions if there were! Her gaze fastened on Donald emphatically making a point.

Sir Alan Armstrong's brow was deeply furrowed as he read the report presented to him that morning by the private detective he'd hired to find out exactly what was going on between Rosemary and young McBain.

It surprised him just how many times the pair con-trived to meet. Going alone with Diane to the local pictures and dancing indeed!

But what really upset him was the detective's state-ment they were having an affair.

According to the detective, friends of the family had been away on holiday during the past few weeks and Rosemary had somehow contrived to get hold of the key to a small guest flat at the back of the empty house where she and Angus had gone on a number of occasions to make love. Peering through a window, the detective had actually seen them in the act.

Laying down the report Sir Alan made a mental note to thank Gemmill for putting him onto this. A reward would come later.

He could forbid Rosemary ever to see McBain again but, knowing his daughter as he did, a face to face confrontation wasn't the way. What was needed here was something subtle, something devious to cause a break between the pair. And break there would have to be and soon if his plans for her future were to have any real hopes of success.

It came back to him she'd once asked him the ins and outs of John McBain's accident. She must have been seeing the lad even then.

A glance at the calendar confirmed there were only a few days left till Christmas. He would use the holiday to think up a plan to get young McBain out of Glasgow and away forever. For if they were as deeply committed to one another as the detective said it would have to be as drastic as that to ensure the affair was over and done with.

Dismissing the matter from his mind, he turned his attention to a sheaf of papers which had arrived in from his solicitor. Some property was about to come onto the market of the sort he'd been looking for as an investment. Within seconds he was totally absorbed by the details of the buildings under proposal.

On Christmas Day Iain and Peter McLaren arrived at Arnprior House with gifts for the girls.

Rosemary and Diane were delighted with what they'd received – perfume in both cases – and somewhat embarrassed by the fact they hadn't thought to buy the McLarens anything.

Iain shrugged that one off with a suitable comment and then changed the conversation by announcing he'd just passed his private pilot's licence a few days previously.

He'd been taking lessons for some time now and had acquired himself the reputation round the aerodrome as an excellent pupil and a potentially outstanding flyer.

Rosemary thought this news marvellous and immediately pressed him to take her up as soon as it could be arranged.

Iain replied he'd be only too happy to oblige providing

Sir Alan agreed, which Sir Alan did.

Watching Rosemary and Iain together started Sir Alan thinking about Angus McBain again and as he thought he played with one of his cuff links which had been a Christmas present from Cordelia. They were twenty-two carat gold inset with diamond chips.

Suddenly it was there, fully hatched in his mind, a plan to take care of young McBain – neat, simple and very thorough. McBain wouldn't have a leg to stand on.

Reaching for the decanter he poured a round of sherries and the toast he proposed was Iain and Rosemary's flight together.

He smiled as he drank because only he was aware of what he'd really meant by that.

Mid-morning of the first day back to work after the New Year Angus was summoned to Sir Alan's private office. He went convinced Sir Alan had at last found out about him and Rosemary and all hell was about to break loose because of it.

For fifteen minutes he was kept waiting in the secretary's outer office before being ushered through to the inner sanctum.

He tried not to wilt under the accusing gaze knifing into him, forcing himself to stand perfectly still.

'I hear you've been taking bets, making book as I believe it's called,' Sir Alan said abruptly.

Relief surged through Angus. It wasn't what he'd been expecting although this was certainly serious enough. 'Yes sir,' he replied.

Sir Alan made a pyramid with his hands and launched into a reprimand scathing in its severity.

There was no way Angus could defend what he'd been doing and knew it. He did point out to Sir Alan, however, that he'd never made book in the company's time.

Sir Alan took the point but countered by saying the important thing was that an illegal act had been taking place on his property which was something he couldn't countenance.

Angus sighed inwardly. Here was the best money-making scheme he'd had to date about to go down the plughole. But if Sir Alan would only overlook it this time Angus gave his word it would never happen again.

Sir Alan grunted and appeared to consider that. He reached for the humidor and took its top off, exclaiming with annoyance when he saw it was empty.

'Wait here,' he snapped and left the room, closing the door behind him.

For a full five minutes Angus was left in the office alone and then the door opened to re-admit Sir Alan puffing on a fat cigar.

In a few short sentences Sir Alan stated he was willing to overlook the matter this once, qualifying himself by adding he hadn't forgotten John McBain had died in his foundry nor that Donald Chisholm was a treasured employee.

With a wave of his cigar, he told Angus to get back to work and he would expect Angus to keep his side of the bargain.

Angus thanked the still glowering Sir Alan profusely and then hurriedly took his leave, thankful he'd been let off so lightly, as he could well have lost his job or even been reported to the police.

He was hurrying back across the yard when suddenly a figure seemed to fly out of nowhere and crash into him so violently both he and the figure went tumbling to the ground.

'I'm helluva sorry, Angus, my fault entirely. I just wasn't looking where I was going,' Tod Gemmill said, springing to his feet and helping Angus to his. 'No bones broken I hope,' Tod added, patting Angus down.

'I'm fine,' Angus replied and shrugged himself away from the questing hands.

Tod grinned wryly. 'No offence?'

'None taken,' Angus confirmed and hastily resumed his way back to the job.

It was just before the lunchtime hooter when another messenger arrived from Sir Alan to say Angus was wanted back again in his office. Thoroughly mystified, Angus trotted back across the yard and up the stairs to be told to go straight through as Sir Alan was waiting for him.

The moment Angus opened the door to the inner office he knew something was dreadfully amiss. Looking like the wrath of God, Big Donald, with cap in hand, stood at one end of the desk while at the opposite end was a constable and what was unmistakably a plain clothes man.

Sir Alan glanced up. 'Come in McBain and shut the door behind you,' he said.

Completely bewildered, Angus stepped forward to stand beside his grandfather.

In a tight, angry voice Sir Alan introduced Detective Inspector Hammill and Constable Forbes, neither of whom gave Angus any sign of acknowledgement. Then with a wave of his hand in the Detective Inspector's direction, Sir Alan sank back into his leather padded chair and proceeded to light a fresh cigar from the now full humidor.

The detective inspector came straight to the point. Earlier on Angus had been called into this office to speak with Sir Alan on a company matter and was it not true that while he was here Sir Alan had left him alone for a few minutes?

'Yes, that's correct,' Angus admitted. He looked at his grandfather hoping for some clue as to what all this was about but Donald refused to meet his glance.

'Would you mind turning out your pockets?'

The question came from the detective inspector and was delivered in such a way as to leave Angus in no doubt that to refuse would be admitting guilt to whatever it was he stood suspected of.

Angus declared he had nothing to hide but before he complied would they mind telling him what this was all about?

Hammill cleared his throat and then went on to say an extremely valuable pair of cuff links – twenty-two carat gold inset with diamond chips – had gone missing that morning from Sir Alan's desk and all those who'd been in the office were being asked to cooperate in trying to solve the matter.

Angus couldn't remember having seen any cuff links and said so, adding that he was only to happy too co-operate as he didn't want anyone thinking him a thief.

There were five pockets in his overalls and the cuff links were in the right leg one.

The moment he felt the unusual bulges he knew with a sickening certainty what they were. He paled and loked from Hammill to Sir Alan, whose eyes were hooded behind a cloud of smoke.

It was the constable who worked the cuff links up the length of the long pocket till they popped out into his hand. He set them carefully on the desk's well polished top for all to see.

They were gold inset with diamond chips.

Donald took a deep breath which he slowly exhaled.

'There's been some sort of mistake,' Angus said almost hysterically, realizing only too well how pitifully inadequate and clichéd that sounded.

'That'll be for the court to decide,' said Hammill, scooping up the cuff links which he informed Sir Alan would have to be taken along and used in evidence.

Sir Alan cupped his chin in his hand and looked thoughtful, a pose he held for over a minute while he stared hard at the squirming Angus.

Finally, with a sad shake of his head, he thanked the policemen for coming along and informed them he'd decided not to make any formal charges.

Hammill tried to argue but Sir Alan was resolute in that he intended dealing with the matter himself. With a disappointed shrug Hammill capitulated and returned the cuff links.

Hammill and the constable then took their leave, both shooting Angus filthy looks as they did so.

'Have you anything further to say?' Sir Alan asked.

'It wasn't me. I swear it!'

'Then how did the cuff links come to be in your over-alls?'

Angus slumped. He had no answer to that one.

Sir Alan puffed on his cigar knowing he now had Angus exactly where he wanted him. In his victory, he allowed the triumph he felt to show in his eyes. Angus, who happened to glance directly into his face at that precise moment, noticed it.

Suddenly everything clicked into place and Angus knew without a shadow of a doubt it was Sir Alan himself who'd had him framed.

He remembered then Tod Gemmill careering into him in the yard and that part of the mystery was solved. So he'd been right to start with. Armstrong *had* found out about him and Rosemary and this was the bastard's way of putting the boot in.

Sir Alan busied himself trimming his cigar and said it was, of course, impossible for Angus to continue working for him. Furthermore he felt it his duty not to give Angus a reference as should there ever be a repeat of this type of incident it would only reflect on his good name.

For the second time within minutes Angus was stunned. Without a reference he was virtually unemployable, not only on Clydeside but everywhere.

Still busy with the end of his cigar, Sir Alan went on to say in view of what had happened to Angus's father and bearing in mind Donald was an employee of long standing he was prepared to give Angus a letter of introduction to an old friend of his who owned a firm similar to Armstrong's down in Newcastle.

The letter would set out the reasons for Angus's dismissal but would also plead he be given a second chance.

'You can go now,' Sir Alan said. 'I'll have the letter typed out this afternoon and taken to your home by hand.'

In a completely flat voice Donald said in all the years he'd worked at Armstrong's he'd never asked for time off but he would like some now if it was possible?

Sir Alan told Donald to go home and not come back

till the morning, saying the request was perfectly under-
standable in the circumstances.

Angus and Donald left the office and went down the
stairs and into the yard where Donald told Angus to wait
while he collected his coat from the foundry.

Angus was lighting a cigarette when he saw a group of
lads hurry out of a door. Amongst them was the unmistakable figure of Tod Gemmill. The cigarette went
spinning as Angus ran across the yard.

Gemmill saw Angus coming and froze. His eyes
bulged and he went white with fright as Angus ground to
a halt in front of him. Guilt was written clearly all over
his face.

The other lads looked on curiously, wondering what
was up.

Angus told himself this was neither the time nor place
to settle with Gemmill. That would be when he could get
Gemmill alone and there were no witnesses to see what
happened.

Reaching out, Angus tapped Gemmill lightly on the
shoulder. 'From now on your jacket's marked,' he said
quietly. Rounding on his heel, he strode back to where
Donald was now waiting for him.

Once out of the works Donald said they would go into
the swing park just a little way down the street. Angus
knew then there was going to be a confrontation between them.

In the middle of a grassy expanse Donald stopped and
turned to face Angus. 'Now tell me the truth. Did you
take those cuff links?' he demanded harshly.

There was no lying to Donald in this sort of mood and
thankfully Angus didn't have to try. Starting at the
beginning he told Donald about meeting Rosemary
Armstrong all those years ago and how things had
developed between them. The only fact he omitted was
he and Rosie were actually sleeping together.

He went on to say Sir Alan must have found out about
their relationship and this was his way of trying to break
them up.

He then described the incident with Tod Gemmill: Tod had planted the cuff links either when they were on the ground together or when Tod had been supposedly checking to see he was all right. He added that was what he'd been chiselling Gemmill about while Donald was away getting his coat.

Donald's eyes never wavered from Angus's as he listened to this explanation. He knew it had to be the truth he was hearing for apart from having an honest ring about it the story was just too fantastic and elaborate to be otherwise.

When Angus finally finished he grunted and, gesturing towards a bench, said they should sit and have a smoke.

As he packed his pipe he asked what sort of girl Rosemary Armstrong was. Angus spoke of her in glowing and loving terms.

They sat in silence for a wee while after that. Donald's heart was heavy, knowing Angus was going to come out of all this an all-round loser. There was no way Angus could thwart a man as powerful and influential as Sir Alan Armstrong.

What Angus wanted more than anything else was to talk things over with Rosemary. She had a way of putting everything into perspective that he badly needed now.

He would go and see her as soon as he'd parted from his grandfather.

Rosemary's cheeks were still glowing with exhilaration as Iain turned his father's car into Old Castle Road.

As promised, Iain had collected her that morning and driven her out to the aerodrome where the Avro trainer was fuelled ready and waiting for them.

With a beautifully smooth take off they were airborne and she was revelling in the sheer gut-wrenching excitement of her first ever flight.

She'd hung on for grim death when Iain looped the loop and then threw the aircraft into a steep left hand bank that sent them corkscrewing towards the ground at an incredible rate.

With plenty of altitude to spare Iain had brought the
Avro out of its spin to send it winging away from the city
and out over the Campsie Hills where snow lay hard
upon the ground. The air buffeting them in the face
seemed to be composed of countless millions of tiny,
stinging icicles.

All too soon the joy ride was over and they were
motoring back to Arnprior House with Rosemary
plaguing the life out of Iain every inch of the way. At
last, as he was opening the door of the car, he relented
and agreed to take her up again soon.

Impulsively Rosemary threw her arms round his neck
and gave him a big smacker full on the lips.

Coming to try and contact her, Angus had seen the car
draw up and had immediately recognized Rosemary in
the front passenger seat. Handsome-looking bugger she
was with, he'd thought, as he'd watched Iain walk round
the car to open her door. He couldn't believe his eyes
when he saw Rosemary throw her arms round Iain
McLaren's neck and kiss him.

In his already tremulous state this was another body
blow which stunned him even more than what had happened in Sir Alan's office.

He stood rooted, watching amazed as the pair of them
ran hand in hand towards the front door.

At the door Rosemary paused to peck Iain on the
cheek and then they had vanished inside with the door
banging shut behind them.

Completely numb, Angus turned and started the walk
back to Holmlea Road.

Rosemary. *His* Rosie, had somebody else!

The horrible suspicion dawned she was the one who'd
told her father about their affair. After all, why should
Sir Alan suddenly *now* discover their secret. Was this
her way of getting rid of him so he could be replaced by
the new chap?

There could be no denying what he'd witnessed back
there in the street, nor that Sir Alan had sacked him in a

way that ensured he had to leave the city if not for good then certainly for a long time to come.

Sweat broke on his brow at the thought of the saturnine-looking chap being Rosemary's lover. Nausea rumbled inside him and he had to stop and lean against a standard lamp where he threw up into the gutter.

'Oh, you bitch!' he whispered.

Outrage gave way to a bottomless chasm of despair. Closing his eyes he saw her face and heard her voice whispering the sort of love talk she'd been fond of using.

Was she saying the same things even now to her new bloke? Had she managed to sneak him up to her bedroom where they were . . . ?

Staggering like a drunken man, he made his way down the street. Seeing nothing. Hearing nothing. Thinking far too much.

He was still beside himself when he came to his close. There was a clattering on the stairs and suddenly Kitty was standing beside him saying he'd just been up chapping at his door wanting to tell him the most marvellous news.

Angus forced some sort of composure into his face as Kitty burbled on that at long last he'd landed himself a real job as a stoker aboard a ship called the *Almuria* which was at the moment tied up in the Govan Docks.

Eyes shining, Kitty said he was hoping Angus would go out with him that night for a celebration drink as it wasn't every day he landed a job or left home.

A good bucket was just what he needed Angus decided. He congratulated Kitty and then arranged for the pair of them to meet up directly after tea.

With a whoop of delight Kitty was gone, rushing down the street like some kid who'd just discovered Christmas.

Angus knew Archie wouldn't be home yet so he decided this was as good a time as any to tell Carrie what had happened. He found her in the kitchen standing over a simmering pot of leek and potato soup which he asked her to leave and come and sit down for a little while.

It wasn't easy but he hadn't expected it to be. Starting at the beginning he told her the entire story exactly as he'd related it to Donald.

'That man!' Carrie said when he was finally finished. Putting her head in her hands, she burst out crying. Angus took his mother in his arms and sat there rocking her back and forth the way she'd often rocked him when he was little.

Harriet had been into town to the pictures and was now on a tram swaying along Argyle Street taking her home. To pass the time, she started to read a magazine containing the latest film news she'd bought in the foyer of the picture hall.

The article on page three drew her eye the way a magnet does iron. In heavy type it stated veteran screenwriter Lou Dansie had recently died of a heart attack in his Hollywood home.

Her hands came up to touch the gold chain round her neck, tracing its length till her long fingers came into contact with the heavy ring dangling from its inverted apex.

Turning out of Argyle Street, the tram rattled northward to come eventually to Byres Road where Harriet got off.

She walked up the street, a tall, ugly-looking woman whose skin was a muddy grey colour and whose eyes burned with a strange intensity.

A wee boy in her way took one look at her face and hastily scuttled round her. The wee boy shivered as he hurried along.

He didn't like woman with faces like that. They gave him the willies.

Angus and Kitty were in a West Nile Street pub when Kitty came up with the suggestion they take a taxi down to the Govan Docks and have a look at the *Almuria*.

Half an hour later they were standing on the quayside staring up at a rusty old heap that should have been consigned to the breaker's yard years before. Both had screwtops in their hands.

Already a little maudlin from drink Angus kept maintaining the *Almuria* was as fine a ship as he'd seen and Kitty should be proud of sailing on her, adding he only wished he was, by God.

Kitty fell silent for a few seconds while his alcohol-soaked brain laboriously worked out the possibilities that had just come to him.

Finishing his screwtop, he threw it into the water. 'Want me to try and get you a job tomorrow when I report on board?' he asked in a slurred voice.

Angus blinked. Here was something that bore consideration.

'I don't know if there's anything going, but it wouldn't hurt to ask,' Kitty said, a huge, sloppy grin plastered all over his face.

'Why the hell not!' Angus exclaimed, thinking he'd rather do anything than be forced into going to Newcastle. It was just he hated the thought of having to comply totally with Sir Alan's manipulations.

'You serious?'

'Never more so.'

'Then I'll ask the morn.'

Angus put his arm round Kitty's shoulders. The idea of going to sea with his old china really appealed and he said so.

Laughing, the pair of them headed in the direction of the nearest boozer.

'Do either of you fellows have the time?'

Angus giggled and was about to make a negative reply when suddenly the tart's face was caught in a shaft of light from a nearby ship. He frowned, thinking she looked familiar, and then with a shock it dawned on him just who it was.

'Sheena?'

They stared at one another, then uttering a cry she flew into his arms.

'I'm sorry,' she whispered. 'I didn't know it was you.'

With a sad shake of his head he told her it didn't matter. Then he suggested they go for a drink over which she could tell him everything that had happened to her. They were lucky enough to find an empty table at the back of the pub. Sheena told them she'd gone to London when she'd left Holmlea Road. Work had been almost as difficult to find there as it had been in Glasgow and for a while she'd lived pretty rough. Sally Ann hostels. Rowton Houses. And even Battersea Park.

From London she'd gone to Cardiff where one night in Tiger Bay she'd been forced – as a means of survival, she said emphatically – to cash in on her one asset.

Angus stared into his drink, shocked by this revelation and feeling somehow guilty as though he was partly to blame.

He then asked her the question that had been bothering him all this time. Why had she upped so suddenly and left Holmlea Road?

Her eyes clouded as she told him she'd known it was only a matter of time before Archie forgot himself and under the influence did something they'd both regret for the rest of their lives.

'Jesus!' said Kitty.

With a shrug Sheena added, 'He was always a randy sod as you well know Angus. And with Carrie in hospital and you over in Tallon Street that left just him and me. It would have been inevitable.'

Far too soon time was being called. Having found Sheena Angus didn't want to let her go again. At least not yet. So he suggested Kitty make his own way back to Holmlea Road while he went on to Sheena's place as he had a lot more to talk over with her.

The tenement Sheena took him to was tall, dirty and cankerous. There were three other females sharing the house with her and all of them were on the game plying the dockside trade.

The room itself was neat and tidy and smelled strongly of Sheena, a smell that brought a host of half forgotten memories flooding back into his mind.

Sheena had an almost full bottle which she produced from behind a fancy cushion bearing the legend 'A Present From Shangai' embroidered on its front.

For a while she spoke about herself and then in a quiet, sympathetic voice asked him what his problem was. She'd always been able to read his face like the proverbial book and had known since early on in the pub something was bothering him.

They talked and drank into the small hours and then when there was nothing left to be said or excuses to be made they went to the well-used bed jammed hard up against one wall. They stripped and made love.

He cried out once but it was Rosemary's name which burst from his lips and not Sheena's.

He came apart then, and mercifully screened by the all enveloping darkness, cried his heart out while she stroked and soothed him.

If he'd searched far and wide he wouldn't have found a better comforter than his step-sister who'd loved him since he was a baby.

Two days later Angus, with case in hand, opened his front door bound for the Govan Docks. Kitty had come up trumps in securing him a stoker's job.

He'd left his money box with Carrie, his instructions being she was to open a bank account in her name which she could draw on if she needed to, or if she decided to buy the house they'd so often talked about and which had long been his obsession.

Her parting present was his father's black leather wallet with the initials J.McB. in faded gold lettering on its front.

What Angus didn't know was the previous day Carrie had been to see Dr Robertson for the results of her latest tests. Her TB was active once more.

With a final kiss on the landing, he was running downstairs with Carrie calling after him, 'Look after yourself, son and mind the company you keep!'

'I will, Ma!' he yelled back. 'And you look after

yourself too!'

Carrie smiled grimly at that. Turning, she shuffled back into the house to make out a list of all the things she would need to take with her to the sanatorium.

Part III

The Digger's Dream
1942–1944

14

Physically Angus had changed considerably during the four years he'd been at sea. Long hours working with the shovel had filled him out and now iron hard muscles rippled where once there had been only boyish skin and bone.

There were three of them in the boiler room and they worked stripped to the waist. Lowest on the totem pole was a young lad called Sanderson whose job it was to trim the coal. Angus was stoker, Kitty steam boss.

The ancient *Almuria* was having to steam continually at full speed to keep up with the rest of convoy PQ 17, and consequently was threatening to shake herself apart in the process.

They'd set sail from Reykavik in Iceland heading north for Jan Mayen Island and Bear Island, beyond which they were scheduled to turn onto a southeast course that would bring them down through the Berens Sea into the White Sea and their destination, Archangel.

PQ 17 was carrying vital supplies to help save Stalingrad.

Angus and Kitty sat on a pile of coal and lit up. Both were too tired to indulge in unnecessary conversation so they savoured their cigarettes and thought fondly of their bunks.

The hatch to the boiler room burst open and a greaser called Hay came rushing in to relate breathlessly that a signal had been received on board – the convoy was to scatter. Furthermore, their Royal Navy escort was to withdraw westward at high speed.

Both Angus and Kitty exclaimed aloud on hearing this news. It could only mean the pocket battleship, *Tirpitz*, had set sail from her lair in Norway's Trondheim Fiord. For the convoy to be told to scatter as opposed to disperse must mean the *Tirpitz* was almost upon them.

But why had their escort been instructed to proceed westward when the *Tirpitz* would be approaching from the southeast?

The penny dropped simultaneously. The Admiralty didn't intend losing any more of its warships by sending them up against far superior firepower which could only result in their annihilation.

PQ 17 had been abandoned to face the full fury of the pride of the German Navy.

'My God!' whispered Angus.

Hay fled the boiler room, shouting over his shoulder he would keep them informed of any fresh developments.

Soon the coal was flying as the *Almuria* made its bid for survival by veering onto a fresh course that would take it to the Russian Islands of Novaya Zemla. The *Almuria's* captain had chosen this heading because he judged it to be in the completely opposite direction to the course the *Tirpitz* must be coming up on.

Shortly afterwards in the wireless room, the operator bent to his task as the stories started flooding in. The scattering convoy was already in deep trouble although the *Tirpitz* hadn't yet been sighted.

Aboard the *Bolton Castle* the ship's gunners were busy firing at circling Focke-Wulfs and Shads when suddenly a Stuka came seemingly from nowhere to straddle the ship from port to starboard, obtaining a direct hit.

To those watching from nearby ships it seemed the *Bolton Castle* virtually disintegrated, although, incredibly, the ammunition she was carrying didn't explode.

Aboard the *Paulus Potter* her British gunners kept

attacking planes at bay until for a third time a stick of bombs dropped close to the ship. Earlier misses had sprung her plates and shifted her engines but these latest bombs blew the ship's rudder off and damaged her propeller. The order was quickly given to abandon ship.

As the afternoon wore on a mist appeared and with it fresh waves of German planes.

The deadly U-boats had also put in an appearance, their torpedoes soon notching up an ever increasing toll.

But where was the *Tirpitz*? That was the question on everyone's lips as they anxiously watched the southeast.

Alarm bells suddenly clamoured throughout the *Almuria* and a lookout was frantically pointing at five torpedo planes flying in on the starboard bow. Oerlikons and Bofors started up as one of the planes peeled off to begin its run into attack.

The plane seemed to stagger in mid-air as direct hits were scored on it. But seconds before it broke in two it dropped a single torpedo which ran straight and true for the *Almuria*.

'Hard a starboard!' hissed the captain on the bridge. Moments later the old lady began to swing agonizingly slowly in that direction.

The same lookout who'd first spotted the plane stood watching goggle-eyed as only a few feet away the torpedo ran on a parallel course with the *Almuria*. But the ship had completed its successful evasive manoeuvre and the torpedo was gone.

Down in the boiler room Angus, Kitty and Sanderson were force feeding their complaining charge in an effort to try and wheedle a few more knots out of the old lady who was sorely resenting their exertions.

Hay reappeared with a bottle of whisky in his hand saying he'd been saving it for a special occasion. But he thought he'd better drink it now as he might never get another chance to do so.

Angus gulped down a belter and rifted. He passed on the bottle before crossing to his jacket. From his inside pocket he took his father's old black leather wallet.

The clipping was yellow and faded, the face staring back at him one he'd always see clearly in his mind till his dying day.

Below the blurred photograph of the happy bride and groom was an account of the wedding reception held in the groom's house in Carmunnock.

Less than a year after he'd gone to sea she'd married the chap he'd watched her kissing that day her father had contrived to fire him. Her married name was Mrs Iain McLaren.

It was Carrie who'd cut the photo and attendant story from the *Glasgow Herald* and sent it to him with a note saying she thought he should see this.

Carrie had been in Bellfield Sanatorium at the time, her second incarceration lasting eighteen months.

But Angus didn't know that. At Carrie's insistence the pretence had been kept up she was fit and well, and life in Holmlea Road was carrying on as normal.

Angus was still staring morosely at the newspaper clipping when there was an explosion aft which knocked everyone in the boiler room off their feet.

The whisky bottle went spinning from Hay's hand to crash against the bulkhead where it shattered.

'We're hit!' Kitty yelled, and came to his feet to discover the ship was listing badly.

Tottering, he staggered for the hatch with the rest of them close behind.

'Torpedo's blown the arse right off her!' a frantic seaman shouted.

There was a second explosion aft and the lights started to flicker and go out one by one. The air was filled with screams and curses as terrified men battled their way up from the lower decks. Kitty stumbled and would have fallen if Angus hadn't caught him by the shoulders. 'Thanks mate,' Kitty gasped.

Then the pair of them ran for another hatch beyond which was the sea deck.

The *Almuria* was heeled over at about a thirty degree angle. The great heartbeat of the engines suddenly stilled and in that moment the grand old lady died. All that remained now was the internment which would follow hard upon the death.

Angus blinked as he burst into bright daylight. Running to the guard rail, he peered over to see a lifeboat and raft filled to overflowing already about twenty yards away. Further down the ship men were leaping overboard.

Turning to tell Kitty there was nothing left for them to do but jump, he found himself alone.

Swearing volubly, he scrambled over the guard rail, and ran along the black painted hull. Reaching the point where it curved away to the sea below, he jumped as far out as he could.

His feet knifed into the water and he went down and down into an inky blackness. His last surprised thought was the water wasn't nearly as cold as he'd expected. He was wondering why that should be when unconsciousness claimed him.

When he came to he was coughing and spluttering into Kitty's lap. There was the most awful taste in his mouth and breathing was excruciating. Every inhalation seeming to fan the inferno blistering the inside of his ribcage.

He took in the fact he was in a lifeboat with Kitty and four others. All of them he recognized as lower deck members.

Kitty used his sleeve to wipe Angus's mouth and while doing so informed him he'd swallowed some fuel oil from another ship sunk in the area.

When he heard that, Angus stared up at the gun metal sky convinced he was going to die. He'd heard fuel oil burned the lungs out and the poor bastards who'd swallowed the stuff died screaming in agony unless lucky enough to be shot through with pain killer.

He asked Kitty if there was a medical kit aboard, knowing from the expression on Kitty's face before his friend could reply what the answer was.

'We'll be picked up soon. You just wait and see,' Kitty

said with a smile. But there was no conviction in his voice.

While Angus tried to rest Kitty explained what had happened during those last few minutes aboard ship.

He'd seen the lifeboat they were now in bobbing for'ard and, running to investigate, had got himself out of Angus's line of sight. At that point Angus had jumped overboard.

Guessing what had happened, he'd rowed the boat round to where Angus would have entered the water to find him floating face up.

After another racking coughing fit, Angus said as he was going down he'd imagined the water to be warm which couldn't be so. And yet if it wasn't, why hadn't he frozen to death before Kitty reached him?

Kitty's reply was the water hereabouts was indeed warm which he could only think must be due to some vagary of the Gulf Stream.

Angus closed his eyes and wondered how long it would be before his pain became intolerable? He was still speculating when a black conning-tower broke surface on the lifeboat's starboard side.

The U-boat surfaced fully and several of its crew emerged to bring machine guns to bear on the lifeboat.

'Oh Christ!' said Kitty quietly, convinced they were about to be riddled with bullets.

The U-boat closed in on the now pitching lifeboat and as it did so an officer cupped a hand to his mouth and, in perfect English, yelled, 'What ship were you? And where were you bound?'

Those aboard the lifeboat glanced from one to the other but no one replied.

The German officer tried again, 'Why do you want to go to Russia? Are you Bolsheviks?'

One of the British seamen shook his head in reply which was the only answer to that line of questioning any of them were prepared to give.

The officer leaning from the conning-tower realized this and, with a wry smile, inquired if they had a compass on board?

It was Kitty who replied they hadn't and it was to him the compass was thrown which, despite the lifeboat's pitching, he deftly caught.

The same officer informed them in which direction land lay. Then he apologized for not being able to take any prisoners on board as he was already full.

In an incredibly short time the U-boat was once more submerged leaving the lifeboat yawing on waves created by its disappearance.

Time passed and they lost sight of the other lifeboat and raft which according to their compass had gone off southwards.

They took it in turns – with the exception of Angus – to row in the direction the German officer had told them was landfall. But as there was only one set of oars and they were all verging on the point of exhaustion progress was pitifully slow.

Hope of survival was fading amongst them when, in the early hours of the following morning, a grey warship was spied heading in their direction.

At first they thought she was German. But when she drew nearer and they saw her markings and the flags she was flying a ragged cheer broke out.

The ship was a destroyer called the *Wahroonga* belonging to the Royal Australian Navy.

When the watching sailors saw the state they were in more than a dozen Aussies clambered down the scrambling nets to help.

'You just give him here, sport,' a rangy Aussie said, taking Angus from Kitty.

Angus groaned as he was draped over the Aussie's shoulder.

Halfway up the nets a sudden spasm seized him causing him to spew the most evil looking mess down the Australian's back from where it spattered onto the destroyer's side.

Dimly Angus heard the *Wahroonga's* engines surge with power and then something cold and sharp was pressing into his arm.

He knew no more.

Lazily and reluctantly Angus allowed himself to drift awake. Still with his eyes closed he listened to the rhythmic beat of the engines, thinking the *Almuria* was sounding very different to what she normally did.

Then in a rush it all came back to him, including the fact the *Almuria* was at the bottom of the sea.

There was an antiseptic smell in the air and on opening his eyes he found himself staring up at a white bulkhead. Putting two and two together wasn't hard. He was in the *Wahroonga's* sick bay.

'Orderly, he's awake!' a thickly Australian accented voice called out from close by.

Turning his head, Angus found himself staring at a man about his own age grinning at him from the next bed. He and the man were the only patients in the sick bay.

'G'day how do you feel?' the man asked.

Before Angus could reply the door opened and the orderly entered. The orderly promptly repeated the question. Angus replied he'd felt better but certainly wasn't complaining. He was pleased just to find himself alive.

After the orderly had gone Angus turned back to the patient in the next bed who informed him his name was Sean O'Rourke from Sydney.

Angus introduced himself and asked if his shipmate Robin Kirkpatrick was all right.

With a laugh O'Rourke said Kitty had spent hours by Angus's bedside until ordered to his quarters for much needed sleep.

Angus then learned he'd been unconscious for nearly seventy-two hours.

The doctor, a middle-aged man, was greeted by O'Rourke with the words, 'Hello there, Tom. You're looking a bit crook yourself today.'

Angus was amazed at the informality between officer

and hand and was later to discover this was very much an Australian characteristic.

While examining him, Dr Speke told Angus he'd been extraordinarily lucky as the fuel oil he'd swallowed appeared to have been greatly diluted by its passage through the sea. And spewing as Angus had done while being carried up the *Wahroonga's* side had emptied his stomach of what fuel oil hadn't yet been absorbed into his system.

The summation of all this was Angus was going to live, although it would be some time before he was back on his feet again.

Before taking his leave Speke warned Angus against smoking stating it would probably take his lungs years to recover and to smoke in the meantime would merely be to court disaster

The look on Speke's face left Angus in no doubt as to what the outcome would be should he refuse to give up cigarettes. With a mental shrug he acquiesced. It was a small price to pay for his life.

After Speke had taken his leave Kitty came roaring in to throw his arms round Angus.

News of PQ 17 was bad. In fact, it was downright disastrous.

It wasn't yet known exactly how many of the convoy had been sunk. But piecing together the reports the *Wahroonga* had picked up if more than a handful of the thirty-one merchantmen had escaped it would be a miracle.

As for the *Tirpitz* it seemed she and the pocket battle-ship, *Scheer* had been sighted by a reconnaissance plane. But the time and place of the sighting made it impossible for either battleship to have been near PQ 17 when the Admiralty sent out the order for the escort to head west and the convoy to scatter.

Angus was appalled. For it surely meant the convoy had been abandoned prematurely if not unnecessarily.

'There must be facts we don't know about,' Angus said, to which Kitty raised his eyebrows and shrugged.

Angus's next question was where was the *Wahroonga* bound? And what was she doing in these waters operating on her own so far from the British battle fleet?

Kitty's reply was quite simply he hadn't been able to find out. He'd been summoned to see the *Wahroonga's* captain to whom he'd given full details of the *Almuria's* sinking. But on inquiring where and when the survivors could be expected to be put ashore Captain Tolman had become evasive, saying somewhat obliquely the *Wahroonga's* course and destination couldn't be disclosed at the present time.

All Kitty could add was there were some Russian civilians aboard and he guessed the *Wahroonga's* mission was somehow tied up with them.

Angus and Kitty looked questioningly at O'Rourke who promptly said he didn't know where they were headed for, nor did he even know where they'd been except it had been bloody cold there.

Kitty went on to say he'd been quartered in with the cooks with whom he was getting on handsomely. So far he hadn't been allotted any duties so he was taking life easy.

Angus asked O'Rourke why he was in the sick bay, to be told the Australian's legs had been machine gunned during a recent action. But more O'Rourke wouldn't say.

The next day they put into Reykavik where the *Wahroonga* was swiftly refuelled. But there was no shore leave allowed nor were any civilians, including the Port Authorities, allowed aboard.

Angus assumed he and the other survivors would be off-loaded here but he was wrong. When the *Wahroonga* sailed again they were still on board.

Angus concluded the *Wahroonga* must be headed for a British port but when an entire week passed bringing them into latitudes unmistakably southerly to Britain he had to accept that wherever else the Australian warship was headed it certainly wasn't Blighty.

When they passed the equator Dr Speke informed

Angus he could try walking now, but to take it easy for a while and not overdo things.

Angus discovered the great majority of Aussies were compulsive gamblers so a new way was found of passing the time by playing brag and pontoon.

It didn't take him long to realize he was a far cleverer gambler than the rest of the school. And this he set out to capitalize on, which he did with enormous success.

A number of times Angus and Kitty saw the Russian civilians, heavy set, broody men who stuck together and rarely spoke to anyone other than themselves. But the *Almuria*'s survivors were never introduced and it became an unspoken agreement between the British and Australians that the Russians were never approached or even referred to in conversation.

It was while steaming in the direction of St Helena that Kitty started having trouble sleeping at nights. So much sweat dripped off him, he commented, it was just like lying in a shallow bath. It forced him to get up and prowl the ship, sometimes talking to the night watch, other times sitting for'ard staring out to sea and enjoying whatever breeze there was.

During one such occasion he decided to go below and have a natter to his friends, the cooks, who were preparing the morning meal.

He didn't stay long as the galleys were indescribably hot but while there was offered an ice cold can of beer which he gratefully accepted.

Halfway through the beer he noticed an opened can of dill pickles which he fell upon, having an enormous passion for this delicacy.

When he left the galleys a little later the pickle can was empty.

Angus and O'Rourke were in the middle of their breakfast when Kitty entered the sick bay to sit between them. O'Rourke noticed Kitty was looking pale under his tan and mentioned the fact. Kitty replied he'd been feeling a little nauseous and lightheaded for the last half hour although he couldn't imagine why.

Thinking he was suffering from heat exhaustion, Angus suggested Kitty go back to his bunk and lie down. Even a number of the heat-hardened Aussies had succumbed, so brutal was the weather.

After some coaxing, Kitty agreed and with a wry, apologetic smile got to his feet and lurched from the room.

Angus called after the departing Kitty he would drop by the cooks' quarters later on to see how Kitty was feeling.

Then he and O'Rourke, having finished their breakfast, got the cards out as the off duty members of the gambling school would shortly be dropping by. Soon the incident faded from both their minds.

Lunch came and went till finally the game was abruptly halted – Angus having made his usual killing – by the arrival of Dr Speke to change O'Rourke's dressings.

While Speke was attending to O'Rourke Angus slowly walked the length of the ship, then descended several decks to where the cooks' quarters were situated.

He found Kitty fast asleep, curled into an embryonic position facing the bulkhead.

Kitty's breathing seemed regular enough so Angus decided the best thing to do was leave him sleeping until he awoke of his own accord.

That evening he checked on Kitty again but this time it was difficult for him to see properly as most of the cooks were already in bed which stopped him from putting on the light.

However, from what he could hear, Kitty's breathing was strong and regular so he decided to leave well enough alone.

The heat broke that night with an electric storm. To the accompaniment of far-off thunder, great, jagged streaks ripped the heavens apart. Then the rain came pounding down to lash the *Wahroonga* from stern to prow.

The next morning dawned blissful and quiet with only

an unaccustomed freshness in the air to remind those aboard the *Wahroonga* of the previous night's storm.

After breakfast Angus waited for Kitty. When he didn't appear Angus decided to go below to see if he was still feeling ill.

The moment he placed his hand on Kitty's arm he knew something was dreadfully wrong. Grabbing Kitty by the shoulders, Angus heaved, causing him to flop over onto his back.

Angus stared down at the mottled face and glazed eyes. He knew his friend was dead. It was unbelievable. Yet there was the gruesome evidence before his eyes.

'Oh Kitty what happened, son?' he said, laying a hand on his friend's icy cheek.

For a while he sat thinking back over the many good times he and Kitty had shared together since meeting on his first day at Holmlea Road Primary. The fights where they'd fought side by side. The adventures they'd had. Running with the milk. Going out as a foursome with Rosemary and Diane. Secrets shared. Money loaned and borrowed. Laughter.

Kitty had been as close to him as a brother. Closer in some ways. And now he was gone. Blown away like so much chaff in the wind.

With tears in his eyes, Angus rose and went looking for Dr Speke.

Kitty was buried at sea that afternoon. His body was weighted and wrapped in canvas, draped with the Union Jack, and after Captain Tolman had spoken a few words from the Bible, dropped overboard.

When Angus got back to the sick bay after the funeral he found a double tot of grog and a sympathetic O'Rourke waiting for him. He drank off the rum and then sat silently on his bed waiting for Dr Speke to come and tell him the results of the autopsy carried out on Kitty's body before it had been committed.

Speke arrived to say his findings were that Kitty had

died from a severe dose of food poisoning in which there had been complications.

Just what these complications were exactly Speke didn't know. As he explained to Angus, he didn't have the equipment on board to carry out the tests for their analysis.

What had been established was the pickles Kitty had eaten were at fault. Samples taken from his stomach had shown them to be toxic in the extreme, probably due to a combination of the severe heat and their being left in the can.

Incredulity was stamped all over Angus's face as he slowly shook his head in disbelief. To think what Kitty had been through since the start of the war, including the PQ 17 debacle and the sinking of the *Almuria*. To end up dying because of some stupid pickles!

It was farcical. A grisly joke no one, least of all Kitty, was laughing at.

15

It was nine pm on a Friday night and Carrie knew she was going to be in for another bad time. Archie should have been home hours ago but as he hadn't yet appeared she could only assume he'd gone to the boozer.

Pay night was just another excuse for Archie who since having returned to the drink was now worse than he'd ever been.

He continually complained of pains in his arms and legs but refused to go and see Dr Robertson to find out what was wrong with him. Instead he consumed more and more alcohol, claiming only drink deadened the pain.

And of course the more bevy he put away the more impossible he was to live with, the beatings he constantly dished out more violent and brutal than they'd ever been in the past.

Sighing, Carrie rose and crossed to the oven to have yet another look at his tea which she was trying to keep warm.

Thinking she would make some fresh gravy to try and keep the meal moist she put on the kettle and then returned to her chair in front of the fire.

Carrie was a changed woman since Angus had left Glasgow to go to sea. Her hair was prematurely white while her face had become permanently gaunt and haggard. But the biggest change was in her body, which was skeletal.

The last incarceration in Bellfield Sanatorium had done the trick of completely curing her TB. But what a price had been exacted! It was as though all her bodily juices had been bled from her, leaving her a walking talking shadow of her former self.

She must have dozed off for suddenly she started awake to hear the kettle whistling and Archie's key scraping in the lock.

Her heart sank the moment he lurched into the room. He was so drunk he could hardly stand up.

Just inside the door he stood swaying for a few seconds before staggering to the table and collapsing onto a chair. In a slurred voice he demanded to know where in the hell his fucking tea was?

It was too late now to make gravy. So she switched off the kettle and placed the meal, dry as it was, before him.

Archie prodded it with his fork while muttering under his breath. With a snort he threw the fork onto the plate, then thrust it all to one side.

Taking the initiative – a ploy that sometimes worked – Carrie asked him what he expected when he came rolling in hours after he was supposed to get home? It was hardly her fault his meal was in such a state and why didn't he away through . . .

Her voice was drowned as, with a roar, Archie snatched up the plate and threw it at the wall where it smashed into smithereens leaving a gooey mess sliding floorward.

Carrie blinked and then hastily retreated. Turning, she ran, intending to pick up her coat in the hall and make for Tallon Street. But she never even reached the kitchen door as Archie was too quick for her.

She gasped as his hand grabbed her shoulder. Then she screamed as he threw her roughly against the wall.

'No Archie! Please!' she pleaded to no avail. His balled fist homed in on her shrunken right breast.

'Fuckin' no use bitch!' he spat. He hit her again, this time on the left breast.

What followed was a nightmare for Carrie as his fist thudded time and time again into her defenceless body.

With a cry she fell to the floor while he crouched above her.

Looking up she had difficulty in focusing and his leering face swam as though she was viewing hit through several feet of water. Both her eyes had been hit with solidly connecting punches.

Archie was suddenly limp inside, the anger momentarily burned out of him. He hurried to the bathroom where he was hideously sick.

Carrie whimpered as she rolled onto her knees and then struggled to her feet. In the hall she tugged her coat from its peg and, heaving it round her shoulders, somehow got herself through the doorway and down the stairs.

It was Mrs Kirkpatrick who found her slumped at the close mouth.

'Oh, hen!' Mrs Kirkpatrick whispered sympathetically when she saw the state Carrie was in.

Carrie rubbed her eyes but it didn't help. Her vision was still blurred and out of kilter. In a croaky voice she asked Mrs Kirkpatrick to help her to Tallon Street.

Taking one of Carrie's arms Mrs Kirkpatrick hooked it round her shoulders and that way the two of them staggered down the road.

Harriet was making her weekly visit to her parents' house and it was she who opened the front door to Mrs Kirkpatrick's frantic knocking. Exclaiming in horror, Harriet helped Mrs Kirkpatrick take Carrie through to the living room where Winnie and Big Donald were sitting by the fire.

Winnie's hand went to her mouth when she saw Carrie. Then she was on her feet helping Harriet and Mrs Kirkpatrick seat Carrie in the chair she'd just vacated.

Big Donald was frozen with shock, sickened by the dreadful state Carrie was in. Her two enormous black eyes puffed out even further as he watched.

'Archie?' he asked, his voice cracking with anger.

'Oh Papa!' Carrie mumbled. Turning to Winnie she buried her head in her mother's skirt.

Donald decided this had gone far enough. When his daughter came home in this condition it was high time for something drastic to be done.

He strode from the room to the kitchen where he groped in the coal bin for the heavy hammer kept there.

He was slipping it into his trouser pocket when Carrie supported by Harriet appeared beside him.

'No, Papa. He's not worth it,' Carrie said through a slash of bloodless lips. 'I'm leaving him anyway. Tonight was the finish.'

For a few moments Donald was undecided. Then he nodded. 'Away ben and I'll be through,' he said. But before Carrie could turn to leave the kitchen he swept her into his arms and hugged her close. It was a massive demonstration of emotion from a man rarely given to showing his feelings.

After Mrs Kirkpatrick had left Carrie was given a hot bath and helped into some clothes of Winnie's.

It worried her she'd left behind Angus's money box still containing most of what he'd left her – she never had got round to opening a bank account – behind in Holmlea Road.

If she was going to be on her own from here on she was going to need that money to support herself until she was able to sort things out and get a job.

Convinced Archie would be dead to the world by now in a drunken stupor she was all for returning to Holmlea Road, but when she told the others of her intention they ganged up on her saying she was in no fit state to make the journey there and back.

The last thing any of the women wanted was for Donald to go, so it was decided Harriet would get the money box.

Harriet's heart was in her mouth as she climbed the stairs her sister had fled down a little earlier.

She listened at the door before inserting Carrie's key in the lock. Quietly the door swung open.

Every light in the house was blazing while from the bathroom came the most terrible stench of sick. She put the door on the latch and tiptoed through to the bedroom where she found Archie sprawled across the bed snoring like the drunken pig he was.

Excitement tied Harriet's stomach up in knots as she took various items of clothing from the wardrobe and chest of drawers and packed them in a suitcase.

Archie moved once, suddenly rolling from one side to the other. But after a snort and cough his snoring became regular again.

Closing the suitcase Harriet stole from the room.

She laid the suitcase by the front door, then turning back went into the bedroom that had once been Angus's. The money box was hidden inside the cabinet of an old broken gramophone player.

Tiptoeing back to the front door, she reopened the suitcase and stuffed the money box inside.

Relieved at having successfully accomplished her mission she was just about to close the door behind her when she remembered seeing a framed picture of Angus in his bedroom and thought it was surely something her sister would want.

Leaving the suitcase outside on the landing she quietly made her way back to Angus's bedroom.

The moment she picked up the picture she knew she wasn't alone. Whirling around, she discovered Archie standing swaying in the doorway.

His face cracked into a grin as he grabbed hold of the door handle to steady himself. Without taking his eyes from her he shut the door behind him and stood with his back to it.

Harriet knew there was no use pleading to Archie's better side. In his present state he didn't have one.

'Shite but you're ugly!' he said, tilting his head to one side to watch her reaction.

He'd always wanted to hurt and humiliate Harriet for no other reason than she was the type of woman who provoked that sort of reaction in him.

Slowly and with great emphasis he began to unbuckle his belt.

'Don't be stupid!' Harriet snarled as Archie advanced on her. 'I'm your wife's sister, man!'

Archie took no heed as he contrived to steer her into a corner.

Suddenly he pounced and she was in his arms. Silently they struggled, landing on Angus's bed.

Even before they'd stopped bouncing his hand was up her skirt tugging at her knickers.

His breath was hot and smelly, his chin a strip of sandpaper threatening to rip the skin from her face. 'You bastard!' she spat.

Strong hands clamped themselves on her rear. Then before she'd realized what his intention was she'd been flipped over and a forearm was pushing her shoulders down into the mattress.

Penetration was quick, savage and incredibly painful.

Later that night feeling utterly defiled and degraded Harriet lay in bed staring wide-eyed at the ceiling.

When she'd returned to Tallon Street she'd been able

to carry it off saying Archie had been dead to the world just as Carrie had said he'd be.

She'd desperately wanted to confide what had happened to her. But that hadn't been possible.

One breath of it to Donald and he would kill Archie. She had no doubt whatever about that. Nor could she speak to her mother who would be bound to tell her father.

That left Carrie but how could she tell her own sister when Archie was Carrie's husband? Carrie's cross had been hard enough to bear without her adding to it.

Nor was there anyone else she could confide in about so intimate a matter.

'Oh Lou!' she whispered. Feeling more alone than she'd ever done in her life, she wept long and bitterly.

In the summer of 1943 Hugh came home on leave.

It was a beautiful day, fresh and clear with a hint of salt wind blowing in from the coast.

It was his first trip home since enlisting and he'd been looking forward to it for months now, ever since it had first been whispered in the mess that a leave was on the cards.

He was humming as he turned into the drive leading up to the Paterson house.

For a brief moment he stopped to stare fondly at the house which looked just grand and exactly as he remembered it. Then he was striding forward hoping Greta was home.

She was. With a great cry of delight she flew into his arms where he birled her round and round.

She took him away through to the kitchen where she put the kettle on and brought out the special home made shortie.

Pouring the tea, she suddenly stopped to stare proudly at him sitting in Aly's old chair. His various flashes and badges proclaiming him a sergeant in the Highland Light Infantry.

He was smiling and laughing a lot but there was something in his eyes which hadn't been there before. She'd seen a similar look in men's eyes after the Great War. Once acquired, the look was never lost.

Hugh was eager to be brought up to date on what was happening in the dairy and on the farm, which Stewart had won exemption to stay behind and run.

'And how is Stewart, the old sod?' he asked.

Greta opened her mouth to reply but no words came. She covered her face as great racking sobs were wrenched from her.

Instantly Hugh was by her side, cooing words of comfort and holding her close while she sobbed onto his shoulder.

Her body shook as she told him Stewart and his entire family – his wife and the three children – were all dead.

'How?' Hugh asked in a whisper.

Greta's hands twined and intertwined as she told the story. Just over a month earlier a German bomber had either got lost or funked the attack which had done so much damage to Clydebank that night. Or perhaps the plane had been damaged and unable to continue.

Anyway, the pilot had decided to jettison his load and return to base.

The house and everyone in it had gone up in one enormous, blinding flash seen for miles in all directions. No trace of any of the bodies had ever been recovered.

Hugh listened to all this in silence. Suddenly the day outside wasn't so bright any more.

Greta had another bubble and while she did he whispered various things he hoped might bring her a little consolation.

When Greta had got hold of herself again she washed her face. Then the pair of them went outside.

What was worrying Hugh was with Stewart gone Greta was having to manage the entire kit and caboodle on her own. But she put his mind at rest saying she had some excellent lads working for her. And then there was Mr KcKeand and Mr Farquharson, two retired farmhands who were proving to be a big help in looking after the cows.

In fact Greta was pleased she had the work to occupy her – she was going out in the lead cart herself every morning – it kept her from brooding too much on what had happened.

Inside the stables Hugh inhaled the well remembered smell he'd missed so much. It was the rarest perfume to him.

Returning to the house Greta took Hugh round the side to the make-shift garage where he found his Wolseley Hornet, resprayed black after the Francey affair. It was a little dusty but otherwise in excellent condition.

Petrol was rationed but Greta had managed to save quite a bit from the dairy's allocations. This she'd stored at the back of the garage in tins.

Showing Hugh where the cache was she told him to see he enjoyed himself while his leave lasted.

She hurried away in the direction of the back door.

The one o'clock hooter had just finished sounding as Donald slipped out of Armstrong's and headed in the direction of home.

He'd only gone a few yards when a motor drew up beside him and a voice said, 'Would you like a lift, Papa?'

Big Donald's gaze swept over Hugh, taking everything in. 'Aye. That would be grand right enough, son,' he replied.

When he was comfortably seated he and Hugh solemnly shook hands.

They found Winnie in the kitchen. She laid down the spoon she'd been using and carefully wiped her hands before taking Hugh in her arms and holding him to her.

'When are you going away again then, son?' she asked.

Hugh laughed. 'You might let me get my foot in the door before you ask me that,' he joked.

'Ach ye ken fine what I mean,' Winnie replied, wiping

her nose with her pinny. She was desperately trying not to cry.

Carrie would be home in a few minutes, Donald informed Hugh. He went on to tell him about the Archie Marjoribanks business and how Carrie, having returned to Tallon Street determined to make her own way, had landed a job back at Balogie Clothing as a supervisor, the same position Jakey Sanderson had once held. Jakey like all the other men who'd been employed at the factory was off fighting.

According to Donald, Carrie had been made supervisor because it had been recognized she wasn't up to handling a heavy sewing machine any more. This, coupled with the fact she had previous experience of the factory and was a lot older than the majority of girls currently employed there, had made her the ideal choice for the vacant position.

As things turned out, it had been an inspired placing as Carrie was one of the most popular and efficient supervisors the factory ever had.

While they ate Hugh told his parents about what had happened to Stewart Paterson and his family.

'Those poor weans,' Winnie said and sadly shook her head.

Donald said Sandy and Mary were also dead, Sandy having passed away in his sleep and Mary succumbing a few months after him from a heart attack.

The door opened and Carrie entered.

For a moment Hugh failed to recognize his sister; her new thick pebble glasses somehow completely altered her appearance.

Although she was drawn and haggard, there was a light-hearted expression on her face he couldn't recall seeing there since those far off days when John McBain had been alive.

Brother and sister embraced, both genuinely pleased to see one another.

For the rest of the dinnertime Carrie kept them in stitches recounting the trials and tribulations of working for Ballogie Clothing.

As the dishes were being cleared Winnie asked Hugh if he'd be wanting the front room while he was home on leave? A flash of pain flitted across her face when he replied he'd be staying out at Muirend.

Seeing her disappointment, he muttered he planned going out with the milk in the mornings, and as there was a great deal to be done round the dairy it was just as well for him to be there close at hand.

With dinnertime over Hugh elected to drive Carrie round to Balogie Clothing where he deposited her at the front door amidst a gaggle of giggling girls.

He then parked the Wolseley and went for a stroll round old familiar streets and places. As he walked he soaked up the Glasgow atmosphere he'd missed so much.

Presuming he came out of the war intact the last thing he wanted was to leave Glasgow. And yet if things turned out as he planned he might well have to.

For hours he walked the streets of Cathcart and Battlefield, biding his time till five o'clock when he returned to the Wolseley and drove to Thistle Street. He parked in front of Janey McIver's close.

He knew from their correspondence she was generally on her way home from work at this time so he lit a cigarette and sat back to wait.

It wasn't long before he saw her familiar shape walking up the street towards him.

She must have been preoccupied for she didn't notice the car and would have turned directly into her close had he not leaned out and said, 'Hello Janey.'

As recognition flooded her face, her mouth dropped open in astonishment. 'Hugh!' she exclaimed excitedly.

Immediately he was out of the car and at her side, and not giving a damn who was watching, he took her in his arms and kissed her.

They moved into the relative privacy of the close mouth where he asked how long it would take her to get ready to go out for a hurl in the car?

In a trembling voice, she said she would need ten

minutes to change. She was back in five.

Once she was seated beside him a feeling of completeness settled on Hugh, dispelling any doubts he might have had. Janey was the woman for him all right. Together they were a couple.

During the drive he told her where they were going and why. On reaching the farm, Hugh parked beside the barn. An old man appeared as though by magic and, remembering what Greta had told him earlier, he presumed this to be either Mr McKeand or Mr Farquharson. It turned out to be Mr McKeand.

Once he introduced himself Mr McKeand immediately relaxed, having heard all about him from Stewart and Greta in the past.

McKeand accompanied them over to where the house had stood. All that was left was a blackened pit filled with scorched bricks, pieces of burnt wood and some lumps of melted metal.

Hugh squatted and silently did what he'd come to do – pay his last respects.

Mr McKeand went off to attend to some matter concerning the cattle so Hugh showed Janey round the farm.

It was a fine evening and as the gloaming came upon them Janey told Hugh that sad as the circumstances were, she was enjoying this breath of fresh air.

With the wind blowing in her hair and bringing a flush to her cheeks Janey looked as though she might have been born to the country. Hugh's heart swelled at the thought of spending the rest of his days with her in an environment similar to this one. He envisioned the pair of them surrounded by an enormous family of boys, happy as two pigs in the proverbial muck.

He lit cigarettes and placed one between her lips. Then straight out he asked if she'd marry him?

Janey caught her breath, momentarily thrown by the abruptness of the proposal.

Collecting herself, she said she had no doubts at all

about what she felt for him. But what about the old brick wall that had always loomed between them in the past?

Hugh's eyes took on a faraway look. He began to talk about some of the things he'd experienced on active service.

He spoke of the men he'd known, all types, shapes, sizes and religions, including a Buddhist who had been a real eye opener for him.

Men with whom he'd shared life and death. Men of many background from all over the world whom he'd seen at their glorious best as well as their worst.

Hugh groped for words. He wasn't a particularly articulate person but he managed to put over to Janey what he'd come to realize.

When you were in a tight spot and a man braved his life to save yours it didn't matter if he was a Protestant or Catholic. What did matter was he'd laid his life on the line for you.

When a man lay dying with both legs blown away it didn't matter what religion he was. You gave him what relief and comfort you could.

When you hadn't tasted water for days it didn't matter what religion the man was who offered you a swallow from his canteen. You accepted and were grateful.

Catholic and Protestant. *The Sash My Father Wore.*
The Soldier's Song. Rangers and Celtic. He had no time any more for that sort of bigoted nonsense. He'd finally come to see it in its true light.

Janey replied that might be so, but it didn't alter the fact this was Glasgow and here such things were given enormous importance.

For a Protestant to marry a Catholic was just asking for trouble and in a halting voice she said so.

Hugh sighed. He wanted Janey as his wife and was prepared to do almost anything to get her, even becoming a Catholic.

She came into his arms and they kissed. She said it wasn't necessary for him to turn his coat as long as he agreed she could continue as a practising Catholic and their children be brought up as such.

Hugh had already considered this alternative and rejected it. He thought it best in the long run for their children if the entire family belonged to the same religion.

He went on to say when the war was over, should they run into any unpleasantness, he was quite prepared to go abroad and start a new life where such things were of less significance.

'And how about your family? How are they going to take it?' Janey asked.

Hugh pulled a face and admitted he was expecting the worst, from his father in particular, but that was something he would have to face and live with.

As they walked back to the Wolseley Hugh wondered what God in His heaven thought of what the Protestants and Catholics and many other religions and branches thereof did in His name. If He had a sense of humour He must be laughing at the sheer hypocrisy of it all. When He wasn't weeping in despair, that was.

16

Sir Alan Armstrong lay back in the plush interior of his Rolls and drew with great satisfaction on a very large Cuban cigar.

He'd just concluded a deal which now made him the biggest single property owner in the Gorbals.

He smiled as the smoke blackened tenements flicked by. When the war was over there was bound to be a building boom. There certainly would be if he had anything to do with it.

He'd kick out the slummies, raze the tenements, and then build for the type of tenant who'd once lived there when the Gorbals had been a superior class of district.

The idea was his brainchild entirely, and one which was going to make him an enormous pile of money.

His enjoyment faded at the thought of the small family supper he was now on his way to attend – once he'd picked up Cordelia from Arnprior House – out at Bearsden where Iain and Rosemary lived.

They'd only been living at Bearsden a few weeks when Iain had announced he'd joined the RAF, a move everyone who knew him at all well had been expecting him to make.

Thinking of Rosemary's marriage brought Angus McBain back to Sir Alan's mind. Rosemary's initial pique at finding herself discarded had quickly given way to anger which in turn had been transplanted by the most awesome fury. In such a state she had been putty in his hands and it hadn't been long before she and Iain were engaged.

It hadn't been a long engagement. He'd seen to that. He'd wanted her wedded, bedded and with an offspring on the way before she regained her equilibrium.

Well he'd succeeded with two of his aims at least. The war and Iain's long partings from Rosemary had so far left the third unfulfilled.

The Battle of Britain had been a personal triumph for Iain: he'd emerged covered in glory and had been swiftly promoted to the rank of Squadron Leader.

After Spitfires he'd been transferred to Lancasters and from there he'd gone on to command a squadron of Mosquitoes. It was in one of these he'd very nearly been brought down by anti-aircraft fire over Caen.

From what Sir Alan had heard, the plane had been extensively hit but against all odds Iain had managed to bring it limping back across the Channel to crash land at his home aerodrome.

That had been a little over a year ago and since then

Iain had been hospitalized from the fearsome burns he'd sustained in the crash.

At first his life had been feared for, so bad were his injuries. But thanks to a great deal of dedicated nursing combined with superb work by the specialist involved he'd been able to pull through.

Iain was due home that evening. The small family supper was in his honour.

Rosemary sat staring into her vanity table mirror, scrutinizing her face which she'd stopped making up for the moment because her hands were shaking so badly.

She was wondering about Iain's face which she hadn't seen, except swathed in bandages, since the crash.

For the umpteenth time in the last hour she glanced at the bedside clock. His expected arrival was drawing inexorably closer. She'd wanted to go to the station to meet him but he'd vetoed that in his last letter saying he much preferred her waiting for him at home.

As she sat staring at herself she thought of the three times she'd been down to the nursing home in the Cotswolds – she'd have gone more often only Iain had been dead against it – where he'd been slowly nursed back to health. The last time the plastic surgeon had taken her aside for a little chat, as he'd called it.

According to him a great deal could be accomplished with plastic surgery but miracles were beyond them. They'd done their best and were pleased with the results. He hadn't elaborated further.

There was a crunching of gravel outside as a motor car arrived. Her mother and father's voices came wafting up. They'd hoped Diane would be able to accompany them but she'd phoned to say she couldn't make it as she had to be on duty. She was an ambulance driver with the ATS.

Hours after he should have done Iain still hadn't arrived and a sort of pregnant depression hung over those waiting as the minutes ticked relentlessly by.

Finally, with an exclamation of annoyance, Sir Hamilton rose to announce this was becoming ridiculous and he was going to ring the Central Station to find out the state of the trains.

Sir Alan poured more drinks in the hope of relaxing the tension holding them all as though they'd been collectively caught in a vice.

Sir Hamilton was frowning when he re-entered the room to say the person he'd spoken to had informed him that, although dreadfully late, Iain's train had arrived in an hour and a half ago. Rosemary began twisting her wedding ring.

'Listen!' said Sir Alan urgently when they caught the sound of a car pulling into the driveway.

All eyes swung to the door as footsteps echoed in the hall.

The door opened and Iain stood revealed. Rosemary's gaze was fixed on the buckle at his middle when she heard the involuntary gasp wrenched from Cordelia.

Slowly, reluctantly her eyes inched up his tunic to be arrested by his neck.

The flesh there was an angry red shot through with streaks of white giving it a sort of marbled effect. It took an almost superhuman effort to lift her gaze that little bit higher.

What caught and held her attention were his eyes. Cold and hard, they glittered like those of a snake. There was a chilling quality about them, so completely different from their previous liquidity.

There were no eyebrows above the eyes. Those had gone, leaving in their place twin lines of puckered scar tissue.

Large patches of skin were shiny yellow. Other areas glistened with the same red and white marbling effect as on his neck.

His cheeks had sunk right in leaving the bones above them jutting out.

He was mainly bald with only a few tufts of coarse hair sticking out here and there.

The overall impression was of a decomposing death's head.

Rosemary was only too aware that Iain was watching her, studying her reaction, waiting for her to say something.

She bludgeoned her numb brain to think of a few kind words. But nothing came. She was completely mesmerized by that death's head with its glittering snake's eyes.

As the silence began to lengthen Sir Alan realized something had to be done and quickly. Snatching up a glass, he poured a very large drink into it and walking swiftly across the room grasped Iain's hand which he vigorously pumped up and down, at the same time saying, 'It could have been worse, lad. At least you're alive. That's the main thing.' He then thrust the glass of whisky into the hand he'd been shaking.

The spell was broken. Lize was suddenly on her feet and rushing to Iain. Large, fat tears oozed from her eyes to run rolling down her face.

Striding across to his son, Sir Hamilton shook him by the hand but couldn't yet trust himself to speak.

Inwardly Rosemary was cursing the plastic surgeon for not giving her more of a warning. Burned and scarred, yes, that she'd been led to expect. But nothing like the horror now confronting her which was straight out of her most terrible nightmares.

She knew what she had to do next and the thought revolted her.

'Welcome home, Iain,' she said, and going up on her tiptoes, kissed the twin lines of scar tissue – identical to those where his eyebrows had been – that were all that remained of his lips.

Wryly Iain said, 'They tell me in time I'll get used to how I look but personally I doubt it.'

Sir Alan went round with the whisky bottle and no one even thought of refusing.

Now feeling in full possession of himself, Sir Hamilton asked Iain what had kept him as his train had arrived a considerable time before he'd shown up at the house.

Iain sipped his drink. Then in a peculiar unemotional voice he requested his mother and father sit as he had some rather bad news for them.

Staring into his glass, Iain went on to say he'd been informed by Sir Hamilton's chauffeur who'd met him off the train that shortly after Sir Hamilton and Lize had left for Bearsden a telegram had arrived in from the War Department. The chauffeur had learned of the telegram having rung Carmunnock on servants' business.

The reason for his further delay was that he'd taken it upon himself to go out to Carmunnock and open that telegram.

His voice remained completely unemotional when he said it was just as he'd feared. Peter who was also in the RAF had been shot down and killed.

Lize sobbed and bit her lower lip. Sir Hamilton's expression was one of complete devastation.

Rosemary thought of Diane who was in love with Peter and had been expecting to marry him when the war was over.

'There may be some mistake? Perhaps he was only shot down?' Lize said hopefully.

Iain shook his head. 'Peter's dead,' he said emphatically.

Collapsing, Lize sank sideways onto her husband's lap where her entire body convulsed with grief.

Sir Hamilton was so stricken by this new blow the best he could manage by way of attempted consolation were some half hearted pats on the back of Lize's head and a few mumbled words it was doubtful she even heard.

A little later their chauffeur took Sir Hamilton and Lize home. And shortly after their departure, the Armstrongs left also.

While Iain went upstairs with the remainder of the whisky bottle Rosemary stayed behind to tidy away a few odds and ends. Finally when she'd run out of excuses for remaining downstairs she took a deep breath and went up to her husband.

The bedroom was in darkness. Iain was sitting on a chair by the window which had its blackout curtains pulled fully back.

As she undressed he said it was perfect flying weather and round about now from all over Britain RAF bombers would be taking to the air and winging towards Germany.

Without changing tone and as though it was the same topic of conversation, he said he would understand perfectly should she want a divorce.

Rosemary's thoughts were whirling at this new turn of events. Here being handed to her on a platter was the perfect way out of what she considered to be their disastrous marriage.

She could remember only too well what had been going through her mind when Iain had proposed. By accepting, she'd imagined she was somehow getting back at Angus, hurting him the way he'd hurt her.

But the only person she'd hurt was herself – and Iain, should he ever find out the truth of why she'd married him.

Here was Iain proposing the divorce she so desperately wanted but with circumstances as they now stood she knew she wasn't going to be able to leave him.

Her original mistake was about to be compounded and there was nothing she could do about it, unless she was prepared to live the rest of her life with his blood on her hands.

That Iain was brave and courageous there could be no doubt. His exploits in the RAF spoke for themselves. But there are more more than one kind of bravery and courage.

If she was to falter now in what he believed to be her love for him she would be killing him as surely as if she'd presented him with a loaded pistol and told him to go ahead and use it.

Within days, perhaps even hours, of her leaving him he'd be dead. A suicide.

She was so certain of that she would have bet her own

life on it.

Here he was prattling on about divorce but in his heart of hearts he was praying she was going to say she would stay on with him.

She knew he didn't think she would. But optimist that he was he recognized there was a possibility she might and because of this had come home instead of killing himself in the nursing home.

She knew he wanted to be certain she was leaving him before he did the deed.

Goddamn you, Angus McBain! She raged inwardly. It's all your fault I'm in this impossible position. Why did you have to run off like you did? And where in hell's name are you now?

Her anger died as suddenly as it bloomed at the thought he, too, like Peter might be dead, a victim of the war.

Realizing Iain had stopped speaking she dragged her attention back to him.

Poor sod whose misfortune it was – apart from this latest tragedy of his face – to love a woman who didn't love him in return.

'Well?' he queried.

With that one word he was asking her whether he was to live or die.

'Come to bed,' she said, fixing a half smile on her face. Perhaps in time they both might get used to the way he now looked. But like him, she doubted it.

'Marry a Catholic!' Donald exploded.

Slowly he climbed to his feet from the chair he'd been slumped in. And as he did the years appeared to melt away from him till he was once more the awe inspiring figure Hugh remembered so vividly from his youth.

Winnie hovered nervously in the background, her eyes fastened on her husband as she waited to see what he was going to do. She was sick with worry for Hugh and terrified of what this might do to Donald who, despite his bravado and self-imposed heavy work schedule – and unknown to Hugh – hadn't been a well man of late.

Donald's nostrils flared, their thick projecting hairs thrilling like a flight of arrows.

'Marry a Catholic!' he said contemptuously. It was a preposterous idea and Hugh must be loony to even consider it. Mixed marriages never worked: they were doomed to failure from the very start.

Hugh's reply was the marriage wouldn't be a mixed one as he intended turning.

Donald caught his breath and for a split second it seemed he was going to stride forward and strike his son. But somehow – and the effort it took was both enormous and evident – he managed to restrain himself.

Picking up his pipe, he began packing it, a device he often employed when wanting time to think.

Hugh seized on this opportunity to try and explain to his father just how much the war had changed him.

Quietly he related to Donald the same experiences he'd told Janey about and how all these had combined to open his eyes about many things, not least of all the sheer ridiculousness and hypocrisy of the Glasgow religious situation.

When Hugh had finally finished there was a brooding silence in the room. It was broken by Winnie asking where he and Janey intended living?

Hugh replied Greta Paterson had insisted they stay with her as there was more than enough room in the big house for the three of them.

Being entirely practical, Winnie approved whole-heartedly of this arrangement.

Donald couldn't help but be impressed by the Hugh the war had moulded, seeing in his son many characteristics he'd always considered missing before. A lot of what Hugh said had struck home, making Donald think again about a lifetime's prejudice.

Donald also reminded himself that in these his twilight years, with Angus grown up, he wanted other grand-children to spoil and get close to.

But *Catholic* grandchildren! It was so completely against everything he'd always believed in and stood for. Winnie caught her man's eyes and silently pleaded with him to make his peace with Hugh – for her sake if nothing else.

It was probably the hardest decision Donald had ever made in his life.

It had hurt him deeply when he and Hugh had been estranged previously. And with a war on who knew what might happen?

He would never forgive himself, nor would Winnie forgive him, should Hugh be killed while sundered from his family. The very thought was unbearable.

They would talk about him at work, of course. That went without saying. See Big Donald Chisholm there. Did you know his son upped and married a fenian and went left footed himself? The bastard actually turned his coat! And they would spit in disgust to emphasize the point.

It would be bloody hard but somehow he'd find a way of living with it. He'd have to. For when it came right down to it he couldn't deny Winnie the only son she had left.

'So when do we get to meet this lassie of yours, then?' he asked.

Winnie's eyes shone when she heard that. Rising, she said she'd away through to the kitchen and put the kettle on. She managed to hold back the tears till she'd hurried from the room and shut the door behind her.

She couldn't remember when she'd been so happy.

When the time came for Hugh to return to his regiment his wife of ten days accompanied him to the station.

They held each other close to the very last minute. Hugh finally boarded the train. A whistle shrilled and the train jerked forward.

He hung out of the window, smiling, blowing kisses and feeling terrible.

Janey waved and waved till the train turned a bend

and disappeared from view.

Turning, she made her way back to the barrier, not yet aware her and Hugh's dearest wish had already been granted them.

She was carrying his child.

17

'Hot by name and hot by nature,' Angus said to the sweat slicked body of the woman he'd just been making love to.

Molly Hotblack laughed, a rumbling, sexual sound that came from deep within her magnificent chest.

Angus stared at her in open admiration. There was a wildness about her which fascinated and attracted him. She was fierce and dazzling like the landscape round the small Queensland township of Bundegai in which they now were. A sun woman who at the height of her passion literally blinded him.

He watched while she lit a cigarette and drew the smoke deep into her lungs. She didn't offer him: he'd given up that day aboard the *Wahroonga* when Dr Speke had told him either to finish with smoking or else it would finish with him.

The *Wahroonga* and Kitty, only a year ago and yet seemingly an eternity away. He never thought of Kitty but it brought a lump to his throat, as it did now.

Molly swung herself from the bed and ran her hands down her golden tanned thighs. Her long, auburn hair danced round her shoulders.

'A shower, I think, and then it's back to the slave mill,' she said.

'You don't have to go back to work again, do you?'

She shrugged. "Fraid so, I promised to cover for Gilly who's down with a crook tum.'

Angus pulled a face. He'd been hoping they'd have a bite together before he headed back for the digging. Usually when he came into Bundegai it was an overnight stop but this time it was merely a flying visit to pick up some provisions.

He put his hands behind his head and watched as she moved towards the bathroom.

'Leave the door open so I can watch you,' he called out.

'Voyeur!' she shouted back.

'Too right!' he replied, and they laughed, both knowing as far as she was concerned it was true. He could've sat for hours just staring at her naked body.

While Molly enjoyed her shower Angus's mind drifted back to the *Wahroonga* and all that had happened to him since the Australian warship had put him ashore at Sydney. For this had been their destination. Once there, the mysterious Russians had been hurried ashore and whisked off in an official looking car.

Angus had been kept aboard until visited by an Australian army major who'd sworn him in under the Official Secrets Act. It had been made crystal clear to him that if he ever so much as mentioned the Russians and the fact they'd been brought to Australia he'd spend the rest of the war behind bars. And from the look on the major's face he knew that to be no idle threat.

After the swearing in bit had taken place he and O'Rourke had been carted off to an ambulance which had taken them to a military hospital in the suburb of Homebush.

A great many tests had been carried out on him. At the end of the first fortnight he'd been taken aside and the news broken to him. His war was over, nor would he ever be fit enough to go back to sea.

What it all boiled down to was that his lungs had taken one hell of a beating from the fuel oil he'd swallowed and would never be the same again. From now on he had to take it fairly easy. Hard graft such as he'd become used to as a stoker was out. Any job he took would have to consist of light duties only.

It had been an awful blow to him but in his heart of hearts he'd been expecting something like that. After all, he knew you couldn't expect to swallow fuel oil and get away scot free. If anything, he'd been damned lucky and could only thank his lucky stars he'd spewed his guts up while being carried aboard the *Wahroonga*. If that hadn't happened Kitty wouldn't have been the only one to have died aboard the warship.

For three months he'd been in the hospital before being declared fit enough to be discharged.

By that time he and O'Rourke had become even thicker than before. And he'd been only too happy to accept O'Rourke's mother's invitation, Mrs Boo as she was called, to come and stay at the O'Rourke home overlooking Manly Beach.

Mrs Boo was an ancient, gnarled old biddy, tough as an old roo skin, according to O'Rourke. Angus came to think very highly of her.

There was no Mr Boo. He'd died some years previously. So with O'Rourke's return there were three of them in the dilapidated wooden house.

By the time O'Rourke was back home Angus had got fed up lying on the beach and generally passing his time doing nothing. So he'd got himself a job as a clerk with a local building firm.

He liked the job and having a quick, not to say inquisitive mind, was soon picking up a great deal about the building trade. So much so that the boss, a man called Bill Pettigrew who was another ex-patriate Glaswegian, took him under his wing. The two of them became good pals outside working hours, drinking together and Angus often visiting Bill's home.

Bill was desperately homesick, although with his new-found prosperity was sensible enough to know he'd never go back to Glasgow except perhaps on holiday after the war. For hours on end he and Angus would sit talking about their beloved city. After a while Bill came to look on Angus almost as a son.

When O'Rourke got home from the hospital Mrs Boo had held a cookout for him in the middle of which O'Rourke had announced his big news. Because of his wounds, he would walk with a limp for the rest of his life and he'd been honourably discharged from the Navy.

It was at that cookout O'Rourke had introduced Angus to Eric Petersson, an Australian of Scandinavian descent, who was pursuing what O'Rourke called 'the digger's dream'.

By rights, Petersson should've been in the armed forces but due to a stomach condition and poor eyesight he'd been rejected.

'Gold!' Petersson had said. 'I know it's up there on the western slopes of the Great Divide. When I was there last I could smell it.'

'Gold!' O'Rourke whispered, his eyes taking on a far away look.

Angus sat entranced as Petersson went on to talk about his two previous prospecting expeditions, the last of which he'd only returned from the week before.

'You're sure it's there?' Angus asked.

'It's there all right. You take my word for it.'

'Eric knows what he's talking about,' O'Rourke said. 'And so he should after the years he spent studying the subject at the university.'

'You're a geologist, then?'

Petersson nodded.

That fact impressed Angus considerably, elevating Petersson to something more than a mere story teller or enthusiastic amateur.

By the time the cookout was over the three of them were well drunk. Petersson said his goodbyes and slouched off.

Alone by the remains of the fire, Angus sat staring up

at the velvet sky thinking about what Petersson had told him.

'Gold!' he said in a voice that was a loving caress. The very word had a magic about it that made the hair at the nape of his neck stand on end.

And with the stars shining down on him he began to fantasize about what it would be like to become a prospector himself.

The next day after work he and O'Rourke went down to the pub for a couple of beers where he discovered it had been a yen of O'Rourke's for many years to go prospecting. In fact if it hadn't been for the war, O'Rourke would've already tried his hand at it.

By profession, O'Rourke was a sub-editor. His last position had been with the weekly *Bulletin* which was basically an outback paper. There was a job waiting for him there now but with his eyes gleaming he confided to Angus he had no intention of going back to spend the rest of his life poring over boring copy.

Angus finished his middy and ordered up another round. 'You're going to Queensland with Petersson, aren't you?' he said.

O'Rourke nodded.

Angus sipped his ice cold beer and studied his friend. 'If Petersson's so sure he knows where there's gold how come he's taking you along? Surely that must mean divvying up the profits?'

'Money, me old sport,' O'Rourke replied with a grin. 'Eric's right out of the stuff. His choice is simple: either he stays over in Sydney for some months putting a new grubstake together or else he takes himself a partner, one who can supply the wherewithal for them both to get going more or less straight away.'

Angus thought about the savings he had stashed. He'd managed to put some money by from his job as clerk and then there was still the bulk of his winnings from the card games aboard the *Wahroonga* – all in all a fair amount.

'Would you and Petersson consider taking me with

you?' he asked suddenly.

O'Rourke looked amused. He'd known this was coming. 'You'd need to put up your ante.'

'How much?'

O'Rourke mentioned a sum well within Angus's means and Angus replied that was fine by him.

'What about your health? I thought you couldn't do any hard work which is precisely what prospecting and mining are?'

Angus replied that was the one big fly in the ointment. Obviously he couldn't do any digging or anything like that. But surely there must be other lighter duties which would need attending to? It would be up to O'Rourke and Petersson to agree to it, of course, but if they would he would do everything that didn't include heavy manual labour.

O'Rourke laughed suddenly. 'Christ almighty, talk about three bloody cripples!' he said. 'You with your bad lungs, me with my gammy leg and Petersson with his rotten eyesight and stomach condition. What a three-some!'

Angus joined in the laughter. It was funny when you thought about it.

They saw Petersson later that day. He said if he was going to take one partner, then why not two? And anyway, the extra money would come in very handy indeed.

All three of them shook hands on it and Petersson produced a bottle of Corio whisky to cement their new partnership.

It took them several weeks to get everything sorted out and during that time Angus took an intensive course in driving. He passed his test first go.

Bill Pettigrew was most upset when Angus told him he'd be leaving, speaking scathingly of the prospectors he'd seen in downtown Sydney, tramps for the most part bumming the price of a beer and only too willing to pay for it with the story of how close they'd come to striking the big one.

Prospecting was a disease, Bill said. It ate into you like a cancer till you could neither live with nor without it. Like the alcoholic who knows only too well that one day the booze will kill him but in the meantime he'll just have one more drink to see him through.

Sure there was gold in the outback. But for every prospector who struck it lucky there were a hundred who didn't.

Petersson was a trained geologist, Angus replied. And what's more O'Rourke believed in him and O'Rourke was well known to be nobody's fool.

Shaking his head, Bill said if Petersson was so damned clever then why hadn't he come up with a strike before now? And from what Angus had told him, Petersson had certainly had enough chances. Once the outback gets hold of you you're lost, Bill went on to say. The outback was the most seductive of mistresses who rarely lets go. And that was where O'Rourke and Petersson were wrong in thinking they'd be the exceptions, that they could get in and out again with the big one under their belts and lie from then on in a bed of roses. ·

It was the same self deception nearly every prospector starts out with. Eventually they learn the truth that they aren't the exception at all. And that there's nothing left for them but to keep on prospecting and trekking till one day the land claims them and they vanish forever.

And wasn't Petersson already lost to that way of life? Everything Angus had told him about the man indicated that was so.

Angus had to admit he was shaken a little by the strength and vehemence of Bill's argument. The last thing he wanted was to end up the sort of bum Bill had described. He thought again of the now countless conversations he'd had with O'Rourke and Petersson and Petersson's absolute certainty that there was gold up there on the western slopes of the Great Divide.

His mind was made up, he said, the opportunity too good to miss. Nothing Bill or anyone else could say would dissuade him from going to Queensland.

But forewarned was to be forearmed. Angus swore to himself he wouldn't let the outback get into his blood the way it obviously had Petersson's

He'd give it a year. If they hadn't struck paydirt by then he'd return to Sydney.

Angus brought his thoughts back to the present as he watched Molly emerge from the shower and start to towel herself dry.

She was a barmaid in the hotel they were now in, the Southern Cross. He'd met her the first day he, O'Rourke and Petersson had arrived in Bundegai.

During the first proper conversation they'd had together she'd told him she was from Perth in Western Australia and was gradually making her way round the entire continent. She barmaided mainly but if that wasn't available then she'd do whatever presented itself.

He'd made a rude comment about that and come close to having his face slapped as a consequence. After that he'd been a lot more careful about what he said to Molly Hotblack.

'How's the prospecting going?' she called out as she started dressing.

'Nothing exciting yet. But hell, we haven't been at it all that long.'

She smiled. 'That's what they all say.'

Angus shifted uneasily at that. Her words were too reminiscent of Bill Pettigrew.

'We'll get there in the end,' he said.

'That's what I'm counting on. And you won't forget me when you strike it rich, will you?' she retorted.

'You sound like you're just after my money?'

Her eyes twinkled. 'Too right, sport. Except at the moment you don't have very much.

'Someday I'll be another Carnegie.'

'So you keep saying.'

'I will. I've sworn it.'

She laughed. 'Crazy bloody Scotchman. But I like you.'

'And I like you too. A lot.'

She paused briefly to stare at him. 'Yeh. I reckon you do.'

Angus knew he was falling in love with her – the first time he'd felt anything for another woman since Rosemary.

He couldn't think of two more contrasting women: Rosemary with her elegance and sophistication as opposed to Molly's aggressiveness and sheer volcanic charisma. Both were full-blooded women but in completely different ways.

He put Rosemary from his thoughts. Even after all this time there was still too much pain in thinking about her.

'Come on, let's be having you,' Molly said. 'Time I was downstairs pulling a few schooners.'

Angus rolled from the bed and quickly dressed. His body was lean and tanned, his hair several shades lighter than when he'd first arrived in Australia.

With every passing month he felt better and better, and even more so since coming north to Queensland. The round the clock fresh air and continual sun did him the world of good. Even if they didn't strike gold the experience would've been worth it for his health alone.

He finished dressing the same time she did and together they went downstairs to the huge tiled bar. It was more like a public convenience than a saloon, Angus always thought. He had a quick beer before saying goodbye to Molly and arranging to meet her on her night off two nights hence.

Out in the hot, pounding sun he made his way across to the post office thinking there might be some mail for Petersson who got a considerable amount of correspondence. To his surprise and delight there was a letter for him from home, the first to reach him since the *Almuria* went down.

He made his way back to the Holden station wagon that was owned jointly by him and his two partners. Seating himself comfortably in the driver's seat, he ripped the envelope open. Eagerly he read.

According to Carrie everyone, including herself, was fine. Hugh had joined the army and was currently abroad although exactly where she didn't know. Albeit well past retiring age, Donald was still foreman moulder at Armstrong's, and would no doubt continue in harness until either unable to carry on or the war ended.

Winnie was just the same while Harriet was doing extremely well with the Scottish Amalgamated Insurance Company, having far more responsible duties than previous thanks to the acute shortage of men.

Everyone sent their love and Harriet the message she'd once very nearly emigrated to Australia and would be eager to hear all about his stay there once he returned home.

Carrie was naturally concerned to learn of his illness and most relieved to hear he'd recovered all right with only minor after effects.

He'd mentioned, but played down, his lung damage in his letters to her.

She went on to say what a shock it had been to them all to learn of Kitty's death and that his parents had taken it badly, Mrs Kirkpatrick in particular.

The rest of the letter was chit chat but the most significant thing as far as Angus was concerned was not once did his mother either mention or refer to Archie Marjoribanks. That could only mean things were bad between them.

Relief at finally having re-established contact with home was overwhelming, even if there was the worry of his mother and Archie.

He whistled merrily all the way back to camp.

Months passed and two things happened to Angus; on the one hand he became more and more dejected that so far they hadn't even come across a trace of gold, and on the other, he fell more and more deeply in love with Molly Hotblack.

There was something about Molly that drew and held

him like filings to a magnet. He could never get enough of her company and it was always his complaint that their time together passed far too quickly.

Five times now he and the others had resited their camp as they worked themselves away from Bundegai in a sort of semi-circle.

Petersson's spirits remained high despite the fact their money was rapidly dwindling. The gold was out there, he maintained. He could smell it.

Although O'Rourke hadn't said anything to him, Angus knew he too was beginning to have doubts about Petersson. And it would be a long time before O'Rourke would say anything, not being a man who admitted to a mistake or misplaced faith lightly.

What Angus didn't realize about Molly was that she wasn't in love with him. She enjoyed his company and going to bed with him, but as far as she was concerned love had never entered into it.

The other thing Angus didn't know about her was that she was getting itchy feet again. She'd been in Bundegai far too long, she thought. It was high time she was moving onto her next port of call which she'd already decided would be the Alice.

Unaware that the cookout she'd suggested was to be the scene of her telling him she was leaving, Angus drove into Bundegai early on her day off to find her lying on her bed sipping from a cold can.

She'd made up a basket of goodies which he loaded into the back of the car alongside the cold beers he'd bought downstairs in the bar.

'You're quiet today,' he said with a smile as the Holden bounced its way out of Bundegai.

She returned his smile and laid her hand on his thigh. 'Where shall we go, then?' she asked.

'You choose.'

It was a scorching day with the sun really blistering down. There was a heavy smell of eucalyptus in the air mingled with the warm, earthy odour that the ground exuded.

'Somewhere there's a bit of shade,' she replied. 'Otherwise we'll fry.'

They'd had many cookouts and picnics together and it had been their practice to tend to head in the general direction of the camp. This time however it was decided they'd go more west. They stopped finally by an outcrop of rock beside which a small stream tinkled by.

A helluva long way from Sauchiehall Street, Angus thought as he unloaded the car.

'Koala!' said Molly, pointing to a nearby gum tree. And sure enough, there was one of the small bears sitting in the gum's branches regarding them quizzically.

Molly opened a couple of cans while Angus gathered a number of rocks for the fire surround.

While he was doing this Molly kept glancing at him surreptitiously. She knew she was going to hurt him badly and was sorry about that.

It didn't take Angus long to get the fire going and once it had died down a little he put on the steaks and sausages.

After they'd eaten they stretched out in a patch of shade thrown out by the rock. The heat and meal had made Angus langorous but sleep was the furthest thing from his mind.

Catching Molly by the halter he drew her to him. His hand sought and cupped her breast.

'Angus,' she said in a soft voice.

Smiling, he laid his lips on hers and kissed her deeply, enjoying the scent of her hair and flesh crowding his nostrils.

Somewhere a kookaburra laughed, a loud raucous noise that caused Angus's eyes to jerk open. He was about to close them again when a yellow glint from the dying fire caught his attention.

Gently Molly pushed him away. 'I want to speak to you,' she said.

Angus's brow was puckered in a frown. 'About what?' he asked vaguely, his attention elsewhere.

'There's something I have to tell you.'

There it was again, the same yellow glint as before. 'Wait a minute,' he said, and rising, made his way over to the fire.

Molly sighed. He wasn't making it easy for her.

Angus knelt and, using a twig, poked at one of the rocks he'd used for the fire's surround.

'What is it?' Molly asked, coming to stand beside him.

'I'm not sure yet.'

Using the twig, he pulled the rock he was interested in away from the others. It was still extremely hot so he kicked it down to the stream and into the water.

The jagged yellow line was less than half an inch long and appeared to disappear into the depths of the rock. Not having a pick handy Angus smashed the rock against another lying on the stream's bank.

The rock from the fire split wide open and what was revealed caused the breath to catch in Angus's throat.

'Bloody Ada!' he swore.

Lifting the two sections of rock he showed them to Molly. The split open surfaces of each were riddled with thin yellow streaks.

Molly licked her lips and then stared at Angus with eyes huge as saucers. 'Is that what I think it is?' she asked.

There was sweat on Angus's forehead that had nothing to do with the heat. He stared in fascination at the dully gleaming yellow streaks. 'You ever seen gold in this state before?' he asked.

Molly shook her head.

'Me neither. Although Eric's described it to me often enough. And from what he's told me, well. . . this could be just that.'

'What are you going to do?'

Angus grinned suddenly. 'I'm going to jump in the car and drive like hell back to camp.' And throwing back his head he let out the most enormous yell after which he swept Molly into his arms and kissed her.

Within minutes they'd loaded the car and were on their way, the two split sections of rock lying in Molly's lap.

They were halfway to camp when Angus remembered she'd been going to say something to him back there under the overhang of rock.

She shook her head when he asked her what it was. 'Nothing important,' she said. 'Nothing important at all.'

'Well?' Angus demanded.

Petersson lifted his glasses off his nose and using two fingers massaged the corners of his eyes.

'So it isn't then?' Angus said, his voice heavy with disappointment.

'On the contrary,' Petersson replied. 'It is and from the looks of it very best quality.'

'Oh my God!' said O'Rourke. Then looking directly at Angus, 'You beauty! You absolute beaut!'

Petersson's hands were shaking as he spread a map before Angus. 'Now pinpoint exactly where you found it,' he said.

Angus studied the map for a few seconds. Then his forefinger stabbed downwards. 'There's the stream and I'd say . . . just about here would be the place.'

Very carefully Petersson marked the indicated spot on the map with a pencil. 'Right. Let's go and have a look,' he said hoarsely.

Angus drove. And as he was later to remark his driving that day was probably the worst of his life.

The next morning found Angus and O'Rourke sitting round a table in the bar of the Southern Cross Hotel with a jug of beer in front of them. Every few minutes Angus glanced nervously at his watch. They were waiting for Petersson.

When they finished their jug Molly brought them a fresh one. 'He's taking his time,' she whispered.

O'Rourke topped up his glass which he proceeded to glower into.

Molly and Angus exchanged a few words and then she moved away to serve a customer who was loudly demanding her attention.

Another half an hour passed and then suddenly the doors swung open and Petersson strode into the bar. Seeing Angus and O'Rourke, he crossed swiftly to sit at their table.

'It's a bitch,' he stated flatly.

O'Rourke groaned. 'Let's have it,' he whispered.

Petersson glanced round to make sure they couldn't be overheard. Then he said softly, 'The strike is on private property. Belongs to Rawlestone who owns the haberdashery shop here in town.'

'Damn!' Angus swore.

Petersson went on, 'A quarter of a mile further east and we could've staked a claim. It's bastarding bad luck but there we are.'

'You're absolutely certain of this?' O'Rourke asked.

'Positive. It's a small property comprising a little over four thousand acres that the Rawlestones sheep farmed at one time. But apparently Rawlestone's stock got wiped out in the drought of a few years back. The story is that sickened him of sheep which he'd never been madly keen on anyway. And he went into haberdashery instead of restocking.'

'Then he should be willing to sell?' O'Rourke asked.

'I don't see why not as from what I'm told he rarely bothers to even go near the place. But two things, Sean. Number one, where would we get the money to buy a property like that? And two, we're known around here now so the moment we start making inquiries about a purchase he'd be bound to realize we were onto something.'

The three men sat in dejected gloom.

Petersson said, 'I've sent samples off to Sydney for analysis and we should get the results back within the week. I'm pretty certain they'll confirm the ore is of highest quality.' His face suddenly contorted with fury. 'Hell and damnation!' he said vehemently.

'Well, there's no use hanging around here,' O'Rourke said. 'We may as well get back to camp and talk things through there.'

'Wait a minute,' said Angus. 'Now look, I know little enough about prospecting but is it possible at all that as the vein is almost slap bang on that small stream there might well be nuggets in the stream itself?'

Petersson looked thoughtful.

'Well?'

'There's a damn good chance of nuggets *and* dust I'd say.'

'So why don't we have another look at that stream and if we're right, then what's to stop us doing some panning there? If the place if virtually abandoned as Eric here says then who's to know providing we're careful?'

'I'm still not with you?' said Petersson.

But O'Rourke was. 'Jesus, that's smart,' he said admiringly. 'You mean pan enough gold out of the stream to be able to buy the property?' he said.

'If it's possible,' replied Angus.

Petersson whistled.

'And of course once we own the place then we can get down to mining in earnest,' added Angus.

'It could just work,' said Petersson.

'Except for one thing,' interjected O'Rourke. 'Let's say we do get enough dust and nuggets to be able to buy the place, there's still the problem that Eric has already mentioned. An inquiry from us is sure to make Rawlestone suspicious.'

'There's a way round that as well,' said Angus, a smile twisting his mouth upwards. 'I've always rather fancied myself as a farmer and now that I'm about to get married and settle down – and as I've taken a great shine, or should I say, my future wife and I have taken a great shine to Bundegai – wouldn't it be the most natural thing in the world for me to approach Rawlestone to see if he'd be interested in selling?'

'I like it, I like it a lot,' said Petersson.

'But *would* you actually get married?' asked O'Rourke.

'Why not? It's been in my mind for the past few

months anyway.'

'Have you asked her yet?' O'Rourke went on.

'No. But I doubt she'll refuse. We're in love, you see.'

O'Rourke sighed. 'Love. There's only one thing better.'

'What's that?' Angus asked frowning.

'Gold!'

The three of them laughed. Then Petersson said,'I don't know that I quite agree. But I'd sure as hell hate to have to make the choice.'

'Poor Rawlestone,' said Angus shaking his head. 'We'll be paying the poor sod with what is in reality his own money.'

'Beautiful,' said O'Rourke. 'Absolutely beautiful.'

They talked further and it was agreed Petersson and O'Rourke would get back to camp leaving Angus to speak to Molly.

Molly took her lunch break and together she and Angus went up to her room where he recounted to her Petersson's news plus the two solutions he'd come up with.

'Hold on a minute,' she said. 'Let me just get this straight. Providing the three of you can pan enough gold out of that stream, assuming there *is* gold to be panned out, that is, you'll use what that realizes to buy the Rawlestone place, the excuse being you and I are going to set up home there?'

Eyes shining, Angus replied, 'I was going to propose to you anyway. This just gives me the excuse to do it sooner rather than later.'

Molly's mind was whirling. To cover her confusion she took her time about lighting a cigarette. And to think how close she'd come to giving him the elbow! She shuddered inwardly.

At long last, her luck had turned as she'd always believed it would. Her ship was about to come home.

Nor was Angus such a bad catch. He was young and fairly good looking. And there was certainly no hardship about going to bed with him.

'You're not going to turn me down, are you?' Angus asked in sudden alarm, thinking she was taking an awful long time in giving him his answer.

Instantly she was in his arms. Her lips brushed against his cheek and then nibbled at his ear. 'I thought you were never going to ask me,' she whispered.

'Does that mean you accept?'

'Of course.'

His hands swept down the length of her spine to encompass her backside. 'You'll never regret this,' he said.

She smiled over his shoulder. 'I hope not.'

'Let's go down to the bar and announce the news.'

'Later,' she whispered huskily. 'For the moment I've got a better idea.'

And pulling him over to the bed flopped onto it with him on top of her.

'Could you just show me again exactly what I'll be getting,' she whispered provocatively, adding, 'And take your time. There's no hurry.'

While Angus made love to her she dreamed behind closed eyes of fancy clothes. A smart car. A big house. All the things she'd ever wanted and never been able to afford.

It wasn't till it was too late that she remembered her contraceptive device which in the elation of the moment she'd forgotten to use.

After further consideration Petersson, O'Rourke and Angus decided only Petersson would pan the stream where dust and nuggets *were* to be found as Petersson had soon established.

The routine they fell into was that every morning just before dawn Angus would drive Petersson to the stream where he would drop him off, returning to pick him up again after dusk and taking him back again to the camp.

In the meantime Angus and O'Rourke kept up the pretence of prospecting round the site where their camp was pitched. They created the impression everything was going on precisely as it had been before.

On several occasions they altered the routine by taking Petersson into Bundegai so he could show his face as he would normally have done.

By this time Angus had started putting it about that he was rapidly becoming disillusioned with prospecting and was seriously considering looking for another line of work.

Then one night Angus came into town expecting to find Molly serving behind the bar of the Great Southern Hotel only to be informed by another of the bar staff that she was upstairs in bed having been taken ill.

He found her pale and wan with a bucket beside her bed into which she'd thrown up several times.

He immediately said he'd get a doctor but she restrained him saying she'd already been to see one. The doctor had confirmed what she'd suspected for the past few weeks.

It hadn't been too difficult for her to put two and two together, she said. Her breasts had swollen considerably and she'd put on weight round the tummy. She'd also taken to feeling nauseous at various times of the day.

'I'm pregnant,' she stated seeing the penny still hadn't dropped.

For a moment Angus was speechless and then his face lit up with joy. 'A baby!' he whooped. 'We're going to have a baby!'

First the gold and now this. Truly his cup was running over.

'That's bloody marvellous!' he cried, kissing Molly on the cheek and then hugging her.

The pregnancy was a mistake, of course. Molly hadn't intended it happening, children not figuring at all in her plans.

If she'd been able to have herself aborted locally she would have done so without telling Angus. But in a small community like Bundegai abortions just weren't to be had.

'We'll have to get married as soon as possible now, Angus said striding up and down the room. The plan had been to wait until they nearly had enough dust and nuggets to buy the Rawlestone farm and then have the ceremony. But as far as Angus was concerned that was now out. The sooner they were wed the better.

'How about this Saturday?' he asked. When she agreed, he added she was to leave everything to him. He would do the organizing.

'I can't tell you how happy I am,' he said, sitting on the edge of her bed.

'Me too.'

'I love you Molly,' he murmured awkwardly.

A smile lit up her pallid face. 'And I love you,' she lied.

The ceremony itself was a quiet affair with only Petersson and O'Rourke in attendance, O'Rourke as best man.

But the reception held in the largest room The Great Southern could provide was a marvellously noisy do with what seemed at times like hundreds of people drinking and dancing and having themselves a grand time.

Early on, before it all got out of hand, Petersson and O'Rourke took Angus and Molly quietly aside. Acting as spokesman, Petersson said they hadn't known what to give the couple as a wedding present, but they hoped this would do.

He then handed Molly a gold nugget the size of a small prune which was by far and away the largest he'd so far panned out of the stream.

Molly was enthralled by it, staring at it in the palm of her hand as though it were the Holy Grail.

'We thought maybe later we'd get it mounted for you and make it into a pendant or bracelet, whichever you prefer,' O'Rourke said.

But in the meantime don't show it to anyone,' Petersson added cautioningly.

'I understand,' Molly whispered.

'The other thing is,' O'Rourke went on, 'when everything's set up we want to call it the Lucky Molly Digging. What do you say to that?'

Her reply was to give O'Rourke and Petersson each a kiss on the cheek.

'The Lucky Molly Digging,' she said, her eyes shining, 'I think it's terrific.'

Their conversation was interrupted by Sam Keller, the hotel owner, calling out to them that the band was about to strike up the Gay Gordons, a Scotch dance in honour of a Scotch bridegroom, was how he put it.

'Feel up to it?' Angus asked.

Molly slipped the nugget into her bra. 'Try and stop me,' she replied.

Laughing, Angus led his new wife onto the floor where despite her pregnancy she wheeched and danced with the best of them.

Well Mister McBain what can I do for you?' Con Rawlestone asked. He was a small man with a bald head and a face that had the map of Ireland written all over it.

'Angus, please.'

'All right, Angus, and you can call me Con.'

They were sitting in the Rawlestone's front parlour, Angus having called after the shop was shut.

It was over four months since Petersson had started panning the stream. It had taken him that long to get enough dust and nuggets together to cover the cost of what they'd worked out the Rawlestone place was worth.

'As you know I recently got married,' Angus started, 'and now we've got a family on the way . . .

'Congratulations!' Rawlestone interjected.

'Thank you,' Angus smiled, then going on, 'I've decided it's time I settled down and stopped prospecting which, to tell you the truth, I've been getting rather tired of anyway.'

Angus then went on to give Con Rawlestone the spiel that had been agreed on and refined over the past few months by his two partners and Molly.

When Angus had finished Rawlestone rubbed his chin and looked thoughtful. 'If I was willing to sell, and I'm not saying I'm not, would you be able to afford it, Angus? I'd be wanting the full market value you understand.'

'Oh aye, of course,' replied Angus, nursing the small whisky Rawlestone had handed him. 'Well what would be your asking price then?'

Rawlestone named a figure which was slightly less than Angus had been expecting. There was more than enough in a Sydney bank – the money had been deposited in Sydney by O'Rourke a few weeks previously. He'd gone on the pretext of seeing his mother but in reality to cash in the gold Petersson had panned and to credit the money to an account in Angus's name.

Angus nodded slowly, as though turning the price over in his mind. Finally he said, 'Aye, well I think that's fair enough, Con. You stick to that sum and we'll call it a deal.'

Rawlestone looked surprised. 'You've got that much?'

'It certainly hasn't come from prospecting, I can tell you,' Angus replied, laughing.

'No, it's money from home in Scotland, a legacy I've had put by for years for just such an occasion as this,' pretended Angus.

That explanation obviously satisfied Rawlestone who poured more whisky, after which it was agreed they'd start proceedings for the sale the very next day.

Leaving Rawlestone, Angus went straight to the Great Southern Hotel where he found an anxious O'Rourke and Petersson in the bar.

'We're on,' he said with a smile.

The three of them looked gratifyingly at one another.

'For us, the digger's dream is about to come true,' Petersson said in a soft voice.

'Amen,' added O'Rourke.

Angus went up to the bar from behind which Molly had been watching him anxiously.

'We'll soon have a home of our own,' he said.

Big as his smile was, it didn't match hers.

The day after the sale was completed Angus picked Molly up from the Great Southern and drove her out to the farmhouse. Her days as a barmaid were now over.

He'd been out to the farmhouse twice that day already, dropping off bits and pieces of furniture and other household items they'd acquired.

Shooing Angus out the door, Molly set about putting everything just the way she wanted it.

As houses went it was a bit of a dump, she thought. But it would do for a start, considering what went with it.

'The Lucky Molly Digging,' she mused aloud. It was music to her ears.

One day a few weeks later word spread like wildfire round Bundegai that gold had been discovered on the old Rawlestone property now owned by Angus McBain.

Con Rawlestone was beside himself with anger when he heard and the first thing he did was consult a solicitor.

He was even more furious when the solicitor told him there was no legal action he could take. Angus had bought the place fair and square. Con had no comeback whatever.

Con then went about telling everyone he'd been cheated as Angus and his cronies must've known there was gold on the place before Angus bought it.

But rather than gaining sympathy for himself all he accomplished was to make people admire Angus. As one of the townfolk put it, who amongst them wouldn't have done the same thing had they been in Angus's shoes.

When Con heard that he thought about it for a while. Then with bad grace he accepted the situation: in his heart he knew Angus hadn't done anything he wouldn't have had the positions been reversed. Still, it was a bitter pill to swallow.

Molly was dishing out the evening meal to Angus,

O'Rourke and Petersson when the first pain came.

Gasping, Molly staggered and clutched onto the sink for support. Instantly Angus was by her side. 'The baby?' he asked anxiously.

She nodded, grinding her teeth together as a second pain seared through her.

O'Rourke came to his feet. 'You get her to bed and I'll get the doc.' Without further ado he was out the front door and seconds later the Holden roared into life and drove off.

Angus helped Molly through to their bedroom where as gently as he could he stripped her and managed to get her into a clean nightie.

'Jesus, these pains are coming quickly,' Molly said. 'I only hope the doc gets here before the baby does.'

'Me too,' said Angus. The thought of having to deliver the child himself was too awful even to contemplate.

Despite her pain, Molly couldn't help but laugh at the expression on Angus's face. She couldn't remember ever having seen a man look so terrified in such a comical way.

While Angus waited with Molly, Petersson put some water on to boil. Having done that, and with nothing else to occupy him in the meantime, he got down to doing the digging's weekly figures and accounts.

The digging was doing excellently, especially since some heavy equipment they'd sent to Brisbane for had arrived, enabling them to work far more efficiently and at greater speed.

Another six to nine months at their present rate and yield and the money would really be rolling in. By then the work would be far too much for the three of them and they'd have to hire more men.

Through in the bedroom Molly jerked her head back and screamed.

Where's the bloody doctor! Angus thought. Knowing even as he did so that O'Rourke and the doctor would be making as good time as was possible.

'There, there, love,' he soothed, holding Molly's

shoulder as her lips stretched back into a fearful grimace, the prelude to another excruciating pain.

Angus was only too well aware that Carrie had had a most difficult birth in delivering him. Indeed she'd come close to losing her life as a result of his having been in an awkward position. He knew this from having overheard a conversation between his mother and Winnie when he was a young lad. His worry now was – and it had been preying on his mind for the past few months – that being his child Molly was carrying she might somehow experience the same difficulty.

'It'll be all over soon,' he said, the smile on his face belying his sweat drenched forehead.

A little later the pains went off and Molly was able to relax somewhat.

'How do you feel?' he asked.

'What a bloody stupid question! How do you think I feel? Like a screeching bloody sheila whose insides are being ripped apart and whose backside feels like it's getting all set to drop off, that's what!'

Angus grinned. It *had* been a bloody stupid question.

Suddenly Molly grinned back. 'This'll teach me to get so hot and bothered I forget my cap,' she said. And they both laughed, relaxing the tension that had been built up in the room.

Ten minutes later O'Rourke arrived with the doctor who banished Angus from the bedroom while he got on with it.

For the next hour and a half Angus paced up and down, watched silently by O'Rourke and Petersson. Twice the doctor called for things which Angus immediately sprang to get. Neither time was he allowed back into the bedroom but handed the articles over to the doctor at the bedroom door.

Suddenly the screams stopped. Those waiting were in no doubt that something had happened. A strange calm settled on the house, a calm that was shattered a few seconds later by the thin, piercing wail of a newborn child.

A few minutes later the doctor emerged looking hugely pleased with himself. 'Congratulations,' he said. 'You've got a son.'

'A son!' Angus echoed.

'As fine a boy as any man could wish for.'

Shaking as though he was the father himself O'Rourke reached for the whisky bottle that had been put out in preparation and poured four large ones.

'Was there any particular trouble?' Angus asked.

'Nope,' the doctor said, accepting a glass from O'Rourke. 'Everything was completely straightforward.

Relief welled through Angus when he heard that.

'To the boy!' toasted Petersson.

'John McBain,' said Angus. It had been agreed between him and Molly that if they had a son they'd call him after his father.

'To John McBain!' O'Rourke, Petersson and the doctor toasted in unison.

'I think you'd better go away in and see them now,' said the doctor.

Squaring his shoulders Angus went through to tell his wife how well she'd done and to see his newborn son.

The months after young John's birth passed quickly for all those involved at the Lucky Molly.

Molly discovered what a full time job it was looking after a baby. With Angus giving what help he could, O'Rourke and Petersson spent long hour after long hour delving ever deeper into the ore bed.

But after such a marvellous beginning things were going from bad to worse, the yield continually decreasing and falling off in quality.

Petersson became gaunt and hollow-eyed with worry, assuring Angus and O'Rourke over and over this had to be a temporary setback and that both yield and quality must pick up again.

Molly lost her exuberance and flamboyance to become more and more withdrawn. When she and Angus found themselves alone during the day he was always aware of her gaze riveted to him as though he was some sort of specimen on a microscope slide.

Then one day their worst fears were realized when the ore bed suddenly and quite dramatically came to an end.

Stunned, the three men stood in the huge excavation they'd created looking at one another.

Petersson attempted a smile which never even came close to coming off. 'Perhaps it's only a break in the bed or then again it might well be that . . .'

'Bullshit!' O'Rourke interjected. 'The fucker's played out. You know that as well as I do.'

'No,' said Peterson, his voice trembling. 'You're wrong.'

'He's right,' said Angus. Then tapping his heart, 'I can feel it here.'

'What do you know about it?' said Petersson scornfully. 'Are you the geologist or am I?'

'You are. But right now you're talking with your emotions and not your head.'

'There *is* more gold down there,' sad Petersson dogmatically. 'There has to be.'

'It looked so promising too,' said O'Rourke wistfully. 'From the way it started I was sure it would go on forever. Just shows how wrong you can be.'

'A bust,' said Angus, shaking his head. 'Who would have thought it?'

Petersson lumbered across to the mechanical digger and climbed into its cockpit. Without another word he set the neanderthal looking machine in action, a look of fierce determination on his face as the digger's metal claw tore and savaged into the hard packed earth they'd discovered beneath the ore bed.

O'Rourke gestured to Angus and together they climbed out of the excavation.

As they walked towards the house O'Rourke said, 'Petersson told me months ago that was the only ore bed on the property. With the quality and yield we were getting then that didn't bother us unduly as we were convinced the bed was a deep one. It seems we were wrong. You might say the Lucky Molly just ran out of luck.'

Angus hated the thought of breaking it to Molly. They'd made so many plans together, built up so many dreams.

Angus said, 'Well we haven't come out of it with nothing at all. There's the property which we can sell plus whatever we can get from the equipment we bought.'

Although the property had originally been in Angus's name it had shortly after purchase been stipulated in the deeds that it was jointly and equally owned by the three of them.

'I think I'm going to get drunk out of my skull,' said O'Rourke. 'And if ever a man needed an excuse for doing that then I reckon we three have a beaut.'

Angus was bemused by what had happened. Although he'd seen it coming it was still a profound shock that it had actually happened. Like the condemned man, he'd been secretly convinced there'd be a last minute reprieve.

Once in the house O'Rourke took himself off to his bedroom with a bottle of brandy. Angus found Molly in the kitchen feeding John.

He sat heavily beside her, slumping forward and cradling his head in his hands.

'The bed's run out,' he said.

The colour drained from her face. The threatened nightmare of recent weeks had become reality. 'That's it, then?' she croaked.

'That's it.'

'You're absolutely certain?'

'Petersson seems to think he can pick it up again but he's kidding himself. The Lucky Molly was a nine day wonder and today was day ten.'

Anger bubbled in Molly which she swiftly brought under control. 'What happens now?' she asked.

'I don't know. We'll have to discuss that.'

Molly plucked the now empty feeding bottle from John's mouth who immediately began to cry. Irritation creased her face as she jiggled him up and down on her lap.

Angus stared lovingly at his son. The wee fellow was the spitting image of him which naturally enough tickled him pink.

'Want me to take him?' he asked.

Molly passed John over and then went looking for a cigarette. 'What a mess,' she said through a cloud of smoke.

'It isn't the end of the world,' Angus replied. 'Nothing ever is. And let's look on the bright side. We've got one another and the baby. As far as I'm concerned, that's worth more than all the gold that was ever dug out of the ground.'

Molly looked sour, her expression making it quite clear she didn't agree.

O'Rourke appeared from his bedroom holding the brandy bottle by the neck. 'You've told the little lady I take it,' he said.

Angus nodded.

'A sad day Molly, eh?'

'You can say that again. And are you going to hold onto that bottle forever or are you going to pass it round?'

Molly coughed as the liquor burned its way down her throat. Handing the bottle back, she crossed to the window and stared out, her eyes taking on a faraway look as though she was seeing something way beyond the horizon.

'Penny for them?' Angus asked eventually.

'Nothing important,' she replied. Her voice sounded as though it came from a far distance.

'Come on, tell me,' he coaxed.

She turned and stared at him. 'I was just thinking of all the things we were going to do. Places we were going to go. The house we were going to have. The clothes. The cars.'

'I'm sorry Molly,' Angus said softly. 'I'd cut off my right arm for you if it would change things. But it

wouldn't. The digging's a bust and we're just going to
have to learn to live with the fact.'

'These little things are sent to try us,' said O'Rourke.
'Very character building you know.'

Molly looked as though she was about to retort angrily
when suddenly John was sick all down his front.

'I'll deal with that,' she said wearily, taking John from
Angus and crossing over to the sink where she began
changing the wee lad.

'She's a wonderful mother,' said Angus proudly.

O'Rourke swallowed some more brandy.

For another week Petersson worked at the digging on his
own before finally admitting defeat.

That evening the three men and Molly held a con-
ference during which it was decided to advertise the
property statewide in the hope they'd quickly come up
with a buyer.

The equipment Petersson would sell through various
private contacts he had.

The night Angus and Molly lay wide awake in bed. 'I
think we should go to Sydney,' Angus said after a while.
'We'll stay with O'Rourke's mother till we can find a
small flat of our own.'

Molly winced at the word small. 'And what about
work?'

'I've told you about Bill Pettigrew who employed me
as a clerk. Bill was very fond of me, looked on me as a
son almost. He said when I left that I could have my old
job back any time.'

'A clerk,' said Molly softly, a hint of contempt in her
voice.

'There are big prospects in the building trade, Bill
says,' Angus went on. 'Give it a couple of years and who
knows? I might even start my own firm.'

To Molly it all sounded like pie in the sky. And suddenly she was feeling trapped and deathly afraid. She
could see the years stretching ahead of her. No more
fun. No more laughter. Instead the worry of having a

child and husband to care for with little money coming into the house. What did a clerk earn? She didn't know but she was sure it was hellish little.

As for the brat now fast asleep in his cot at the far side of the room, she'd never wanted him in the first place. Oh, the idea of a child had been bearable when it had seemed she wouldn't be tied down to him indefinitely. A nanny or baby nurse had been high on her list of priorities once the money started flooding in.

But with the collapse of the Lucky Molly there would now be no nanny or baby nurse which meant she personally would have to continue looking after the brat who seemed to be never endingly performing at one end or the other.

And as for Angus, her knight in shining armour had turned out to be like so many other men she'd known in the past. Namely a dead loss. Big on promises but very short on delivery.

Angus with bundles of money was one thing. But Angus as a clerk in a small building firm was quite another.

Christ! she raged inwardly. What a Godawful mess she'd got herself into. Well she was damned if she was going to let herself be sucked into playing the suburban housewife with sprog. The very thought was anathema.

What she wanted was freedom. Laughs. Fun! Godalmighty she was still young yet with her whole life stretching ahead of her. And who knew what might be waiting for her round the next bend? Or should she say *who?*

'Molly, you still awake?'

'Uh-huh.'

His hand slipped up her thigh and into the nest of her crotch.

Despite what she'd been thinking she found herself wanting him.

'I'll give you all the things we talked about Molly. I'll find a way. I promise you.'

'Of course you will,' she replied, wriggling under his

probing fingers.

She accepted him into her arms, enjoying what he did to her and how he made her feel.

And as they made love she worked out the best time for her to leave next day to catch the mid-morning bus that went through Bundegai.

Directly after breakfast next morning Molly said she wanted to go into Bundegai to get some things from the chemist's. And as Angus wasn't working would he mind looking after John?

The three men had already decided during breakfast that they'd spend the morning drafting letters to the various agents and newspapers with whom they were going to advertise the property. Petersson had the additional job of writing to his personal contacts regarding the equipment. So it was no great trouble for Angus to take care of the wee lad.

Angus did wonder briefly why Molly was taking a small case with her but at the back of his mind put it down to some other business she probably had in town.

''Bye then,' Molly said when she was finally ready.

'Don't I get a kiss?'

Smiling, she came back from the door and kissed him on the cheek. Then as an afterthought she bent and kissed John.

'Don't be too long,' Angus said.

Molly smiled again, but didn't reply.

With John cradled in his arms Angus stood and watched the Holden roar off towards Bundegai.

'Now shall we get down to it,' said O'Rourke who was seated at the table beside an extremely morose looking Petersson.

Angus turned his attention to the drafting of the advertisements.

Lunchtime came and went. She must've got tied up, Angus thought. But when afternoon gave way to evening he began to get worried.

'Maybe she's had an accident?' he said to O'Rourke.

'Car's broken down most likely,' O'Rourke replied.

'Aye, no doubt you're right,' said Angus, relieved at this most obvious of explanations. After all, hadn't the same thing happened to Petersson a few weeks previously?

A little later Angus put John down for the night, after which the three men sat playing cards.

At one Petersson went to bed shortly followed by O'Rourke.

For hours Angus kept vigil in a chair facing the door. He dropped off just as dawn was breaking.

The next thing he knew he was being shaken by O'Rourke saying John was awake and crying.

He changed the baby's nappy and fed him. Then the three men had breakfast.

'That's the trouble with not having a phone,' O'Rourke said over coffee. 'Makes situations like this a lot more dramatic than they are.'

'I was thinking just before I nodded off,' Angus said slowly, 'if Molly did have to leave the car in the garage overnight surely they would have loaned her one till she picked the Holden up again? I mean isn't that what they usually do when someone lives out of town?' And when O'Rourke didn't have a reply to that he added, 'I'll give her till ten then if you'll watch John for me I'll start walking into town.

On the stroke of ten Angus set out for Bundegai. He trudged for an hour and a half before being picked up by a passing vehicle which dropped him outside the Great Southern.

There were three garages in Bundegai and he was en route to the nearest one when he spied the Holden parked outside the post office. The car's doors were locked but there was a piece of paper jammed up against the inside of the windscreen which said: 'Angus, keys in post office.'

Having retrieved the keys he opened the car door and slid inside. The piece of paper in the windscreen turned out to be a letter.

As he read his head grew numb. It seemed as though he was standing in the middle of an ice cold wind although it was broiling out.

He read the letter through twice, then folded it and put it into his trouser pocket. Seeing and hearing nothing, he drove the Holden out of Bundegai and back to the farmhouse.

As he drew up O'Rourke came out onto the porch with John in his arms. 'Has she been taken crook then?' he called out on seeing Angus was alone.

Angus joined O'Rourke on the porch, taking John from him and holding the wee fellow close.

'She's gone,' he said, his voice trembling.

'What do you mean, gone?'

'Just that. Lit out for parts unknown.'

'You mean she's left you and the baby?'

Angus nodded.

'Why, the rotten galah!' O'Rourke exploded.

'I found the car with a letter in it,' Angus said after a few seconds. 'She says she's sorry but she couldn't yet face life as a suburban hausfrau as she put it. Before leaving she withdrew what money we had in our joint account. She apologized for that but pointed out I'd have my share from the sale of this place to keep me going.'

'I don't understand,' said O'Rourke.

'I do . . . now. I thought she loved me but I was wrong. What she was in love with was the money she saw The Lucky Molly bringing in.'

O'Rourke swore vehemently, his face flushing and his eyes sparking with anger.

Angus stared down at John who was gurgling happily in his arms. 'Well I'll never desert you, boy. You can stake your life on that,' he said.

'You mean you're going to look after the kid all by yourself?' O'Rourke asked.

'I may need some help. But I'll never have him adopted or fostered. He's my son and we're staying together.

That's the way it's going to be.'

O'Rourke remained on the porch while Angus took John inside. He couldn't remember when he'd last been so moved.

During the next month several people turned up to look the property over but none of them made an offer.

In the meantime Petersson had sunk into a deep depression and had taken to camping out at night all on his own. Going walkabout at one point, he disappeared for over a week.

O'Rourke tried his hand at panning the stream but his efforts produced little dust and no nuggets. Petersson had taken out nearly all the gold there was to be had there.

One month became two and still they hadn't found a buyer. Then one afternoon while Angus was changing John and O'Rourke was busy trimming the lamps an excited Petersson burst into the house.

'We've done it! We've done it! We've bloody well done it!' he yelled, dancing on the spot like an Irishman trying to keep pace with a demented fiddler.

'Done what?' queried Angus.

'All this time staring me in the face and me not having the wit to see it!' crowed Petersson.

O'Rourke caught Petersson by the arm and forced him to stand still. 'Will you please tell us just what it is you're raving on about?' O'Rourke demanded.

With eyes seeming about to burst from his head Petersson said, 'I first noticed it early last week. Although God knows I should've seen it long before then. The trouble is I suppose when you're looking specifically for one thing you just don't take in what else is there. Or at least I didn't.'

'I'm lost,' said Angus.

'When it finally did dawn I took samples from all over the property and sent them to Sydney for analysis. I've just come from Bundegai now. The results of those analyses were in today's mail.'

'You haven't found more gold?' O'Rourke asked quickly.'

'Not gold. Bauxite!' Having said that, Petersson looked from O'Rourke to Angus. But if he was expecting a reaction then he was disappointed. Angus and O'Rourke both stared at him blankly.

'Bauxite,' Petersson repeated.

'What's that?' Angus asked.

'The stuff they smelt aluminium from.'

Again there was no reaction.

'Alufuckingminium!' Petersson shouted in desperation. 'There's a war on and that's one of the metals the government is crying out for. And this entire farm is sitting square on top of a mountain of the stuff.'

Slowly it dawned on Angus just what Petersson was saying.

'Does that mean we're going to be rich after all?' he asked.

'Rich! The three of us are going to be each as rich as Croesus!' Petersson roared.

O'Rourke made a sort of gobbling sound and sat heavily on the nearest chair. He looked like a man who'd just been hit over the head with a sledgehammer.

Like O'Rourke, Angus was completely stunned by this bolt out of the blue. 'You're sure there's no mistake?' he asked in a whisper.

'Not this time,' Petersson replied, and whooped with joy.

Angus took a deep breath and then glanced down at John cradled in his arms. That was who the money would benefit in the long run. He'd make sure of it.

The very best of everything. That would be John's life thanks to a mountain of Bauxite and Petersson's unswerving digger's dream.

He thought of Molly then and the irony of her having left when she did. He could just imagine her face when she heard the news.

Then suddenly O'Rourke was on his feet screaming and yelling and dancing an impromptu jig with Petersson.

Angus hugged John tight against his chest. Later a great deal of serious thinking would have to be done, plans to be made, but for now he was content to give himself over to the madness Petersson had brought into their midst.

Part IV

Goodbye Yesterday
1946–1947

18

Carrie was dying and was reconciled to the fact.

She lay in bed thinking of the letter Harriet, on her instruction, had written Angus a few months previously informing him of the situation.

His reply had come by return saying he and John would be sailing on the first available ship.

Carrie gritted her teeth and stifled a groan. The plaster corset round her middle was giving her gyp. It had done ever since it had been put on. The corset was to help the sciatica the doctor said she had.

But there was a lot more to her condition than merely that. Her body was completely worn out. The ravages of years of TB and mistreatment at the hands of Archie Marjoribanks had finally taken their toll.

She was forty-five years old and looked sixty.

There was a photograph standing on her bedside table which she glanced at occasionally. It showed Angus holding up young John outside the farmhouse where they lived. It had pleased her enormously that Angus had called his son after his father. Thinking of it never failed to bring a lump to her throat.

Over at the window Harriet stood staring out. She was dressed in her inevitable black with her hair drawn severely back in a bun. Like Carrie, she was thin and wasted, but in her case it was entirely self-inflicted by her almost constant diet of cigarettes and tea. Her thoughts were with the Scottish Amalgamated Insurance

Company and its Glasgow branch, in particular. She'd been in charge of the branch for a number of years now. But with the war over and the men returning home she would soon have to step down and resume her previous position of secretary.

She was going to miss dreadfully the power and responsibility. But there was no way the company was going to promote her officially into an executive position, albeit her ability was well proven.

It was one thing for her to step into her boss's shoes in wartime. Another entirely for her to stay there or assume another position of that nature once peace had been achieved.

She saw it as one more major frustration in a life filled with them.

Carrie started coughing, dry, racking spasms that shook her entire frame. The hand she held to her mouth was skeletal, each bone distinct. The skin covering those bones was yellowishly opaque and like an old leaf to the touch.

Harriet immediately left her vantage point by the window to help Carrie reach a glass of water. As she held Carrie close she knew the only thing keeping her sister alive was Carrie's dogged determination to see Angus again and hold her grandson for the first time.

When the coughing fit was finally over Carrie lay back on the bed and closed her eyes. As she drifted off she thought how much more comfortable she'd be without the damned corset. But she also knew she wouldn't order Dr Robertson to remove it in case she somehow reduced the precious time left her.

When she fell asleep she dreamt of the happy days when she'd been married to John McBain and life, though hard, had been glorious for the pair of them.

Through in the living room Donald was sitting in his chair reading the day's paper. He was retired now having been told directly after VJ day his time at Armstrong's was finished.

He had taken over an allotment after Winnie had gone

on at him incessantly to do so. But his heart wasn't really in it. Growing vegetables on a wee plot was fine as a hobby but it was hardly a day's work for a man.

He missed unbearably the bedlam of the foundry, the roar of the blast furnaces, the dazzling liquidity of molten metal, the pride of a job – his type of job – well done.

Rising, he made his way through to the hall where he stood wondering whether or not to go through and see Carrie. He decided against it when he heard the sound of soft snoring coming from her room.

With Harriet in the house to look after Carrie should she wake he decided to take a dauner along by the Cart. That should fritter away a good hour which would bring him home just as Winnie returned from getting in the messages.

As he walked down the close stairs he thought about Alex being the first of their brood to go. And now Carrie was about to be the second.

The one blessing was she wasn't in the least scared of dying. If any thing, she was looking forward to it as she was convinced somewhere in some form John McBain would be waiting for her.

He could only hope and pray she was right.

Clad in a badly fitting demob suit Hugh stepped off the train at the Central Station. He still couldn't believe he'd emerged from the war completely unscathed. After what he'd been through it seemed a miracle to him he was actually home again in one piece.

Not only that, but there was a wife waiting to greet him and a wee baby daughter whom he hadn't yet seen.

It had been a great disappointment to him to learn Janey had given birth to a girl. But he'd consoled himself in the knowledge the wee lassie was perfect in every detail. And there was nothing to stop him and Janey having a boy next time round.

He made for the Broomielaw from where he'd be able to catch a tram for Muirend. On a sudden impulse he continued on down to the suspension bridge which took him over the gently flowing Clyde and into the Gorbals.

To another's eyes, the dirty, squalid tenements – the air hard and rasping from the sooty smoke belching out of their innumerable chimneys – might have jarred. But to Hugh they were a joy to behold as they confirmed he was home again in the city where his roots ran deep and which he so loved.

He walked as far as the Star Bar and Plaza dancehall opposite. My God, he remembered that night all right! He ran the last few yards to a stop where he caught a tram. As the tram rattled on its way he thought of Kenny White who'd introduced him to Janey. He'd been killed in North Africa.

Janey was scraping potatoes when she heard the front door open and close again.

At first she didn't recognize the man standing in the kitchen doorway staring at her in such a quizzical fashion. Then with a cry she dropped the knife and potato and rushed across the floor into his arms.

There was so much she wanted to say but for the moment no words came.

Lifting Janey's chin, Hugh kissed her, not a passionate kiss but rather one of sheer pleasure at their reunification.

Breaking away, Janey used the edge of her hand to wipe the tears from her face. Still too overcome to speak, she beckoned him to follow and hastened towards the door.

The child lay fast asleep in her cot, her face pink and angelic, the mouth puckered up as though she was blowing him a kiss on this the event of his seeing her for the first time.

'Mary Agnes,' Janey said, the words trembling from her mouth.

She was a bonnie baby with a definite look of the Chisholms about her. His heart went out to the wean and he quickly put to the back of his mind the regret she wasn't a boy. A lassie would do him just fine – for the moment.

Janey would have woken Mary Agnes but Hugh restrained her. They returned to the kitchen where Janey busied herself brewing a pot of tea.

She was putting this by to mask when he asked her where Greta Paterson was? He was looking forward to seeing his old friend again.

Janey turned a suddenly stricken face towards him and asked if he hadn't got her recent letters?

He replied that the last letter he'd received had been a little over six weeks previously.

Janey poured him a cup and as she handed it to him said Greta had been dead and buried a month now. Death, according to the autopsy, was due to kidney failure.

Janey went on to say how close she and Greta had become during the past few years, particularly after Mary Agnes had been born as Greta had doted on the child. She'd seized on Mary Agnes as a substitute for her own grandchildren so tragically killed by German bombs.

Janey said Hugh had taken the place of the dead Stewart in Greta's mind with herself replacing Stewart's wife. Greta had come to think of and refer to their small family as her own.

Hugh was well pleased his old friend had found some comfort in having Janey and Mary Agnes to stay with her. That at least went a little way to repaying the multitude of kindnesses she and Aly had lavished on him.

Hugh frowned suddenly, the thought striking him their position here at Muirend was now extremely precarious. After all it was unlikely the new owners – presumably Greta's next of kin – would be keen on their presence in the house and no doubt they'd be given notice to quit.

It was also quite feasible a new manager would be appointed in his place – new broom and all that.

A soft, loving smile curled the corners of Janey's

mouth as she stared at the dejected Hugh. It was almost worth her last letters going astray so she could tell him the good news herself.

Her smile widened as she told him that directly after the funeral she'd received a communication asking her to call on Greta's solicitors. On presenting herself she'd been ushered into the presence of the senior partner who'd told her in accordance with his late client's will the entire Muirend estate plus the farm on the East Kilbride road had been left to one Hugh Chisholm, a Paterson employee currently serving with His Majesty's Armed Forces.

So taken aback was Hugh he made Janey repeat what she'd just told him.

'My God!' he whispered when she'd finished for the second time. Crossing to the window, he stared out over the yard to the stables beyond. To think all this was now his was simply unbelievable! And the last thing in the world he'd expected.

He knew Greta had some distant relatives but Janey said that Greta hadn't wanted them to have the place as they would've only sold it. And anyway, they were more than comfortably off and didn't need any addition to their bank balances.

Hugh and Janey both loved the house and dairy and because of this she preferred everything to go to them, just as it would've gone to Stewart and his family had they still been alive.

Hugh was suddenly aware of Janey standing by his side, her face beaming as she stared up at him.

Catching her in his arms he announced his intention of taking her upstairs to bed to celebrate his safe return and their stroke of stupendous good luck.

They were halfway up the stairs when Janey remembered to tell him on top of everything else there was also £2653 in a joint bank account she'd opened in their names. This was the cash savings Greta had left and which had also come their way.

Their combined laughter was so loud it woke Mary

Agnes so they didn't get to bed right away after all. . . .

Three weeks to the day after Hugh arrived back in Glasgow the late train from London brought Angus and John. With them was a girl from Bundegai called Dawn Schroeder who'd been acting as nanny to John since shortly after Molly had flown the coop.

Having disembarked from the train Angus booked them into the Central Station Hotel where Angus had no trouble getting them a suite with two bedrooms, one for him and the other for Dawn and John.

After being shown to their suite Dawn busied herself with John who'd been fractious during the latter part of their long journey up from Southampton.

While Dawn got John ready for bed Angus stood by a window looking out on the city, which gave the impression of having had its life juices bled from it. The people he'd seen so far had thin, pinched faces as grey as the buildings surrounding them.

Tanned and fleshed out, he might have belonged to another species altogether so stark was the contrast.

Sighing, he poured himself a glass of whisky. As he sipped, his mind flew back to Australia and his affairs there. The bauxite strike had been everything, and more, Petersson had said it would.

The original digging had been abandoned and a new site opened. This had grown rapidly into what was now known as the Lucky Molly Bauxite Mine – LMBM for short – employing close on a hundred people.

O'Rourke had taken over as overall administrator and was proving superb at the job. As for Petersson, once the mine had been opened, he'd moved on to pastures new. He'd been last heard of up on the Northern Territory prospecting for silver he was convinced was to be found there.

Of course Petersson didn't need to do any further prospecting as he, like Angus and O'Rourke, was now a very rich man with the prospect of those riches reaching mind boggling proportions. But with the outback and prospecting deep in his blood he needed – as Bill Pettigrew had once warned Angus nearly always happened to prospectors – to keep up his erstwhile mode of life the way a junkie needs another fix.

O'Rourke also had caught the bug although to a lesser degree than Petersson. With him it was merely the outback. As he often said, he could no more imagine himself going back to live in an urban situation than he could flying in the air.

If asked, Angus would have had to admit he too had almost fallen for the seductions of the outback. But what had saved him was an older love and craving – that for his native Glasgow which surmounted all else.

As for Molly, and he smiled grimly thinking about it, she'd been back like the proverbial shot once she'd learned of the bauxite strike. In vain she'd pleaded with him for them to take up where they'd left off but he'd have none of it.

He'd loved her once. But that love had been blown away like so much chaff in the wind the day she deserted him and John. Stripped of the emotional tie he'd even come to feel quite repulsed by her.

In agreement for a divorce he'd made a reasonable settlement on her, far more than she deserved, he reckoned. But she had given him John and for that he owed her something.

Angus's musings were interrupted by Dawn calling out to say John wanted to be kissed goodnight. This he did with all the warmth and love he bore his son.

It didn't take John long to drop off, worn out as he was by the journey and excitement.

Dawn joined Angus for a drink. The relationship between Angus and Dawn was strictly a business one. They liked one another, enjoyed one another's company, but that was as far as it went. The truth was that physically neither was particularly attracted to the other.

Angus nervously paced up and down the room, desperate to go out to Tallon Street and see Carrie.

When he told Dawn he was considering going on his

own she pooh-poohed the idea saying it was far too late
and all he would succeed in doing was waking his mother
when no doubt what the poor woman needed was all the
sleep she could get.

Dawn was right, he decided reluctantly. It was best he
bided his patience till the morning when he could take
John with him.

It was a decision he'd regret for the rest of his life.

Tallon Street was smaller and meaner than he remembered it.

His heart was thudding as he rapped on the so familiar
door at the top of the close. Behind him Dawn wiped
John's nose and checked the wee fellow was neat, tidy
and a credit to his father.

The door opened and Winnie was there staring at
Angus as though he were a stranger. Then the penny
dropped.

'Oh, son!' she said in a tremulous voice.

He knew then he'd come too late. 'When?' he asked.

'Last night,' Winnie replied. Had he come to Tallon
Street when he'd wanted to he would have caught Carrie
just before she'd died.

Realizing she was keeping them standing on the door-
step Winnie brought them in, gesturing towards the
living room where she said Donald and Harriet were.

Hugh had already been but had returned to Muirend
to see to the milk. He'd be back as soon as he could.

The family knew all about Dawn, Angus having carefully explained about her in the last letter he'd written.

As John came abreast of Winnie she bent and swept
the wee fellow into her arms. Kissing him on both
cheeks. Then holding him at arms' length she said, 'A
fine lad, the living image of his dad. Carrie would have
been so proud.'

Donald was waiting just inside the living room door
and the first thing he did when Angus entered the room
was to throw his arms round Angus's shoulders and
squeeze his grandson tightly. All he said, was 'Aye, well

there we are, then.'

Harriet had been crying as was obvious from her red rimmed eyes. She embraced Angus after her father had let him go.

When everyone had been introduced and a bit of a fuss made of John, Donald said to the very last Carrie had been smiling and joking, assuring everyone they weren't going to get rid of her until she'd seen Angus again and held the wee chap named after her John in her arms. But she'd been wrong.

When she died Angus's name was on her lips.

Dawn was distraught remembering it was she who'd dissuaded Angus from coming the previous night. But he dismissed her self condemnation saying the argument she'd put forward had been a valid one.

If he blamed anyone it was himself. He should've followed his instincts.

He asked to see his mother's body and Harriet volunteered to take him through to the bedroom where Carrie was laid out.

He'd brought a number of presents along and one of these he now sorted out from the rest.

It was a leather handbag he'd scoured Sydney for, knowing precisely the type and design Carrie would like.

Entering the bedroom, he came to an abrupt halt, his face plainly registering shock. If he'd met his mother alive in the street he'd have walked straight past her.

She was so *old* looking! A crone nearer Winnie's age than the actual forty-five she was.

Stiff-legged, he walked forward to sit on the edge of the bed. Slowly he unwrapped the handbag and laid it on the pillow beside her head. 'A wee minding, Ma,' he said.

Coldness gave way to heat which exploded into a blast furnace of bubbling anger. 'What happened to her?' he demanded, his voice a thrumming stretch of wire.

Harriet wilted under his terrible gaze.

'It was Archie, wasn't it?' he hissed taking hold of the front of Harriet's dress.

All this while Harriet had kept her dark secret, never

once breathing a hint of it to anyone. Time had pushed it
to the back of her mind where, like a bad dream, it had
gradually faded to nothingness.

But seeing Carrie dead had brought it all rushing
back. Her skin crawled with the memory of what the
animal had done to her. And how many awful times had
Carrie endured the same?

Her nerve shredded. It came out in a rush, the words
tumbling from her mouth.

When she finally finished speaking she gave a great
shudder as though an enormous weight had been lifted
from her.

Angus whimpered. His mind filled with dreadful
pictures. It was unbelievable. Inconceivable. And yet
Harriet said it was true.

He dashed from the room and before anyone realized
what was happening was through the front door and
running down the close stairs.

Behind him Harriet wept volubly.

Once out in the street, he hesitated, not quite knowing
what to do next. Then remembering it was a Sunday and
there was a good chance Archie would be at home, he
ran, all the while thinking of the life Archie had given his
mother. It had transformed Carrie into the raddled
corpse now laid out in Tallon Street.

The time had finally arrived for the reckoning. He was
no longer the wee boy Archie could contemptuously
knock to one side. It would be man to man and he
doubted there were many could have stood up against
him the way he felt right then.

Reaching the front door he formed a fist and hammered. And hammered. And hammered.

'Christalbloodymighty, I'm coming!' the well remembered voice called out followed by a dragging sound as
though Archie was pulling something heavy across the
floor.

The moment the door started to open Angus leapt at
it, hitting it hard with his shoulder so it was thrust
suddenly and violently back in on itself.

For an instant he glimpsed Archie's startled face. Then, with a cry, Archie toppled backward to fall heavily onto the manky floor.

Angus advanced on his quarry. He was going to enjoy this.

'You!' Archie exclaimed, his face contorted with what Angus mistakenly thought was hate.

'Get up!' Angus spat.

Archie's hands scrabbled for two rubber tipped sticks lying next to him. Using these he tried valiantly to regain his feet.

Angus frowned, wondering what his step-father was playing at. Why the sticks?

For the first time he noticed how twisted and grotesque – the legs especially – Archie's limbs had become.

Raising his eyes he saw a wheelchair standing further along the small hallway.

Finally, having tried repeatedly and failed, Archie sank back onto his bottom. Glaring, he said he couldn't get up under his own steam and that Angus would have to help him.

Sitting there almost helpless as a babe Archie was a pitiful sight, and one which drained the tumultuous anger out of Angus. It just wasn't in him to ladle into a man in this condition.

Angus took Archie by the hand and after something of a struggle got him back on his feet.

Angus asked what had happened and Archie replied his old pains which had bothered him for years had been the early stages of arthritis. He turned and shuffled – making the dragging sound Angus had heard while waiting for the door to be answered – to the wheelchair which he sank into with a sigh of relief.

There was a certain classic irony about all this which wasn't lost on Angus. That Archie's arthritis caused him continual, excruciating pain was plainly evident. The man who'd caused so much misery and suffering to others was now doomed to suffer miserably himself.

Staring at his step-father Angus could find no forgiveness in himself. The picture of Carrie was too fresh in his mind. And anyway he wasn't the forgiving kind.

He hoped Archie lived to a ripe old age, and during every day of the time left him suffered all the pains and agonies of hell.

'She died last night,' Angus said abruptly.

Archie blinked and frowned. 'Who?'

'My mother.'

Archie's lips shrivelled into a thin line and he dropped his head to stare at the floor. Nor did he lift his head again until Angus turned to go.

Revenge had already been exacted on Archie and in a far more terrible manner than anything Angus had had in mind. His hand was on the doorknob when Archie suddenly spoke softly behind him.

'You may be grown up but don't think you know it all yet. In my own way I loved your mother even though I did treat her badly from time to time. For what it's worth I'm truly sorry. She'll be sorely missed for she was a good woman.'

When Archie had finished speaking Angus walked from the house out into the street where he stood feeling sick. He wondered why Harriet hadn't told him about Archie's condition.

The simple answer was she hadn't known. Archie Marjoribanks had become virtually a taboo subject in Tallon Street as Carrie couldn't bear to hear his name mentioned. Consequently Harriet had been in the dark about his illness.

Just then a face from the past arrested Angus's gaze and instantly rekindled his anger.

He watched as Tod Gemmill strolled by on the opposite side of the street. Tod was another he owed and now was as good a time as any to repay that debt.

Crossing the street he hurried after his man. When they came to Angus's old primary school, Angus maintaining a respectable distance behind Tod while he waited his chance, Tod suddenly headed off at a tangent.

Being Sunday and at a time of the morning when most

folk were either still abed or else getting ready for church the streets were more or less deserted, which suited Angus down to the ground.

Breaking into a trot he caught up with Tod in front of the Rialto picture house and tapped him on the shoulder. 'I'm claiming you,' he said.

Recognizing Angus, Tod's jaw literally fell open.

Angus jerked his thumb towards the ash and cinder track leading round the back of the picture house and Tod got the point. With a shrug Tod walked in the direction indicated.

Angus had always had extremely fast reflexes and it was these that saved him now.

In a well practised movement Tod whipped the cap from his head and flicked the brim straight at Angus's face.

Angus registered the blur and hastily jerked his head back. The cap brim missed his eyes by a few inches. Realizing what it was Tod had tried to hit him with he closed on Tod.

Tod flicked the cap again and this time its brim brushed against Angus's outstretched hand. A large gash suddenly opened up from wrist to little finger.

Grunting in surprise, Angus backpedalled.

The next time the cap sliced the air in front of him he glimpsed a flash of metal which told him the brim had been doctored in some way.

The two men circled one another, Tod swaying from side to side holding the cap bunched in his hand with its brim projecting outward.

The rim contained a row of razor blades stitched between the two layers of fabric so only their cutting edges protruded.

Suddenly Angus's opening was there as Tod overreached himself and stumbled. His hands automatically dropped to steady himself and as they did Angus leapt.

He got round behind Tod to put a crushing stranglehold on Tod's windpipe at the same time securing the hand holding the cap.

For a few seconds they struggled. Then Angus brought his heel smashing down on Tod's right instep.

Tod screamed and bucked. Dropping the cap, he reached back with both hands to tear and claw at Angus's face.

Angus exclaimed as a thumb jabbed him in the eye. Shifting his grip, he grasped Tod by a shoulder and using a combination push/pull movement, knocked him off balance. Then he threw him over his leg onto the ground.

He dropped his full weight onto Tod's chest, landing on his knees, which brought another scream from Tod.

'I give up! I give up!' Tod pleaded.

'Like fuck you do,' Angus said, drawing his fist back with the intention of bursting Tod's nose.

'I can tell you about your Da!' Tod wailed.

Angus's fist stopped in mid punch. He thought he couldn't have heard correctly. 'What did you say?' he demanded.

'Your Da,' Tod sobbed.

'What about him?'

'Promise you'll let me go?'

'If it's worth it,' Angus said slowly.

Tod sucked in a breath and groaned. He licked his lips.

'Well?'

'Your Da on the gantry, no one ever knew why he was up there.'

There was a vice in Angus's chest. 'Go on,' he whispered.

'Armstrong himself gave the order. It was to inspect something or other. I know for a fact because *my* Da overheard.' Tod gulped. 'He could never tell your Grandpa or speak up. It would've meant his job.'

So there it was. Sir Alan *had* owed Carrie compensation and the bloody man had never said a dickey bird. He'd kept stum to save himself a pittance, for that's all it would have been to him.

'Please?' Tod pleaded. 'You'll keep this to yourself? If Armstrong was to find out. . . .'

But Angus had stopped hearing. Rising, he started

back for the street, his anger completely gone leaving a great calm behind.

'He'll pay, Ma. I promise you,' he whispered.

He'd never meant anything more in his life.

19

In Scotland the best summer months are often May and September. It was the middle of May now and the sun was cracking the skies.

Diane Armstrong stood in the downstairs bay window of her sister's house in Bearsden watching several blackbirds squabbling over a worm one had dug up.

Rosemary was sitting by the fireplace mending a slight tear in one of Iain's best shirts. Diane said, 'By the way, an old friend of yours has been making inquiries about buying a house that's up for sale in Newton Mearns.'

Rosemary was engrossed in her task, nimbly sewing the tiny stitches required. 'Who's that, then?' she asked.

Diane sprung her bombshell. 'Angus McBain.'

The shock that swept through Rosemary was like having a bucket of ice cold water emptied over her head. 'Is that a fact?' she replied and somehow continued sewing.

In a quiet voice Diane went on to say Angus was apparently interested in buying a mansion that had only recently come onto the market. It was an old property with something like twenty rooms, a conservatory and outhouses.

Rosemary said it couldn't be the Angus McBain they knew as he couldn't possible afford anything like that.

But Diane was adamant. It was the same Angus McBain who'd lived in Holmlea Road and run off leaving Rosemary in the lurch.

A lump filled Rosemary's throat as she pretended to be still interested in her sewing. But she wasn't fooling Diane one little bit and she knew it.

She asked Diane if she knew where Angus had been and what he'd been doing? But these were questions her sister had no answers for.

All Diane could tell her was that Angus was back. And if he was able to consider buying a house like the one in Newton Mearns it was to be presumed he wasn't still the poor lad he'd been when they'd known him.

Rosemary smiled grimly to herself. Angus had always sworn he'd one day be a somebody with lots of money. It would seem he'd at least got the money.

Further discussion was halted by Iain's entrance.

Now he was back in civvy street Iain was being reluctantly drawn more and more into running his father's property business. Both his parents had virtually lost all interest in everything since the night he'd returned home from hospital to give them the combined shock of seeing the ruin his face had become and telling them the news of Peter's death.

Hyper-sensitive about his looks, he'd become something of a recluse, only leaving the house when absolutely necessary. The telephone was his lifeline through which he conducted the vast majority of his dealings with the outside world.

His personality had changed considerably since leaving hospital. He'd always had a tendency to be brooding and introspective: Now it wasn't unusual for him to spend days locked away in his study.

After Iain had left them the two women chatted for some time about the reappearance of Angus McBain.

Then, having seen her sister off, Rosemary went into the garden where she strolled deep in thought. Questions crowded her mind. Had Angus altered much? And if so, what did he look like now? How had he made enough money to be able to contemplate buying a mansion?

And, of course, the big question that had plagued her this long time – why had Angus run off the way he had?

As Rosemary wandered through her garden thinking about Angus, he was mounting the stairs to the solicitors who were dealing with the sale of the Newton Mearns property.

The house was an old one with an enormous amount needing done to it. But rather than being a black mark against it this appealed to Angus as it gave him the excuse to have the place modernized to his own specifications

The house was to be the first stage of the promise he'd made the day Petersson announced the bauxite strike. His son was going to have the very best of everything which naturally included a place to live.

Having stated to the solicitor that he wanted to purchase, he was entertained with sherry and digestives over which he was informed the legal documents would be drawn up in due course.

Before leaving he inquired about rented accommodation and was told the matter would be looked into right away.

Feeling well pleased with himself and the way things were going, he drove out to Cathcart and Tallon Street. Winnie was in but Donald whom he'd really come to see was at the allotment.

Over a cup of tea Winnie told him Hugh and Janey's big news. He said he'd drop by Muirend and see them after he'd had a word with Donald.

Angus found his grandfather at the plot. The two sat on an old wooden bench and for a wee while they blethered about inconsequentials, Donald using the respite to enjoy a pipeful of tobacco.

Retirement was proving a heavy burden for Donald to bear. Despite constant nagging from Winnie he was beginning to neglect himself. It was this personal neglect which was worrying Angus and had given him the idea of

how he could help his grandfather and at the same time
do himself a good turn.

In a mild voice Angus asked Donald if he'd be interested in holding down a job again?

Donald slowly took the battered briar from his mouth
and turned to stare at his grandson. Trying desperately
hard not to betray his eagerness he asked just what it was
Angus had in mind?

Angus explained about buying the house in Newton
Mearns and the state the place was in. Once an architect
had drawn up plans for modernization a gang of workmen would have to be employed to carry them out. What
he wanted was Donald to be gaffer over this lot.

Rubbing his jaw Donald said it was certainly an interesting proposition but had Angus forgotten all his
experience was in the foundry?

It was fair comment and one Angus was pleased his
grandfather had made. What he wanted Donald on the
payroll for was Donald's expertise in handling men and
getting the best out of them. Any problems over the job
in hand and all Donald had to do was refer back to him.
He'd soon get on site and work it out. After all, Donald
was a practical man who'd worked with his hands all his
life. He didn't have to be a journeyman in a particular
field to know if a job was well or badly done. Common
sense and a craftsman's eye would tell him that.

Donald nodded. Taking out his smoker's knife he
busied himself cleaning the briar's bowl and while doing
so quietly asked about money.

Angus replied he'd pay his grandfather a pound more
per week than whatever Donald had been earning at
Armstrong's

Donald was completely taken aback by this generous
offer and for a second actually gawped. Pulling himself
together, he resumed cleaning his pipe. After a suitably
dignified time had elapsed he cleared his throat and said
he'd be happy to accept.

Angus said Donald could consider himself on pay as
from the following Monday although it would be a wee

while yet before actual work started.

Together the pair of them left the allotment. Donald walked very straight and with his head held high. Back at Tallon Street an excited Donald broke the good news he was a gaffer again.

Angus made it quite clear to his grandfather the job had a limited life span after which he couldn't promise anything.

Donald said he fully understood. Then he hurried away through to the hall cupboard to root out his boiler suit for Winnie to wash and get ready for when it was needed.

Out on the landing Winnie drew the door behind her and Angus. There was more than a hint of tears in her eyes. 'Thank you, son. God bless you!' she whispered. Then wiping her face with the hem of her pinny she retreated swiftly to the hall where a voluble Donald was demanding to know where in the name of the wee man his boiler suit was!

As he dove out to Muirend Angus reflected Donald was a gaffer *par excellence* and would see to it every man jack gave a full day's work for the full day's pay they'd be collecting. Furthermore, with Donald in charge, he could rest assured no materials would go for a walk nor would there be any other petty finaglings of that ilk. The money and time saved would more than cover his grandfather's wages.

Humming to himself he arrived at the dairy to find Hugh in the stables attending to the horses. He loved coming to the dairy for the marvellous memories it held for him.

Looking round it wasn't difficult to hear and see himself and Kitty as young lads. There was a choke in his throat when he congratulated Hugh on Janey expecting again.

They found Janey in the kitchen baking and the first thing Angus did was to sweep her into his arms and give her a big hug and kiss.

Hugh was jubilant he was to be a father again. He kept

saying this time it was sure to be a wee boy.

After ten minutes non-stop talking about the forth-coming baby Hugh was told to shush by Janey who said he was beginning to sound like a big jessie the way he was going on.

Hugh mumbled something about not being able to help how pleased he was. To change the subject he said a little defiantly he was regularly attending classes down at the chapel where he was doing just fine. The priest had told him only the other day if he continued at his present rate of assimilation it wouldn't be too long before he was eligible for confirmation into the Catholic church.

Screwtops were opened and while Hugh did the honours Janey said she'd had some worrying news about Thistle Street. One of her sisters had been over to say her mother and father were near beside themselves because of the rumours flying round that the entire area had been bought up and the new owners intended giving them all notice to quit.

There were a dozen conflicting stories about what was to happen once the rows of tenements were finally empty.

One said they were to be demolished and new private middle-class accommodation built in their stead, another that a huge works was to be constructed on the site. Yet another rumour was that a Corporation scheme was to be erected in which many of the former inhabi-tants were to be rehoused.

As to who'd been buying up the area there were as many candidates as there were rumours to support them.

Those who favoured the housing scheme idea natur-ally enough said it was the Glasgow Corporation while others were adamant it was a titled Englishman out to exploit Scotland the way his hated race had always done.

Those believing the works story insisted it was a con-sortium of Scottish businessmen, the most well known of whom was Sir Alan Armstrong. Angus's ears pricked up the moment Sir Alan's name was mentioned.

Janey went on to say her father was terrified of losing

his job. At his age and with the surplus of young man-power suddenly swamping the market as a result of thousands of demobbed soldiers looking for work, the chances were he would never get another job again.

Hugh's bonhomie and wellbeing gradually faded as he listened to all this. Much as he liked his in-laws he didn't particularly want them descending on him for what might turn out to be an indefinite period. He chided himself for the unworthy thought. Nonetheless it was how he felt.

Angus decided he was going to have to have Armstrong's rumoured involvement in the Gorbal's investigated. Anything Armstrong had his snout into interested him.

As it happened he already had a private investigator called Otis Bitu under hire. When he next saw Bitu he would ask him to take on this new assignment.

They spoke about the McIvers possible predicament a little while longer, then Angus excused himself, saying it was high time he went.

Motoring up the drive he decided on impulse to visit Carrie's grave which was close by.

Having parked the car, he walked down an incline past row upon row of graves until he came to the one where Carrie and his father were buried.

The gold lettering recently scored into the marble headstone shone and glinted in the sun. The grave itself still had a freshly dug look about it.

To have come all the way from Australia only to miss her by a few hours! It was heartbreaking.

There had been little of Carrie's he'd wanted to hang onto: her wedding ring, the one his father had given her and not Archie's, several hand stitched pictures she'd done herself, and the tug-of-war medal his father had won against the City of Glasgow police.

What had been his other treasured possession, his father's wallet with the faded initials J.McB. on its front, was at the bottom of the sea, having gone down with the *Almuria*.

All in all not a lot to be the only keepsakes he had of his parents, but for Angus they were enough.

Sir Alan Armstrong was being entertained by his mistress in the house he'd bought her in Partickhill.

Margaret Cunninghame was twenty-four years old, the same age as Rosemary, whom she'd been to school with. Margaret had been the other girl with Rosemary all those years ago when Angus and Kitty had saved the two Parkie lassies from the toughs in the Queen's Park reccy ground.

She was a tall woman with mouse brown hair, frightfully well spoken, and languid in all her movements.

She was a war widow. Her husband, an officer in the Scots Guards, had been blown to smithereens by a German landmine.

Her family were landed gentry, at least they had been until just before the war when everything they owned had disappeared into the open maw of the Glasgow stock market which her father had played addictively and badly.

As a result of her family's penury Margaret had married for money. But her husband had been killed before he'd come into his inheritance and, as she hadn't got on at all well with her in-laws who'd guessed her reason for marrying their son, she'd found herself more or less back to square one.

Being Sir Alan's mistress was a solution to her problem. It was an indolent life she led but then she was an indolent person. Her only worry was keeping Sir Alan happy when he visited her every Tuesday and Friday nights.

His permanent alibi was that he travelled through to Edinburgh on those nights to stay with friends with whom he conducted east coast business. And in case Cordelia ever decided to ring him there a plan had been worked out whereby his friends would say he was tied up and would ring her back. They would then contact him and he would ring her from the Partickhill house pretending he was speaking from Edinburgh.

The reason Sir Alan had taken a mistress was a quaint one: having made a great deal out of the war he had to think of new ways in which to spend and enjoy his money. The idea of a mistress had originated from one of his friends who'd let drop in conversation that a third party they both knew had installed a fancy lady in the West End.

Now Sir Alan's marriage was a happy one with which he was well pleased. Nonetheless the thought of another woman was an exciting one. So there and then he'd decided he too would have a mistress.

Propositioning Margaret had taken him ages and caused him much anxiety in case he was making a mistake as to the sort of person she was.

In the end it was Margaret, no fool at seeing what was in a man's mind and what his intentions were, who'd steered a conversation between them in such a way it had seemed the most natural thing in the world for him to suggest she became his mistress.

Later he'd wondered just who had propositioned whom?

Sir Alan sat back and gazed into his glass of whisky while through in the bedroom Margaret went about making down the bed. He reflected life had been extraordinarily good to him of late, thanks to the war.

Business in the works was falling away, of course, now the conflict had come to an end. But he'd diversified his capital into property. He positively swelled with pride and pleasure thinking of the amount of property he now owned. Nearly half a square mile belonged to him and soon it would be time for the tenements to be razed and the new constructions started.

The one fly in the ointment was there were still several streets eluding a Phoenix takeover.

With a smile of gratification he pictured the plans his architects had drawn up for the area. Once those bright, shiny houses were built they would radically alter the face of south Glasgow, at the same time earning Phoenix

Development Ltd a massive fortune.

The Gorbals would return to what it had been originally – an area where decent middle-class folk lived rather than the appalling, festering blot on the landscape it had degenerated into.

A frown creased his face at the thought of that pocket of resistance holding out on him. It was owned by a cantankerous old besom called Miss McCallum with whom he'd crossed swords in the past, and who, despite a number of most generous offers, steadfastly refused to sell.

Unfortunately the streets owned by her were situated slap bang in central Gorbals, occupying the prime site of the redevelopment area.

The one good thing was she was eighty-six years old with one foot in the grave from stomach cancer. It was thought she wouldn't last out the year.

Once she died he intended stepping in and buying her properties from her next of kin, a nephew in Inverness whom he'd ensure would be only too happy to sell.

The Gorbals! A name as hard as the people currently living there. Well, he was going to arrange it so the name was eradicated forever. It would become a mere historical reference.

Hutchesontown was the correct name for the district and the one he intended it to be known as in the future.

Leaving John and Dawn in the excellent rented accommodation, a house in Barrhead the solicitors had acquired for them, Angus drove into town to Otis Bitu's office. He rather liked Bitu, tiny, dark-haired, swarthy American of Middle European ancestry.

Otis Bitu had come to Scotland as a flyer with the United States Air Force and had married a Scots lassie by the name of Morag. Tall as he was short he worshipped her as though she was a goddess come to earth.

When Morag had announced at the end of the war she had absolutely no intention of leaving Glasgow – she wanted to stay near her Mammy – he'd seen no alternative to remaining behind while the rest of his comrades went home.

Born and bred in Lansing, Michigan, he'd done well for several years until being drafted.

Finding himself a civilian again and unable to practise his profession in Scotland, he'd elected to work as a private investigator for the simple reason it was a crazy sort of job which suited him down to the ground.

He enjoyed getting out and about and meeting people from all walks of life, finding it a sort of balm after the rigours of war.

It was through having performed some minor services for the Central Station Hotel that he'd come to be recommended to Angus. For here Angus had stayed on his return from Australia.

Angus knocked on Bitu's office door, letting himself in when Bitu called out the door was open. Bitu was on the phone and gestured he sit in the visitor's chair. Cradling the phone, Bitu launched into a verbal report outlining the results of his investigations on Angus's behalf.

To begin with he'd gone to the address Angus had given him down by the Govan Docks where he'd found the house still inhabited by prostitutes. But none of them had ever heard of Sheena Marjoribanks.

In a local shebeen where only red biddy –a lethal concoction of rough red wine and meths – was served he'd come across a played out brass called Wild Irish Maeve who for the price of a Parazone bottle filled with the nightmare mixture told him Sheena had left the Govan address to move to the Gallowgate.

Again it had been doing the rounds, asking in shops, speaking with the local police.

He'd come up with another address which had taken him out to Pollokshaws where he'd learned Sheena had moved on to Egypt, an area between Shettleston and Tollcross.

In Egypt he'd discovered Sheena had flitted yet again, this time to the centre of town because she'd landed a job as a barmaid in a boozer called the Capitol Bar.

Angus had never actually been in the Capitol Bar but knew it had a reputation as being a place where a lot of hard men drank. At least that's what it had been like before the war.

Angus was pleased with Bitu and said so. Producing his cheque book, he wrote out the balance of the American's fee, adding a tenner because he appreciated a task well done.

Handing over the cheque, he asked if Bitu would be interested in doing another job for him?

Bitu was only too happy to oblige and hurriedly got out some scrap paper and a pen to take down the details.

Leaving Bitu's office, Angus drove up Sauchiehall Street to just before Charing Cross where he turned off left.

The Capitol Bar was grimy outside but then so was nearly all of central Glasgow. He parked the car and went inside to discover there was an upstairs and downstairs bar. Sheena was in neither.

Thinking she might appear at any time he stayed in the downstairs bar and ordered a pint of heavy. He could have asked for Sheena but didn't want to, preferring to give her a surprise. When at the end of an hour she still hadn't put in an appearance he decided to leave it and return later.

After the evening meal he drove back to the Capitol Bar which was packed.

Downstairs he found an arty crafty crew far different to the hard men he'd been expecting. The clientele had been so sparse in the morning it had been difficult to judge what sort now frequented the place.

He squeezed past two young lads talking about Cubism and sidled up to the bar.

She was dressed entirely in black and standing directly facing him pulling a pint. As she lifted the pint onto the bar she looked straight into his eyes. As she did so her own eyes filled with amazement, then pleasure.

'Another pint of that when you're ready,' he smiled.

When she took his money their hands briefly touched.

She nodded as if to say it was as though he'd never been away.

Handing him his change, she whispered, 'Can you hang on until we're closed?'

He replied that he could. So she added if he'd wait for her outside the front door she'd meet him there.

At a quarter past nine the doors to the pub opened and she slipped out. Without any hesitancy she came into his arms and he held her close.

'A long time, Angus,' she said.

'It is that,' he replied. 'Did you know Carrie's dead?'

She stiffened and then pulled herself away from him. Slowly she shook her head.

There was far too much to talk about standing out in the road like this so he asked her if there was somewhere close by where they could go? She replied she had a wee place only a few streets away.

The room was a large kitchen with a box bed tucked away at the far end. It was neat and tidy and shone like a new pin.

While she hung up her hat and coat Angus sat and studied his step-sister. She was certainly older looking with a few splashes of grey in her hair. She was carrying a little more matronly weight than he remembered. And the stamp of a terrible loneliness was on her.

She produced a bottle of gin from which she poured two generous measures into tumblers. They drank it neat because she had no mix.

Missing nothing out he told her all that had befallen him since they'd last been together.

After he'd finished they sat for a few minutes in silence. Then he prompted her to tell him what had happened to her during the long years of separation.

At first she was reluctant. But he got round her with a bit of coaxing and slowly she began telling him her tale.

She'd remained on the game for quite a while after he'd gone to sea until getting an awful scare by coming down with a bad dose of VD.

The cure had been excruciatingly painful but had

brought her to her senses. When she was discharged from hospital she'd gone looking for a straight job, ending up as a conductress on the trams again.

For a time there had been a man. Then one day he just wasn't around any more and she'd had to accept he'd gone for good.

The funny thing was she hadn't been sleeping with him, having insisted they wait until after they were married. What she'd wanted more than anything was his respect.

She could only think he'd disappeared out of her life because he'd got fed up being denied sex or else had somehow found out about her past. She was inclined to think it was the latter.

'If you're interested I'd like you to be John's nanny,' Angus said. 'That's been in my mind since I knew I was coming home and Dawn who looks after him now, wants to go travelling.'

'Look after your wee boy?' Sheena said, her voice cracking with emotion.

'Would you like that?'

'Oh yes,' she whispered. 'You know damn well I would.'

'Then it's settled. When can you start?'

'I've got to give forty-eight hours notice at the pub. I wouldn't run out and leave them, you understand. They've been decent to me.'

Angus nodded. He would've expected nothing less.

There were tears in Sheena's eyes as they made the arrangements. She would overlap with Dawn for a week and then Dawn would be free to start her tour of Europe.

Later, when Angus had gone, Sheena went to bed taking the remains of the gin with her. And there she cried her eyes out. Thanking God time and time again for this new chance.

In the morning she felt a woman reborn.

Donald stood with his arms akimbo staring up at Craiglea – the name of the Newton Mearns house –

which now belonged to Angus. It was a handsome place albeit in his estimation a wee bit dark and forbidding.

He couldn't help but be filled with pride to think *his* grandson was the owner of such a fine mansion. My God, it was a far cry from the hovel he'd been born into in Invershuie or the one Winnie had first seen the light of day in in Fanagmore!

The family had come a long way in three generations. There was Angus with his grand Newton Mearns mansion and his Australian bauxite mine. And Hugh the owner of a prosperous dairy as well as an equally thriving farm out on the East Kilbride road.

Mind you, Hugh had been enormously lucky in having Greta Paterson leave him the dairy and farm but that didn't detract one whit from the achievement. After all, Hugh had grafted damn hard to get in her good books in the first place and Greta had left him what she had knowing full well he'd make a go of it.

He'd come to think an awful lot of his son these past few years although it still pained him greatly that Hugh had married a Catholic and even worse, was in the process of turning one himself.

Not that he could fault Janey on anything bar her religion. Apart from that flaw he couldn't have asked for a better daughter-in-law.

With regards to Angus, it saddened him enormously that Angus's marriage had folded, and so quickly too. The poor boy's mother had gone through so much in that department you would've thought he'd be spared similar problems.

Donald was inordinately proud of what Angus and Hugh had achieved but there was another side of him that was highly suspicious of the way in which they seemed to be joining the capitalist classes.

He still considered it wrong and grossly immoral for individuals to be so well off when countless others in the world were either starving or else barely getting by on subsistence level. In Britain, at least, with a Labour government under Clem Attlee in power, the future looked good and getting better all the time for the working classes. He firmly believed the corner had been turned and what the country was now witnessing was the dawn of a glorious socialist age.

In the meantime he had a job to get on with – and the irony wasn't lost on him – thanks to his capitalist grandson.

He made his way across to where the first of the workmen he'd hired were waiting to be told what to do.

20

Angus was whistling as he parked his car and ran up the stairs leading to Bitu's office, where he found the American primed and ready for him.

Bitu said his inquiries about the Gorbals had thrown up the name Phoenix. He'd gone to London where he'd spent an entire day in Companies House in the City Road where a record is kept of every company formed in Britain. Eventually he'd turned up a company called Phoenix Development Ltd which had two directors, Sir Alan Armstrong and Sir Hamilton McLaren. Between them these two gentlemen now owned nearly all of the Gorbals.

Angus nodded his satisfaction. Bitu had again done well. The question now was what did Sir Alan and Sir Hamilton – whom he knew to be Rosemary's father-in-law which made it even more interesting – propose doing with the properties they'd acquired?

Bitu's new brief was to find out precisely what these

proposed plans were. It seemed a safe bet to assume something had to be in the wind to account for the many rumours currently flying round the area.

They shook hands at the door as Bitu promised to be in touch as soon as he'd come up with something.

Back on the street Angus walked round the corner to a little coffee shop he'd fallen into the habit of frequenting at this time of day when he'd been living at the hotel.

The coffee shop was in the rear of a barber's and was extremely masculine. It was mainly patronized by businessmen who in their pin-striped suits and starched collars blended in perfectly with the wood-panelled decor and faded genteel atmosphere.

He was surprised to see a woman sitting alone at a table. Even a woman in the company of a man would've been unusual as it was just not that sort of establishment. He was even further surprised when she smiled at him.

For a moment he thought she was a high class tart. Then with a start he realized he recognized the face.

'Hello Angus,' she said, extending her hand to be shaken.

She'd changed a lot since they'd last met but then so had he. 'Hello Diane,' he replied. And having sat, he waved to the hovering waiter to bring coffee for him and a refill for her.

They smiled and stared at one another. Finally Diane said, 'I heard on the grapevine you'd bought Craiglea so I went out there this morning hoping to see you but met your grandfather instead. He told me if I was to come here at around this time I might well run into you.'

Angus raised an eyebrow. 'Does Grandpa know who you are?'

'Oh yes. He's seen me many times in the past.'

Angus wondered about Donald knowing he frequented this particular coffee shop. He couldn't remember ever having mentioned the fact to his grandfather. But then that was Donald all over, always full of surprises.

Her voice suddenly betraying her eagerness, Diane

asked if Kitty had returned to Glasgow with Angus and, if so, how was he?

'Kitty's dead,' Angus replied and watched her face crumple in on itself. She and Kitty had been extremely fond of one another.

Angus had always presumed the Armstrong girls would have found out he and Kitty had gone off to sea, but apparently not.

Starting with the *Almuria* he spoke briefly of what had befallen them up to the point where Kitty had died from eating poisoned pickles aboard the *Wahroonga*.

'My God!' said Diane, shocked at the absurdity of Kitty's death.

Angus could hold his own question back no longer. Affecting a nonchalent attitude he asked, 'How's Rosie?' adding what he hoped appeared as an after-thought, 'Didn't I hear or read somewhere she'd got married?'

'She's fine, And yes she is.'

Angus lowered his head and sipped his coffee. He didn't want Diane to see his face.

Diane knew only too well she'd been manipulated by her sister into this meeting. Rosemary's intention was that while Diane was inquiring about Kitty she'd also find out the answer to the question tormenting Rosemary all these years: namely, why had Angus run off and left her the way he had? Without frills or preliminaries Diane now put it to him point blank.

Angus blinked and sat back in his chair. That Diane had needed to ask the question gave him a great jolt.

He remembered the intense anger and wounded pride he'd felt that day in the Old Castle Road when he'd witnessed Rosemary kissing the man later to become her husband, and whom he'd presumed ever since she'd been two timing him with.

And yet staring into Diane's frank, open face the first suspicions of doubt began to niggle him. If what he'd believed was true all these years then why was Diane demanding an explanation from him as though *he* were the guilty one?

He knew then he was going to have to tell Diane his side of the story. He started with the episode of the cuff links.

As his tale unfolded Diane's reactions couldn't have been more genuine. Disbelief was followed by incredulity which in turn gave way to anger.

In a voice cold as winter she said her father would never have done such an underhand trick and he must be mistaken!

But Angus continued describing how feeling wretched and completely distraught he'd gone to Arnprior House only to witness Rosemary and Iain McLaren kissing in a way that could hardly be described as platonic. It hadn't been difficult to put two and two together.

Diane's face creased in a frown as she searched her memory. As for the reason behind the kissing she couldn't say. But she was certain Rosemary and Iain hadn't been involved at that point.

They sat in silence for a while, accusation and denial having given them both a great deal to think about.

Finally Diane said she would do her best to get to the root of all this and when she'd done so she'd contact Angus again and tell him of her findings.

Then by mutual consent they changed the subject.

For a while Diane talked of herself and what she'd done during the war. Then she tried to pump Angus as to how he'd come by enough money to be able to afford a house the size of Craiglea.

He skilfully parried all her questions with vague answers. For the time being he didn't want any of the Armstrongs, even friendly ones, knowing how wealthy he'd become.

They said goodbye on the street corner.

Diane was nearly a block away when, like a bolt from the blue, it came to her her father did indeed own a pair of cuff links horribly similar to the ones Angus had described.

Furthermore, unless her memory was playing her

false, they'd been a present to him from her mother the very Christmas before the January during which Angus and Kitty disappeared.

She would go straight to Rosemary's to relate everything Angus had told her.

Sir Alan knew the moment he walked into the room and saw Rosemary's face something was dreadfully wrong.

When he asked her if she'd care to join him in a drink she didn't reply, instead holding out her right hand on the palm of which lay two small objects.

Intrigued, he came closer until he could make out what they were. When he recognized them he knew immediately what this was all about.

'Well?' she snapped, her eyes flashing cold fire.

'How did you find out?'

'So it's true,' she said.

He shrugged and busied himself at the decanter. Almost casually he said, 'It was for your own good, lass. McBain was a nothing, a nobody. And you after all are *my* daughter.'

She'd realized long ago he'd manipulated her into marriage with Iain but she'd always believed he'd merely capitalized on Angus's disappearance. It had never crossed her mind he'd engineered that disappearance.

Bile churned in her stomach and it took every ounce of self control she possessed not to fly at her father and rake him with her nails.

Through the open window she could see the very spot where Iain had parked Sir Hamilton's car that fatal day she'd kissed him as Angus had looked on.

If only Angus had come to her she could've explained. Instead he'd run away to sea and out of her life.

Her hand whipped in a savage sideways motion to send the cufflinks sailing out the window to fall somewhere in the garden.

Without another word she walked stiffly from the room.

She was halfway home when the dam broke and her

pent up emotions overflowed in a flood of hot, salty tears.

Iain banked the Tiger Moth and brought her onto a course that would take him directly over Stirling Castle. The plane was a recent acquisition he'd been lucky enough to snap up at a bargain price.

The sky was duck egg blue with clumps of cumulus moving at between 4000 and 5000 feet. He was flying at 3000 so the cloud wouldn't interfere with the splended panoramic view spread below him.

He tried to get up as often as he could for only in the air did he feel whole again and at peace. In the confines of the cockpit he could forget about his face for a little while.

If it had been possible for him to remain airborne for the rest of his life he would've elected to do so. His only regret would have been losing Rosemary who was his strength and whose very strength he found so comforting.

Once over Stirling he executed a wide turn, bringing him onto a south-westerly course that would take him back to the small aerodrome in Renfrew where he kept the plane.

It was worrying him that Armstrong was insisting they start demolition work in the Gorbals as soon as possible, albeit they hadn't yet been able to acquire Miss McCallum's properties.

He wasn't at all convinced starting work at this juncture was wise. He much preferred the prudence of actually waiting till the old woman was dead and Phoenix actually owned her properties.

It also bothered him how obsessive Armstrong was becoming over this particular project.

As a means of self-preservation he'd learned to be extremely chary about this type of subjectivity while in the RAF. Fanatics might make excellent Kamikaze pilots but were hardly the best co-pilots when you yourself weren't interested in becoming part of the Divine Wind.

353

If only he'd been able to turn to his father for advice. But Sir Hamilton absolutely refused to discuss business, declaring that side of things to be his responsibility now.

He considered his father's attitude a great pity as there was so much he could have learned, and indeed desperately needed to learn, from Sir Hamilton, whom Iain was convinced wasn't long for this world.

During the war he'd become sickeningly familiar with the peculiar aura exuded by many people who have an approaching rendezvous with death. His father had been exuding that aura for months now.

When Otis Bitu met up with Angus some weeks after being instructed to find out what Phoenix Development Ltd had planned it was to report failure.

Try as he might, he just hadn't been able to uncover what Sir Alan Armstrong and Iain McLaren – whom he'd established was acting on behalf of Sir Hamilton McLaren – intended for the Gorbals

Demolition had already started near Ballater Street where a great many families had been evicted and a sizable area razed in the short time the bulldozers and wrecking crews had been at work.

Bitu went on to say he'd even gone as far as making inquiries of the Clerk of the Dean of Guild Court. But according to that worthy, Phoenix hadn't yet submitted plans for re-development.

While Angus digested this Bitu coughed and, looking vaguely embarrassed, shifted several times in his seat.

When asked by Angus what was on his mind he replied he'd accidentally stumbled across a piece of information which if Angus cared to exploit it might just be the key to solving the problem.

Prompted by Angus to continue he went on to say he'd discovered Sir Alan's chief accountant, a man called George Hetherington, was deeply in debt to a bookie by the name of Joe Field.

Angus grinned to hear Hetherington, whom he re-

membered well, had taken to playing the gee gees. A dry
stick of a man, Hetherington always gave the appearance of being the very epitomy of self-righteous pres-
byterianism. It seemed Hetherington wasn't such a dry
stick after all.

It was a few minutes past eight pm when Angus knocked
on the door of Hetherington's house in the smart district
of Clarkston, not all that far from Muirend where Hugh
and Janey lived.

Hetherington himself answered the door and asked in
a not particularly friendly manner what Angus wanted.

It was plain Hetherington didn't recognize him so he
introduced himself and asked if he could come in as he
had a business matter to discuss.

Hetherington was startled to find out who Angus was
and after a moment's hesitation started closing the door
in Angus's face.

He exclaimed in surprise and annoyance when Angus
first jammed his foot in the door, then leant heavily
against it. Smiling softly, Angus told Hetherington he
wasn't being very polite towards someone who'd come
to do him a good turn.

Extremely agitated, Hetherington wasn't at all sure
what to do next. Finally he decided prudence was the
better part of valour and with bad grace invited Angus
through to the parlour where they could discuss whatever it was Angus had in mind.

Angus had already been to see Joe Field – spinning
him a yarn that had opened the bookie's mouth – to get
the facts and figures right. So he came straight to the
point.

'How would you like to earn £419?' he asked.

Hetherington gulped and had to hold onto a chair for
support. The figure was too precise for there to be any
mistake.

In a trembling voice he asked how Angus had found
out about his gambling debts and what Angus intended
doing about it? Both he and Angus knew if this came to

Sir Alan's attention he'd be sacked immediately.

Before Angus could reply the door opened and Mrs Hetherington entered. She was a kindly looking soul although shockingly thin with a positively haggard face. She was the sort who is always cheery with never a bad word to say about anyone. Angus warmed to her right away and wondered how she'd got tied to such a dreich colourless man as her husband was.

Seeing Hetherington wasn't going to do the honours, Angus introduced himself and shook Mrs Hetherington by the hand.

She was taking her leave to put the kettle on when she started to cough and wheeze simultaneously, causing her to stop and bend over in an effort to catch her breath.

Straightening up again she said to Angus it was just a wee dry tickle she had in her throat. Throwing him a beaming smile, she hurried away through to the kitchen.

Angus sat unbidden facing the accountant and while Hetherington stared concernedly after Mrs Hetherington he went over what he'd learned from Donald that afternoon regarding the man.

During the many years he'd been with Armstrong's Hetherington had made a name for himself as being highly conscientious and exceptional at his job. He thrived on anything to do with figures, having a natural understanding of money matters and all their various facets.

He also had a shrewd head on his shoulders and was often consulted personally by Sir Alan. And more often than not his advice was acted upon.

As chief accountant he was naturally in charge of the Armstrong books. What Angus was hoping was that he was also in charge of the Phoenix ones, or at least privy to their contents.

Hetherington slowly brought his attention back to bear on Angus. As he did so guilt and apprehension crept over his face.

Licking his lips, he asked what Angus intended doing,

adding dourly that if it was money Angus was after then Angus was out of luck as he didn't have any.

Angus shook his head. On the contrary he was hoping to give Hetherington some in exchange for a little information.

Hetherington was clearly puzzled and asked how an ex-apprentice fitter could afford to hand over the sort of money he was in debt to the tune of? Unless, of course, Angus was working for someone else, in which case who?

Angus replied he was working for no one but himself. When he saw Hetherington didn't believe him he crossed to the telephone and gave the operator the number which would connect him with the solicitor who'd handled the purchase of Craiglea for him.

When the man came on the line Angus told him what was required. Then gesturing Hetherington over, he left it to the solicitor to confirm his financial *bona fides*.

Hetherington returned to his chair to admit grudgingly it would seem Angus was now a man of considerable means.

Angus wrote out a cheque for £419.00 which he passed over to Hetherington. He wanted the accountant to hold his salvation in his hands for the psychological effect it would have on him.

The door opened and Mrs Hetherington wheeled in a trolley overflowing with goodies. She helped Angus and her husband to what they wanted and was about to help herself when Hetherington said gruffly he wanted to be alone with Angus.

Without a word of argument or dissent Mrs Hetherington left the room. Hetherington stared after his wife. There was something very poignant and touching in his expression which impressed Angus.

Hetherington's gaze dropped to the cheque still clutched in his hands.

Angus smiled and said for reasons of his own he wanted a friend – Hetherington winced at the euphemism – in Sir Alan Armstrong's camp and was willing to pay handsomely for the service.

If Hetherington agreed the £419 would only be a down payment with regular monthly sums to follow.

When Angus mentioned the sum of fifty pounds Hetherington looked startled for a second, then quickly nodded.

There was something wrong here. Angus could feel it. Although having little choice in the matter of capitulation Hetherington, for the man of honour and integrity Donald assured him he was, had done so too easily. That bothered Angus so before putting his question about the Gorbals he demanded to know why it was so?

Hetherington took so long in replying that Angus was beginning to think he wasn't going to. But suddenly he started to speak in such a low voice that Angus had to strain to hear.

Hetherington said his wife had always been asthmatic but her condition had worsened drastically during the war years as a direct result of the prevailing conditions. Her asthma was now so bad that unless they could move to a warm climate within the next year her chances of surviving much beyond that were extremely slim.

As Hetherington spoke Angus felt awful about how he'd misjudged the man. He'd presumed Hetherington to be just another punter with gambling fever whereas the truth of the matter was it had been a frantic effort on Hetherington's part to try and raise the money to take Mrs Hetherington to the sort of climate the doctor said was necessary for her survival.

Angus asked if they owned the house, thinking they could have sold and raised capital that way. But the answer was no. Like the vast majority of Glaswegians the Hetheringtons rented.

What little savings they'd had had gone on financing his gambling venture which Hetherington had hoped and prayed would bring them in the sort of return to solve their problem.

It had been clutching at straws, of course. And Hetherington had come horribly unstuck when, after a short winning streak, he'd hit a seemingly non-stop losing one.

That left the obvious question. Why hadn't Hetherington gone to Sir Alan for the sort of money that would enable him to send Mrs Hetherington abroad while he remained behind until the loan was repaid?

Hetherington replied he had indeed approached Sir Alan only to be callously turned down. He thought Sir Alan considered him far too valuable an employee to lose which would've eventually happened had the loan been forthcoming.

As an afterthought, Hetherington added he'd actually considered embezzlement and would have committed it had he thought there was any possible chance of getting away with it. But there wasn't thanks to a checking system he himself had introduced.

Angus asked why Hetherington had elected to try Joe Field's when surely the Stock Exchange would have been a far more suitable hunting ground for a man of his abilities?

Hetherington's reply was that the Exchange was still very firm after the conditions imposed on it during the war. As such it would've been virtually impossible, in the relatively short time available to him, to turn his small amount of savings into the capital sum needed.

Angus now appreciated why the poor bugger had caved in so easily.

Much as Sir Alan prized Hetherington as an employee he would be forced to sack him, especially if Joe Field made the matter public as Field was threatening to do.

Besides, from Sir Alan's point of view Hetherington would now be untrustworthy. Not only would Hetherington be sacked but undoubtedly there would be no letter of recommendation – and how that brought back memories for Angus! – which would mean the middle-aged accountant would never work again.

Angus's proposal was this. He would advance Hetherington over and above the £419, one year's money which amounted to £600, enabling Mrs Hetherington to go abroad right away.

Hetherington was dumbfounded. He stared incredulously at Angus, hope dawning joyously in his eyes. 'Why?' he croaked.

Angus explained it was merely a case of each of them having something the other wanted; Hetherington money, himself access to Sir Alan's innermost financial secrets. It seemed stupid for them not to help one another to their mutual advantage.

There had been a time when Hetherington would've refused outright in the name of loyalty to have anything to do with such a deal. But Sir Alan had forfeited that loyalty in turning down his plea for a loan, and condemning his wife to an early grave.

Angus and Hetherington shook hands on the agreement. Then Hetherington told Angus everything he wanted to know about the Gorbals project.

En route home it came to Angus there were parts of Australia – although unfortunately not Queensland – ideal for Mrs Hetherington's condition. He would put it to Hetherington the next time they spoke that she go there.

It had been a fruitful night which had brought him one step closer to Sir Alan's jugular. He wasn't quite sure yet just how he was going to effect his revenge. But he was certain that he was on the right track.

The next morning Angus was up early and, having breakfasted alone, collected the mail from the postman as he made his way out to the car.

It was a beautiful day so he thoroughly enjoyed the run down to Largs on the Firth of Clyde's coastline.

Arriving in Largs he embarked on the P.S. *Jeanie Deans* for Rothesay on the Island of Bute.

Halfway across a sudden squall came up. Leaving the outdoor passenger deck, he made his way to the aft saloon where he settled himself amongst the rose pink furnishings and light oak woodwork.

Remembering the letters he'd stuffed in his pocket earlier, he pulled them out. It was the last letter which interested him most coming as it did from Diane Armstrong and suggesting they meet again in the same coffee shop where she'd previously waylaid him. She said she'd be there on the following day at the same time unless she heard from him – her telephone number was enclosed – to the contrary.

As she'd said she would contact him again when she'd investigated the allegations he'd made about her father, Angus was curious to hear what she had to say.

When the boat docked Angus drove ashore. He had to ask directions twice before he found the house he was looking for.

He knocked, knocked again, and then again.

He was on the point of turning away thinking there was no one at home when the door opened to reveal an ancient, gnarled crone with a crabbit face.

'Miss McCallum?'

'Aye, sonny. What do you want?'

Angus hated people who called him sonny in that patronizing way. Nonetheless he fixed a smile on his face and introduced himself, asking if he could come inside as he had some business to discuss.

Miss McCallum looked suspicious and it was only when she realized he had a car – he could only wonder what association that had in her mind! – she agreed to let him in.

The place stank appallingly which was hardly surprising considering the clart and general debris littered everywhere.

There were the remains of a multitude of meals now covered in a virulent looking fungus atop a table. The sink was stacked high with unwashed dishes. There was another load piled in a cracked and mottled basin under the open-faced sink stand.

From the state of the house's interior it wasn't difficult to believe it had been many years since a cleaning hand had been raised in anger against it.

The *piece de resistance* was a rabbit hutch complete with long-eared rabbits tucked away in the far corner of the living room.

Miss McCallum asked if he'd like a cup of tea which he hastily refused. She sat down in a threadbare armchair whose bottom was threatening to fall out. A grizzled scotty dog nuzzled at her feet until she picked it up and deposited it in her lap. Gently she stroked the animal.

Angus wasn't quite sure what he'd been expecting – probably some genteel old lady amid a quaint Victorian setting. Instead he was faced with someone who might have stepped straight out of the first scene of *Macbeth*.

Opening the conversation, he said he understood she'd been ill and in the circumstances had been surprised to learn she was still at home. Surely she would have been far more comfortable in a hospital?

Miss McCallum replied waspishly that might well be so but hospitals didn't take in dogs and she had no intention of leaving dear Bella here to fret and pine which the beast would do if the two of them were parted.

In a whisper she added – perhaps she thought Bella would overhear and understand – her wee friend was also getting near the end of her days. They chatted for a while about Bella.

Then Angus brought up the object of his visit. He was interested in purchasing the properties owned by Miss McCallum in the Gorbals and was prepared to make a generous offer for them.

Miss McCallum snorted, replying he was the second person who'd wanted to buy those houses in recent years, the other being a certain Sir Alan Armstrong whom she couldn't abide at any price, being a rude and horrid man.

Angus said he knew Sir Alan and stressed he and Armstrong were far from friends.

Suddenly and without warning Bella was sick all down Miss McCallum who exclaimed in sympathy. She explained Bella had been suffering from a gyppy tummy of late which she thought had been cleared.

Leaving Bella whining in the chair, Miss McCallum hurried to a cupboard to fetch a far from clean cloth.

Hating to see the animal in distress Angus crossed to it and stroked its head. Then Miss McCallum was back wiping away the sick and fussing over the stricken beast.

Angus recalled a conversation he'd once heard between some Australian associates, both of whom were mad keen on dogs. It included a tip for canine upset tummies which he told Miss McCallum about. The mixture was warm milk with a tablespoonful of bicarb of soda stirred into it.

Miss McCallum had never heard of this particular cure and decided to give it a try. Luckily she had both ingredients to hand.

When the mixture was ready it was placed in a saucer before Bella who after a tentative sniff and taste eagerly lapped it all up. The dog appeared a little eased after that, soon curling up and falling asleep.

Miss McCallum was full of Angus's cure and insisted he take a glass of sherry with her. The sherry was sickly sweet and cloying, the glass it was served in manky. Somehow he got it down.

Again he broached the subject of the Gorbals properties to be told although he was a nice young man who'd just done her a service she had absolutely no intention of selling.

She'd originally purchased these properties on the advice of her man of business, a Mr Tait, now deceased, who'd told her never to part with them under any circumstances as they were the best possible investment a body could have.

The more she talked about this Mr Tait, who came over as having the wisdom of Solomon and the business acumen of a Rothschild, the more it became obvious she'd been a wee bit in love with him.

She said she sympathized with Angus and would like to have helped him as opposed to Sir Alan who in his efforts to get her to sell had caused her severe harassment in the past. But what it all boiled down to was her

Mr Tait had sworn her to holding onto these properties for the fine investment they represented and the regular income they provided.

She was adamant. She would hold onto these properties until her death after which they would go to her only surviving relative, a nephew living up in Inverness.

Angus asked if she was sure the nephew wouldn't sell to Sir Alan? But she pooh-poohed the idea, saying she'd written to him a number of times making it quite clear he was to abide by her wishes in this matter.

Angus could see there was no use discussing the subject further. So having left Miss McCallum his rented Barrhead address with the instructions to contact him should she ever change her mind, he climbed into his car and returned to Rothesay Pier where he awaited the next boat to Largs.

He was bitterly disappointed for he'd seen this as the perfect opportunity to initiate an attack on Sir Alan. Still it would seem Armstrong was going to have enough problems to contend with if Miss McCallum's nephew kept faith with her wishes.

According to Hetherington Sir Alan was confidently expecting to pick up the properties at bargain prices once Miss McCallum was dead and the houses transferred into the nephew's name.

With massive initial investment already sunk into the project and demolition work under way it was going to be a terrible headache to Phoenix to discover things weren't going to quite fall out as they'd planned after all.

During his return trip to Glasgow Angus tried to be philosophical about his failure. Other ways of getting at Armstrong would present themselves. All he needed to do was recognize and grab hold of them when they did.

He suddenly burst out laughing at a thought which flashed through his mind. Wouldn't it have been marvellous to have knocked down Miss McCallum's properties and built a glue factory in their stead!

He would love to have seen Phoenix try and sell their middle-class houses with that little lot belching out the most noxious fumes right in their midst.

Mid-morning the next day at precisely the time Diane had stated in her letter Angus presented himself in the coffee shop.

He was halfway to the table where the solitary woman was sitting before he was able to glimpse her face. The moment he did so it was as though he'd been hit a sledge hammer blow in the solar plexus.

He stood by the table and they stared at one another. Angus drank in every well remembered feature of her face.

'Hello Rosie,' he said and sat.

A waiter approached and, seemingly from a long distance away, he heard himself ordering coffee and biscuits.

'I was very upset to hear about Kitty's death,' Rosemary said.

Nothing had changed between them. It was the same as it had always been, the same empathy, the same ease. They fitted.

Taking a deep breath he launched into the tale which ended with Kitty's death aboard the *Wahroonga*.

The impulse to touch her, to hold her, was almost overpowering.

When he finally concluded she was sad and withdrawn. She said she hoped he didn't mind her coming in Diane's place but she'd felt it only right she did.

Jesus, the smell of her was so good! Time had dulled his memory of it. He inhaled to let it wash through him.

Continuing, Rosemary said she'd challenged her father about the cuff link incident which he'd admitted to.

Angus grunted.

The entire affair had been a complete set-up to get rid of Angus and have her married to Iain McLaren.

'And the kiss?'

She smiled bitterly and said she had, indeed, kissed Iain McLaren that day. But not for the reasons Angus had thought.

The kiss had been a purely spontaneous action because she'd just talked Iain into taking her flying again. That was all it had been. She gave him her oath on it.

'Aye, well there we are then. We were both played for a right couple of mugs,' Angus said, his intense hatred for Sir Alan Armstrong deepening even further.

That Rosemary hadn't been two timing him was a relief on the one hand and galling on the other. If only he'd kept his head how differently things might have turned out! As it was, he'd played right into Armstrong's hands.

Rosemary said Diane had told her Angus had married an Australian girl from whom he was now divorced. And that he'd brought his boy back to Scotland with him who, from all accounts, was a right smasher.

Angus dug in his wallet for a snapshot he carried of himself and John. John was positively beaming into the camera: it would have been impossible to find a bonnier or more appealing wee laddie anywhere.

Rosemary smiled as she stared at the snap. But it was a smile belying the pain lancing through her. She couldn't help but think if only circumstances had been different this wee chap might well have been hers.

'I'm sorry about the divorce,' Rosemary said.

Angus shrugged. 'Just one of those things.'

'Are you over it?'

'Oh yes.' Then to change the subject Angus said, 'He's a good looking chap, your Iain. I hope you've had and continue to have a lot of happiness together.'

For a split second she thought he was sticking the knife in. Then she realized from his expression he genuinely didn't know about the tragedy that had befallen Iain.

She considered telling him and decided not to. The last thing she either needed or wanted was his sympathy.

They talked for a little while longer, each dragging the minutes out and hoping the other wasn't noticing.

Finally after four cups of coffee and being nearly awash they ran out of excuses for prolonging the meeting any further.

Angus paid and then ushered Rosemary outside where they stood blinking in the harsh sunlight. There were creases round her eyes and mouth he hadn't noticed inside. She too had aged.

She pecked him chastely on the cheek and, without further ado, turned and went.

His heart in his mouth, he watched her till she'd rounded a corner and disappeared from sight. He'd thought she might look back. But she hadn't.

He remembered then Otis Bitu kept a bottle in his office for emergencies. If feeling the way he was didn't constitute an emergency he was damned if he knew what did.

A few weeks later Angus received a letter date stamped Rothesay. It came from Miss McCallum.

Miss McCallum had given a great deal of thought to their conversation and as a consequence had written her nephew in Inverness ordering him to travel down and see her. The nephew had come hot foot only to find himself subjected to an immediate interrogation. Riddled with guilt, he'd soon confessed to having been approached recently by Sir Alan Armstrong's partner with whom he'd made a gentlemen's agreement regarding the Gorbals properties once they became his.

Miss McCallum had been furious and lambasted the poor unfortunate who in an effort to make her see his side of things had explained he wanted to expand the wee grocery shop he owned and if possible open up another. The income from the Gorbals properties, while steady, was low whereas what he wanted was a lump sum in his hand.

After thoroughly vilifying her nephew for planning to go against her wishes Miss McCallum dispatched him back to Inverness with a gigantic flea in his ear, threatening to leave everything to a charity for dogs should he have anything further to do with Phoenix Development Ltd.

The upshot of all this was Miss McCallum was more determined than ever Sir Alan wouldn't get his hands on her properties. The cheek of the man and his partner going behind her back like that!

So to spite Sir Alan and this Iain McLaren she'd decided to sell to Angus, the proceeds of which would go to her nephew whom she still had a soft spot for. And his wish for a lump sum would then be fulfilled.

Angus was delighted by this. It meant it was now possible for him to move against Armstrong and hit the man where it would hurt most – in the pocket.

This operation he would tie in with another, something he and O'Rourke had discussed at length and come to agreement on before he left Australia. A great deal of what LMBM was producing was being exported. The bulk of what was going abroad came to Britain.

What Angus and O'Rourke intended was for Angus to set up a UK office of LMBM to handle the importing of the bauxite ore and its distribution. With the various middle men cut out they reckoned the company's British profits would leap by as much as one hundred per cent.

Angus intended setting up the company office in Glasgow for two reasons. The first was that he would be the chief executive of that office and Glasgow was where he wanted to live. For the time being, though, he would remain anonymously in the background, not wanting Sir Alan to know he was the puppeteer pulling the strings. His second reason was that LMBM ore coming into Clydeside would be work for the Docks, his small contribution to the prolonged life of his beloved city's main artery.

What he needed now was a front man, a lieutenant who'd apparently be in charge but in reality be under his command. And he was convinced he'd found just such a man in Otis Bitu whom he was sure would grab at the opportunity as Bitu's private investigation line of work – outside what Angus was putting his way – wasn't proving too lucrative.

The idea of the glue factory came back to Angus

making him laugh out loud. Glue factory it would be!

21

Sir Alan Armstrong stared lovingly at the plans for the new Hutchesontown spread before him.

These plans had actually been ready for some time but he'd always managed to find some small additional improvement to suggest which necessitated sending them back to the architects for incorporation.

When he finally came to submit the plans to the Dean of Guild Court he wanted them perfect in every detail. He wanted to submit a work of art which would reflect on him personally.

He started slightly, then smiled benevolently as Margaret Cunninghame slid her arm round his waist.

She said she enjoyed seeing him this way when he was so obviously happy, but thought sometimes he derived more pleasure from these plans of his than he did from her company.

Breaking away, he crossed to a trolley laden with drinks and poured them each a stiff one.

Handing Margaret hers he told her to sit and he would try and explain what the Gorbals project meant to him.

The engineering works was his father's creation. Sir William had conceived and brought into being the works of which he was now owner.

Armstrong's might be his responsibility but it wasn't his brainchild. The Gorbals project was. The fact he was deriving enormous self satisfaction out of it was enough.

But there was a lot more to it than that.

By building this whole new housing redevelopment scheme he was leaving his personal mark on Glasgow. For the next hundred years or so there would be a great slice of the city owing its existence to him – his memorial so to speak.

Not that he wouldn't be making a huge profit out of the redevelopment. He would. But the money wasn't primarily what this was all about.

The project was going to be the pinnacle of his life – what he would be *remembered* for.

Angus discussed the matter thoroughly with Hetherington who'd advised him to exploit without further delay the fact Sir Alan hadn't yet lodged the plans for the redevelopment of the Gorbals with the Dean of Guild Court.

Angus had therefore instructed the same architect working on Craiglea to cannibalize a past design into one for an animal by-products factory.

The reason it was necessary for him to lodge his factory plan first was by doing so he would have precedence over anything coming after, even something on such a grand scale as Sir Alan's plans. The smaller wouldn't have been allowed to intrude on the larger had the larger already been established.

Speaking further with Hetherington, Angus had been able to establish that one member of the Dean of Guild Court if approached the right way – by which Hetherington meant the man took backhanders – could be persuaded to argue their case, more or less ensuring LMBM's factory plan won aproval.

Otis Bitu – who'd accepted the job and who to all intents and purposes was now the UK representative of LMBM (Pty) Ltd – had consequently approached a civil engineer called Graeme McAskill who'd agreed to give LMBM's case due consideratioon.

This was McAskill's way of saying he was waiting to see what was offered before committing himself. Bitu had then suggested he and McAskill get together for a few drinks to solidify the situation. McAskill readily agreed.

McAskill's sweeteners usually came in the form of hard cash. But Angus intended introducing another element into the proceedings which he was convinced would really win McAskill over to LMBM's cause.

Angus explained to Sheena what he needed and asked if she could help? Sheena laughed and replied with her contacts from the old days it was the easiest thing in the world for her to arrange.

That Saturday night Bitu met McAskill in a pub. The pair of them made their way to a hotel where Sheena and a beautiful prostitute were waiting for them in the best suite the hotel had to offer.

Janice was what is known in Glasgow as *a right brammer*. She was petite with finely chiselled features and a figure any movie actress would've been proud of.

Perhaps her most winning asset – bearing in mind many middle-class Scots such as McAskill are most impressed by this sort of thing though they deny it – was her accent which was so refined as to be almost good enough to pass for a southern English one.

One look at the gorgeous Janice and McAskill was completely smitten. Glancing across at Bitu he was tipped the wink he wasn't misreading the situation.

For appearances sake and to help matters along Bitu had been paired with Sheena. But this was only a façade for McAskill's benefit. Neither Bitu nor Sheena intending anything other than a few drinks and conversation.

McAskill wasn't a widely experienced man when it came to women and Janice was something out of his wildest dreams. She had tricks to her repertoire that left him pop-eyed and gasping for more.

And more he got in abundance. When morning finally came McAskill was a man who'd already tasted paradise.

After the women had left, Bitu handed McAskill a wad of used fivers with the promise there would be more plus another party with Janice as soon as LMBM's plan for an animal by-products factory was given the go ahead.

As Bitu later reported to Angus, they could be certain McAskill would wax most eloquent on their behalf. Janice had seen to that.

The same night McAskill was being entertained, Hugh and Janey were wakened a little before midnight.

They lay in silence for a few minutes listening. Then they heard quite distinctly the chink of a foot knocking against a stone followed by the furtive whisper of voices.

Thinking burglars were paying them a call, Hugh swung out of bed and reached for his dressing gown.

In a whisper Janey asked if she should ring for the police?

Hugh replied he didn't think that necessary. He crept downstairs to the hall stand where a stout walking stick was kept. Grasping this, he stepped out into the night chill.

Again he heard voices, this time off in the direction of the dairy. Being as quiet and stealthy as he could he tip-toed towards them.

Suddenly a dozen or so figures erupted out of the darkness to go hurtling past. Although he managed several good swipes with his stick he failed to make contact with any of the ducking and weaving bodies.

Several of the figures turned in the driveway. It was evident they were teenage lads. They called out:

'Fenian bastards!'

'Left footed whoor!'

'Ya fuckin' turncoat!'

Hearing these vitriolic mouthings, Hugh knew with a sinking heart what this was all about. Taking a deep breath, he returned to the house, confident whoever those boys were they wouldn't return that night.

Janey was waiting for him at the top of the stairs to say Mary Agnes hadn't been disturbed.

They went back to bed where he told her what had been shouted at him downstairs.

Suddenly he was deathly afraid, not for himself but for

Janey, Mary Agnes and the unborn child.

Next morning they were up at their usual early hour.

When Hugh stepped outside what he saw stopped him dead in his tracks.

The sides of the house plus stables and dairy had all been daubed with various slogans in bright orange paint.

Catholics ya bass!

King Billy won at Benwater!

Remember the Boyne!

Clutching Mary Agnes to her bosom Janey came out to stand at Hugh's side. 'Holy Mary Mother of God!' she whispered.

Hugh felt sick. He'd secretly dreaded this happening.

The news of his defection to the Catholic church had finally come to the ears of those who weren't prepared to sit back and allow such a thing to happen without exacting some sort of revenge. The bully boys and wild element had become involved.

'Hugh?' Janey whispered. Leaning close and staring up into his face, she was remembering the terrible sights she'd witnessed in the Gorbals and elsewhere when the Green and Orange had clashed.

Men with faces shredded by razors. Others being carted away with hatchets embedded in various parts of their anatomies.

Quite clearly she recalled the awful picture of a man lying dead with a knife sticking out of his chest. Mindlessly drunk, the silly bugger had worn a bright blue suit and shouted 'Up the Gers!' at a dance where those present had been predominantly Catholic.

'Never mind, lass. It'll soon scrub off,' Hugh said. And giving her a squeeze he went in search of a bucket to fill with hot water. He wanted to erase as much of the daubings as possible before the milk boys came.

As he worked up a sweat scrubbing it came to him it would be a good idea to get a guard dog to let loose on the premises at night when they were all indoors.

He laughed suddenly thinking he would get a brute of an alsatian whom he would call King Billy.

Let those lads come back and he'd give them King Billy all right, a mouthful of slavering fangs where it would hurt like hell, in the arses of their trousers.

Whistling, he bent to his task, the situation not appearing nearly as black as it had done a few minutes previously.

King Billy! He couldn't wait to tell Janey.

Iain McLaren sat across from Rosemary in the drawing room of his parents' house. Upstairs with his mother and a specialist in attendance his father lay dying. According to the specialist it was doubtful if Sir Hamilton would last till morning.

He and Rosemary had been with Sir Hamilton for some hours but had broken their vigilance to come downstairs for a much needed cup of tea and smoke.

There was a knocking on the outside door which the butler answered. Sir Alan's voice filled the vestibule.

Sir Alan burst into the room with a face like fizz. He was about to launch into a tirade when, remembering the solemnity of the occasion, managed to keep himself under control long enough to ask what the up-to-date position on Sir Hamilton was?

Unable to contain himself any longer and not even making a pretence of listening to Iain's reply, he exploded with his news.

The old bitch Miss McCallum had gone and sold to some Australian firm who that very afternoon had been granted permission to build an animal by-products factory on the site where her properties now stood.

'A bloody glue factory!' he fumed.

Purple with rage, he stalked over to the whisky decanter and poured himself a large one.

Staring at the irate Sir Alan, Iain was filled with contempt for the man's insensitivity.

Sir Alan strode up and down the room furiously trying to think.

He would have to put in a bid to this LMBM (Pty) Ltd for the properties involved. Perhaps they would be understanding once he explained the situation to them. After all, there had to be a hundred places in Glasgow where such a factory could be sited without causing undue inconvenience.

What he could suggest was he give them the benefit of his local knowledge in their purchase of an alternative strip of land. Naturally he would ensure it was worth their while financially obliging him this way.

Coming up with a possible solution mollified him somewhat and whirling on the whisky decanter he poured himself another.

Turning back to Iain he began to explain what he had in mind only to be brought up short by Iain saying firmly no business would be discussed in this house that night.

Sir Alan had been somewhat dismissive of Iain in the past but hearing the steel now in Iain's voice caused him to pause and look at Iain afresh.

Part of the trouble was Iain's badly damaged face was so damned difficult to read because it so rarely betrayed the emotions behind it.

In a flash of insight Sir Alan realized there was far more to Iain McLaren than he had previously given him credit for.

Iain rose and stared at Sir Alan who was suddenly acutely aware their business relationship had just undergone a shift of emphasis.

Never again would he be able to ride roughshod over Iain who was on the brink of succeeding to the family title and, more importantly from his point of view, fortune. A large part of that fortune was pledged to the building of the Gorbals project.

Rosemary sat quietly amused by this silent interplay. It was a rare sight to see her father stopped dead in his tracks.

Sir Alan coughed, using that as an excuse to turn his eyes away from Iain.

He laid his glass beside the decanter. Then acting as though nothing had happened, declared he must be getting on his way as it was getting late and Cordelia would be worried.

At the door Sir Alan said if there was anything he could do Iain wasn't to hesitate getting in touch. But it was an offer he should've made on entering the house rather than on leaving.

Iain had just seen Sir Alan out when the specialist appeared at the top of the stairs. 'You'd better come quickly,' the specialist said.

Iain took the stairs two at a time with Rosemary coming up behind him as fast as she could. He was only a few feet away from his parents' bedroom when an agonized wail erupted from within.

They found Lize lying prostrate over her husband's body. She was weeping profusely, quite beside herself with grief.

Next morning tragedy struck the McLaren family afresh when Lize, the shock of losing her husband having proved too much for her, was discovered dead in bed.

Her face was in repose, a soft smile on her lips, as though she'd just seen someone she hadn't expected to see again so soon.

Angus wheeled his car in Craiglea's front drive. Switching the engine off, he sat back to listen to the cacophony of sound made by hammers and saws all going nineteen to the dozen.

It pleased him that within forty-eight hours of LMBM having been granted permission to build an animal by-products factory an approach had been made to Bitu by Phoenix Development Ltd.

Bitu's reply to the letter had been LMBM hadn't been aware of Phoenix's plans. But now these had been made known to them he was certain Mr O'Rourke, LMBM's head man in Australia, would view Phoenix's offer with sympathy.

This was a purely delaying tactic to allow Angus to come up with the next move.

Angus made a fist and gently bashed his thigh. Now he

knew what was niggling him.

All this was very well but where was it ultimately leading? Was he merely going to use the former McCallum properties to eventually extort a monstrous profit out of Armstrong or was there a way in which he could use this lever to hurt the man even more?

What he wanted was a gutting stroke – the infliction of maximum pain combined with maximum damage.

Suddenly what his goal should be came to him and the very rightness and irony of it caused him to exclaim. It should have been obvious to him all along!

It would be an incredibly difficult coup to pull off, and one that in the end might even prove impossible. Only Hetherington would know its feasibility so the sooner he saw the chief accountant the better.

Hetherington was full of the letter he'd received in the morning's post from his wife who'd arrived safely in Perth, Western Australia.

According to Mrs Hetherington her health had picked up almost immediately she crossed the equator. And now she had experienced the warm, dry Westralian climate she had no doubt it would improve her condition immensely.

Angus allowed Hetherington's excited chatter about Mrs Hetherington to run its course before sitting the man down and disclosing his idea.

Hetherington was dumbfounded. Then ever so slowly his face cracked into a grin and he began to laugh.

'You really do hate Sir Alan, don't you,' he said: it was a statement, not a question.

Angus thought of his father, dead without compensation; his mother married to that sadistic bastard, Archie Marjoribanks, and the life he and she had undergone as a consequence; and at last but hardly least, the incident with the cuff links which had cost him Rosemary.

'Yes, I hate him,' Angus replied grimly.

Hetherington wouldn't be rushed into giving an answer and insisted on making a pot of tea in order to give himself time to think.

Finally he said what Angus had in mind was possible if handled the right way and luck was on their side.

Armstrong's weakness lay in being short of ready capital, having only a fraction of the works' war profits left. The rest had been ploughed into buying up the Gorbals.

Some time ago Sir Alan had gone to the London Merchant Banks and various private financiers in the hope of raising building capital. Much to his consternation he'd been turned down flat by each and every one of them.

The general consensus of opinion had been the Gorbals project was not a viable one and could only be doomed to failure. None of them could believe with the terrible name the district had that middle-class people would ever be persuaded to live, far less buy private homes there.

Despite a great deal of correspondence and to-ing and fro-ing on Sir Alan's part, he'd been unable to make the money men change their minds. Rebuffed by London, Sir Alan's solution to his problem had been to approach Sir Hamilton McLaren – already involved in a minor way – and propose Sir Hamilton put up the money.

The Phoenix partnership had then been drawn up with each director having equal standing. Sir Alan's capital had bought the Gorbals. Sir Hamilton's would redevelop it.

Excited now, Hetherington leaned forward to say Sir Alan's dependency on the McLaren fortune was the key to his possible undoing. If one could somehow be separated from the other, Sir Alan would have to fall back on his own resources which would leave him with only three options.

The first was to abandon the project altogether and in time recoup his investment by selling off the Gorbals piecemeal. This Hetherington was convinced he wouldn't do as he was so committed to the project that as long as there was a way open for him to continue he would use it.

Apart from the Gorbals, Sir Alan's other major asset was the works on the River Cart and this he could raise money on by either mortgaging buildings and plant or else going public. These were his second and third.

In his privileged position as chief accountant Hetherington would be expected to give advice on the matter. He would strongly advise the latter which Sir Alan would undoubtedly plump for once it had been explained to him a greater amount of capital could be raised that way.

Angus asked why Sir Alan hadn't approached Sir Hamilton in the first place? Hetherington's reply was that Sir Alan had never wanted to share the glory of redeveloping the Gorbals: this he would be forced to do with another prominent Glaswegian in partnership with him.

Hetherington went on to say a detailed plan of action would be needed and this he'd get cracking on from the financial point of view. It was agreed they'd meet several days hence to discuss the matter further.

On an impulse Angus drove down to the Cart where he stopped, facing Armstrong's. Emerging from his car he crossed the road to stand by the iron railings over which he'd climbed to get to the river countless times as a boy.

Lines from an old street song he'd sung in his youth came suddenly to mind: 'I'm the king of the castle, and you're the dirty wee rascal!'

He glanced across to the brooding pile on the opposite bank – the king of that particular castle was about to discover just how dirty this ex-wee rascal could be.

And it wasn't hygiene he was referring to.

When Angus and Hetherington next met, the accountant had already drawn up rudimentary financial plans for Angus's eventual takeover of Armstrong's. These he would continue to work on.

In the meantime, phase one of their ultimate realization was to cause a breach between Iain McLaren and Sir Alan.

Angus had been thinking about the correspondence Sir Alan had conducted with the London Merchant Banks and private financiers. He was now able to verify from Hetherington that the contents of this correspondence had never been disclosed to Sir Hamilton either before or after Sir Hamilton had pledged McLaren money for the Gorbals project.

What Angus wondered was if Sir Iain (Iain having succeeded to the title) were to see that correspondence now would it persuade him to pull out of the Gorbals venture?

For a start, withholding vital information was hardly conducive to inspiring future trust within a partnership.

Secondly, London were certainly no fools when it came to matters of investment. So if it was their opinion the Gorbals project was a non-viable one that opinion just had to be given deep and careful consideration.

According to Hetherington this correspondence was kept in a locked filing cabinet in Sir Alan's office to which Sir Alan had the sole key.

Hetherington was in a position to remove this correspondence but for him to do so, and it subsequently turning up in Sir Iain's possession, would necessitate giving himself away. His future use to Angus within Armstrong's would be non-existent which was the last thing Angus wanted.

So Angus decided to call in an expert to acquire the correspondence for him. But before going into action he had a little ploy up his sleeve which would be the opening shot in his bid to sunder relations between Sir Iain and Sir Alan.

It was the morning of Sir Hamilton and Lize McLaren's funeral: Sir Alan was dressing to attend when he was informed there was an urgent telephone call for him.

Otis Bitu was on the line to say he'd received a telex only minutes previously informing him Mr O'Rourke was ringing through at eleven am and wanted to speak personally with Sir Alan about the former McCallum properties.

This put Sir Alan into a terrible quandary as he naturally wanted to settle the McCallum business – and from Bitu's tone he guessed it was going to be in his favour. On the other hand, it would be a dreadful insult to the McLarens if he was to turn up late for the funeral.

Bitu expressed sympathy with Sir Alan's position, then pointed out as the funeral service didn't start until twelve-thirty surely Sir Alan would have time to speak with Mr O'Rourke *and* attend the service?

Sir Alan was uncertain. Bitu said he could understand if Sir Alan didn't come into the office but O'Rourke might not.

The insinuation was crystal clear. Sir Alan assured Bitu he would be on his way shortly.

Angus was in the new LMBM office which Bitu had moved into listening to Bitu on the phone to Sir Alan. When Bitu hung up and turned to him with a smile he knew the bait had been swallowed.

As it would be a little while before Sir Alan arrived they lingered over a cup of coffee. Then Angus left the office to go across the road to where his car was parked. He settled back to wait the arrival of his adversary.

The Rolls Royce was different to the one he remembered. As Sir Alan climbed out of the Rolls he was afforded a clear view of the face he hated so much – the face he'd last seen the day he'd been framed for the supposed theft of the man's cuff links.

As Sir Alan disappeared into the building where the LMBM office was Angus got out of his car and crossed to the Rolls. It was a trick he'd learned as a lad, effective now as it had always been. He waited till the coast was clear. Then bending down to the nearside front tyre, he whipped the valve cap off and rammed a matchstick into the valve itself so it was jammed in the *on* position.

He did this with all four tyres, waiting a little way off

until the last one was flat. Hastily he removed the matchstick evidence before returning to his car.

When he was again settled in the driving seat a glance
at his watch told him it was one minute to eleven.

At eleven am precisely Morag Bitu dialled her husband and, pretending to be the operator, said a call was
coming through for LMBM on the radio link with
Australia. It would be delayed for a few minutes due to
trouble on the Australian side.

Bitu relayed this to Sir Alan and then urged him to tell
him more about the alternative site for the animal by-
products factory Sir Alan had discovered out in
Polmadie.

Sir Alan went on at length praising the virtues of the
site which in his estimation was ideal for LMBM's
purposes.

Morag called again at eleven fifteen to say the call
from Australia was still delayed but should be coming
through any minute now. This an apologetic Bitu relayed to Sir Alan.

At eleven thirty Morag rang to say the call was on the
line but due to appalling interference they were holding
it for a few minutes more in the hope the interference
would clear itself.

By now Sir Alan was becoming extremely agitated
and kept glancing repeatedly at his gold hunter.

Bitu talked non-stop, pointing out again and again it
would be ridiculous for Sir Alan to leave now and
jeopardize the Phoenix position when Mr O'Rourke
would no doubt be getting through at any moment.

Outside the next phase of the charade had appeared in
the shape of a black cab whose driver Angus had sought
out and bribed earlier. The driver would now wait a little
way up the street until Angus tipped him the wink.

The minutes ticked by and as they did so Sir Alan
became more and more frantic. When yet another look
at his hunter told him it was noon he knew he was going
to be late for the service.

And still Morag kept ringing to say the call was being

variously held or detained and should be coming through loud and clear directly. Finally at twelve fifteen she rang to say the Australian party had cancelled.

Sir Alan was apoplectic, Bitu full of apologies but argued that no fault could be attached to him for what had happened. The blame rested fairly and squarely with the telephone people.

At the door Sir Alan muttered hasty goodbyes, then went galloping downstairs intent on getting out to Carmunnock to join the other mourners who'd been invited back to the McLaren house.

The moment the Rolls started forward he knew something was wrong.

Bringing the car to a halt, he got out to examine the tyres thinking one of them had gone soft. When he saw all four were completely deflated he jibbered with anger.

Cued by Angus, the taxi moved forward to be hastily flagged down by a relieved Sir Alan. The taxi disappeared in the direction of Carmunnock – not that it was ever going to arrive there.

Once out of the city and at a rural spot previously agreed on, the driver would suddenly take ill and insist on dropping Sir Alan so he could return to Glasgow and his bed. From there, Sir Alan would have to walk a good two miles to the nearest public transport which was infrequent at the best of times and downright non-existent at others. It would be a miracle if he succeeded in reaching the McLaren house before the mourners dispersed.

Angus was well aware there were elements of farce about all this and it seemed more like a schoolboy prank than the action of one grown man against another. But there was a serious side to this apparent frivolity concerned directly with loss of face.

Even though Lady Armstrong had been present at the service and gathering after, the fact Sir Alan had elected to go off and attend a business meeting would be seen as a lack of respect for the deceased. Sir Iain couldn't fail but take offence.

Returning to the LMBM office, Angus found Bitu on the phone congratulating Morag on her successful excursion into amateur dramatics. Angus congratulated her also.

Hanging up, he announced what he needed now was a first class burglar and could Bitu please find him one?

The smile on the American's face changed fractionally to become a trifle strained. So far Bitu had done everything Angus requested with no questions asked. But now he thought it time to be told what all this was about.

Angus had been intending to confide in Bitu as more and more he was coming to think of him as a friend rather than employee. So he started at the beginning with his father's death.

In Angus's estimation Hetherington had done a brilliant job on the financial plans. If they worked as well in practice they would make him, as majority shareholder, head of Armstrong's.

This was going to take an enormous amount of capital so to ensure enough was available he'd approached the Bank of Scotland to arrange an advance set against his future earnings from LMBM which were guaranteed into the next century.

He'd also asked the Bank of Scotland to act on his behalf regarding a large number of shares he intended purchasing in the new year.

Besides the Bank of Scotland he'd also approached a number of other Scottish banks, none knowing about the other's consent to act on his behalf with regards to shares yet unbought, and all of them had agreed.

Another part of Hetherington's plan called for Angus to set up a construction company which Angus duly did, registering it under the name of Jocar Ltd whose directors were listed as D. Chisholm and W. Chisholm. Donald and Winnie had only reluctantly agreed – after Angus had pleaded with them, saying it was of vital importance to him to have people fronting the firm whom he could trust implicitly.

The name Jocar was a play on words as well as being a combination of parts of Angus's parents' Christian names, Jo/hn and Car/rie coming together to make Jocar. Angus's joke was to be at Sir Alan's expense.

As Angus intended they would never meet, he thought it highly unlikely Sir Alan would tumble to the fact D. Chisholm and W. Chisholm were his retired foreman moulder and wife.

Hetherington had explained to Angus in the first instance Sir Alan would no doubt retain fifty-one per cent of the shares issued, thereby giving him the majority holding. Jocar had been brought into existence to trick him deviously later into relinquishing this majority.

In the meantime there was still the business of engineering a split between Sir Iain and Sir Alan which the success of everything else depended on.

The man Bitu eventually found was called Shughie Reid who'd been a cat burglar all his life.

A layout of Armstrong's office and the exact location of the filing cabinet containing the correspondence was drawn by Hetherington.

To disguise the real motive behind the burglary Shughie was instructed to take other bits and pieces including the petty cash kept in Sir Alan's secretary's office.

One week after Bitu had first contacted Shughie Reid the burglary was successfully carried out and Bitu able to hand over the correspondence to Angus.

The correspondence verified everything Hetherington had said. London was unanimous in its opinion that the Gorbal's project was non-viable in its present form and could only turn out to be a white elephant.

Certainly if Angus himself had been considering investing money in the project this would have turned him completely against it. He could only hope it would have the same effect on Sir Iain McLaren.

* * *

The ball was being held in the home of the Duke of Renfrew, a stately mansion just outside the small village of Carmunnock.

Angus had received his invitation at Craiglea the previous week and after dithering over it had finally decided to attend. Now that he belonged to this strata of Glasgow society he might as well find out whether he liked it and vice versa.

The ball was on behalf of the area Conservative and Unionist Society. The night it fell on was Hallowe'en.

Angus parked his car amongst the Rollses, Bentleys and Armstrong-Siddeleys, then made his way to the front door and the liveried flunkey in attendance there.

Standing beside Iain with whom she'd had a terrible battle earlier on in order to get him to attend, Rosemary saw Angus the moment he entered the great hall. Although she continued making the correct responses to a couple talking to her and Iain, her eyes were riveted on Angus.

Sensitive to all his wife's moods, Iain noticed immediately the change in her focus of attention. When he was able to, he glanced swiftly across at the man she was staring at but failed to recognize him.

Diane Armstrong was talking to her mother and father when out of the corner of her eye she spied Angus. Initial surprise gave way to pleasure and, excusing herself, she crossed to where he was hovering on the periphery of a group who were talking about what a disaster it had been for Winnie to be defeated at the polls the previous year.

Angus was delighted to see someone he knew, greeting Diane warmly and affectionately. He was brought up short when she asked him if he'd spoken to Rosemary yet?

Just as he was shaking his head he caught sight of Rosemary and a man with a hideous face moving slowly in their direction.

He knew from Bitu's report – compiled since his meeting with Rosemary in the coffee shop – that Sir Iain had been disfigured in the war. But it was a shock to see just how hideous the actual disfigurement was. He couldn't help but feel sorry for the poor sod.

A few minutes later he sensed Rosemary intended to joining them and wondered if Sir Iain knew about him.

'Angus, what a pleasant surprise!'

The moment Iain heard Angus's name he knew why Rosemary had been showing such great interest in the man.

She believed he didn't know about her and Angus McBain but he did, having learned it from his brother Peter who'd wormed it out of Diane when she'd inadvertently let something drop one night during the early war years.

He'd made discreet inquiries and found out Angus McBain had vanished suddenly from Glasgow although for what reason he'd been unable to determine.

Since then he'd come to suspect Rosemary retained a great deal of feeling for McBain which hadn't bothered him unduly as McBain was safely out of the way and out of her life.

Only now McBain was back.

During the ensuing chat Angus turned to Sir Iain and said he understood Sir Iain was interested in flying?

Replying, Iain told Angus about the Tiger Moth he'd recently bought and what a joy she was to fly.

Throwing leading question after leading question, Angus encouraged Iain to talk about flying which he did with enormous keenness and passion.

Sir Iain was waxing lyrical about Mosquitoes which he'd flown during the war when he was interrupted by a new voice asking to join their circle.

Angus went ice cold inside. Glancing across at Rosemary he saw she was frowning sympathetically at him.

The muscles in his face were rigid as he turned towards Sir Alan and Lady Armstrong.

Sir Alan stared directly into Angus's face, his brow creasing in thought as he tried to place where he knew this young man from.

Unable to help herself, Rosemary smiled sweetly and said, 'Surely you remember Angus McBain father? You loaned him a pair of cuff links once.'

Inwardly Sir Alan cursed her for her impertinence. McBain! Where in God's name had *he* come from!

The atmosphere between Angus and Sir Alan was almost a static crackle. They were like two fighting dogs suddenly come face to face in an alley.

It was Sir Iain who saved the explosive situation from erupting altogether. His scarred and mangled face lit up in a gruesome smile as he asked Diane for the pleasure of the next dance. Casually he suggested Angus might like to take the floor with Rosemary.

The ferocity of the looks Angus and her father were exchanging sent shivers racing up and down Rosemary's spine. Hurriedly she took Angus by the arm and steered him in the direction of the dance floor

The arm in hers was like a steel pole.

Later that night as Rosemary sat brushing her hair in front of her dressing table Iain approached her from behind to put his hands on her shoulders.

'Tell me about the cuff links?' he asked.

She started but swiftly recovered her composure. Shrugging, she said it was something that had happened a long time ago and wasn't worth talking about now.

'I'd still like to know,' Iain said softly. Adding when he saw she intended to prevaricate, 'I know all about what went on between you and McBain if that's what's holding you back.'

This time she wasn't able to recover her composure. She was rattled and clearly looked it. 'How did you find out?' she whispered.

He told her. Then he asked again.

Rosemary nervously lit a cigarette. She had enormous affection for Iain and didn't want to hurt him in any way. But if he knew part of the story it was probably best he knew all.

Hoping she was doing the right thing she started at the beginning – the time Angus and Kitty had saved her and Margaret Cunninghame from the louts in Queen's Park Recreational Ground – and told him everything with the exception of having met up with Angus in the coffee shop. That and the fact she was still in love with Angus.

For Angus the night at the ball had proved constructive in one respect: he'd discovered just how passionate Sir Iain was about flying.

He therefore continued to hold on to the burgled correspondence while Bitu went on yet another quest for him.

Some LMBM business had come up which took Bitu to London anyway and while he was there he contacted a number of planemaking firms and flying organizations whom he enlisted to his aid.

It was finally through the Handley-Page people that he came to hear of a young man call John Muir who lived in Kilwinning, a small village in Ayrshire.

Like Sir Iain, Muir had been in the RAF during the war only instead of flying as Sir Iain had done he'd been one of the backroom boffins.

Since the war and working entirely on his own Muir had come up with a design for a revolutionary new passenger plane intended for the Middle and Far East runs. He'd tried every planemaker in Britain but his design had been turned down flat by all of them.

The simple reason for this was that money was desperately short in the planemaking world and what capital the planemakers had was already committed to schemes of their own.

According to Handley-Page who'd kept tabs on Muir he was now back in Kilwinning where he was contemplating going to America to see if they would buy his design.

What Angus had been looking for, and was sure he'd now found, was an alternative investment to the Gorbals project for Sir Iain. And where better to look for that potential investment than in the world of aeroplanes in which Sir Iain was so interested?

Janey was kneading dough when the pains started. She
gasped and bent over the table till the first one had
passed. Then very carefully she crossed to a chair and
sat.

She gritted her teeth as the second searing pain tore at
her insides. When that pain had passed away she came to
her feet and stumbled to the door and out into the front
yard. There was no need to worry about Mary Agnes for
the moment. The wean wasn't long down for her sleep.

Hugh was in the stables mucking out.

Yet another pain exploded in her. As she lurched into
his arms her fingers dug deeply into his flesh.

'It's coming!' she whimpered.

She was a hefty lump but Hugh would've managed
had she been twice the weight. Staggering, he carried
her back to the house and up to their bedroom where he
laid her on top of the bed.

He flew down the stairs to the telephone and rang Dr
Robertson's surgery to be informed by the receptionist
the doctor was out doing house calls but should be
ringing in soon.

His second call was to a neighbour in Tallon Street
who'd go and tell Winnie that Janey's labour had started
and she was needed right away.

He was filled with a curious combination of fear and
elation as he raced back up the stairs to Janey. The baby
was several weeks early.

Winnie and Dr Robertson arrived almost simultaneously to find Hugh with the situation well in hand. Mary
Agnes was playing quite happily down in the kitchen on
her own while Janey was sitting up in bed wearing a clean
nightie and sipping a cup of tea between spasms.

Banished to the kitchen, Hugh strode up and down
like the proverbial cat on a hot tin roof. Winnie told him
to go back to work and she would give him a shout when
there was news. But he would have none of her
suggestion.

Suddenly he burst out he and Janey had agreed to call the baby Alexander after his dead brother providing it was a boy which of course it would be.

Winnie was most touched by this gesture and said it was a grand idea. She knew Donald would be pleased and said so.

Exactly six hours after the pains had started the baby was born without any complications.

When Dr Robertson handed it to Janey there were tears streaming down his face as a result of what he'd had to tell her after his examination of the wee one.

'I'll send Hugh to you,' Robertson said, turning in the doorway to add, 'I'm awful sorry, lass.'

The moment Hugh saw the doctor's face he knew something was wrong. 'Well?' he demanded, his voice suddenly harsh and ugly.

There were times Robertson hated being a doctor and this was one of them. 'Janey and your baby daughter are both well,' he said.

'A girl?' Hugh replied quickly and Robertson nodded affirmation.

Hugh was bitterly disappointed but consoled himself with the fact they could always try again and next time it was *bound* to be a boy.

As though reading Hugh's mind Robertson said unfortunately Janey wasn't going to be able to have any more children.

The he dropped the real bombshell. The wee girl was a mongol.

For a few seconds the whole world spun and the only thing Hugh was aware of were the doctor's pitying eyes.

'Oh, son!' said Winnie.

'I think you'd better away up and see Janey,' Robertson said. 'She needs you now.'

'Aye,' said Hugh.

He trudged up the stairs with shoulders hunched and head low. His face was grey and lined. He seemed to have aged a dozen years in the past few minutes.

He knew it was selfish but the thought running

through his mind was there would be no immortality for him after all.

'Why are you crying, Granny? Aren't you happy I've got a new babby sister?' Mary Agnes asked.

Winnie couldn't answer, the words sticking in her throat when she tried.

Dr Robertson let himself out.

John Muir wrote to Sir Iain McLaren who replied asking him to present himself at Carmunnock which Muir duly did.

They started talking mid-morning and became so involved in the conversation they missed lunch. Undoubtedly they'd have missed dinner as well had Rosemary not interrupted to demand their presence at table.

After dinner they disappeared back into Iain's study where they continued talking till well after midnight when Rosemary interrupted again to say Muir had better stay the night and that a bed had been made up for him.

Iain's conversation with Muir resumed over breakfast and continued through till late afternoon, at which time Iain suggested they go for a walk to clear their heads with a breath of fresh air.

On the return leg of this walk Iain thought to ask about the American Muir had mentioned in his letter who'd recommended Muir to contact him.

Muir explained the man had arrived at his door one day out of the blue with some knowledge of his design. To begin with he'd thought the man represented one of the American aero firms but it had transpired this wasn't the case.

The man had been extremely vague about just who and what he was. His one definite action was to recommend in the strongest terms that Muir contact Sir Iain McLaren whom the American was convinced would be interested in the design, perhaps even to the extent of financing its production.

Sir Iain was intrigued by this report and couldn't help but wonder who this mysterious American was who seemed to know so much about him.

Then he thought of the correspondence that had arrived anonymously through the post a few days previously regarding dealings Armstrong had conducted with London banks and financiers.

Suddenly he began to smell a rat. All this was too pat and far too coincidental.

Over a month had passed since the correspondence burgled from Sir Alan's safe had been mailed to Sir Iain. According to Hetherington there was as yet no sign of discord between these two worthies.

Angus was beginning to despair that his plan had failed and that he would have to find some other way of splitting the two Phoenix directors when suddenly his telephone rang one morning with Sir Iain on the line suggesting they meet.

Angus was taken aback by this invitation, but nonetheless agreed to do so the following afternoon.

Angus arrived dead on time to find Sir Iain waiting for him. They strolled for a little while in silence. Then Sir Iain's glittering, snake-like eyes swung slowly round to fix themselves on Angus's face.

They were cold as ice those eyes and made Angus wilt a little inside. In a voice as chilly as his gaze Sir Iain said he would be obliged if Angus would tell him just what in the hell Angus was up to?

The fact Sir Iain was accusing him meant the man knew something. But how much?

Angus phrased his reply in such a manner he neither pretended innocence nor committed himself in any way.

With a sigh, Sir Iain said he'd been able to prove conclusively that Otis Bitu of LMBM and the mysterious American who'd visited John Muir at Kilwinning were one and the same. And weren't Angus and Bitu often to be found in one another's company?

Furthermore, a cablegram to an Australian contact

had eventually resulted in this contact discovering that one of LMBM (Pty) Ltd's directors, who employed Bitu in Glasgow was one Angus McBain. And hadn't Angus recently returned from Australia?

Taking all this into consideration plus the fact LMBM owned the former McCallum properties which Phoenix Development Ltd were desperately after – not to mention some incriminating correspondence he'd received regarding his Phoenix partner whom Angus quite understandably hated – had led to the logical conclusion. Angus was the common denominator in all these events with the exception of the correspondence which Iain suspected Angus was also involved in but couldn't prove. Angus was up to something and would Angus please tell him precisely what that was?

Angus digested this, thinking his convoluted machinations had come to naught. Or had they?

He asked Sir Iain quickly if Sir Alan was aware of his connection with LMBM?

'Not as far as I know. I've certainly said nothing to him,' Sir Iain replied.

That was an enormous relief to Angus as it meant all wasn't yet lost. If only he could win Sir Iain to his cause he might still carry off the plan Hetherington had devised.

They walked a little further, Angus with head bowed in thought as he tried to work out how best to put what he wanted to say to Sir Iain.

Finally Sir Iain said, 'I found out about you and Rosemary a long time ago although it wasn't till recently I discovered how Armstrong separated the pair of you. Will that make it any easier?'

Angus nodded, grateful to Sir Iain for clarifying the position.

'Let me say I bear you personally no malice whatsoever. It was hardly your fault the way things happened and how they turned out. It's Armstrong I'm after. Him and him alone.'

And having said that, Angus launched into an explanation of his recent actions.

*   *   *

Iain was jealous of Angus and had been ever since Peter had told him of the milk boy who'd been having it off with the girl who was later to become his wife. Of one thing he was now certain – Rosemary and Angus still hankered after one another. The signs were all there and not too difficult to read.

So what should he do? Should he put a spoke in Angus's wheel by ensuring the Gorbals project went ahead as planned? Or should he follow the dictates of common sense and jettison Armstrong as Angus had been trying to manoeuvre him into doing?

There were no words to describe what he felt at the thought of losing Rosemary. On the other hand he didn't want her staying with him out of pity and doubly so when there was another man she wanted to be with.

He decided the best thing he could do was not to put the boot in as far as Angus was concerned. He wouldn't do anything against Angus that could later be held or used against him in any way.

He was only too well aware this course might prove disastrous in the long run. But it was the one he was determined to pursue.

Iain heard Angus through to the end, then said he would see Armstrong the following week and dissolve their partnership.

He'd never been happy in property anyway, and especially since Armstrong had become so fanatical about the Gorbals project.

John Muir's aeroplane was far more to his taste as an investment and it was into that he would now channel his energies and capital resources.

Nor was he doing this for Angus's sake but rather because of the correspondence Angus had sent him.

He wouldn't allow himself to remain in partnership with a man he didn't trust to be as honest with him as he was in return.

Angus asked Sir Iain to keep his own involvement in all this quiet, which Sir Iain promised to do.

They shook hands on what had passed between them and without a further word Sir Iain strode off.

Angus's breath misted the air as he rubbed his hands together in self congratulation. He would telephone Bitu with the good news immediately and later Hetherington.

His head whirling with plans, he followed Sir Iain out of the park.

22

Angus and Bitu waited till the end of the week after Angus's meeting with Sir Iain before Bitu telephoned Sir Alan to say he'd now had the go-ahead from Australia to sell the former McCallum properties to Sir Alan provided terms could be agreed.

Sir Alan was still in a state of shock when Bitu rang. He had been since Sir Iain McLaren had confronted him with the various letters stolen from his office which Sir Iain had said had come to him anonymously through the post.

It had been a terrible blow to have the McLaren money withdrawn from the project which, in a momentary panic, he'd suddenly seen as having to be abandoned.

Then he'd somehow pulled himself together again and forced his benumbed brain to consider the financial alternatives.

In grey despair he turned over all the possibilities in his mind – which individuals he could approach with a view to making them a partner, including the proposal put forward by Hetherington that he turn Armstrong's into a public company.

His initial reaction to this had been one of rejection. But the more he thought about it the more it appealed.

He'd never wanted the McLarens or any other local individuals involved in the first place. And it was only dire necessity that had made him approach Sir Hamilton.

But here was a viable alternative which would ensure all the eventual credit and glory would fall squarely to him. It would be just as he'd always seen it. His project and his alone. The new Hutchesontown. *His* creation!

He summoned his secretary and told her to fetch George Hetherington. He had a host of eager questions to ask his chief accountant about the technicalities and ramifications of going public.

The Monday following his telephone call Bitu was ushered into Sir Alan's office. Bitu repeated what he'd already told Sir Alan on the phone – O'Rourke had finally agreed to resiting the proposed animal by-products factory and selling the former McCallum properties to Sir Alan.

However, there would be several stipulations, one of which was that the actual sale didn't take place until after the old woman's death, as knowing how she felt about Sir Alan, they didn't want to cause her any further upset and pain.

Bitu then mentioned the price LMBM wanted for the properties. Sir Alan replied hoarsely that such an astronomical sum was way above their real value.

Bitu smiled thinly and said of course it was way above their real value. But what Sir Alan had to consider was their value to *him*.

Sir Alan made some rapid mental calculations. He could just afford to buy the properties out of the remainder of his capital. But it would mean his financial resources were more or less wiped out.

Still smiling, Bitu stuck the knife in even further by saying if Sir Alan wasn't agreeable to an immediate purchase his instructions were to raze the site and start building the factory within the month. Once that happened, the opportunity to buy would be lost forever.

Fearing the worst, Sir Alan asked what the remaining stipulations were?

There was only one, Bitu declared, which was that a construction firm called Jocar Ltd whom LMBM had connections with be given the overall contract for the Gorbals project.

Sir Alan naturally seized on this second stipulation as a bargaining point – as Angus had foreseen, hence the outrageously high asking price – to beat down the figure for the former McCallum properties to a little over half what had been initially demanded.

Angus didn't really care what price he got for the properties as they were now merely a device to secure Jocar the contract.

As it transpired he still made a substantial killing.

It was a Saturday afternoon when Angus drove John and Sheena into the driveway at Craiglea to find Donald waiting for them. Only hours previously the finishing touches had been completed and Craiglea was now ready to be moved into.

After the tour of inspection was over and the appropriate comments made, Angus sent Sheena and John into the kitchen to make tea while he took Donald to one side.

'You've kept on the Craiglea workforce like I told you?' he said.

'Aye, that's right.'

'Good. Now what I want you to do is expand that gang to at least ten times its present size.' Angus laughed a little when he saw the mystified expression on his grandfather's face. 'Jocar's been contracted to rebuild the Gorbals.'

'Help ma bob!' exclaimed Donald.

'But somehow I don't feel it's going to be a very long job,' said Angus mysteriously. He hadn't yet confided in Donald as to what his ultimate goal was nor what part Jocar was to play in achieving that goal.

'Are you going to tell me what this is all about?' Donald demanded.

'Not yet. I want it to be a surprise.'

'Always did have a mind like a bloody corkscrew,' Donald muttered later after the tea had come.

Angus smiled broadly. 'Flattery will get you everywhere.'

'Away to hell!' Donald retorted but secretly he was highly chuffed as it meant he was still in a job.

Later that night after John had gone to bed Sheena came to sit opposite Angus by the fire.

Although Angus had the evening paper up in front of him he was actually thinking about Hannah – Hugh and Janey's new wee girl – whom he was in the habit of dropping by to see whenever he could.

He felt so sorry for Hugh who, although trying to put a bold front on things, was a changed man since Hannah's birth.

He thought again of that little face and shuddered.

According to Dr Robertson a mongol could live a good twenty years or more. Poor soul, he thought, then poor Hugh and Janey.

'Angus?'

Dropping his newspaper, he discovered Sheena smiling at him.

'I've never really thanked you for asking me to look after John. Doing so has made me very happy, in fact happier than I've ever been before,' she said.

He returned her smile, a wealth of understanding between them.

Crossing to his chair she kissed him tenderly on the forehead, then left the room for her bed.

Angus stared after his step-sister. Next to Rosemary he loved her more than any other living female.

*　　*　　*

Sir Alan was in his dressing gown having just enjoyed a piping hot bath. He sat now on the toilet seat with a glass of whisky in his hand watching in admiration as Margaret climbed into a freshly drawn tub.

From time to time he enjoyed talking to her about business which was what he was now doing.

That very day the manifesto for the new public Armstrong's had been issued. It had finally been decided between himself and Hetherington there would be 1,500,000 one pound shares selling in the first instance for fifteen shillings per share of which he would retain a majority holding of fifty-one per cent.

The remaining forty-nine per cent would be made available on the Glasgow and London Stock Exchanges on a day still to be decided the following month.

There would be a board of directors of which he would be chairman. And to accommodate the monthly and annual general meetings he was having a boardroom built as an extension onto the side of his office.

There was also good news concerning Miss McCallum who'd finally reached the stage of being unable to continue on her own. She'd been admitted to a hospital in Greenock: her end was evidently imminent.

All of a sudden he grunted in agony and bent over double, his face suffused with blood.

'Alan!' Margaret exclaimed in alarm. Clambering from the bath, she quickly crossed to enfold him in her wet, soapy arms.

'It's nothing, lass,' he wheezed. Disentangling himself from her embrace, he sucked in a large lungful of air,

She wore a worried frown as she studied him. 'Can I get you anything?' she asked.

'Have you any antacid powder or milk of magnesia?'

She shook her head.

'Then a glass of water,' he smiled.

While she got the water he massaged his chest.

Within a minute his face was back to its normal colour. And within five they were laughing at the terrible fright he'd given her.

It was only a bad attack of indigestion he assured Margaret. And not the first he'd had like it either.

Usually the antacid powder or milk of magnesia cleared it up. But as she had neither he was just going to have to settle for another glass of whisky.

He started talking about the Gorbals project again and soon the incident had passed from both their minds.

Angus entrusted the drawing up of the Jocar contract to Otis Bitu.

There were two important clauses incorporated into the contract. One featured reasonably prominently while the other was buried deep in the mass of small print comprising the latter part of the document. The first clause stated all aluminium used in the constructions to be built had to come from bauxite ore originating from LMBM (Pty) Ltd.

The reason Bitu would give Sir Alan for the clause's inclusion was that LMBM wanted to encourage the importation of their ore into Britain and this was a device to set the ball rolling.

Angus, Bitu and Hetherington all agreed that Sir Alan would accept this clause as he would think it the reason why LMBM had stipulated Jocar get the Gorbals contract. He would imagine it was a case all round of 'If you scratch my back then I'll scratch yours'.

The trick was going to be to get Sir Alan to sign the contract without tumbling to the timebomb ticking away in the small print.

Directly Angus learned Miss McCallum had been taken into hospital he drove to Greenock to check she was being properly looked after and to see if there was anything she needed.

'Oh it's yourself, sonny,' she whispered out of the crabbit face he remembered so well.

He'd brought her a bunch of flowers plus a bottle of

lavender water which he'd suspected correctly she would like.

She thanked him for these gifts then launched into a tirade against the tyranny that insisted on carting her off to hospital away from the rabbits and poor Bella whom she missed so much and was so worried about it fair made her heart hurt.

Angus inquired who was looking after the animals? A distraught Miss McCallum told him that having collapsed in the street she'd been wheeched off to hospital without being allowed home to make arrangements for the poor beasties.

Angus earned her eternal gratitude by saying he would go to Rothesay straight from the hospital and, having collected Bella and the rabbits, would take them back to his house where he would see they were well provided for.

When he added he had a wee boy who'd be delighted at the prospect of having pets to play with Miss McCallum replied she couldn't have asked for anything more for them. 'And God bless and look after you, sonny.'

He stayed and chatted with her for about half an hour, then as he'd promised, he left the hospital to drive down to the quayside from where he caught a boat for Rothesay.

He found Bella in a pitiful state lying whining in the old woman's bed. It was patently obvious neither dog nor rabbits had been fed or watered since Miss McCallum had last done so.

Once Bella and the rabbits had been attended to Angus put the hutch into the back of his car. Then with a satiated Bella lying beside him he made the journey back to Craiglea where he and the animals were welcomed by an ecstatic John.

That night Angus wrote to Miss McCallum assuring her all was well with her animals and she could now set her mind at rest.

He also wrote to Sean O'Rourke telling O'Rourke what he wanted done, when it was to happen and why.

O'Rourke's brief was to arrange matters so that on a signal from Angus all LMBM ore to Great Britain would be blacked indefinitely by the Mine Workers' Union.

The actual securing of the Armstrong shares when they appeared on the exchanges was conducted by Angus with all the thoroughness of a military operation.

A number of brokers in Glasgow and London were instructed to snap up the shares the moment they became available, which the brokers did with such success that within one minute of their appearing Angus owned forty-six per cent of the forty-nine sold.

The remaining three per cent somehow eluded Angus's brokers to be bought on behalf of a Major Cattermole residing in Richmond, Surrey who, despite the offer of a most handsome profit, stubbornly and steadfastly refused to sell.

This didn't worry Angus unduly as he considered forty-six per cent a more than satisfactory haul..

The next step was to parcel the shares out to the various banks he'd previously approached and whose managers would now be acting as his nominees.

None of the nominees knew the others were also acting on his behalf or that they all had the same instructions – to rubber stamp *everything* Sir Alan proposed.

When Armstrong's board of directors was finally announced it consisted of Sir Alan as chairman, four men of his choosing of whom one was Hetherington, and the four bank managers acting as nominees on Angus's behalf.

At the beginning of December the Greenock Hospital phoned Angus to say Miss McCallum had sunk into a coma the previous day and had passed away in the night.

He thanked the Sister for ringing him and asked if she'd let him know what funeral arrangements were made as he wished to attend.

Three days later he went to Miss McCallum's funeral

in the local Greenock cemetery where he was the only mourner.

It seemed the nephew hadn't wanted the additional expense of shipping the body back to Rothesay. Nor had he even bothered to put in an appearance, having arranged everything by telephone from Inverness.

'Bastard!' was Angus's sole comment when he found this out.

A week after Miss McCallum's death the contract from LMBM for the sale of the former McCallum properties plus the Jocar contract arrived simultaneously on Sir Alan's desk, both of which he immediately handed over to Hetherington for perusal.

The same morning Bitu rang Sir Alan to give LMBM's reasons for the inclusion of the ore clause in the Jocar contract. This explanation Sir Alan readily accepted.

Hetherington sat on the contracts for several days, then returned them to Sir Alan saying as far as he could see they were both perfectly straightforward.

Hetherington had already warned Angus that Sir Alan would give the contracts to a solicitor whose job it would be to go over the documents with a fine tooth comb. To prevent this happening and the delay clause being discovered Angus had come up with a plan which now swung into operation.

Informed by Hetherington that the contracts were now back with Sir Alan, Bitu made another phone call to Armstrong, consisting in the main of a well rehearsed speech.

With panic in his voice Bitu said he'd just received an urgent cablegram from Mr O'Rourke saying for reasons unspecified there had been a change of heart about the former McCallum properties which were not now to be sold under any circumstances.

Sir Alan reacted exactly the way Angus anticipated in replying it was too late for LMBM to go back on the deal as the contracts had already been signed and witnessed.

Having inveigled Sir Alan into committing himself,

Angus further pressured the man by having Bitu announce he was leaving for Armstrong's right away and would expect to see the signed contracts on arrival.

Hanging up, a smiling Sir Alan immediately signed both contracts. Hetherington witnessed them. They were then laid aside for Bitu who arrived half an hour later seemingly frantic and consumed with worry.

Within days of the contracts being signed Donald and the Jocar workforce started building on part of a Gorbals site previously razed by a demolition firm contracted to Sir Alan.

Word went swiftly round that Jocar were looking for time served men. Within hours of work being started there were long queues of eager applicants.

Acting on Angus's instructions, Donald hired a large number of these hopefuls to further double the Jocar manpower before the week was out.

As was traditional, the Jocar men toiled over Christmas then got three days to themselves at Hogmanay, *the* festival in the Scottish calendar.

Normally Donald wouldn't have dreamt of leaving his own house on that night of nights. But when Hugh and Janey invited him and Winnie up to Muirend they decided to go for wee Hannah's sake.

Harriet was also invited, as was Angus. So too were Sheena and John but she swiftly declined saying she'd had enough of partying to last her the rest of her life. And anyway John should be in his bed, Hogmanay or not, and not up to all hours. So Angus left Craiglea on his own on Hogmanay and drove to Muirend where he was the last to arrive.

Nobody spoke much about Hannah but it was understood they were all there as a sign of family unity and strength for which Hugh was pitifully grateful.

After a while it was suggested by Hugh the men go to the pub for an hour to allow the women to have a good old blether amongst themselves.

The pub was jam-packed with alcohol being consumed as though it were going to be banned come morning.

A group of men started to sing but were told to keep quiet by the landlord as they knew damn well singing was against the law.

Donald insisted on getting the first round in so while he fought his way to the bar Hugh asked Angus how John was getting on?

Angus gave Hugh a quick rundown on the wee fellow's latest exploits and activities then subtly changed the subject, thinking that the wisest thing to do in the circumstances. He knew only too well what a bitter and compounded disappointment Hannah had been to his uncle.

While they chatted Hugh was thinking about the gang of teenage boys who'd daubed his walls earlier in the year. They'd tried again another night only to encounter King Billy, a huge fearsome black beast whose very growl was enough to chill the marrow.

He didn't think he'd be seeing them or their like back again which was a relief. But it was still depressing to be the object of so much scorn and hatred. Nor could he even emigrate now as no country would accept a family which included a mongol. For better or worse he would have to stand his ground and take whatever was dished out.

When the pub closed they drove back to Muirend where they settled down to await the bells which would start to dead on the final stroke of twelve.

At ten to twelve Janey decided she wanted Angus to be their first foot. So armed with shortie, a lump of coal and his bottle he had to go out into the yard where he would have to wait till the bells.

Earlier in the day it had been freezing cold. But during the past few hours the temperature had risen considerably making Angus think they might well be in for a fall of snow.

He took a deep swig from his bottle then listened lovingly to one of the horses snickering in the stables. He had so many fond memories of this place which had been such an oasis to him in the dark days of Archie

Marjoribanks.

He remembered again the many mornings he and Kitty had cycled here to run with the milk.

Thinking of those times inevitably brought Rosemary to mind. As it did now. Raw emotion rose in his throat which he forced down again with several more swigs from his bottle.

'Oh, Rosie love,' he whispered to the wind. Having met up with Rosemary again he'd come to realize that what he'd felt for Molly Hotblack was a mere counterfeit when put up against the real thing.

Suddenly the bells were pealing in the far distance. With the broadest of smiles plastered all over his face he chapped the door.

'Happy New Year!' he said to Janey when she answered.

And having been solemnly invited in he equally solemnly presented her with the shortie, coal and whisky after which he swept her into his arms and hugged her tight.

For the next several hours Angus drank with a savagery awesome to behold. Dram after dram vanished down his throat. And each time it seemed to those watching he must surely have reached his capacity. But he dumbfounded them by again reaching for the bottle.

Hugh was another hitting the cratur as though he intended drowning himself in the stuff. And the more he drank the more morose and sullen he became.

At a little past three Winnie and Donald decided they'd had enough and, overhearing this, Angus insisted on driving them home.

A few friends and neighbours had dropped by so there was something of a party going on. Angus announced to Janey that he wouldn't be long.

His excuse for taking a bottle along with him was he might bump into someone he knew en route in which case he'd have to exchange drinks as was the custom.

There were quite a few people out and about first footing and visiting but luckily not many cars on the road. Angus drove with a drunken concentration and somehow – much to their obvious relief – managed to deliver Donald and Winnie home all in one piece.

Waving goodbye he turned the car around and headed back the way he'd come.

His thinking was completely muddled and confused now. Every so often he spoke aloud addressing Kitty as though Kitty was sitting there in the car with him.

He confided to Kitty he was on his way to the bear cave where he was to meet Rosie just like in the old days.

He swung the car away from Muirend in the direction of the Linn Park. Things became indistinct and hazy after that. But he was aware of parking the car and then climbing a wall down which he dropped on the other side.

The River Cart was black and ominous as it moved silently on its way. A slight wind had sprung up causing the denuded trees to rustle and sway. Somewhere close by rooks were cawing.

He staggered through the long grass almost to the water's edge. Something wet hit and clung to his face again and again. In his befuddled state it took him a little while to realize it had started to snow.

Within minutes the snow had intensified to such an extent it was difficult seeing more than a few yards ahead.

His foot slipped once and he went tumbling over and over to end up sprawling only inches from the lapping water. Luckily he wasn't hurt nor was his bottle broken. To celebrate he treated himself to another drink.

The snow had started to lie immediately and even before he reached the bear cave the world had turned white and he was a stumbling snowman.

It was warm inside the cave where he sat huddled listening to tiny rivulets of melted snow running down its sides.

She would come soon he told himself. And when she did they'd make love just like they used to.

Once he thought he heard her and smiled in anticipation. But it was only a fall of snow or else some creature being less stealthy than it should.

After a while he could fight the tiredness no longer. His head slumped forward as he pitched into a deep and troubled sleep.

Sheena was in the process of giving John a late breakfast when Angus stumbled into the kitchen.

His face was grey and pinched, his eyes red rimmed with red bags under them, his clothes muddy and wet as though he'd been rolling around on the ground.

A long shuddering spasm wracked his body. 'Christ, I'm so cold,' he mumbled. Then suddenly all arms and legs, he slumped to the floor.

The briefest of examinations confirmed he had a raging temperature. Grasping him under the arms, Sheena dragged him across to the fire and there began stripping him.

John stared in horror at his prostrate father. He began to wail in a high, shrill voice.

Angus was soaked through and positively stinking of alcohol. Sheena stripped him stark naked, then getting a large towel from the press, rubbed and buffed him dry.

Somehow she got him into clean pyjamas which, within minutes, were wringing wet from the sweat suddenly oozing from him.

He was a good fourteen stones to her eight and a half but alternatively coaxing and shouting at him she managed to get him to his feet where he stood swaying and clinging to her for support.

Buckled under his weight, she manoeuvred him out of the kitchen and into the hall. Ascending the stairs to the first floor landing, in through the door of the closest bedroom and onto the bed.

His teeth began chattering as she wrapped the bedclothes round him. Every so often his body jerked as though an electric current had been shot through it. Each time that happened he gave a horrible groan.

Running downstairs she hurriedly put the kettle on for hot water bottles. Picking up the telephone she rang Dr

Robertson's surgery, to get no reply.

Cursing, she hung up and redialled, this time the doctor's home number.

She was profuse in her apologies in disturbing him at a time like this but she was sure it was an emergency.

After hearing her description of Angus's condition Dr Robertson said she was quite right to ring him and he would be at Craiglea within the hour.

With that weight off her mind Sheena hung up to find John standing by her side clutching her pinny. His face was streaked with tears and his eyes huge with concern as he asked her what was wrong with his daddy?

She replied she didn't know but the doctor was coming to find out. So John would have to be a big man and let her get on with organizing things for the doctor's arrival.

When she returned to the bedroom she found Angus writhing deliriously repeating the same word over and over again.

'Rosie . . . Rosie . . . Rosie . . . '

On arrival Robertson gave Angus a thorough examination at the conclusion of which he looked most grave.

In his opinion Angus had a pleurotic involvement compounded by an almost certain local pneumonia. Angus should really be in hospital but he was against moving him as to do so now would undoubtedly cause further complications.

He intended giving Angus an intra-muscular penicillin injection for the pneumonia. He would return in several hours with further medication.

John bit his lip and clung to Sheena as the needle slid into Angus's flesh. He whimpered when the needle was withdrawn and a spot of blood spattered the sodden whiteness of the bed's bottom sheet.

'Is there any chance of him . . . ? I mean, is it possible he could . . . ?' Sheena stumbled over the words, not quite knowing how to put the question without it seeming over-melodramatic.

Robertson looked up from where he'd stooped to

ruffle John's hair. 'Yes, it is possible,' he said evenly.

After the doctor had gone she rang Hugh and Janey to say she needed help and could Hugh go and fetch his mother for her? Hugh said he'd leave for Tallon Street right away.

Harriet was still at Muirend and offered to come over. But Sheena declined, thinking the domineering Harriet would try and take over, which she didn't want.

In his delirium Angus talked of many things. But time and time again he came back to Rosemary, calling for her and asking where she was.

Winnie and Hugh arrived and sometime after that Dr Robertson returned with a freshly charged syringe of special anti-toxin.

Robertson injected Angus after which he contrived to make him swallow several pills. He then took Angus's temperature.

Robertson perched himself on the edge of the bed and said he would hang on for a wee while as he wanted to observe the effects of the jab.

Half an hour later Robertson again took Angus's temperature, shaking his head when he saw it was unchanged.

There was a look in his eyes which told Sheena and Winnie he was becoming more and more concerned for Angus's life.

They were sitting drinking tea Winnie had made when Robertson asked who this Rosie was Angus was continually asking for? And was it possible to get this Rosie here as her presence just might help?

Sheena's gaze was riveted to Angus's sweat slicked face as she considered that. 'It's worth a try,' she said eventually. She went in search of Angus's address book.

When Rosemary came on the line Sheena explained who she was and why she was ringing.

Rosemary was taken aback to get this call so out of the blue. When she mentioned Angus by name she was aware of Iain raising his head from the book he was reading to stare at her.

Her heart was thumping when she finally hung up.

Iain sat apparently engrossed in his book but his eyes remained fixed to one spot on the page.

'Iain?'

'Yes, my dear?' he replied, looking up and smiling.

Rosemary sat and related precisely what Sheena had told her. When she was finished she waited for Iain's reply.

That the telephone had announced a crisis point in their marriage Iain had no doubt. He could feel it with a certainty that was absolute. His smile became strained as he considered what his reaction should be.

Finally and with a lightness he certainly didn't feel he said if Angus was as ill as his step-sister purported then Rosemary had better get over there to be of what assistance she could.

Rosemary's heart went out to Iain. She knew how difficult this must be for him. Kissing him quickly on the forehead, she turned and strode from the room.

For a long time after she'd gone Iain stared at the doorway through which she'd vanished. He'd known since the night of the Ball this moment was going to come when Rosemary would have to make a choice.

When he tried to concentrate on his book again what he saw was a blurred page from which Angus's face stared up at him.

On arriving at Craiglea, Rosemary was met at the door by Sheena. For an instant the two women stood eyeing one another. Then Sheena stretched out her hand and said how good it was of Rosemary to come.

As they walked up the stairs Sheena explained that Angus had needed someone to look after him and John and had very kindly asked her to be his housekeeper.

Rosemary had known Angus and his step-sister were close but hadn't been expecting whatever it was she now saw in Sheena's face.

In a moment of insight it came to her that Sheena was in love with Angus in a more than sisterly way and yet less or perhaps differently than she herself felt towards him. Surprisingly she sensed in Sheena she had an ally.

Angus lay bathed in sweat, his eyes open but unseeing, his face flushed to a ripe shade of candy pink.

Rosemary's stomach flipped as she stared down at him. Her whole instinct was to take him in her arms, gather him to her and tell him everything was going to be all right now she was here.

'He's been desperate for you to come,' Sheena said.

'I'll stay as long as I have to,' Rosemary replied simply.

Sheena nodded. They understood one another. 'I'll be downstairs if you need me. Just call,' she said, and flitted from the room.

Angus didn't know where it was he'd been but he'd wanted to stay there forever. But someone had called him back. He wasn't ready for that other place yet. There were still things to be done here.

'Rosie?' he croaked.

A hand tightened round his. 'I'm here,' she replied.

He blinked, feeling so weak it was an effort even to open his mouth.

When he tried to focus, his vision became blurred and watery. 'Is it really you? I mean, I'm not dreaming, am I?'

'You're not dreaming,' she replied.

Closing his eyes to stop his head going round and round he said he'd gone to the bear cave to wait for her but she'd never come.

She replied softly no such arrangement had been made between them.

'Must have been the bevy then,' he said. 'So many dreams and imaginings. Hard to know just what was real and what wasn't.'

She bent over to wipe his forehead and suddenly found their lips scant inches apart.

'What have we done to one another?' he asked in a whisper.

She bent her head further and their lips met in a kiss.

There were tears in her eyes when she finally drew away.

He struggled higher up the bed onto his pillows, a fever in him now that had nothing to do with the illness. 'It's still not too late,' he said urgently. 'Leave Iain and come to live with me. We'll get married just as soon as you can get divorced.'

Before she could reply the door opened and Sheena ushered Dr Robertson into the room. They both exclaimed with surprise and pleasure when they saw Angus was sitting up and talking.

Dr Robertson felt Angus's forehead, then said he'd prescribed the right medicine in asking Rosemary to come. A check with the thermometer confirmed Angus was now on the road to recovery.

Sheena announced Winnie had some leek and potato soup on downstairs and Angus was going to have some whether he wanted it or not.

'Bully!' Angus called after her and grinned.

Rosemary was in a turmoil inside. There was nothing she wanted more than to come and live with Angus. And yet she couldn't help but think of the poor man she'd left at home. She knew Iain would be sitting there, watching the clock, fearing the worst.

Before taking his leave Robertson gave Angus another injection. To observe the proprieties Rosemary stepped outside while Angus bared his bottom.

She was just about to go back into the bedroom when Sheena appeared with the bowlful of soup.

Thrusting the bowl into Rosemary's hands Sheena told her to take it, adding Angus was probably too weak to feed himself so she would have to do it.

Sheena was at the top of the stairs when she suddenly paused to say over her shoulder, 'And thank you for what you did. I think we might have lost him if you hadn't been there for him to come back to.'

As Rosemary rejoined Angus and Robertson it was to hear the doctor say he'd return the next day but from now on he expected it to be all uphill for Angus. What Angus needed was rest and plenty of it.

After the doctor had gone Rosemary sat on the edge of the bed with the intention of feeding Angus. But before he would accept any soup he demanded to know the answer to his question. Would she leave Iain for him?

They were right together and always had been, he said – like bacon and eggs they fitted. They were a natural couple.

'Well?' he demanded, and when there was no reply, 'It's now or never, lass. Let this moment go and we'll both rue it the rest of our lives.'

She was so choked with emotion she could hardly get the words out. But eventually they came in a tight crackling whisper. 'Yes, I'll live with you,' she said.

'When?'

With her thoughts whirling she replied it would be best if they waited a little while, at least until Angus was better.

Telling Iain she was leaving him wasn't going to be easy. She needed time to work out just how she was going to do it.

Angus wanted to kiss her again but she said there would be more than enough time for that once he was better. What was important now was he got this hot, nourishing soup inside him to build his strength back up.

He laid his head against the headboard and accepted the first spoonful into his mouth. With Rosemary feeding him he ate every last morsel.

Over the next fortnight Angus grew steadily better until finally Dr Robertson announced he could be taken off the sick list.

During those two weeks Rosemary came to see him every day and each visit was an inspiration to him. He was happier than he'd been in years which went a long way to aiding his recovery.

Early on he told Sheena that Rosemary would be coming to stay and eventually they planned to marry.

Sheena was genuinely pleased to hear this news. She

knew what Rosemary meant to him.

She said it would be best if she left as she wouldn't be needed now. But Angus wouldn't hear of it and nor would Rosemary.

As the days passed Angus pressed Rosemary to tell Iain. Again and again she put it off saying it was her prerogative to choose the right moment.

Iain grew desperately morose and despondent during this time, sitting in his study and staring vacantly at the wall for hours on end.

Even his enthusiasm for John Muir's aeroplane waned as he became more and more resigned to the fact Rosemary had taken up again with Angus McBain and consequently it was only a matter of time before she left him.

Finally Angus forced Rosemary into naming the date she would come to Craiglea.

On the coming Saturday she would ensure she and Iain were alone for the evening and tell him then. Angus would be outside waiting for her in his car.

On the Friday Rosemary paid her daily visit to Craiglea to discover Sheena had gone into town taking John with her to do some shopping. This meant she and Angus were alone in the house.

When she saw the gleam in his eye she knew right away what he had in mind. Nor was she averse to it providing his health was up to it which he assured her it was.

He took her by the hand and led her up to the bedroom where they both stripped and hurriedly crawled beneath the bedclothes.

He was nervous to begin with as was she. But soon those barriers fell away and it was even better than it had been all those years previously.

Life was truly wonderful after all, Angus decided.

By lunchtime on Saturday Iain knew this was the day Rosemary had chosen to tell him she was leaving. He could feel it. Sense it. Read it in her face.

He'd already decided he'd make it easy for her. There would be no row or vain pleadings – merely the statement he wanted her to be happy and if she thought being with Angus McBain would bring her happiness then so be it. He wouldn't stand in her way but rather wish her well.

Dinner that night was a sombre affair, the main course a great favourite of his, a last minute sop, he thought grimly.

After the meal they sat round the fire, he waiting for the prepared speech she was so obviously working up to.

Eyeing the clock, Rosemary knew Angus would be outside waiting for her. Upstairs she had a small case packed ready for the moment of departure.

All that was left for her to do was speak. And yet, for some reason she couldn't.

She loved Angus and always had done. There was absolutely no doubt about that. If things hadn't turned out the way they had she would've undoubtedly married him all those years ago.

As coldly as she was able, she examined her feelings towards Iain. She didn't love him in the grand manner she loved Angus. But she was inordinately fond of him – loved him in a minor way.

Over the years she'd come to accept her situation and together she and Iain had built a successful life by many people's standards. If Angus had never reappeared their marriage would have gone marching on without even a hiccup to disrupt it.

There had been the time she was going to leave Iain. But that had been before his disfigurement.

If the break had been made in those early years it would've been neat and clean. But she'd been unable to bring herself to leave him after his crash, knowing to do so would be to literally sign his death warrant.

The intervening years had altered Iain, however. He was now far tougher mentally and had come to terms with his disfigurement. This time there would be no question of him killing himself.

Staring into the fire's cheery blaze she thought of the good times she and Iain had enjoyed together. There had been many.

She remembered the innumerable kindnesses he'd done her, the way he'd always been there to give her strength and support whenever she'd needed it, the love he'd unabashedly and unstintingly lavished on her.

It came to her that their marriage was a number of daily bricks they'd built together and which formed a bond between them, a bond consisting of many little things put together to comprise a whole.

And it surprised her, thinking of it like that for the first time, just how strong and worthwhile that whole was.

Then there was the question of need. Angus loved and needed her. That was indisputable.

But Iain loved and desperately needed her too – and if she was honest about it – undoubtedly more than Angus did. For it was always possible Angus could find someone else whereas in Iain's case it was either her or no one.

Another item to be taken into consideration was that Angus was a born survivor. Naturally he could be wounded and deeply. But he was the type who would overcome that wound and flourish despite it.

Iain, on the other hand, like some plant whose roots have been badly damaged, would eventually fade and wither away.

She would be happy with Angus but her happiness would be marred by the knowledge that it had been achieved only at Iain's expense. She would be forever feeling guilty and might that not be the fatal flaw that would ultimately destroy her relationship with Angus?

For she knew herself only too well. Once her guilty conscience was activated it would gnaw and gnaw away at her with never any relief except the eventual one of death. She just wasn't the sort of person who could walk out on a marriage and conveniently forget the devastation she'd left in her wake.

What had seemed so easy only hours before, and

especially the previous day in bed with Angus, was now a skein of complications.

However, of one thing she was certain. Angus had been right when he'd said it was now or never. If she didn't make the break tonight she never would.

She glanced across to where Iain sat apparently immersed in a newspaper. He didn't fool her. They'd been together too long for that. She knew he knew and was even now waiting for her to utter the death knell to their marriage.

It was funny how she'd grown accustomed to his face over the years, she thought. To begin with it had horrified and revolted her. Now she hardly even noticed it.

She knew then she was going to stay with Iain and not go off with Angus.

For better or worse she was married to Iain. That was where her commitments lay.

With a sigh she rose and straightened her dress. For a few brief moments she considered going out to the car and telling Angus her decision face to face. But in the end she chose not to, whether because of cowardice or a reluctance to put her decision to such an immediate test she wasn't quite sure.

'I'm going to bed. Are you coming?' she said.

Iain tried to hide his surprise. Had he been wrong? Had her intended decamping been a product of his imagination?

Looking deep into her eyes he saw he'd been right and for some reason she'd changed her mind and was staying with him.

Pity? He didn't think so. He could see many things in her eyes but pity wasn't one of them.

'I'll be right behind you,' he replied, his voice not betraying one whit of the drama that had just passed unspoken between them.

He checked the gas and electricity as he did every night. And only when he was certain everything was as it should be did he climb the stairs to his wife whom up until minutes previously he'd been convinced he'd never sleep with again.

Outside in his car a chilled Angus frowned as the lights in the house went out one by one. His frown deepened to puzzled perplexity when the last one blinked off to leave the house in total darkness.

Something must have gone wrong. There had been a fight. Iain was forcing her to stay against her will.

These and a dozen other explanations for Rosemary's continued non-appearance flashed through his mind.

The minutes ticked by and, as they did so, came the horrible realization Rosemary wasn't going to come with him after all. Nor was she being held against her will. She'd *elected* to stay on with Iain. That had to be the way of it.

His head sagged forward to rest against the wheel. His breath was laboured and there was a burning sensation in his chest.

He would be daft to stay here further considering he wasn't all that long out of a sick bed, he told himself.

But still he hung on, hoping against hope he was wrong and she would suddenly appear full of apologies and saying she'd been detained for some reason or other.

Midnight came and went. Then one o'clock and finally two.

At the back of two he admitted defeat. He headed for Craiglea and the bed that was going to seem empty even when he was in it.

The drive home remained a blank in his mind for the rest of his life.

By June of 1947 Angus had Sir Alan over the proverbial barrel.

Jocar had built a considerable amount of houses in the Gorbals by this time, none of which were finished thanks to the fact all aluminium bits and pieces – and there were a great many in each unit – couldn't be installed due to LMBM's ore being blacked at source from coming to Britain.

O'Rourke had done his job well.

Sir Alan grew more and more worried as his remaining capital rapidly dwindled. His plan had been to sell off blocks of units as they were completed thereby financing the next section to be built. With nothing being sold it was all outgoings and no incomings.

In vain did Sir Alan contact D.Chisholm and Bitu – he spoke to the former a number of times on the telephone and never recognized the voice as being that of his one-time foreman moulder – to try and get them to use British aluminium in the meantime until the Australian ore could reach this country and be processed.

But Donald and Bitu – carefully stage managed by Angus – were adamant. According to the contracts only aluminium derived from LMBM ore could be used. And that was the way it was going to be.

Feeling he had no other recourse left to him, Sir Alan notified Jocar that all further construction was to be cancelled until such time as the Australian ore was in this country and processed ready for use.

Angus then played his trump card – the delay clause buried deep in the Jocar contract small print.

From now on until construction started again all costs incurred by Jocar – including the wages of the entire Jocar workforce – were the responsibility of Sir Alan who as contractor was liable.

Beside himself, Sir Alan had looked up the named clause. Apoplectic with rage, he consulted his solicitor to be informed the contract was wholly binding in law and as such he was liable for all Jocar's delay costs whether he liked it or not.

At the end of the first delayed week a massive wages bill was sent to Sir Alan which he had no option but to pay.

By the end of the second delayed month Sir Alan had been so reduced financially he was actually considering approaching the Glasgow Corporation to try and offload his Gorbals holdings for whatever price they would pay.

At this point word arrived from Australia – again

carefully orchestrated by Angus – that the end of the union's blacking was imminent. All being well, the first consignment of ore should be on the high seas within the next few days.

This news put Sir Alan into a terrible quandary. If only he could lay his hands on enough capital to tide himself over until the ore arrived in Britain, was processed and made up, all could yet be saved.

It was Hetherington who again came up with the solution. He pointed out that the members of the Armstrong's board had proven themselves to be a most accommodating lot; without exception they'd approved of everything Sir Alan had either suggested or put before them. With so much control over the board, why didn't Sir Alan put it to those directors representing outside interests that he sell them a further twenty-five per cent of his shares with the proviso that those shares would never go on the open market and could only be sold back to him?

According to Hetherington's calculations, the money so raised would be sufficient to allow Sir Alan to ride out his current financial nightmare.

Of course this would necessitate Sir Alan losing his majority holding in Armstrong's. But with such an amenable and malleable board of directors what did that matter as he would always get his own way anyway?

In desperation Sir Alan came to the conclusion that Hetherington's suggestion was his only salvation.

So he called an extraordinary general meeting of the board in which he put it to them he was willing to sell another twenty-four per cent of his shares – this a further refinement of Hetherington's – and would offer each director acting as nominee for outside interests the option on six per cent of them.

This way he could still retain – so Hetherington had smoothly argued – the most individual shares and therefore the right to the position of chairman.

The nominee directors agreed to inform their various clients of this development. All came back saying their clients were willing to take up the options.

It was a day Angus had long been looking forward to. It was the first of August and on the twelfth of the month he would be twenty-six years old. He felt twice that age.

The day dawned warm and sunny with blue sky stretching from horizon to horizon. He ate a leisurely breakfast before returning to his bedroom where he dressed himself in a brand new suit he'd had made especially for the occasion.

Outside in the drive stood something else he'd bought especially – a 1932 Rolls Royce in immaculate condition.

When it was time to leave he went downstairs where he shook John solemnly by the hand and kissed Sheena on the cheek.

Whistling merrily, he went out to the Rolls and eased himself behind the wheel.

En route, he thought of George Hetherington now on his way to Australia where his wife was eagerly awaiting his arrival.

Hetherington had taken with him a nice little additional nest egg courtesy of Jocar and Angus. Angus reckoned he'd earned a good bonus.

At the gate into Armstrong's Angus was automatically waved through by the guard. The guard was someone he'd known all his life and yet he went by unrecognized. It seemed guards didn't look too closely at the faces of those who drove a Rolls, the car being credential enough.

He drove slowly across the yard, glancing briefly at the spot where Tod Gemmill had bumped into him and planted the cuff links in his overalls. He smiled grimly at the memory.

He parked the Rolls beside Sir Alan's and climbed out into the sunshine. A glance at his watch told him the meeting was scheduled to have started one minute previously. He had timed it to perfection.

He strode up the stairs that brought him to Sir Alan's office where in a small reception area a middle-aged secretary asked him what his business was?

He replied he'd come for the board meeting and he looked so much the part he was shown straight through. When he entered the boardroom he did so as though to the manner born.

As he expected, there were four of them grouped round the table – Sir Alan plus Sir Alan's three tame directors. He stared boldly at Sir Alan.

'You!' Sir Alan exclaimed and looked thunderstruck.

Angus took his time about walking to the seat furthest away from Sir Alan. He smiled softly and waited.

'Just what in God's name do you think you're doing here, McBain?' Sir Alan demanded angrily.

Angus laid his brief case on the table and slowly opened it.

The penultimate twist of the screw had been applied to Sir Alan that morning in the form of a telegram from O'Rourke informing him the Mine Workers' Union had reconsidered their position. As a result they were once more blacking all LMBM ore to Great Britain.

This was in effect the death blow to the Gorbals project for it was impossible for Sir Alan to financially survive the consequences of this action.

Angus leant across the table to hand the man nearest him certificates and statements showing the absent four nominee directors had all been acting on his behalf. With seventy per cent of the Armstrong shares he was now the majority shareholder.

Having noted the contents of these papers Sir Alan closed his eyes. It was as though he'd been reduced to a shell with a cold wind blowing through the empty spaces where flesh and blood had once been.

Angus reached into his pocket and pulled out an old pair of cuff links which he threw down on the table where they came to rest about a foot in front of Sir Alan. 'Also for Rosemary and the compensation you owed but never paid my mother,' Angus said.

The three directors watched spellbound the drama being played out in front of them. From the expressions on their faces Angus might have been the very devil incarnate.

Angus went on, 'As the new majority shareholder I claim the position of managing director and as such will assume responsibility for the running of the firm. As you, Armstrong, still own twenty-seven per cent of the shares I hereby offer you the post of assistant managing director which your holdings entitle you to.'

Having said that, Angus swung his gaze onto the three directors sitting gawping at him. 'In the circumstances there will now be no further need for a board of directors which makes you redundant, gentlemen,' he added.

Sir Alan squared Angus's certificates and statements into a neat pile before coming to his feet.

Without uttering further he walked from the board-room into his office. His secretary's voice was heard a few moments later asking if he was all right as he looked awful.

Mumbling something incomprehensible, Sir Alan took a last fond look round his office, then left it for his car parked outside.

The three directors took their leave almost directly afterwards. En route one of them explained to the secretary there was a change of management and Mr McBain was now in charge.

After the directors had gone Angus strolled through to what had been Sir Alan's office, plonking himself down behind the man's desk.

Strangely there was no feeling of elation but rather a sense of the anti-climactic.

There was a framed photograph on the desk which he picked up and studied. It featured a grown woman and two young girls – Rosemary and Diane as youngsters with their mother.

His heart crowded into his mouth as he stared at the young Rosemary's face. With a sigh he slid the photograph into a desk drawer and called out for the secretary to come through.

The woman entered all wide-eyed and timorous. He

introduced himself and told her to take a memo, copies of which were to be distributed throughout the works.

In the memo he informed the workforce of the change of management, then went on to allay any fears they might have had regarding the sort of internal upheaval often occurring in circumstances like these.

He instructed her to tell all heads of departments and gaffers to present themselves in his office in half an hour's time. He wanted to introduce himself to these men without delay.

When Miss Morrisson had left he crossed to the window and stared out. There was an enormous amount he was going to have to learn about running a business like this. But learn it he would and quickly.

He was going to see Armstrong's prosper like it had never prospered before. Before he was finished Armstrong's was going to be a by-word not only in Glasgow but throughout Britain and beyond.

'Mister McBain?'

He turned to find himself staring at a pretty blond lassie of about twenty-two or -three.

'I'm Miss McPhail, Miss Morrisson's assistant. I was wondering if you'd like a cup of tea? We usually have one about this time.'

There was something about the girl, a certain unmistakable Glasgowness, that appealed to him. 'What's your Christian name, Miss McPhail?' he asked.

She blinked in surprise. 'Irene.'

'Well, Irene, I'd love a cup of *coffee*,' he said.

She smiled hesitatingly, then was gone.

Angus rubbed his hands briskly together. The sun was shining outside and he'd achieved what he'd set out to do. True, he'd lost Rosemary but then perhaps there was a law somewhere which stipulated a man couldn't have everything he set his heart on.

Looking on the bright side there was an awful lot he had to be thankful for including a smashing wee son whom he idolized and would have sold his soul for.

Returning to his desk he mused he was going to need a

personal assistant-cum-secretary now, someone clever and efficient to be by his side as he constantly flitted between LMBM and Armstrong business.

He wondered if the pretty Irene McPhail would be interested?

For three days after Angus's coup Sir Alan sat at home and brooded. Surly and taciturn, he refused to discuss the situation with anyone, including his wife, Cordelia.

He drank a great deal, consuming bottle after bottle of his favourite malt.

On the evening of the third day he announced abruptly that he was going out.

He drove to Partickhill, having a desire to see Margaret Cunninghame, and as this was one of his usual nights for going there he'd decided to keep the tryst.

Not feeling the same sense of shame with Margaret as he did with Cordelia he was telling her everything within minutes of his arrival.

Appalled, Margaret fetched him a stiff drink, made sure he was sitting comfortably and generally fussed over him.

They talked and drank, he downing the whisky as though it was water. The more alcohol he consumed the more flushed and agitated he became.

Like many courtesans, Margaret eventually related most things to sex and bed. To her, intercourse was the great panacea which, if not exactly the cure for all ills, couldn't fail but help.

With that in mind she began coaxing Sir Alan to come to bed.

To begin with he wasn't interested but when she began touching him in a way he especially liked he soon became aroused.

As she'd intended, all thoughts fled from his mind other than lust and bodily satisfaction. Hand in hand they hurried to the bedroom where they both quickly undressed.

Their lovemaking was fiercely urgent – far more so

than normal.

Suddenly, he gave a long, shuddering sigh and collapsed on top of her where he lay heavily pressing her into the bed.

'Oh love, that was wonderful,' Margaret crooned, stroking the side of his sweat slicked neck.

She continued stroking him, then frowned when she got no reply.

'Alan?'

For the first time it dawned on her there was something peculiar about the way he was lying so heavy and unmoving.

'Alan?'

Her hand groped for the bedside table and the lamp sitting atop it.

His face was suffused with blood, the way it had been when he'd had the previous attack in her bathroom.

His eyes were wide open and bulging as though being forced outward from internal pressure of some kind. The expression was a grotesque parody of sexual ecstasy.

There could be no mistaking he was quite dead.

A few days after Sir Alan's funeral Angus stood by the man's grave in the Linn Park Cemetery with a huge bunch of magnificent red roses in his hand.

For a long time he stared down at the grave. Then turning he made his way to another part of the cemetery where his mother and father were buried together.

On top of their grave he laid the roses.

It was a puerile thing to say but he said it nonetheless. 'You got your compensation at last, Ma. Armstrong finally paid up. And with interest.'

Tears oozed from his eyes which he hurriedly wiped away. It wouldn't do for anyone to see a grown man greeting like a wean. They'd think him a big jessie.

Taking a deep breath, he thought Armstrong's death was the passing of a personal era. Yesterday was now gone. Tomorrow lay fresh and inviting before him.

It was with a light heart that he made his way up the

path to the cemetery gates beyond which his Rolls was parked. Off on the horizon he could see the grey pall of chimney smoke that hung forever lowering over central Glasgow.

It might be a dirty horrible violent place but he loved it.

It was home.

Bestselling Women's Fiction

☐ Destinies	Charlotte Vale Allen	£2.95
☐ Hester Dark	Emma Blair	£1.95
☐ Nellie Wildchild	Emma Blair	£2.50
☐ Playing the Jack	Mary Brown	£3.50
☐ Twin of Fire	Jude Deveraux	£2.50
☐ Counterfeit Lady	Jude Deveraux	£2.50
☐ Miss Gathercole's Girls	Judy Gardiner	£2.50
☐ Lisa Logan	Marie Joseph	£1.95
☐ Maggie Craig	Marie Joseph	£1.95
☐ A Long Way From Heaven	Sheelagh Kelly	£2.95
☐ The Gooding Girl	Pamela Oldfield	£2.75
☐ The Running Years	Claire Rayner	£2.75
☐ The Pride	Judith Saxton	£2.50

ARROW BOOKS, BOOKSERVICE BY POST, PO BOX 29, DOUGLAS, ISLE OF MAN, BRITISH ISLES

NAME ....

ADDRESS ....

....

....

Please enclose a cheque or postal order made out to Arrow Books Ltd. for the amount due and allow the following for postage and packing.

U.K. CUSTOMERS: Please allow 22p per book to a maximum of £3.00.

B.F.P.O. & EIRE: Please allow 22p per book to a maximum of £3.00.

OVERSEAS CUSTOMERS: Please allow 22p per book.

Whilst every effort is made to keep prices low it is sometimes necessary to increase cover prices at short notice. Arrow Books reserve the right to show new retail prices on covers which may differ from those previously advertised in the text or elsewhere.

Bestselling Fiction

☐ Toll for the Brave	Jack Higgins	£1.75
☐ Basikasingo	John Matthews	£2.95
☐ Where No Man Cries	Emma Blair	£1.95
☐ Saudi	Laurie Devine	£2.95
☐ The Clogger's Child	Marie Joseph	£2.50
☐ The Gooding Girl	Pamela Oldfield	£2.75
☐ The Running Years	Claire Rayner	£2.75
☐ Duncton Wood	William Horwood	£3.50
☐ Aztec	Gary Jennings	£3.95
☐ Enemy in Sight	Alexander Kent	£2.50
☐ Strumpet City	James Plunkett	£3.50
☐ The Volunteers	Douglas Reeman	£2.50
☐ The Second Lady	Irving Wallace	£2.50
☐ The Assassin	Evelyn Anthony	£2.50
☐ The Pride	Judith Saxton	£2.50

ARROW BOOKS, BOOKSERVICE BY POST, PO BOX 29, DOUGLAS, ISLE OF MAN, BRITISH ISLES

NAME ....

ADDRESS ....

....

....

Please enclose a cheque or postal order made out to Arrow Books Ltd. for the amount due and allow the following for postage and packing.

U.K. CUSTOMERS: Please allow 22p per book to a maximum of £3.00.

B.F.P.O. & EIRE: Please allow 22p per book to a maximum of £3.00.

OVERSEAS CUSTOMERS: Please allow 22p per book.

Whilst every effort is made to keep prices low it is sometimes necessary to increase cover prices at short notice. Arrow Books reserve the right to show new retail prices on covers which may differ from those previously advertised in the text or elsewhere.

Bestselling Fiction

☐ Dancing Bear	Chaim Bermant	£2.95
☐ Hiroshima Joe	Martin Booth	£2.95
☐ 1985	Anthony Burgess	£1.95
☐ The Other Woman	Colette	£1.95
☐ The Manchurian Candidate	Richard Condon	£2.25
☐ Letter to a Child Never Born	Oriana Fallaci	£1.25
☐ Duncton Wood	William Horwood	£3.50
☐ Aztec	Gary Jennings	£3.95
☐ The Journeyer	Gary Jennings	£3.50
☐ The Executioner's Song	Norman Mailer	£3.50
☐ Strumpet City	James Plunkett	£3.50
☐ Admiral	Dudley Pope	£1.95
☐ The Second Lady	Irving Wallace	£2.50
☐ An Unkindness of Ravens	Ruth Rendell	£1.95
☐ The History Man	Malcolm Bradbury	£2.95

A Selection of Arrow Bestsellers

☐ A Long Way From Heaven	Sheelagh Kelly	£2.95
☐ 1985	Anthony Burgess	£1.95
☐ To Glory We Steer	Alexander Kent	£2.50
☐ The Last Raider	Douglas Reeman	£2.50
☐ Strike from the Sea	Douglas Reeman	£2.50
☐ Albatross	Evelyn Anthony	£2.50
☐ Return of the Howling	Gary Brandner	£1.95
☐ 2001: A Space Odyssey	Arthur C. Clarke	£1.95
☐ The Sea Shall Not Have Them	John Harris	£2.50
☐ A Rumour of War	Philip Caputo	£2.50
☐ Spitfire	Jeffrey Quill	£3.50
☐ Shake Hands Forever	Ruth Rendell	£1.95
☐ Hollywood Babylon	Kenneth Anger	£7.95
☐ The Rich	William Davis	£1.95
☐ Men in Love	Nancy Friday	£2.75
☐ George Thomas, Mr Speaker: The Memoirs of Viscount Tonypandy	George Thomas	£2.95
☐ The Jason Voyage	Tim Severin	£3.50

ARROW BOOKS, BOOKSERVICE BY POST, PO BOX 29, DOUGLAS, ISLE OF MAN, BRITISH ISLES

NAME ....

ADDRESS ....

....

....

Please enclose a cheque or postal order made out to Arrow Books Ltd. for the amount due and allow the following for postage and packing.

U.K. CUSTOMERS: Please allow 22p per book to a maximum of £3.00.

B.F.P.O. & EIRE: Please allow 22p per book to a maximum of £3.00.

OVERSEAS CUSTOMERS: Please allow 22p per book.

Whilst every effort is made to keep prices low it is sometimes necessary to increase cover prices at short notice. Arrow Books reserve the right to show new retail prices on covers which may differ from those previously advertised in the text or elsewhere.